Unbidden Her Body Awoke to Him...

"A woman like you serves only one purpose!"

Shocked, she watched him drag his doublet off and fling it aside. Pulling off his blouse, standing naked to the waist, he muttered, "Now I'm going to use you for that purpose."

"Never, you swine!"

It was impossible for her to run. He barred the way. As he came toward her, Lily grabbed her brush and hurled it at him.

She missed, and he roared with laughter. "True to form, Lily! An uncontrolled wildcat!" He ripped his breeches off, kicked his shoes under the bed. In one stride he had caught her in his arms. As though she were a toy, he tossed her onto the bunk. "Now you're going to pay a little for the mischief you've done!"

He was like a man possessed, and seconds later, she knew her sensuousness was betraying her. . . .

Also published by POCKET BOOKS/RICHARD GALLEN

Heather Song
  by Nicole Norman

The Love of the Lion
  by Angela Gray

Helga Moray

PUBLISHED BY POCKET BOOKS NEW YORK

A POCKET BOOKS/RICHARD GALLEN *Original* publication

POCKET BOOKS, a Simon & Schuster division of
GULF & WESTERN CORPORATION
1230 Avenue of the Americas, New York, N.Y. 10020

Copyright © 1958, 1980 by Helga Moray

All rights reserved, including the right to reproduce
this book or portions thereof in any form whatsoever.
For information address Pocket Books, 1230 Avenue
of the Americas, New York, N.Y. 10020

ISBN: 0-671-41780-0

First Pocket Books printing December, 1980

10 9 8 7 6 5 4 3 2 1

POCKET and colophon are trademarks of Simon & Schuster.

Printed in the U.S.A.

To
Judith Voessler
with love and admiration

EIGHTEEN-YEAR-OLD Lady Lily Deveraux sat on a tapestry stool as her serving woman dressed her thick dark hair. The sides were permitted to hang in long graceful curves over her shoulders, while the remaining ringlets were swept high on the crown of Lily's head.

"Two strange knights have ridden into the castle to shelter for the night," the girl told her maid, Marion. "Who knows, they may be brave and handsome. I might even fancy one of them," Lily said, her large green eyes sparkling with laughter.

"And a lot of good it will do you when your father has already decided on Sir Roger Huet for your husband," Marion sniffed, not in the least amused by her mistress's teasing. "You don't think that great man traveled all the way from London to Wales at the earl's invitation to hunt buck, do you?"

"I don't care what he came to hunt, but he'll not have me for a wife! The suet-faced Puritan. Why, this afternoon I bested him at fencing. He may be strong but he's not very nimble or skillful." She laughed suddenly at the recollection. "He hated it that I won. He said fencing was not for females."

"Sir Roger is right!" Marion went to a tall oak closet and took out an embroidered red-velvet gown, suitably warm for the damp March weather. "You'd better realize that you'll *have* to marry him. It's your father's wish, and no one dares disobey Lord Deveraux."

Lily's eyes blazed. "You forget we're living in 1636, and thank the merciful Almighty, our Welsh law forbids any girl to be married against her will."

"No matter, no matter. You will obey the earl."

"I'm damned if I will! I'll never marry Sir Roger! I swear that by the Holy Virgin."

"Hush, girl. Are you mad? Do you want it known that you, your mother and I are Roman Catholics? Do you want to land us in prison?"

"Don't be so nervous, Marion. After all, the queen is a Catholic." Lily stepped into the full-skirted dress and turned to make it easier for Marion to do up the corset tapes.

Suddenly the arras were thrown roughly open and the heavy figure of the earl of Deveraux, wearing a blue-velvet doublet, walked into the chamber. One of the mightiest lords of southern Wales, feared by the thousands of men whom he ruled, he was a physically powerful, hard-drinking, wenching man. But now he stood for a moment of appreciation of his daughter. With her huge emerald eyes, wealth of dark hair, creamy skin and half-exposed breasts like white doves, she was enough for the tastes of any king on earth. His fatherly pride told him he would have no difficulty in finding a proper husband for Lily.

She turned her head angrily to look at him. She knew what was on his mind and that she could not permit herself to give in to his selfish desire to protect his position and his property. He did not care that she wanted to both love and respect the man she wed. Her temper got the better of her. "What age must I attain, Father dear, before you knock before entering my room? I'm no longer a child."

"You're an insolent little bitch." He chuckled, amused at what he believed was her joke.

But to Lily, his presence, always smelling of wine, seemed to diminish the beauty of the crimson damask wall hangings, the tapestry-covered chairs, her mother's portrait by Chantereel, and Queen Henrietta's gift of the marble font that Lily could never dare fill with holy water.

Feet apart, Rhys Deveraux came to stand over Lily as she sat on the stool. As his eyes took in the sight of her rounded white breasts barely contained in the red velvet bodice, he said, "Yes, yes, indeed, it's quite obvious you are no longer a child. And as you are definitely a woman, it's time you married. You know my wishes about Sir Roger Huet, so be sure that you encourage him tonight."

Rhys's heavy fingertips gathered snuff from a gold box. He held the powder to his nose and sniffed noisily. "The latest news is that the king will be forced to summon Parliament, and Roger will be a prominent member in it. That's why I need him! I've told you that coal is rapidly replacing wood as fuel in England. My Welsh output sells well in London. But the cursed London faggot-mongers, having lost their wood trade, are trying to monopolize coal transportation . . . and that will hurt me!"

"But what can Roger do about all that?"

"A great deal. Huet is one of the finest legal brains in the country, and with him as my son-in-law in the Commons—and me in the House of Lords—between us *we* could secure the transportation monopoly for southern Wales! It would mean untold wealth for me!"

Lily swiftly understood the extent that her father needed Huet, for both commerce and politics interested her. "Father, of course I want to help you, but just the idea of being Roger's wife, of having him embrace me, makes me feel ill."

"Christ damn me! What rot! On your wedding night you must get soused on wine so you'll forget it's Roger who's bedding you." Rhys's heavy face, his mud-brown eyes, looked amused at his own shrewdness. "Then you'll quickly bear him an heir, and with my rich Welsh blood in your veins and not just your Italian mother's religious water, you'll toss around between the sheets with some man to your liking."

Although accustomed to her father's vulgarity, Lily was now disgusted. She rose to face him. "How can you suggest such things? You, my father!" She glared at him with burning, reproachful eyes.

"Your popish prudery bores me." He was growing angry, and his temper, when crossed, could be almost uncontrollable. "Listen to me. You've been sought after by every eligible bachelor in the country and you've refused them all. You should have married at fifteen, like other girls, and given me male issue." His voice thickened sarcastically. "Hell and damnation, just who is the beautiful Lady Lily saving her great treasure for? The treasure that every woman born has between her legs. Just what kind of man do you want?"

His vulgar tirade was powerless to crush her. "I want an honest, brave, intelligent man, not a rabid Puritan nor a conceited drunkard."

Somewhere, as a child, she had seen a man she wanted—taller than other men, shoulders wider, his head capped by a mass of bronze-gold hair, eyes blue as a summer sky. He had spoken wisely of England's politics, but he had also been amusing. Who he was she did not know, nor where she had seen him; she only knew that such a man must be her husband or despoiler.

"God in heaven, Lily! The devil enjoyed his joke letting you live while my sons were all stillborn." Sometimes Deveraux almost hated Lily for being alive when his sons were dead. His voice was bitter. "At least you can try to make retribution for my disappointments with a marriage that will benefit me!"

"Truly, Father, you know well that since I was a small child I've tried to be like a son to you. For your sake I dared to ride the wildest horses, I learned to shoot, to fence. You've said yourself I excel at mannish pursuits. I want to be adaptable to your wishes, but don't ask me to marry that—"

"Sir Roger has appealed to me for your hand," Rhys interrupted, "and I have promised it. He's a fine man, only twenty-three, very influential, well born, wealthy. He's a splendid match for you. Don't be a fool, girl! When he asks you to marry him, accept him. That is my command—remember!"

Lord Deveraux turned and strode from the chamber.

Trembling with rage, Lily picked up her hand mirror and smashed it down against the dressing table. Staring at the pieces of shattered mirror around her feet, she muttered, "Never! I'll never marry Roger! By all the ancient spirits of Wales, I swear it."

"God have mercy on us," Marion murmured. "You were born with a clenched fist—the sign of an evil temper. Someday you'll suffer for your willfulness. Now let me finish fixing your hair."

Laughter and loud chatter filled the great hall of Breck Castle, which was lit by hundreds of candles. At long oak tables set with pewter tankards, wooden spoons and trenchers, and large saltcellars, Lord Deveraux's two hundred retainers sat eating meat. Smoke from two huge fireplaces at either end of the hall mixed with aromas of roasted flesh as servants in Deveraux livery stepped over sprawling dogs to serve platters of marrow bones, joints of mutton and veal, fowl, pullets and larks, neat's tongue, fritters and anchovies. Great oak dressers were filled with tarts, prawns and cheese.

At one end of the large hall, three fiddlers played. At the other a heavy tapestry curtained off an alcove with a round table set with a white cloth, silver candlesticks, tankards, trenchers and spoons. Here Lily sat with her parents, Geraldius the family bard and Sir Roger Huet, as well as the two elderly knights who had ridden in earlier that day.

At the first introduction to them, Lily had mentally eliminated them along with Sir Roger. Surely somewhere between Scotland, England and Wales there is a man to bring the blood racing through my body, she thought impatiently. Perhaps the next time I go to court in London, I might meet such a man!

Watching Roger in his black doublet with wide lace collar as he conversed with her father, Lily thought, He is so pale; his skin, his golden hair, his gray eyes—all pale. Yet months ago at a court masque she had allowed him a swift kiss, but then he had shouted about his Puritanical ideas. From then on she always seemed to detect a self-righteous expression on his face, an accusing look in his eyes as if everyone but he were a sinner.

In his clipped speech he was complaining, "It's scandalous. King Charles and Archbishop Laud have brought back Church plate, pulpits and fonts—even painted glass images of the Virgin and saints." He bit into a piece of mutton, then tossed the bone over his shoulder to the dogs. "It's imperative that our Anglican church be reorganized along Geneva lines!" Roger looked as though he were passing a law.

As he stared amorously at Lily, it amused her to think of his shock should he learn she was a papist.

"But is the king's church policy all wrong?" Lady Deveraux's beautiful dark eyes threw an almost apologetic glance at her husband. "Because of Puritan abhorrence of Roman trappings, so many churches are sadly misused. Squatters turn tombstones into cheese presses. Dogs, hawks and horses are brought to divine service and pigs are pastured in graveyards."

"Poppycock, Angela! You know nothing about it," Rhys barked at his delicate wife, whom he sometimes hated for having borne four stillborn sons. Now he turned placatingly to Roger. "I believe one of your ancestors is mentioned in Fox's book of martyrs dealing with Mary's bloody reign." His glance took in the knights. "I understand how King Charles's leaning toward papacy must infuriate Sir Roger."

"But my lord, when King Charles married Henrietta Maria, he gave her a promise to lessen oppression against Catholics," one of the visitors remarked, "but Parliament stopped him."

"Excuse me," Roger snapped, "but what about the intervals between his three Parliaments? Charles certainly aided the Catholics then. Jesuit and Franciscan priests have seeped into England." Roger's thin fingers selected a lark from a dish piled with the tiny birds. "But with a papist wife, what can one expect? Charles probably intends returning to Rome."

"No, no, no, he hopes the pope will admit his errors and join the Anglican church," the silver-haired Geraldius said with a chuckle, and the visitors joined in. "Recently a man was fined five thousand pounds for asserting that His Majesty attended mass in the queen's private chapel."

"Amazing how you get news, Geraldius," Lord Deveraux laughed affectionately, "even though the king has banned newspapers."

If Father cares for anyone, it's Geraldius, Lily mused. But how could anyone not love the old sage who had warmed her life with his devotion, developed her mind with his learning?

"What an awful position Charles has landed England in," Roger went on grimly. "For over seventy years the Hapsburg dynasty of Spain and Austria have been crusading against the Protestants, while the French Bourbon Catholic king supports the Protestants, and the Vatican upholds France against Spain." Roger's thin nostrils quivered angrily. "In Germany and Flanders the Protestants' cause is fought by Swedes and Dutch, on the Rhone by the French, while England under Charles does nothing!"

"Oh, but Roger," Lily burst out indignantly, "the king has accomplished much good at home. He's improved the Poor Law; he tried to prevent the spread of epidemics, to avert famine such as the corn dearth created, and he's controlled bad building."

"That's quite true, Lady Lily," one of the visitors agreed while his eyes bathed Lily in longing admiration.

"Charles imagines his goodwill alone upholds the people—" Roger felt he was favorably impressing Lily with his wisdom—"but he forgets that laws are administered by judges, justices of the peace, sheriffs, constables and lord lieutenants."

"Oh, judges! They're no longer what Bacon called them, lions under the throne," Rhys Deveraux said disagreeably. "I know too well as a judge of the Council of the Marches that if the king dislikes our roar, he removes us."

"Yes, he appoints and removes judges, but still he cannot control the law!" Roger's clenched fist struck the table. "At the Assizes his judges instruct local justices on royal policy. But supposing they were to oppose the king—could his council remove the entire bench?"

"Of course not!" Deveraux smiled enigmatically at Roger. "Who would rule the countryside?"

Bored by Roger's hatred of the king, Lily exchanged an understanding look with Geraldius and was thankful that servants were passing tarts and the meal was ending.

"I blame the Royal Council for the unfair laws that extract fines," one of the knights said. "The worst is reviving the Elizabethan tax of ship-money, although of course the navy required strengthening to protect the southern coast from Corsairs and channel shipping from Dunkirk pirates." He held his greasy fingers out for a servant to pour water over them. "But it was taxing the inland towns for ship-money that started trouble."

"More than trouble, my good sir." Roger seemed to be enjoying himself. "King Charles is pushing us toward war."

"War!" Lady Deveraux exclaimed. "Oh, no! With whom?"

"With Scotland, Lady Deveraux. The Scots refused to obey Charles's proclamation to reform their church. The covenant was signed by Scotland's principal lords, ministers, gentry and thousands of citizens. It means the Scots will resort to arms!"

As the men heatedly discussed this possibility, a servant bent and whispered to Lady Deveraux. "The poor await you, my lady."

THE TEMPEST LILY

Angela Deveraux made a signal to Lily. They rose and left the chamber, for it was an ancient custom for the remains from the noble Deverauxs' repasts to be distributed by their womenfolk to the poor.

"Roger is frightening with his talk of war," Lily's mother said, once they were in the hallway. "A civil war is a terrible thing."

"Don't be upset, Mother, by Roger's gloomy talk." Lily linked her arm through her mother's. "He really enjoys spreading such talk. It puffs him up, makes him feel important. You'll see. The king will bring the Scots to heel without resorting to arms."

"I pray you're right, my darling."

Later Lady Deveraux and Lily sat down in the comforting warmth of an upstairs chamber, where Geraldius was playing the harp while Lord Deveraux and the other men talked.

As Roger detached himself from the group and came toward Lily, she whispered to her mother, "I don't feel like talking to him tonight."

Sir Roger bent over her with a smile. "Ah, you're back, so now we can speak, dear Lily."

He was about to sit down when she said, "Not tonight. I've a cruel headache."

"I'm very distressed. I leave for London tomorrow and it's imperative that I talk to you. I've already told your father that—"

"Yes, yes, Roger," she interrupted. She could sense her father's eyes watching her. "Let's ride together in the morning and talk then. Good night, Roger." Lily rose and gave him her hand.

Roger raised her fingertips to his lips. "Until tomorrow, then."

His meaningful look repelled Lily as she dropped a curtsy to her parents and the guests, then hurried away. She could not bear the confrontation tonight. In the morning she would feel more able to defy her father by refusing Roger.

2

THE NEXT MORNING, followed by two grooms, Lily and Roger rode slowly out of the castle's grounds toward the village, which was sheltered beneath the castle's great walls. The winter sharpness had left the air. Wisps of blue swirled between chiffoning clouds; brown mountains and valleys boasted of an underlying spring greenery.

Out here, removed from her father's nearness, Lily's defense against Roger's marriage proposal was stronger. Even so she was surprised at how swiftly he began.

"My beautiful Lily, lovely as the Deveraux lands are, I want you to know the Huet lands in Sussex. Your visit with your mother last year was far too brief. I feel so deeply about you that I want you to be . . . my wife."

"Look! There's been a fire ahead." She cantered forward and, though annoyed, he was obliged to follow until they reached a group of partly burned cottages. Reining in and speaking Welsh, Lily asked the peasants what had happened.

"No lives were lost, thank heaven," she told Roger. "They say a witch started the fire. Anyhow, neighbors are aiding with the rebuilding. It's an ancient custom called *cymmorthau,* when a whole neighborhood turns out to help someone."

THE TEMPEST LILY

With a smile and a nod to the peasants, Lily continued riding, and Roger fell in beside her.

Still annoyed with her rude interruption, he said, "You speak Welsh, but half a century ago gentlefolk stopped speaking it."

His contemptuous tone sparked her anger. "Father speaks it to the tenantry and mine workers, and I always shall. It's a lovely language. But today is Market Day, so let's ride down the village street and not argue."

Lily led her horse past the wicker stalls displaying russets, kennets and whites made from Welsh sheep and goat wool. Ignoring Roger's grim face, she pointed out a stall where a man was energetically extracting a tooth from a groaning woman, while a line of grim-faced villagers waited to have boils lanced and corns cut.

"The visiting peddler is busy today," Lily remarked.

"It's all very backward," Roger said stiffly.

It seemed that everything he said aggravated her. As they continued riding, she decided to take pleasure in annoying him in return. "Since Roman times eagles have sharpened their beaks on this stone," she said, pointing to a boulder, "before feasting on men slain here in battle. The villagers say an ancient prayer to counteract the evil spirit. 'Over the mountain, the cold mountain, we see blessed Mary with her head on a pillow, digging a space between every soul and hell.' "

"What a lot of popish superstition!" Roger said scathingly. He was upset, for all morning she had been baiting him. He glanced at Lily, looking so lovely in her black riding garments as she gazed down at the valley with its winding stream. The quiet was broken only by bursts of laughter from the villagers hidden from view by a swelling of land.

"Why can't people be like nature?" Lily murmured as they dismounted, "and tolerate each other's ideas. The stream is moving but it doesn't quarrel with the banks because they remain stationary."

"Ah, Lily—that's truly profound. You know, my dear, somehow you are more lovely in this rather stark countryside than in fashionable court life." Roger's usually cold voice had grown warm. "Your wild beauty seems to belong with mountains, scurrying clouds, an uncertain sky."

"Why, that's quite poetical, Roger."

"It's you who make me poetical. It's not just your beauty but your spirit that's invaded my being. Months ago when I first realized I loved you, I could think of little else." His voice choked. He coughed, trying to hide his emotion. "I took your face into the Temple, into Lincoln's Inn, everywhere I went. In court, pleading a case, the judge's face would suddenly fade, and I'd see *you*." He laughed unhappily. "Then you refused to marry me, and I fought to try to forget you. But useless! I shall never love anyone but you!"

"That's poppycock. Of course you will." She despised him for dramatizing himself.

"Oh, Lily! I beg you to marry me! I'll do everything to make you a good and worthy husband." Suddenly he leaned over and caught her in his arms, pulling her to him, his mouth hard on hers. She did not struggle against him because she was curious to see if his kisses could please her. No. They meant nothing, just like every other man she had kissed. He bored her, and she pushed him away.

"Roger, I told you before, I don't want to marry you. In any case, we're such opposites. You love prayer meetings and Bible reading. I love theaters, music, dancing, the horse races in Hyde Park—all things you disapprove of. What happiness could such opposite characters give each other?"

"But you are young. I'll teach you the folly of dancing, singing and such frivolities. You would learn to relinquish them!"

"I most certainly would not! You think you know me but you don't. There's a wildness in me that you'd hate. Sometimes I gallop madly over the earth, loving the pounding of the horse's hooves, the feel of its great muscles contracting and expanding. Other times I walk for miles—bareheaded—and cry out to the wind, rain and hail as they toss me about." Lily shrugged. "I

THE TEMPEST LILY

assure you, you could never be happy with my strange moods."

"You really mean that your answer is no again?" He muttered angrily in his disappointment.

"I'm afraid so, Roger."

"But Lord Deveraux has accepted my proposal!"

Lily burst out laughing. "Then marry him, Roger. Marry him!"

She jumped up and went racing around the rock to where the grooms waited with the horses. She wanted to go home, to have the inevitable angry scene with her father finished with.

An hour later Lord and Lady Deveraux and Lily stood on the castle steps waving good-bye to Roger as he left in his carriage for London.

"In the library, Lily!" Lord Deveraux muttered.

Angela surreptitiously caught and squeezed Lily's hand, for she feared her husband's temper, but Lily was braced for trouble.

Inside the shabby book-lined room, Lord Deveraux opened his attack. "I'd like to break every bone in your rotten body! How dare you disobey me? Now you'll sit down and write and tell Roger you've changed your mind and you will marry him. The letter will follow him to London."

"But Father, surely you can persuade him to help you obtain the monopoly on coal transportation without sacrificing me?"

"Don't dare give me advice! I need Roger Huet for more than that, and marry him you will."

Outraged justice fed Lily's rebellion. "I'll *never* marry him, Father! He's a cold hard man and he's half-mad with Puritanism!"

"You dare defy me? You she-devil!" Without warning Rhys's big hand slapped her cheek so hard that her head spun around as if snapped from her neck. Leaning over Lily, her father's brutal face filled her world as he muttered, "Perhaps you understand now? I said you will write and tell Roger you accept him."

Aided by the strength of hate, for now she hated

her father, she gasped, "I loathe you! You harbor thieves and murderers to do all your foul deeds. You terrify everyone, but not me! You forget that I have your rotten blood in my veins. I'll . . . never . . . marry . . . Huet."

Rhys's second blow knocked her unconscious. When coherent thoughts seeped slowly back to her, there was a drumbeat in her head, and her jaw felt broken. She gradually realized she was lying on a couch with her mother's weeping face on one side of her and Geraldius's sad face on the other.

"Lily, Lily, oh, my darling," Angela sobbed. "The fiend, the cruel brute to have struck you like that."

"For sixty years I've served the Deveraux clan," Geraldius said while applying cloths dampened in vinegar to Lily's forehead and jaw, "and I tell you it's devil's poison that runs in their veins—not human."

"Hush, Geraldius. Hush," Angela begged. "Praise God there is no devil's poison in Lily. My darling child, drink this wine. It will help to revive you." Angela held the pewter mug to Lily's lips, and she managed to swallow some of the liquid.

"Alas, my child, you will have to obey your father," Angela half-sobbed.

"No!" Her determination was a hundredfold stronger. "Mother, I'll get away from Breck Castle—find a ship. I'll sail to your mother in Capri. Father will never find me there."

"Poor child, escape is impossible for you," Geraldius whispered. "Your father is returning here within an hour to make you write that message to Sir Roger; otherwise he threatens to imprison you."

"Imprison me! His own daughter! Even he would not be so rotten!" Fury almost choked Lily. "I'll resort to law! Geraldius!" She grasped at his thin old arm. "The law will uphold me, won't it? I can't be forced to marry against my will, can I? Welsh law forbids—"

"Yes, yes, child, the law would uphold you, but where is there a lawyer in southern Wales who'd dare fight against the powerful earl of Deveraux? Most law-

THE TEMPEST LILY 15

yers up here exist because of his patronage!" The sage sorrowfully shook his silver head. "I fear you'll have to suffer imprisonment for a while until I find a way out of this trouble for you."

In complete darkness Lily lay in a dungeon deep below Breck Castle. Cold and damp seeping through the stone floor made her bed matting constantly wet, and the ache in her bones gave her a foretaste of old age.

Before her imprisonment she had despised her father for his wenching and neglect to her mother, but now, with all of her heart, brain and soul, she hated him. Her one continuous prayer was for God to let her escape from Breck and Wales.

Lily passed the time reciting poems that Geraldius had taught her. In recalling lines from plays of Shakespeare that she had recently read, she thought much about her ancestors who had built Breck Castle and this very dungeon. Had they also imprisoned their relatives? Even murdered them down here?

Denied communication with anyone, she lived for the sound of Geraldius's harp and his songs, which he sang regularly at a certain spot in the yard from where they floated down through the castle's foundations. Today he sang in Latin, not Welsh, for he was confident the retainers did not understand Latin. He was singing a message to Lily, saying that Lord Deveraux was away hunting. Then Geraldius instructed Lily to dispatch her jailor to Lord Deveraux upon his return, saying that she repented and would marry Roger. The balance of the plan to avoid the marriage Geraldius would divulge later.

Obeying him, her release came some hours later. Now back in her own chamber, her eyes still blinking from the unaccustomed light after three weeks of darkness, Lily enjoyed the comfort of her bed as she lay listening to Geraldius.

"You must simulate affection for Sir Roger when he arrives, and accept him; then later you will incense him to such an extent that *he* will break the betrothal, thus making it impossible for your father to force the marriage."

"But I've sworn to the Virgin that I shall escape from Breck. I can never live again with my father. I feel I might kill him."

"Yes, poor child, I understand." Geraldius nodded. "Trust me. I am arranging for your escape, but you must exercise great patience and deceit, no matter how you hate doing it. Remember, your father is no fool. He will be watching your every motion."

"Don't worry, Geraldius, I'll give not a sign to alert him."

But that night it took all her control to greet her father civilly when they met at supper.

"I'm glad that at last some sense entered your cursed, obstinate head."

"Yes, Father, a dungeon is a good place in which to develop second thoughts."

Content that he had broken her rebellious spirit, he went on to talk of other things.

A few days later, when Roger arrived, Lily convincingly acted her part, pretending to have grown to care for him in his absence. She now did everything to please him. In the next ten days she relinquished all pleasures and, cursing inwardly, sat beside him enviously watching her friends dance the pavane and saraband. Because he disapproved of displays of affection, she ignored her favorite dogs. She did not attend the Eisteddfod, although for a year the whole countryside had been preparing for it. In the great hall, when Geraldius played his harp and everyone sang, she sat silently beside Roger.

"Lily, I am so happy." Roger's pale face now glowed with joy. "This change in you is miraculous. Has my love really influenced you so much?"

She smiled, inwardly thinking, He knows nothing of my imprisonment nor how it has taught me to act the lie.

When he attempted to pull her into his arms, she

remonstrated. "Remember, Roger, we promised to deny our affection until we're married." This part of the practice of denials had been her suggestion. "Roger dear, now I want you to do a little thing for me." She forced a demure smile, although actually her blood was flaring with excitement, and she sang a silent *Te Deum,* for soon Geraldius's plan would be put into action. "Ride with me over a part of the land that I'm particularly fond of?"

His tall, black-clad figure stiffened. "But, my dear, you promised to ride only when it was essential, that you would relinquish riding for pleasure."

"I know, and within a few weeks we'll marry and leave here and I'll stop riding, so please favor me this once."

He unwillingly agreed, and when the hour came, Lily tried to look calm as she mounted a wild black stallion. Barely breathing, she watched Roger mount a frisky chestnut she had chosen for him. Followed by grooms, they left the castle sward and passed through the outer gates. As soon as they reached open countryside, Roger commenced complaining that his mount was too lively.

"The wilder they are, the more I love them," Lily laughed. "In the south you don't have our mountains, so your horses are quieter. Come, Roger, let's ride to my favorite spot." She touched a heel to her stallion, causing him to break into a gallop.

The blue-gray mountains, the sky with shifting clouds, the wind on her face—she loved them all, and beneath her the horse's great muscles contracting and expanding. Life! Glorious life warmed the animal. It was the joy of horses that cursed Roger planned to deny her, but soon she would escape from him and her brutal father.

Digging her heels into her mount's sides, she called out, "Faster, Roger. After me, Roger! After me!" and she set the stallion straight at a pile of bracken.

"Wait! Wait! Lily! Why . . . ?"

The rest of his words were lost in the horses' thundering hooves. Her blood surging through her, Lily set the stallion's head at the bracken which she knew hid a ditch. Only a fine rider familiar with the jump could hope to clear both. Roger's chestnut had often carried her across and would follow her now if Roger would permit it to.

"After me, Roger! After me!" she yelled as she felt her stallion's great muscles gather themselves together for the decisive spring. Landing safely across bracken and ditch, she whirled the stallion around to watch Roger.

As the chestnut gathered itself to make the leap, Roger, suddenly afraid, dragged at the reins so that the horse cleared the bracken but missed the further bank. The crash of man and horse falling was terrifying.

"God in heaven!" Lily swore. Geraldius had planned to terrify Roger, not kill him. Sick with apprehension lest he be dead, Lily rode to Roger and with relief found he had only suffered a broken leg—as Geraldius had imagined he would. The grooms came, and she commanded them to lay him face down over his horse and bring him back to the castle while she rode ahead to make preparations to receive him.

Acting the part of a half-distraught fiancée, she told her father what had occurred. When Roger was brought in and Geraldius called upon to attend to the leg until a doctor arrived. Lily still acted out her worry over him.

"You must be possessed of the devil!" Roger spat. "I swear you deliberately tried to kill me! I was saved by the mercy of God. No power on earth would ever make me marry you!"

"Oh no—no Roger," Lily cried out and collapsed in a simulated swoon. She was carried to her chamber, leaving a mystified, incensed Rhys trying to placate Roger.

Immediately upon reaching her room Lily pulled off her female riding attire and changed into boy's breeches and doublet. Well cloaked, she and Marion disappeared through a little-used side door of the castle. Fast horses awaited them outside the great walls. The women were swiftly carried a safe distance away from Breck Castle to where Geraldius had arranged for a carriage to meet them. The next morning, in Cardiff, they boarded a ship bound for Naples.

Once out at sea, staring up at the ship's great white sails, Lily blessed Geraldius. His arrangements had been perfect, but she and Marion had still to risk all the possible horrors that attended travel—shipwreck, mutiny, starvation, capture by pirates. But in her joy at being free, Lily gloried in the voyage. After several weeks they dropped anchor in Naples.

Here they remained for two days so that Lily could purchase female attire, and then they crossed the bay in a small boat to the island of Capri, where, at the palazzo of the marchesa da Lucca, Lily's maternal grandmother, she was welcomed with glorious surprise as a heaven-sent angel.

⟝ 3 ⟞

ON THE SUN-DRENCHED piazza, shaded by an expansive olive tree, Lily reclined in a basket-weave chair. Her eyes, filled with pleasure, swept down the terraced hillside over gardens of brilliant flowers bordering vineyards, their bushes heavy with grapes, their chalky white paths like fingers pointing down toward tangled vegetation and black rocks plunging into the Tyrrhenian Sea. Sentinel of Capri's loveliness was Monte Solaro, two thousand feet of purple-black peaks and ravines softened by silver aloes.

Breathing deeply of the scented air, Lily stretched her bare arms to the sun. Wonderful! Yet Capri was too small to hold her for long. From here she would sail to the British colonies in the New World. In Virginia she would somehow earn her living.

"My lovely Lily, you seem lost in dreams."

As the old marchesa da Lucca joined her, Lily sprang up. "I was thinking, Grandmother, how gorgeous Capri is, though still so aloof from the rest of the world."

Settling in a deep wicker chair, the elderly woman arranged her black silk skirts about her feet while Lily slipped cushions behind the lace-covered silver head.

"You enjoy Capri's loveliness, my child, and I enjoy yours. That Capriote costume of white chemisette and red skirt is so becoming to your black hair and pale skin. Yes, yes, your mother's fine Italian blood shows in your eyes, your long throat, the tilt of your head. You would excite Michelangelo were he alive."

"Dearest Grandmother," Lily laughed, showing her even, white teeth. "I was painted by Van Dyck, who's so fashionable at King Charles's court, but the portrait is horrible." After a pause she said, "You know, actually being here makes me feel at last as though I'm half-Italian."

"Ah, yes, your sweet mother. . . . It's been more than twenty years since she sailed away," the marchesa sighed, "but it's all as clear as yesterday. Your father had been traveling through France and Italy, completing his education, when his ship, running from a storm, sheltered in Capri. Important visitors always come to our palazzo, and the moment Lord Deveraux saw my Angela he fell in love with her. Of course I regretted that he was not a Roman Catholic, but he promised that he would always aid her and any children they might have to practice the faith."

"Well, he kept that promise," Lily said dryly.

At that moment the sound of laughter and male voices came from an unseen path. "What is all of this?" the marchesa demanded.

Rounding a clump of scarlet hibiscus came a group

THE TEMPEST LILY

of fishermen wearing brightly colored caps on black hair, white shirts and knee-length breeches in greens, blues and reds. In their center a huge man with shoulder-length golden hair glowing in the sunlight was striding toward the piazza, making the fishermen run to keep pace with him.

The marchesa sat up. "Ah, he's back! What joy! What joy!"

Lily's eyes eagerly appraised the magnificent-looking man with great shoulders stretching his cream doublet, his long legs in black breeches and the boots of a gentleman, which made the Capriotes' bare legs and feet look as thin as boys', but his well-groomed cavalier appearance was incongruous with his suntanned skin. A strange feeling of recognition came over Lily. She knew this man. Somewhere, they had met. A shiver ran the length of her body.

Leaving the fishermen at the foot of the steps, he sprang up to the piazza, grasping both the frail hands the marchesa extended to him.

"Welcome! Welcome!" she laughed like a delighted girl.

"Loveliest of all ladies." His voice was deep. He bent to kiss the marchesa's mottled hands.

"You've been gone two years," the old lady complained. "I've missed you so much."

Straightening, the man glanced down at Lily and she looked up into eyes—the deep blue of a summer day—eyes that she had seen once and never forgotten. His searching allover glance was so swift she could not be certain he had made it. The bold admiration in his eyes was almost impertinent. "I would have returned to Capri sooner had I known the island held such loveliness." He smiled intimately at Lily.

"Ah, let me present you to my granddaughter, Lady Lily Deveraux, a countrywoman of yours."

Very excited by what she could swear was her recognition of "her man," Lily gave him her hand. The strong grasp, the warm lips brushing her skin were unnerving.

"Lily, this is Lord Clune."

"Then *that* is your name!" Lily exclaimed. "You're the son of the earl of Severn!"

"Why yes—" the blue eyes looked quizzical—"and delighted to be at your service." He lowered his great frame into a chair, thinking what a beauty she was.

"I know you! Oh . . . I *know* you!" She tried to calm her excitement. "Years ago you visited us at Breck Castle . . . but I didn't know your name."

"Breck Castle!" What eyes, what skin, what breasts thrusting impatiently at the thin white chemisette. "I am Adam Clune, but I swear by God I never saw anyone as lovely as you at Breck."

"Thank you." Lily laughed heartily. "But I was a gawky twelve-year-old then, and we did not meet. I only peeked through a slit in an arras at my father's guests." Even then, with extraordinary precocity, she had longed to hold Adam Clune's head against her tiny sprouting breasts, to kiss his smiling mouth. Now, at last, she was looking at him again! It did not seem possible. It seemed like a fantasy.

Their eyes caught and held. Adam smiled widely, with teeth as white as blanched almonds, while the marchesa ordered a servant to bring wine.

Finally he said, "Wine also for my friends, please," and he gestured toward the fishermen. "They accompanied me up all the steps from the Marina Grande."

Waving the fishermen toward the kitchen, the marchesa turned to Adam. "How strange that you and Lily have met before. But tell me, when did you put into Capri?"

"At dawn, once my affairs were under control, I came straight here. We'll stay several weeks to give the *Fearless* a thorough careening." He turned to Lily. "Whatever are you doing so far from Wales?" He knew Lord Deveraux for a hard, brutal man. How ever had he allowed this beauty to travel to Capri?

"Visiting my grandmother and enjoying this paradise."

Damnation, there was more to it than that, Adam

THE TEMPEST LILY

guessed. "But it's not possible that you traveled alone? With your beauty, every man on board would have been a menace to you."

"I was with my serving woman and disguised as a boy."

"A boy! You!" He chuckled, unbelieving, as his gaze sensuously traveled over her opulent breasts. "That must have been difficult." Seeing the swift anger fly to her green eyes, he added, "I mean with your wealth of hair."

"Oh, I kept it rolled up under a peasant cap. But do tell me if my memory is correct. When you came to Breck, hadn't you recently come from Oxford, having just joined the navy with plans to sail to the New World?"

"Your memory is flattering." What a desirable wench she was. And what bloody luck to find her here! Was she a virgin? Never! Not with that voluptuous body, those wild passionate eyes; but was some man following her? "Tell me, have you been here long?"

She was irritated with herself for flushing under his admiring scrutiny. "Three days."

"Ah, then it will be my pleasure, if you and your grandmother permit it, to show you around the island."

"Adam has been coming here for years and knows Capri well. His tales about it will enchant you," the marchesa offered.

Pleasure softened Adam's granitelike face. "Lady Lily, your grandmother speaks with an embroidered tongue. I shall call for you at nine in the morning." He had arranged to bed a voluptuous islander, but he would postpone that; the Deveraux girl was more of an exciting challenge.

"Adam, sup here tonight and bring your nice first mate," the marchesa suggested. "Shall we expect you about eight?"

"Life could offer no greater pleasure." He unfolded himself from a chair and stood like a tower above Lily. He kissed the marchesa's fingertips, then Lily's, and the brief physical contact sent tendrils of warmth shooting through her.

Then she watched him run down the steps and stride across the garden. Her eyes clung to his tall figure as, nearing the flowering hibiscus, he turned, waved his arm high above his head and disappeared. Absurd! Ridiculous! But the garden suddenly seemed so forlorn.

"Well, well, well," the marchesa chuckled kindly. "So you too, Amora, are charmed by Adam. That man attracts women as a magnet attracts iron. Two of your Roman cousins met him here and they never ceased quarreling about him.

"He is not married?"

"No. Had he married while he was away, he would have told me."

Lily felt absurdly relieved, then blurted out, "Why does an English naval ship come here so often?"

"Dear child, I would rather he answered that question."

The three-hour interval before dinner seemed like years to Lily. Wanting to look particularly appealing to Adam, she decided a warm, scented bath would be a general tonic for her skin. When Marion came in and saw her in the round porcelain tub, she sniffed disapprovingly.

"It's not decent, Lady Lily, to immerse the whole body like that."

"But I'm glad Grandmama introduced me to the bath. It's so refreshing. Oh, Marion, could you please lay out my white satin gown with the silver embroidery, and send a maid to the garden to pick some white camelias for my hair?"

When at last her toilette was complete, Lily sat in the candlelit drawing room with her grandmother, impatient for Adam's arrival.

As soon as he and his first mate, Daniel Salter, arrived, Adam's eyes played appreciatively over her. After kissing her grandmother's hand and then Lily's fingertips, he presented Salter to her. Then they went into the dining hall, where, through the wide windows, the setting sun's rays tinted to rose the white walls and the white in the mosaic floor. Barefoot maids moved silently about, bearing silver plates laden with fish. Lily sat at one end of the gray marble table set with Venetian red glassware and silver dishes, while the marchesa was seated opposite her. Adam and his shy-looking mate were seated between them.

"The sunsets here enthrall me," Lily said, gazing out at the distant sea shot with shades of opal.

"As a seafaring man, I enjoy visualizing the Greek vessels that sailed these waters three thousand years ago," Salter said, a half-apologetic expression on his pleasant face.

"Capri is surely Homer's Siren Isle." Adam's blue eyes danced as he looked fully at Lily. "Unlike Ulysses, I don't need to bind myself to the mast nor fill my ears with wax to deafen them to the siren's tempting calls, because, unfortunately, they've never summoned me."

During the general laughter, Lily shot a searching glance at Adam, whose blue satin doublet with wide lace collar fastened at the neck by a cluster of diamonds emphasized his bronze skin. His face was like an eagle's—high forehead, almost hook nose, lean cheeks blending into the strong, jutting jaw. He was a man all women would become excited over.

Suddenly he turned toward Lily and caught her studying him. She felt herself tremble as he said, "When the men of Naples and Rome get word about you, they'll follow you here as the waters of the Atlantic follow the moon."

"How delightful, Lord Clune. I see you mix Welsh poetry with Irish flattery." She forced her eyes away from him and stared at her plate.

"My father is Welsh and my mother Irish. But that was not flattery. You *are* extraordinarily beautiful —but of course you've been told that many times."

Lily was glad she was wearing the low-cut white satin bodice drawn provocatively across her breasts and the voluminous white skirt which was tight around her small waist. Her black hair, well oiled, was caught back in curls held up with strands of pearls and white camelias. Let Adam Clune stare.

"Oh, Adam, I must tell you that Lily is most curious about you," the marchesa said playfully.

"Grandmother—"

"I'm honored," Adam smiled. "Lady Lily, perhaps you're familiar with the Welsh saying that three things reveal a man's soul: what he fears, what he tries to conceal and what he takes pride revealing." Derision tinged his smile. "I take pride in revealing that I captain a privateer."

Shock filled Lily's eyes. "You! But it's not possible!"

Throwing his head back, Adam laughed deep in his throat. "You sound as scandalized as if I had said I was a pirate."

His amusement disillusioned her. Annoyed, she retorted haughtily, "I see little difference, Lord Clune, between privateersman and pirate."

"Ah, there is a *great* difference." Adam leaned toward her. "Drake, a privateersman, brought back one million five hundred thousand pounds, enough to defray the expense of a seven-year war. The Spaniards cursed him as a pirate. To the English he was a hero."

"I see," she said slowly. "It's just that since I was a child I imagined you as a naval hero and—"

"Damn my soul! But a privateer is a wartime auxiliary to the navy! I sail under the king's letter of marque, which authorizes me to board and take as prize any ship but our own."

"Lily, dear child," the marchesa said gently, "remember your king shares in Adam's profits and, thank heaven, so do I."

"*You*, Grandmother! But surely this is a jest!"

"But, Amora, when the young of the family traveled out into the world, how could I make the vineyards pay? So I gladly invested in Adam's syndicate. Without the profits he brings me, I could not manage, and many islanders depend on me."

"Yes, I understand, Grandmother." Still a little

shocked, Lily struggled to spear the quail on her plate with a two-pronged fork, but for her the Italian innovation was difficult to master, whereas Adam seemed expert at it.

"Now, Adam, tell us about your voyage," the marchesa eagerly prompted.

"When we left here, we headed for eastern waters, and during the first couple of months we took several small prizes. Then we suffered a long blank period when we sighted no foreign ships." Adam leaned back against the high chair. "Water and food began to run low, and altogether things were not too pretty, when luck came in the shape of a tall ship. We ran her down and fired across her bow and ordered her to lower her topsails!"

With shining eyes the marchesa murmured, "Yes, yes, what happened?"

"She refused to surrender, so we gave her several guns, and then she struck her colors. She was native-owned from Surat."

"And the amount of the prize, Adam?"

"Thirty thousand pounds' worth! Your share will be delivered tomorrow." He smiled at the old lady's pleasure.

"Bravo, bravo!" The marchesa delightedly clapped her thin hands. "And will you return to eastern waters?"

"No." Adam slowly shook his head. "Even for a hardened sinner like myself, privateering in those parts is too harsh."

"It was odd what happened to our crew out there," Daniel said reflectively. "They never committed atrocities on white captives, but immediately they touched a brown or black man, they became merciless."

"I dislike torture, whatever a man's color is." Adam was massaging his forehead. "The natives on the Surat ship refused to divulge where their treasure was hidden, so our men lost patience and performed vile acts. We could not stop them, so I've decided I'll have no more of it."

"But as master of the ship, surely the crew had to obey you?" Lily said with obvious disgust.

"Not at all. On a privateer such matters are put to the communal vote, and the vote was torture."

As the marchesa and Daniel became involved in conversation, Lily changed the topic. "Do you know there is still fear of war with Scotland?"

"I'm afraid so, for neither the Scots nor the king has budged. Instead Charles instructed the lord lieutenants of the six northern counties to muster trained bands."

"Will the king subdue the rebels?"

"I doubt it. They've been drilling for months and, like the king, buying arms in the Low Countries and north Germany."

"Where are your sympathies, with the king or Scotland?" Her eyes searched his.

Adam's long brown fingers twirled the stem of his goblet. "I dislike Charles's belief in his divine right, but I like his aim of making the British dominions one state in morals, religion, foreign policy and prestige. Authority in his hand—I agree with. He has created a navy but, alas, no army, and this is a terrible weakness. Anyhow, Lady Lily, I am definitely a king's man," Adam ended cheerfully.

"I'm glad, for now we have something in common."

"I hope so." His glance, almost as intimate as a caress, made Lily look away.

"If you are all finished," the marchesa said as she rose, "shall we go and sit on the piazza? It will be cooler there."

In the scented air, settled into deep-cushioned chairs, they watched darkness enfold sea and land. Then, from behind a somber hill, a luminous glow slowly rose and the moon, a great silver disc, flooded the valley of Tagara. The white radiance highlighted precipices that dropped straight down into the sea; it found deep valleys and made flat-roofed houses seem like ivory miniatures. Far below, the sea was a silk of silver.

Between Adam and Lily's chairs stood a life-size marble figure of Aphrodite rising from the waves. Her beautiful breasts just caught the moonlight, which also accented the triangle of the statue's thighs. The naked figure became embarrassing to Lily, for Adam stared at it with burning eyes. Then he turned his head and looked directly into Lily's eyes, and she could not pull her look away from his. She felt mesmerized. I've drunk too much wine, she upbraided herself.

"Aphrodite, goddess of beauty, love and laughter," Adam whispered.

"Yes . . . I know a little of the Greek myths from our family bard, Geraldius." Willing herself not to look at Adam, she scanned the sea and valley. "What a magical night." And what a magical man, she thought, her entire being affected by him beside her, the scenery, the moonlight.

"It's a strange thing, Lady Lily, but on Capri the Greek myths seem to take on reality. One becomes something of a pagan. When I'm old, I'd like a home here," Adam observed. "But with the immense obligations my ancestors left me of restoring our lands, I'll have first to find a prize like Drake's Plate Fleet!"

"Drake's story is every sailor's dream," Salter said enviously, and the others laughed.

The moonlight was glinting off Adam's silver-tipped pipe, off the diamonds at his throat. The rest of him was in darkness. Do his looks represent his character, Lily wondered, brilliant in spots, but mostly dark? Otherwise why has he turned to privateering?

After a few minutes of general conversation, the marchesa said, "Now it's time for an old lady like me to retire."

As she was giving Salter her hand, Adam swiftly bent and whispered to Lily, "The night is too lovely to retire so early. My valet has discovered which room you're in. I know it. Be at the window and I'll lift you out and we can enjoy the moonlight."

Without hesitation she gave a nod of assent; the

man and the enchantment of the island had bewitched her.

Within minutes the good nights were over. Both Salter and Adam supposedly had left, carrying lighted lanterns. The marchesa was in her quarters. Trembling with excitement, Lily stood in the dark at her open window, breathing in the scented air, undisturbed by Marion's snoring coming from the adjoining room.

Then, silent as a cat, Adam appeared under the window. "Stand on a chair," he whispered, "so I can reach up and grasp hold of you."

She did as he instructed, and his strong hands clasped her around the waist and lifted her lightly out and onto the ground. He did not release her but crushed her in his arms against his ironlike body with his mouth hard on hers.

She had never known such an embrace—such kisses. Her head was dizzy, her whole body was limp in his arms, but when his hand slipped down her bodice and touched her bare breast, she fought to stop him.

"Don't be a damned little ninny. Why pretend? You want me. I know it. All night your eyes have been shouting at me to take you."

"You're a madman," she cried. Ignoring her, he picked Lily up as if she were a doll and started carrying her toward a dark clump of bushes. Adam seemed oblivious to her fists hammering against his shoulders. Damn him to hell to be so sure of her! "I'll scream if you don't put me down this minute!"

"I think you're just bitch enough to do it." One huge hand clamped tight over her mouth and chin, preventing Lily from making any noise. She wanted his lovemaking, but not like this. Now he was frightening. Reaching the concealing bushes and keeping her mouth covered with one hand, he easily laid her on the warm earth, holding her down. Now she fought wildly to escape.

"Don't struggle. I'm going to have you, Lily. Even if I have to rape you, I'll have you, by God! All night you've been encouraging me, leading me on with

THE TEMPEST LILY

those great eyes, and by Christ I won't be played for an idiot."

"I never encouraged you," she mumbled behind his heavy hand, but he was ripping her corsage open. Then his mouth was on her breasts. He was licking them, drawing her nipples erect. The sensation, so new to her, was bewildering, making her feel dizzy as if drunk with too much wine. He pinned her to the earth, her arms beneath her body.

She wanted to fight him, scratch his face, but she was powerless to move, he was so heavy. Now he was flinging up her skirt, his hand feeling her between her legs. She would kill him later for this. He ripped off his satin breeches and within seconds he was covering her completely, his powerful legs pushing hers apart. Then his hand released her mouth but his lips immediately covered hers, sucking them into his own so that screaming was impossible.

She felt delirious with his hands exploring her body, it was all happening so swiftly. It had no reality until he pushed himself high up inside her and she moaned with a moment's pain. Surprisingly, it was followed by a surging heat flooding her from head to toes. Oh Lord, it was wonderful, exquisite, the throbbing of her inside self.

Rape! He was raping her! But what a strange joy was the blood rushing through her—extraordinary, pulsating. As his great body gyrated on hers, the earth seemed to move and some pagan spirits sped her up, up, up to know complete bliss.

Minutes later he was still; then he rolled off her and lay on his back, breathing heavily beside her. "I suppose an apology is due you, Lily . . . but by Christ I didn't think you were a virgin. There was nothing virginal in the looks you were giving me all night."

"Damn you to hell! Does the king's letter of marque state that you may rape your countrywomen?" Never must he know how he had transported her with joy. She was dragging her skirt down to hide her nakedness, pulling her bodice over her breasts.

He gave a little laugh. "I'll bet by all the saints or Greek myths that you enjoyed it. You're made for coupling and every little part of you rose to welcome me. Hell and damnation, you may be inexperienced, but your responses would put Aphrodite to shame. You're as beautiful inside as you are outside."

She wanted to berate him and forced herself to get to her feet. "How dare you talk to me as if I were a common bawd! You're a rotten brute to have forced yourself on me."

"Don't lie to me, Lily. You wanted my lovemaking. You wanted the whole thing. You're as passionate as any woman I've ever known. I don't see how you were still a virgin." With a swift motion he knelt and ran his hand up her skirt, up her naked thighs to between her soft legs. Though loving his touch, she still pulled away from him. Her own nature was frightening to her. Then he was on his feet, grasping her in his arms.

"Come on, lovely devil, don't be shy with me." He covered her face with his warm kisses. His hand on her buttocks was pushing her body up against his swollen manhood. "You want me inside you but you don't want me to know it. Come, my lovely one." He laid her back on the grass and dragged her skirt off. "Let me see your body. By the Almighty, you're exquisite." In the moon's radiance her skin seemed to glow.

She lay trembling as he stared at her, but she wanted to see his body too. A naked man was new to her. She wanted to see the part of him that had helped to lift her to such heights. As he knelt beside her, he stripped off the last of his clothes. He was unbelievably magnificent, but she must not give the arrogant brute the satisfaction of knowing how she felt about him.

She grabbed at her satin skirt. "Adam, let me up! Let me go! I don't want—"

"Lovely little liar, you *do* want it all over again, but this time with tenderness. Let me teach you what real lovemaking is like."

THE TEMPEST LILY   33

He bent and started to kiss her breasts, and it was so wonderful that she could not stop her arms from cradling his head against them. Never had she believed lovemaking could be like this. Was it the same for everyone? Impossible! No man was a lover like Adam. Then he kissed her lips as his hands caressed her burning body.

Later, when he entered her, he taught her how to hold her legs up for more intense enjoyment, and when they were climaxing together, she moaned with delight as she clung to his shoulders, digging her nails into his flesh until she reached dreamland. Then she lay limp beneath him.

From far off across the ravines, over the precipices, floated the sound of an ancient church clock tinnily chiming five times. In half-sleep Lily counted and somehow managed to raise her heavy eyelids. Wherever was she? Then the extraordinary happenings of the night flooded her mind. She saw that she was lying on the earth, her nakedness covered by Adam's blue-satin doublet. He must have done that as she slept. Her head was resting on his great bare chest, his arm encircling her body. They had made love again and again, then fallen asleep.

So her maidenhead was gone—taken by Adam. As he had raped her, she had no need to upbraid herself for having sinned, but she knew she lied, for she had joyously sinned with him for hours afterward.

Now a soft underlying grayness was lightening the heavens. A tongue of flame shot across the sky and dawn started to roll back the night.

She glanced at Adam's handsome sleeping face, like a bronze carving, and suddenly she was infuriated with him. He looked so sure of himself. Damn him to hell! He had taken her last night as if she had been a whore! Worse, she had allowed it; and he was well aware, the arrogant swine, that she had reveled in his lovemaking.

But that girl of last night, as if bewitched by moonlight and the magnificent man, was not the true Lily Deveraux; he would find that out.

The sound of tinkling donkeys' bells alarmed her—grape pickers approaching the vineyards! They must not discover her. Gently she loosened herself from Adam's arm, grabbed her torn dress and swiftly wrapped the skirt around herself and pulled on the bodice. Let the workers find the great Lord Clune sprawled by the bushes, unclothed. They would have a jest for months to come, believing he had been tossing a serving girl who had left him.

Lily crept away, then ran across the garden to her window. In dismay she suddenly recalled that it was several feet off the ground. She must climb up the wall to the ledge.

Her hands reached up and grasped at a jutting piece of masonry, then searched with her feet for a hold in between the rough stones. She found two spots and started to climb, but her hands slipped and she slid down, badly scraping her bare arms. How the devil would she reach the ledge?

She tried again and slipped again, further tearing the skin on her arms. Without warning, powerful hands encircled her waist from behind.

"Allow me to assist you." Adam lifted her lightly and placed her inside the window.

Amazed, she looked down at him; he was dressed and must have silently followed her.

"Not very considerate of you," he whispered, "to have left me to be discovered sleeping like a barbarian."

"Barbarian! That's how you behaved!" She angrily threw the whisper down at him.

"I'll be back to take Lady Lily on our tour in a few hours." He grinned up at her, then gave her a mock sweeping bow.

4

LYING IN BED, too excited to sleep, Lily's mind relived the happenings of the night. Ever since childhood she had watched for Clune's return to Breck, measuring all other men beside a twelve-year-old girl's infatuated memory.

She could not make herself regret what had happened. Although she regretted having sinned, she did not linger on this aspect of the affair. Now Lily wondered, when he came to collect her and Marion, how best to behave toward him.

Haughtily? To punish him, letting him know she now accompanied him merely to please her grandmother? Coldly? Should she ignore him to show her disapproval of him? Normally? Acting with casual friendliness as if last night's lovemaking had never been? That would be wisest! That would be shattering to his self-assurance.

After a breakfast of melon, bread and coffee, Adam arrived, and Lily felt quite ready to confront him. He looked even more attractive in a plain cream doublet than in last night's satin. Her own appearance satisfied her—in a pale gray dress and a wide-brimmed hat held on with blue ribbons.

His pleasant good mornings, then his kisses of the marchesa's hand, then Lily's, were those of a friend, nothing more. He behaved exactly as if he were continuing their acquaintanceship started yesterday, and only once did she catch his eyes sweeping over her tightly laced bodice.

"Where to first?" he asked her. "Have you any special desires?"

"Yes, to visit the church of San Constanza, where my parents were married."

They set off, with Marion following at their heels. They spoke lightly of the island's beauty as they passed through shady lanes massed with lemon, fig and olive trees and then descended to a labyrinth of narrow streets, where small dwellings nuzzled into the hillside.

The tiny town of Capri was surrounded by a waist-high wall. The verdant hill on which it rested dropped to the sea half a mile below. In the sun-drenched marketplace, dark-skinned women in gaily colored garments with barefoot children clustered around stalls piled with fruits and cakes.

A stout, important-looking man marched into the square blasting on a trumpet. Instantly everyone flocked around him.

"What's that all about?" Lily asked Adam.

"It should be to announce that beautiful Lady Lily is here," he smiled teasingly, "but it's to announce that a cow has fallen over a cliff and it's for sale. A cow must die accidentally before the islanders have meat." Before Lily or Marion could comment, he changed the topic. "Ah, we've reached the steps. Three thousand years ago they were hewn out of the mountainside. They start at the beach, break here at Capri, then continue up to Anacapri."

They stood gazing up at Anacapri, where dwellings like eagles' nests balanced on the rocky heights. Holding the sides of her hat, her head thrown back, Lily asked, "Whatever made people build up there?"

"The higher up they went, the more security from invaders," Adam told her.

"Even to escape invaders I wouldn't live in such isolation. I'd stay to fight and even die." Lily searched for a safe footing on the roughly hewn steps.

"But Breck is isolated. You must have been lonely there."

"Not at all. I had many interests. Hunting, fencing, shooting. There were balls, the Eisteddfod, duties to the poor and sick and the splendid seasons in London and at court."

They all stood aside to allow a line of Capriote women, balancing big stones on their heads, to ascend the stairway. "Most houses up here have been carried up on women's heads," Adam noted. Then as the women called, *"Buon giorno,* noble lord," he smiled broadly and bowed.

Commendable of him, Lily thought; most noblemen give dogs better treatment than peasants.

"The Capriotes are my friends," Adam remarked.

"I'm amazed. Aren't the women terrified that you will press their men onto your ship?"

"On the contrary; that's what they want. I've a dozen Capriotes in the crew who always return with treasure for their avaricious wives."

The stairway wound around a bend, and the sea stretched before them. A few more steps brought them to the beach, which was dotted by gaudily painted fishing boats. Brown nets were spread to dry as their owners repaired them. Farther along the shore a crowd was gathered in a sheltered cove.

"They're admiring my ship!" Adam said softly, and Lily wondered if those wonderful blue eyes ever held such affection for a woman. "Would you like to see the *Fearless?* She is being careened, though, and no beauty looks her best undergoing treatment."

He strode so swiftly over the pebbly beach that Lily almost had to run to keep up with him, and Marion was even farther behind.

The vessel lay on her side in shallow water. Blocks and tackle tied to the mast had been strung through a grove of nearby trees, allowing the hull to have been pulled over. Dozens of sailors, stripped to the waist, stood knee-deep in water, scraping the ship's bottom.

"The top mast, guns and equipment have been removed to those tents," Adam said, nodding farther up the beach where armed seamen stood on guard.

"But why ever are your great guns mounted on earthworks?"

"While the *Fearless* is being careened she's vulnerable to attack from the sea, so she has to be protected. Here comes Salter."

"Good morning, Lady Lily, Mistress Marion. Forgive my appearance," Salter said as he glanced down at his soiled blue garments, "but today's a busy day." He looked at Adam. "I'm sorry, sir, but the carpenter says the teredo worm has a stronger hold than we feared."

"Curse the pest! When we're rid of it, we'll seal the sheathing with a mixture of tar, tallow and sulfur. That might repel the worm in future."

"Aye, aye, sir."

Bidding good-bye to Daniel, they continued walking toward a thickly wooded area at the mountain's base.

"Daniel Salter seems an honest fellow," Lily said with an air of innocence. "Strange that he's an officer on a privateer."

Adam knew she was trying to needle him. "Obviously a grave misfortune is responsible," he mocked. "Salter was serving in the Royal Navy, but after a battle he was captured by Turkish Corsairs. I took the ship several years ago and released him from the galley oars."

"You're probably an improvement on the Turks."

He grinned. "That's a great compliment." Glancing back at Marion walking a few feet behind, he said, "I told you about myself yesterday, so now tell me—why is beautiful Lady Lily on a lonely island?"

What should she say? She decided to tell him the truth, and when she finished he gave a low whistle.

"What courage there is in that delicate-looking body. Roger Huet and I were at Oxford together. We didn't like each other, but he's one of England's most eligible bachelors. Most women would consider him manna from heaven."

"I have no appetite for manna," Lily retorted. "Is

THE TEMPEST LILY 39

that San Constanza ahead of us?" She felt strangely moved at the sight of the little building half-hidden by cypress and pines. It was shabby with age and the moods of the elements.

"Yes, that's San Constanza," he said, "hardly changed in a thousand years."

Stepping into the shadowy interior, Lily suddenly wondered if he knew that she and Marion were Catholic. No matter; this was not England, so she need not hide her Catholicism. Dipping her hand into the holy water font, she was amazed to see his brown fingers beside hers. She stared up at him as he made the sign of the cross on himself.

He smiled, grasped her elbow and guided her deeper into the dim nave. "Architecturally there's nothing really to see."

At the stone altar rail, worn smooth by ten centuries of worshipers, the three of them knelt. Lily was absorbed with tender thoughts of her mother, a fifteen-year-old bride, kneeling here to whisper her marriage vows. And she had of course been a virgin. Shame swept over Lily at her sin committed with Adam, and she made a solemn vow never to lie with him again. Then her mind went to her father. Even then was he so brutal? The solemn proceedings must surely have irritated him.

Outside again in the sunshine, Adam chuckled. "You both looked so amazed when I blessed myself. Of course the marchesa had told me you were Catholic."

"Praise be to God that you are one of us, my lord." Marion's round face looked approvingly at Adam.

"I'm so glad, Adam." Words bubbled out of Lily as they crunched over the pebbles. "How good that we can talk openly."

"My family has always practiced the faith. That's why Queen Elizabeth punished us and robbed us of some of the richest estates in England and Wales. It was then my people turned to privateering. With prize money they were able to buy back some of our lands." His face hardened. "Not until every inch of Severn earth, every stone of Severn property is ours again, will I relinquish sailing the seas!"

Lily now understood him better. "Your vow is commendable. I hope you recover all of your land. But now where do we go? It's far too early to return to the palazzo."

"I suggest the Villa Jovis, if you don't mind the climb."

Their way lay through masses of fig trees that led to a height where the enormous ruins of Caesar Tiberius's palace sprawled over the peak of the thousand-foot-high Lo Copo.

"Really, Lady Lily, my feet won't go a step farther," Marion complained, "they're swollen already."

"Then sit down and be comfortable on that matted ivy. We shan't be long," Adam promised.

When he and Lily reached the summit, they stood catching their breath and gazing at the two-thousand-year-old ruins, chaste pillars, graceful stairways, tessellated courtyards, all open to the sky. Everywhere vegetation encroached on the once hallowed foundations.

"Just think of the people who lived in this great villa," Adam said. "What hate, love, jealousy. Now they are all dust. Perhaps Tiberius was standing on this very spot when word reached him of Christ's crucifixion."

Lily's eyes widened at the enormity of the thought. "You've seen so much in your travels, Adam; could Wales ever satisfy you again?"

"Damn my soul! What a question." He ran long fingers through his golden hair. "I put in often at Milford Haven and at nearby Ben Fras. It's connected by an underground passage with the castle where my father is governor."

"I suppose you offload prize goods at Milford Haven?"

"Exactly, fearing nothing from the castle's guns, which would fire on any other ship landing merchandise."

"How clever of you. But why must you enter Wales surreptitiously when you go freely about London?"

Her eyes upturned to him were provocative. Her slim beautiful body, the whole of her was so provocative.

"The *Fearless* has taken some prizes around Cardiff and Bristol, and the shipowners there have labeled me a pirate." He spoke dryly. "You know about pirates. They're hanged at Tyburn."

His words stabbed at her, but how ridiculous! Why should his fate worry her?

They continued walking across the tessellated courtyard to stand at a low wall at the edge of the precipice, looking into the sea far below.

Waving out across the vast glittering blue to the purple-blue outline of distant shores, Adam told her, "Far away over there is Venice, Virgil's grave and Tasso's birthplace. Tasso claimed that man had the right to embrace all beautiful things, love being the most beautiful."

Her eyes, turned up to his strong, handsome face, were almost mesmerized by him. Quickly he caught her in his arms, but she struggled against him.

"No, no Adam! Never again! I've made a vow."

Still he crushed her against his hard body. "Why not? In God's name! Be like Tasso and embrace love."

"No, no, please let me go. I can't sin like that again."

"By the Almighty, don't be insane! Here among the ruins of the dead. It's a lesson to us. One day we shall be dead and forgotten."

"I don't care, just let me go!"

But he pressed his lips onto hers as one hand caressed her breasts. And even as she fought to be free, he lowered her to the warm earth. Suddenly she weakened and betrayed herself, for she *wanted* to lie with him, wanted to feel him inside her again.

She had to stop herself from unlacing her corsage and instead let him do it. And when he started kissing her breasts, she knew this was the only thing in life that mattered to her. She was on fire for his lovemaking and helped him lift her full skirts up to her waist. Eagerly she spread her legs as he ripped his breeches off. When his huge body covered her, she could barely wait for him to thrust himself inside her. "Ah," she gasped as his swollen manhood filled her and made her throb with the exquisite sensation still so new to her, that sent her into a delirium of swirling happiness.

After a few minutes, when they were both lying quiet, he raised himself on an elbow and smiled down at her somnolent, contented face. "So last night was real," he murmured. "All day I've wondered if I'd been dreaming, but it's true. You are the most gloriously passionate woman I've ever had the joy to cover. I can't get enough of you, beloved."

"I'm glad. To me it's all so new and wonderful, I can't really believe it. But shouldn't we leave, lest Marion grow anxious?"

"She won't. Anyhow, she won't climb up here, so we don't have to worry."

"Oh, Adam, what would it be like to keep you inside of me for hours and hours on end?"

"Sounds like a game for the Greek gods. Let's try it again."

"Do you love being inside me?"

"You should only know how much!"

For the next two weeks Adam spent some hours each day showing Lily over the island, while each night he supped at the palazzo. Then later he and Lily lay hidden behind flowering bushes and made love. While she grasped at this wonderful happiness, she banished thoughts of the future from her mind. When Adam sailed away, she would just have to leave Capri, too, and travel to the New World.

"Adam seems fascinated by you, Amora," the marchesa said one morning over breakfast as Lily awaited his arrival. "He's never called here so frequently before." The lady's eyes were clamped on her beautiful granddaughter as she wondered whether Lily was in love with Clune.

"Oh, Adam enjoys being with a countrywoman, and I like being with him. He's so knowledgeable about the island."

Don't let Grandmother suspect the truth of our love-making, Lily prayed.

At that moment a servant brought Lily a note from Adam.

> Forgive me for not coming today, but it is essential that I remain to oversee the righting of the ship.

Why hadn't he asked her to watch the *Fearless* being righted?

Disappointed, she read the letter aloud, and the marchesa nodded. "It's a most important business for him. He sails shortly. His time in Capri is running out."

Lily deliberately changed the subject, "You know, Grandmother, my Italian is improving. Of course I knew a little from Mama, but now I can converse. I think I'll go into town with your maid Lucrezia if I may."

"Of course, dear child, she is now *your* servant."

A little later, with Lucrezia for chaperon, Lily left for the Marina Grande. She wanted to watch the *Fearless* being righted.

The ship's hull was half-hidden by an excited crowd. Undeterred, Lucrezia pushed to make a place where Lily could watch.

The ship was being slowly righted. Seamen, sweat pouring down their bodies, strained on ropes.

Searching the crowd for Adam, Lily's eyes easily found him, his head and shoulders above the rest. He was stripped to the waist as he moved swiftly from man to man, calling, "Easy there! Easy!" As the men pulled and the ship's sticks slowly began to point skyward, he shouted, "Put her down gently, by God!"

"Aye, aye, sir," the men grunted as the sharp edge of the keel crunched and bit into the pebbles.

"Bring her up slowly, by the Almighty!" Adam yelled, running from place to place. "All right! Ready now? . . . Then let her go!"

Men guiding the ship's hull jumped backward, splashing clear as the *Fearless* suddenly floated upright, its masts pointing to the sky. The crowd cheered excitedly, and Adam clapped bystanders on their backs. Fawning girls surrounded him, grabbing at his bare shoulders and arms. Lily gasped as he planted a swift kiss on a laughing girl's mouth. As others fought to be kissed, anger drove Lily rushing over the beach, back to the palazzo.

She then sent Lucrezia with a message to Adam, saying she was suffering a touch of sun and could not see him that evening. For a while she enjoyed her little triumph, but as the night dragged by, she cursed herself for having wasted it.

She was on the piazza the next morning when Adam strode around a cluster of red-flowered cacti, and she had to restrain herself from running to him.

"Lovely Lily, I'm delighted you've recovered." He kissed her hand. "I've planned a visit to the cave of Mithras."

It would be ridiculous to acquiesce immediately, so she said, "Marion also has a touch of sun." This was true.

"Then Lucrezia can accompany us."

The walk over the verdant, sweetly smelling hills was delightful.

"How noisy the cicadas are today." Adam smiled. "The tiny creatures are rubbing their legs together, and their funny sounds say, 'We—love—Lily. We—love—Lily.' You see, you've enchanted them too."

Laughing, they came upon an open space covered by an immense net stretched on tall poles. "It's to snare quails," Adam explained. "For centuries Capri has been their resting place on their spring and summer migrations."

"Even poor birds are victims to piracy." Lily laughed.

"Why should they escape? Watch for their arrival in the morning or evening. Like all tailless birds, they fly in a straight line." He nodded toward birds in boxes atop the poles. "They've been blinded, so they'll sing and decoy the others in."

A flight of ancient steps, remote, with a magnificent view of the sea and far-off islands, led to the cave of Mithras. Inside, between cracks in antique yellow masonry, luxuriant vegetation sprouted. Shadowy alcoves exuded an atmosphere of unending solitude timed by the rhythmic drip of water.

"Some say Caesar Augustus built this temple to honor Cybele." Adam's voice was almost an affront to the silence. "Others maintain that many centuries before the Romans came it was dedicated to the sun god Mithras." His warm fingers gripping her arm were welcome to Lily as they penetrated the eeriness.

"Those look like seats, as though this has been a small arena." Lily pointed out steps leading to a gallery.

"Undoubtedly, and this alcove held the sacrificial altar, and the blood ran down this marble drain."

"Alas, alas! There the lovely maiden Theano was sacrificed as her lover Upates watched her die." Lucrezia spoke in Italian. "Then he swore that their spirits would forever return to consummate their love, and he drowned himself. Now the ancient lovers' enchantment has fallen upon my lord and lady!"

"You talk with a fool's tongue!" Adam snapped, guiding Lily into a chamber so dark that details were indistinguishable, and Lucrezia did not follow them. "This cave has a happier legend, my darling," he murmured. "Those who kiss here will never be parted in spirit."

His arms caught her to him. He kissed her eyes, her cheeks, her throat, her mouth.

"Lily, Lily," he breathed. "By God you're exciting! All my life I've dreamed of a woman like you! You're lovely, lovely."

Kissing him passionately in return, her arms clung to his great shoulders. Far off, the sea pounded the rocks. Adam's heart thumped louder against her shoulder. Alone . . . alone, he and she. Alone in their togetherness. She loved this man. With all of her being she was *in* love with him. Now his arms were dropping her back to lie on the earth, and expertly he undressed her.

In the shadowy, ancient cave, his hands on her burning flesh were caressing, bringing her to life in a way that only he could. She sank her fingers into his thick hair, lost herself in his all-absorbing mouth. She curved her body to his to be one with him as he thrust his marvelous maleness into her, and then together they soared above earth, above all human happenings.

Later they lay side by side, almost too lethargic to move. After a while he said, "God knows what time it is, but we should be leaving." He got to his feet, then helped her up and assisted her to dress. As she bundled up her long hair and secured it with her silver combs, she suddenly ached to know if he was in love with her. He must be. He *must* be! The wildness of his lovemaking was surely proof. But supposing he was not. Absurd! Yet he had not told her that he loved her.

He guided her out of the cave into the sunlight. A little way off Lucrezia had fallen asleep under a fig tree. Laughing, they woke her and started on their way.

"We must hurry," Adam said. "My crew is victualing and watering, and I've a lot to attend to on the ship."

"You're leaving so soon, Adam, and you've never invited me aboard."

"But the *Fearless* was only righted yesterday; besides, it's a rule that women don't come aboard unless they are hostages. Sailors think they're bad luck—a Jonah." He grinned down at her. "Of course you could be an exception. We'll see how the victualing goes tomorrow."

"I hope you'll be supping with us tomorrow, darling. Lucrezia's sister is marrying, and Grandmother is giving her a fiesta."

"Certainly I'll be there."

As he went ahead of her to make a path through the tangled vegetation, Lily felt a creeping uncertainty taking hold of her. Would Adam leave Capri without declaring his love for her? Yet supposing he did *not* love her? Possibly he had only just discovered his love and would tell her later. Strange about the legend of the poor ancient lovers Theano and Upates. Could spirits really return to consummate their love through living beings? If so, had the spirits entered into Adam and herself? She shivered, even though the sun was still hot, for Theano's and Upates's lives had ended so tragically.

5

WHILE THE MARCHESA'S household prepared to fete the bride whose family had served the da Luccas for four generations, Lily watched vainly for a messenger to invite her to the *Fearless*.

Annoyed, she dressed for supper, wearing a sea-green satin bodice, the shade of which was flattering to the white skin of her bare shoulders and throat. Oiled eyelids made her eyes a luminous green. Her lips needed no reddening. Heavy pearls were entwined through her hair and worn low on her neck. She stepped back from the mirror, spreading out the pearl-embroidered skirt. She hoped Adam would think she was as beautiful as she felt.

Later at supper, with its eighteen varieties of fish, birds, fruit and savories, Lily fretted, longing to be alone with Adam, whose admiration for her glowed in his eyes. In cream damask, he was fascinating the other guests, an elderly count and countess. Music was coming from the great tent in the gardens, and the marchesa suggested they join the celebration.

In the marquee, lit by lanterns on poles, fresh flowers festooned the canvas walls, the refreshment table and the musicians' dais. Brightly dressed people, including the very old and very young, occupied chairs around the dance space. The marchesa's party moved to specially reserved chairs.

"An unusual wedding." Adam pulled his chair close to Lily's. "The bride is Capriote and the groom Anacapriote. For centuries their people have hated each other, and until his betrothal the groom had seldom left Anacapri."

"Then how did he meet the bride?"

"Anacapri has no wells, and its water comes from Capri. The groom was a water carrier, and that's how he met his bride. Watch now, the tarantella is beginning."

Alone on the dance floor, the bride faced the groom, who seemed uncomfortable in tight red velvet garments. Then tambourines rattled and castanets clicked. The groom bowed supplicatingly, but the bride scorned him. Several more supplications were refused until, relenting, the bride threw her arms around him.

The guests shouted their delight, the music went wild and the bridal couple broke into a whirling dance. Then other couples joined in, and soon the tent became a tapestry of shining, laughing faces, flashing eyes and teeth, swirling colored head cloths of the men, long hair of the women flying out. Men's white-hosed legs were hidden by bright swinging skirts.

"It's the gayest thing I've ever seen," Lily called excitedly to Adam.

"Shall we try it?" he asked eagerly, and Lily turned questioningly to her grandmother, who smilingly nodded.

With Adam's powerful hands grasping her waist, her hands gripping his forearms, Lily felt she was dancing as if by magic. Adam was expert at the tarantella, and

THE TEMPEST LILY

he almost lifted her from the ground as he swung her around. She laughed up into his admiring eyes as her hair loosened and fell to her waist.

The dance ended and they sat down, Lily's slim fingers trying to rearrange her hair as Adam took wine from a servant. "Leave your hair. It's beautiful hanging around your shoulders." In a dream she took the goblet of wine from him. "I've never seen you so lovely, so desirable." His voice was a caress. "I shall always remember you just like this."

At that moment the marchesa's hand touched Lily's arm, jerking her back to reality. "Dear child, I shall retire, but you may remain." She looked over at Adam. "This is *a rivederci,* Adam. Remember, let your rosary grow smooth and your sword grow rusty." She smiled. "Let's not have riches splashed with blood. God go with you, dear Adam."

Before sadness had a chance to settle on Lily, the music started, and once more she and Adam danced, and again she entered a dream. The wine, music, perfume of flowers—all affected her so strongly that she silently rebelled against time. Why couldn't she and the huge laughing Adam be like this forever? Why must there be a tomorrow of reality?

In a whirl Adam maneuvered her through a flap and into the garden. The night was so still only a wisp of scented breeze touched their cheeks. The lanterns had burned out, and the moon and stars lit the world. Arms around each other, they wandered along the flower-decked terrace. Half a mile below the sea was shiny, still, inscrutable. High above towered the dark mass of Monte Solaro.

"Look at the stars, Lily," Adam murmured. "Everywhere else in the world they are silver, but in Capri the stars are gold."

"What a lovely thought."

"It's not just a thought, my beloved, it's true. Look!" He stopped walking, and his arm held her against him as they stood staring up at the heavens. "You see, Lily, they are gold."

"How wonderful, they really are! Oh, Adam, this time tomorrow I shall be looking at them . . . alone! You'll be gone."

"Yes, and I'll be thinking of you. Your voice, your walk, the proud hold of your head, your wonderful green eyes. I'll be missing everything about you, all your secret beauties that only I know."

As he pulled her closer, she told herself, Now he will say I love you.

He chuckled and said, "My mistress, the sea, will be jealous of you."

"Damn the sea! Damn your ship! Damn your prizes!" The words burst from Lily. "Are these things all-important to you? I love you, Adam!" She grasped his arms. "Does that mean nothing to you?"

"Love? By God, Lily!" Then he gripped her shoulders, forcing her head back to stare into her face. "You mean that?"

"With all my being! Oh, Adam!" Her eyes searched his dark face, which was silhouetted against the moonlit sky. "You love me, I know it! Why won't you tell me?"

"Love you! Damn my soul!" he muttered thoughtfully, "yes, perhaps I do love you, but alas, love can have no place in my life yet! I'm tied to an oath! The Severn estates! I've got to work to get them back!"

"But, beloved, that doesn't stop you loving me!"

"Lily, God knows you're the most desirable woman I've ever known. Yet even loving you, what can I offer you? I can't ask you to spend your life waiting for me."

"I'll wait for you forever, Adam! Always! Always! I'll—"

"Hush, Lily! Hush. You don't know what you're saying."

"I do! Time is nothing when we love each other. That's all that matters. Oh, darling, I'm so happy! Now, one more thing. I must see the *Fearless*."

"At this hour! It's impossible!"

"It's not! I can slip away and be back before I'll be even missed. Oh, please, Adam darling! While I'm awaiting your return, I've got to be able to imagine you in your surroundings." She was determined to go.

"It's madness," he chuckled, "but I'll get Lucrezia from the tent to act as your chaperon."

The moon's rays lit the glassy water with a stream of light. The *Fearless* lay in the shadows, looming like a phantom ship. Adam rowed Lily and Lucrezia from shore.

When they stepepd on deck, the watchman saluted Adam and scowled at the sight of the women. Lily gazed at the vessel's structure, illuminated by pools of lantern light. "The ship I sailed on looked quite different."

"She was a passenger ship, with deckhouses," Adam explained with a laugh. "Our decks are clear for action and our gunwales have been raised to give protection when fighting." Grasping Lily's elbow, he led her past great guns glinting in the lantern light. She picked a footing between rows of ringbolts fastened to the deck for the attachment of guns' tackle.

Under a lantern seamen squatted, throwing dice. A couple of the crew bore the letter *T* branded on their cheeks, showing they had been caught as thieves. They acknowledged Adam with respect, though it was obvious they resented the presence of women.

"What a terrifying-looking lot," Lily whispered.

"They're not altar boys, my beautiful darling. The crew's a mixture—Welsh, English, Irish, a couple of Newfoundlanders, a Jamaican, Neapolitans, Capriotes. In fact, any good fighting seaman is welcome if we've space for him."

With Lucrezia trailing them, they descended a ladder, walked down a corridor, and Adam flung open a door. "Here's my cabin."

The way he grinned at Lily told her he knew she had been curious to see his quarters. Smiling in the same mood, she stepped into a small, low-ceilinged room, lit by a center hanging lantern. A walled bookshelf, a desk, a carved chest, a washstand, chair and cot were the only furnishings. The masculine severity pleased Lily. If she ever lived aboard with him, she would not change it.

"It has a monastic atmosphere," she told him.

"Ah, because I seldom have feminine visitors," he replied with an intimate smile.

"But what about women you take from prize ships at sea?" Her jealousy toward complete strangers surprised her.

"They are kept practically isolated," Adam said, throwing her a teasing look, and left the cabin. "No man may touch a woman against her will on pain of death."

"That's on a privateer." She smiled provocatively up at him, and he gave a low laugh.

"I still say you encouraged me on that first night. Now these doors lead to the crew's quarters," he pointed down the corridor, "although sometimes we're so crowded that men sleep on deck. They prefer sailing on a privateer to the navy. There's no torture. Instead, they receive fair treatment, and decent food and clothing is provided by the syndicate. It takes fifty percent of prizes and fifty percent goes to officers and men."

They passed through the main cabin to the quartermaster's room.

"Salter will be happy to see you." Adam opened the door. "And what man wouldn't, eh?"

Despite the late hour Daniel was at his desk. "Lady Lily, this is an honor." He swiftly cleared papers off a chair for her.

"We'll have some wine with Mr. Salter," Adam suggested, "then continue our tours." Pulling a silver whistle from a pocket, he blew it, and a cabin boy appeared. While Adam ordered, Lily signaled Lucrezia to sit on the floor beside her chair instead of standing.

"Is everything satisfactorily stowed aboard, Mr. Salter?" Adam asked.

"Everything is shipshape, sir. We've taken on plenty of water and wine, fruit and beans. Also a large supply of quail and fowl have been stacked in brine. As usual, there's no meat to be had."

THE TEMPEST LILY 53

"We'll manage without for a while." Adam turned to Lily. "Perhaps you'd like to glance at the Privateer Articles."

"Indeed I would!" She joined him at a table, where he opened a large leather-turned book, but a furious gust of wind suddenly rocked the ship, sending the volume to the floor. Lily's insides seemed to drop, and she noticed Adam and Daniel exchange questioning glances.

A shattering clap of thunder followed by a blast of wind seemed to lift the *Fearless,* then dash it down. The lantern was blown out, and the next second, as though demons were attacking, a gale was screeching around them.

"Poente!" Lucrezia screamed. "The devil storm! It comes all at once!"

Adam rushed the girls toward the door. "You must go ashore immediately."

On deck Lily's skirts were blown above her head as she struggled toward the gangway. Already the sky was a moving mass of angry clouds. Then lightning, like a bloody scar, split the heavens and lit the sea—a churning, boiling cauldron. Suddenly the ship started shifting.

"She's dragging her anchor!" Adam roared. "She'll dash against the rocks! All hands on deck!"

Like maddened shadows, men sprang on deck yelling, "Aye, aye, sir!"

"Up anchor! Set the foresail!" Adam yelled. "Stand out to sea!" Pushing Lily and Lucrezia in the direction of the companionway, he shouted, "Go below."

With the ship's tossing Lily lost her footing and pitched down the steps. Men rushing to get on deck knocked her down when she tried to get up. She yelled to Lucrezia but her voice was nothing in the bedlam of driving rain, thunder, the wind's shriek.

Anchor up and foresail set, the *Fearless* was now battling to tack into the wind to carry her out to sea. Rising to the top of a mountainous height, she shivered there for terrible seconds before she crashed down into a deep abyss. The torturing motion was continuous.

Snatches of cries from deck told Lily that Adam had

saved the ship from the rocks. But what could they hope for from the maddened sea, she wondered. "God be merciful. Preserve us. Preserve us!"

Rolling from side to side in the corridor, nausea blotted out fear, but retching brought no relief. Her head ached beyond endurance. Water sloshing down from the deck drenched her. Feeling sick to death, she lay there until a gray dawn light showed Adam, soaked clothes clinging to his muscled frame, hair plastered across his face, leaning down to pick her up.

Thank God he had not been washed overboard, Lily's bemused mind thought as she clung to him while he somehow maneuvered the journey to his cabin.

He dropped her on the cot. "Hold onto the sides!" he yelled, lurching out the door.

Alone in a demented world, she clung to the bed. She had no idea where Lucrezia was. The ship climbed a watery mountain, heaving her up, up, up so that her insides shook as though wrenched loose. Then she was cruelly flung down again.

For untold hours the torture continued. It seemed impossible that the *Fearless* could withstand the sea's savage poundings. She must split open! The roar of wind and sea and the ship's groaning timbers added to the horror.

Darkness ruled until a cabin boy with a swinging lantern struggled to the cot, clutching a bowl that he wedged into the crook of Lily's arm. Then, his lantern swaying drunkenly, he disappeared. Lily's fingers scooped up some cold gruel that she managed to swallow, but, as the ship pitched forward, the bowl crashed to the floor.

Was Adam safe? How could men remain on deck? Surely the sea must wash them away. Adam! Adam! God, don't let him die! Stop the storm! Lily prayed.

Light came, but still the cataclysmic storm raged on. Then it was dark again, and the boy brought more gruel, and always there was the storm. This was actually hell, Lily's benumbed mind told her. For her sins she would perpetually suffer this screaming wind, this madly tossing sea.

Gradually, unbelievingly, she became aware that the punishment was not quite so furious. The waves were not so gigantic, the wind's roar was lessening, then the rain ceased and, God be praised, a few hours later it was over! The only sounds were creaking timbers and wind in the rigging as the *Fearless* plowed through the long swells. Thank God the ship had come through! But what of Adam? Was he all right?

"I've brought you some broth, your ladyship." Lily's eyes flew open to see a young sailor by the cot offering her a bowl. "It's hot. Made over our first fire for four days."

"We've been at sea for four days?" Lily gasped. "The captain! Is he all right?"

"Sleeping like a babe! I'm Valentine Dawson, your ladyship, and in fifteen years at sea I've never known such a storm. Blew us out of the Mediterranean and into the Atlantic!"

"Where is Captain Clune sleeping?"

"In the quartermaster's cabin. He never left the deck until a little while ago! You've never seen the like of him, with his hair blowing in the wind, swearing he would not let the storm take his ship." Valentine was enjoying himself. "The wind drove us so we covered a ten-days' ordinary journey."

"Then we won't be back in Capri for ten days?" How wonderful to have this unexpected time with Adam.

"We're not going back to Capri." Valentine laughed. "We're West Indies bound, hoping to fly at high game!"

"Inform Lord Clune as soon as he awakens that I wish to see him."

"Don't fuss yourself, your ladyship. The cap'n will see you enjoy the voyage." Valentine's lewd wink was infuriating, but before she could reprimand him, he had left the cabin.

West Indies? Was Valentine right? she asked herself. If so, did it mean that Adam did not wish to be parted from her? Wonderful, exciting speculations presented themselves. Where could they be married? Would they live on the *Fearless?* Anywhere with him would be heaven. Though she was exhausted, she wanted to remain awake, reveling in the marvelous possibilities, but sleep mastered her.

When she awakened, the cabin had been cleared. Splintered furniture was gone, Adam's precious books that had been awash on the floor were piled next to a wall. Through the open window, blessed fresh air was pouring in. There was a basin of water and soap and, next to them, a doublet, breeches and hose, obviously Adam's, were laid out for her to change into.

She washed and changed quickly, enjoying wearing his huge clothes. Then, taking some of Adam's sodden books, she sat at the window separating and drying the pages as she excitedly awaited him. She had loosened the pages of three books when he arrived. His face was strained, his eyes shadowed; a bruise was turning purple.

"Adam, darling!" She jumped up, catching his arms. "You were hurt!"

"Sit down, Lily—please." He shook her hands off.

His rudeness was almost like a physical blow, and her temper flared. "How dare you behave like this?"

As he sat down, he shot her a swift allover glance, but the sight of her in his apparel brought no amusement to his eyes. "Just how do you expect a man to behave who's battled a four-day fury? With a helmsman washed overboard, a hand killed by a falling spar and four others seriously injured?"

"I'm sorry about the losses, Adam." There was reason, of course, for his ill temper. "But it was wonderful how you brought the ship through." Why was he looking at her so coldly? "When will we reach Capri?"

With calculated deliberation he crossed one leg over the other. "A year . . . perhaps more . . . probably two."

"Oh darling, does that mean you want me with you?"

"It's not what *I* want!" he snapped, feeling trapped.

"The entire company of eighty men voted to hold you for ransom."

Shock momentarily constricted her throat. Her great green eyes stared into Adam's hard, impassive face. Involuntarily a spiral of high-pitched laughter broke from her. "Ransom! I don't believe it!"

"I'm sorry, Lily. I tried everything to prevent it. At first the crew blamed you for the storm. Sailors are very superstitious. Some of them were for tossing you and Lucrezia overboard until they realized your potentialities as a valuable prize. On a privateer everything is decided by general vote. A captain has sole command only in battle." He shrugged. "There's nothing I can do, though by God I tried to save you."

"How can they hold me for ransom? If they know we are to be married—"

"Married!" He stared so coldly at her that she felt death brush her heart. What had happened to him?

"What else? I told you I'd wait for you. You swore you loved me and—"

"Stop, Lily! I said perhaps I love you."

"You swore you loved me! That you would return for me." Shock, disillusionment and humiliation sickened her. "I should have known that a thief would also be a betrayer!"

"Listen to me, Lily!" He jumped up, shaken. "When you made your unexpected avowal of love to me, surely I would have been ungallant and a lout not to have pretended I loved you."

"Pretended!" Suddenly she hated this insulting brute in all his arrogant maleness. If she had had a horsewhip, she would have lashed it across his face. "I demand that you return me to Capri! My grandmother will pay your filthy ransom money!"

"Five thousand pounds? As part of my syndicate, she would hardly appreciate that." He laughed dryly. "Anyhow, we can't waste the time. My commission from the king has less than four months to run. Time is of the essence. We must keep heading for the West Indies. I assure you I don't relish having a beautiful woman like you and your attractive maid on board. It can cause trouble, so I intend putting you ashore as soon as possible, at Jamaica. From there Lord Deveraux can ransom you with a draft on a London bank."

Ridiculous! Impossible! Adam *could not* look at her, talk to her, like this—this man who had so desired her.

As though reading her thoughts, he said, "I wish I could make you understand. The syndicate and the men have got to come before my personal feelings."

"You coward, to sacrifice me."

"I'm sorry. I don't want to." He shrugged impatiently. "You'll receive honorable treatment. I'll relinquish my cabin to you, and a guard will be posted continually outside your door."

Lily laughed, not hysterically but with irony. "Adam, hasn't the thought crossed your avaricious mind that my father won't want me back?" Her voice rose. "I'd swear he'd not give a halfpenny for my ransom."

"I had considered that, so I shall also write to your mother, and if she cannot raise five thousand pounds, she'll probably appeal to Roger Huet for a loan."

She must be going mad, Lily thought, as disgust sickened her. "Get out!" she muttered, her eyes like accusing lights glaring from an ashen face. "You low, rotten cur!"

Without another word he left, cursing the bloody storm that had kept her aboard and forced him into this degrading position so that he must act contrary to the way he felt.

6

WITH THE RETURN of normal weather, life aboard assumed a pattern. Adam moved into Salter's cabin. Lily occupied Adam's bed, with Lucrezia sleeping on a mattress on the floor. At night Valentine stood in the corridor, lest seamen hungry for women should creep along. Their meals were served in the cabin, and their clothes-shortage problem was solved by the quartermaster producing lengths of dirty-white linen from his stores, which Lucrezia made into bodices and skirts.

Though wishing to avoid any contact with the powerful, almost swaggering figure of Adam as he walked the deck, Lily was driven by the smallness of the cabin to sit on the quarterdeck in a hammock chair Adam had instructed the carpenter to make. Officers on watch, including Daniel, were aloof. Sailors pretended she was not there. Her face half-hidden by a book, she watched Adam as he conducted the ship's business. Where was the happy, wonderful lover of Capri in this stern man? Twice he approached her and attempted conversation, and she found satisfaction in ignoring him and his invitation to eat in the dining salon.

After a few more days with only Lucrezia's chatter, boredom defeated pride. Making the best of her appearance in a white linen dress made by Lucrezia, she entered the low-ceilinged dining salon, her head, adorned with bunches of ringlets, held high. Adam placed her on his right hand, then made the introductions.

"Lady Lily, may I present Mr. Liam Traherne, second mate?" On deck Lily had noticed the big man whose eyes were as black as his hair. He bowed stiffly, and she nodded. Adam went on, "And our doctor, Glynn Moody." Lily thought his face suited his name. She inclined her head to him. "Mr. Abraham Watts, our sailing master." Lily nodded curtly to the disagreeable-looking man. "Mr. Salter you of course know."

Though despising these men who held her captive, she was soon grateful for their intelligent conversation.

"Well, Captain, to return to the subject of Harvey's theory of blood circulation," the doctor said, "and Glisson's ideas on anatomy . . ."

"Yes, yes," Adam nodded, "the study of natural science is growing. Digby is inquiring into the nature of bodies, I hear. Asking how the vital spirits are sent from the brain into intended parts of the body without mistaking their way."

She sensed that Adam was deliberately concentrating on Moody to demonstrate that her presence meant nothing to him. Well, she would simulate interest in the other men. Watts was lost in his food and rum. But Traherne, handsome in an unpolished way, and Salter were nice.

She used her charm and wit to put the young men of modest background at ease with a titled woman.

"Mr. Traherne, I know some of Mr. Salter's history, but none of yours. I'm sure it's exciting."

"Well now, Lady Lily, it's not really exciting." The big man looked abashed as his fork dug at an oyster. "My Irish parents settled in London. Later, Father was pressed into the navy and left Mother with eleven children. For years we mourned him as dead while he was suffering floggings, stinking food, small pay and no shore leave in case he jumped ship." Traherne's face looked bitter. "Then his luck changed when pirates seized the ship and he joined up with them. In four years he had enough treasure to quit the seas, and he came home—poor fool!"

"Was he caught and hanged?" Lily was genuinely sympathetic.

"No, he landed secretly in London. What a miracle it was to us that he was alive and we were rich!" Traherne laughed nastily. "He entrusted his bags of jewels to merchants to sell, but they cleared off and Father died penniless."

"How cruel," Lily murmured, "how very cruel."

"I was pressed into the navy, too, but after a few years, thank God, I landed on *Fearless*."

"When Traherne has made his pile, it's Tortuga for him." Salter spoke teasingly as though this was an old joke between them.

"Ah, that's an island right out of heaven." The Irishman's eyes became almost loverlike. "High mountains, tall trees, wine from coconut palms, wild pigeons in plenty and fine crabs litter up the shore." His voice took on a lilting tone. "I'm going to build a house in the sun—bring my mother and sisters out of London's fog. Have fruit trees, a boat and do a bit of fishing."

His dark eyes suddenly burned challengingly into Lily's face and she sensed he wanted to discover if, from her position of wealth, his ambition seemed pitiable.

"What a wonderful idea," she said enthusiastically.

He smiled half-apologetically. "Of course all of that is nothing to someone like you. Anyhow, I'm a long way off from settling on Tortuga."

"I hope not." Advising herself not to neglect Salter, she said, "The fiddlers are excellent, Mr. Salter." She nodded to the two players. "Is it permitted to dance after supper?"

Salter's stolid face lightened. "You're very kind, Lady Lily, but I'm afraid I'm a poor dancer."

"She would make a splendid teacher," Adam observed, and Lily congratulated herself. Despite his absorption, he had listened to her conversation. She would fascinate Salter and Traherne, not just to irritate

Adam, but might they not help her escape when the *Fearless* put into Madeira to repair some of the recent damage? She would promise them a reward from her family if they aided her.

Upon reaching Madeira, Adam gave orders that she be locked in her cabin.

She stared angrily through the window at Funchal Island, with its green mountains towering over the little harbor. Ships with naked masts were taking on fresh water and fruit. Traherne had promised to arrange for one of the vessels to carry her letters to her mother. To banish nostalgic thoughts Lily forced her attention on the sun-browned children, who dived from rowboats for coins sailors threw into the water.

Leaving Madeira, the *Fearless* caught the northeast trade winds, which it was hoped would carry her swiftly across the Atlantic. The first afternoon out Lily was permitted on deck again, where she enjoyed watching hundreds of porpoises cavorting beside the ship, looking absurdly like fat women.

The rigging sang with wind. Unseen fiddlers played for the crew's amusement. And laughter accompanied a friendly game of dice. Staring up at the great sails, Lily thought that this trip would have been lovely had Adam been the same man he had been on Capri. On the sanded, dazzling white deck, a shadow fell across her feet. Lily looked up at Adam's great height rising like a tower beside her, the sun glinting on his thick red-gold hair.

"I wanted you to know, Lily, that at Madeira I dispatched a message to your parents. If they respond at once, you should not be kept long in Jamaica."

For a moment her eyes blazed up at him. Then she lowered them to her book, pretending to read.

"This is ridiculous!" he blurted out. "We'll be together for several months. It's childish to maintain this quarrel."

"I have no quarrel with you, only contempt!"

"Damn my soul! Matters would have been worse for

you if you'd fallen to Sallee pirates, who'd have clapped you into a harem or offered you on the slave block."

"At least I wouldn't be disillusioned by the Turks' betrayal!"

"No, by God! But you wouldn't like their treatment. On *Fearless* you're protected."

"And the bed is soft and the food fresh," she spat at him.

"Lily, for God's sake!" Her presence was disturbing to him. He recalled her in her lovely nakedness. "Do you think I enjoy holding you for ransom? There are eighty men against me. What can I do?"

"You could have freed me in Portugal."

"You are impossible!" He swung around and strode off to an unhampered spot, where he commenced pacing the deck, hands clasped behind his back.

Shaken by the knowledge that he had actually sent the ransom demand, she was about to go below when Traherne came up to her, his grin spreading almost to his ears.

"Your letters to your mother will not be long in reaching her," he said in a low voice, glancing cautiously at Adam.

"I'm most grateful. Do stay and talk if you have time."

"And if I did not, I'd pirate it." He laughed, settling cross-legged on the deck at her feet.

"Tell me what the news was in Madeira."

"A brigantine out of Plymouth says Charles will soon march against Scotland. The armies are gathering."

"How awful!" What would her father's position be? By feudal law noblemen must either lead troops into the field on the king's behalf or give money.

"I took the liberty when I was ashore of buying you some brocades." Traherne flushed with embarrassment. "And some hose. I've given the package to Lucrezia."

"How very thoughtful of you!" Gazing into Traherne's sea-weathered face, the adulation she saw there aroused her shame. It was wicked to encourage him too much. "You will allow me to refund you the cost . . . when I'm able to."

"Don't talk of that," he said proudly. "It spoils my pleasure."

"That's the last thing I want to do."

To cover the embarrassing moment they both glanced over at Adam, pacing the tiny space. There was a change in the curve of the sails, and he rapped out a reprimand to the man at the wheel for not noticing it.

Traherne must know so much about Adam that she did not, Lily mused. "*Fearless* is the captain's first love," she said lightly.

"His only love! Begging your pardon, but I've known some heartbroken females because of it."

Who were these women? Lily wanted to ask. Her green eyes followed Adam as he moved closer and joined the helmsman to examine the slate, which showed the hourly casting. Later he would note speeds of three to five knots in his log.

Lest Adam had gone there to overhear her conversation, she said, "The very emptiness of the sea is wonderful, Mr. Traherne. Here there's nothing to show of time's passing, no sign of man's efforts."

"Such empty seas are bad for a privateer. Sometimes I've wondered if the lookouts atop the masts are asleep."

"Tell me, why do I always hear the sails taken in just before dawn?"

"Because sensible captains show no lights at night. Until daybreak we don't know what to expect on the horizon, so we lie ahull."

Adam left the deck.

"The sea is running high and the roll seems steeper," Lily noted, "so I think I'll go below. Besides, I'm eager to see your lovely gift."

"I look forward to talking to you again, your ladyship." Liam smiled broadly, then walked away to take up his duties.

Inside the cabin Lucrezia was lovingly laying out

THE TEMPEST LILY

lengths of brocade. "Mr. Traherne is so clever. This rose color is good for my lady."

Taking off her bodice, Lily draped the brocade over her bare shoulders to survey the effect in the small hanging mirror when there was a rap on the door.

"See who it is," she told Lucrezia, and as the door opened, she saw Adam's reflection filling the doorway.

He shot a swift glance at her, then closed the door behind him and dropped a large bundle on the cot.

Pulling the fabric closer over her breasts, Lily swung around. "Of course this is *your* cabin, but while I occupy it under duress, be good enough to wait until I ask you to enter."

Not taking his eyes from Lily, he muttered, "Leave us, Lucrezia!" The startled girl slipped out. "I saw that you were ready to receive anyone, Lily, so I came in. Just why do you persist in behaving like a spitfire? I've tried to explain that I am powerless to save you from this situation. My mistake was to have permitted you to come aboard."

She eyed him rebelliously. "I understand you are obliged to hold me for ransom, that you find it necessary to lock me up in port, but why do you invade my privacy?"

By his taut jaw muscles she knew she had sparked his pride. "You persist in this stupid attitude, so I'll leave you to enjoy it. Thinking you were short of garments," his big hands angrily ripped open his bundle, "I bought you these in Portugal." He pulled out beautiful silks. "But I see your wants have been amply supplied." She was so desirable he ached to have her that very minute.

He was jealous! Was not jealousy the angry child of love? "Yes, I have been amply supplied." Swinging back to the mirror, she assiduously draped Traherne's brocade about herself. "Be sure to add the cost of your package to my ransom price!"

His face stiffened with rage. "God blast you! Since you insist upon behaving like a baggage, I'll treat you like one!" With a swift movement he ripped Liam's gift off her, revealing bare breasts and shoulders.

"How dare you!" she gasped. Springing to the cot, Lily swept his silks into her arms, dashed to the window and tossed them into the sea.

"You she-devil! By God, I'll cure you of your insolence!" He gripped her shoulders, his fingers digging into her flesh. "I'll teach you I'm no Roger Huet!"

Her clenched fists pounded his chest, but his steel-like arms crushed her to him, pinning her fists against his chest. His hot mouth was harsh on hers. She must get away from him! He was treating her like a harlot. He did not love her, did not wish to marry her. Yet the terrible truth was that she did not want to part from him.

When he lifted her onto the cot, she had almost stopped struggling. But when he lay beside her, she lashed her pride to rescue herself. He only wanted her body to appease his desire—her title for ransom. "Adam! Let me up!" she beseeched.

She felt his whole body stiffen. After a moment's pause he let her go. She sat up, wrapping her slender arms around herself, her dark hair cloaking her shoulders. "You told me you don't love me—and you'd flog any man of your crew who used a woman like this," she murmured.

The expression in his eyes was incomprehensible to her as they raked hers. Questioning, loving, repentant? Slowly he swung his legs to the floor. Sitting on the edge of the cot, elbows on his knees, he dropped his head in his hands. He didn't move for several moments. She ached to take his hand to her breast, to tell him she was his if he loved her.

Adam lifted his head, his face showing his inner turmoil. "Lily, I'm sorry." He stood up. "Never before, I swear, have I ever acted the brute." He straightened his doublet, then ran a finger between his shirt and his neck as though trying to let air in. "You're dangerous—blasted dangerous! I'd forego any prize money to rid my ship of you."

Gathering some brocade around herself, Lily murmured quietly, "And I'd relinquish all my inheritance if I could undo having met you." At this moment she spoke the truth; no man had humiliated her, made her suffer as Adam had. No other man had the power to stimulate her like he had.

For a moment he stared at her as though he were going to say something else. Then, as though deciding against it, he walked to the door and left.

At least this time she had triumphed over her sensuousness. She went to the window to stare out at the rippling sea. What awaited her when she reached Wales? Her father's anger because she had run away, his insistence that she marry Roger if Roger still wanted her? Whatever it was, she would confront it without fear.

Lucrezia, entering the cabin, broke into her musings. Smiling knowingly, the girl started folding the fabrics. "My lady, it is funny. Valentine will not leave me alone. He has promised me gifts from the first prize the ship takes." She tossed her curly head flirtatiously so that her brass loop earrings tinkled. "But I do not let him know how I like his big shoulders and little hips."

Lily laughed at her coquetry. "You are unfaithful, Lucrezia. Your lover is probably weeping for you in Capri while you encourage another man."

"Ah, my lady, he will not weep for long. Come, let me sew something for you from Mr. Traherne's material." She winked impishly. "It will make him happy and Lord Clune feverish with jealousy."

7

As the sun strained through a heavy mist curling over the Atlantic, in the dimly lit cabin the officers sat disconsolately at the card table.

"Cursed luck!" Watts's mottled face was darkly furious. "For weeks we've encountered nothing but British ships. Now with our first prize, what happens? An unseasonable fog comes up so she gives us the slip!" He slapped his cards down on the table.

"Damnable." Adam spoke casually, taking his silver pipe from his mouth. "But there'll be other prizes." Determined to take the men's minds off their grievances, he remarked, "Interesting pipe, this—Raleigh's gift to my grandfather after they'd sailed in the Cádiz expedition." His thumb tamped tobacco into the bowl. "Great man, Raleigh. I'm proud to carry on in his tradition—never to allow the Spanish to assume divine right to the New World's trade!"

"I agree, sir!" Liam was vehement. "No enterprising British mariner would tolerate it!"

"Indeed? You speak as though you command a ship." Adam frowned.

Liam's face stiffened. Lily felt it was unnecessary for Adam to demean him. "Are there no men with more noble purposes than trade who wish to populate the New World?"

"In twenty years of sailing I've never met a man who

didn't act for profit," Watts said nastily. "And if we don't seize a prize soon, the fine manners of the gentlemen aboard will disappear."

"Visibility is getting worse." Eyes on the window, Adam scraped back his chair. "If you'll excuse me, I'll see what's happening on deck."

The doctor, Watts and Salter left with him. Turning to Traherne, Lily said, "It's rather like a London fog."

"Nothing is as bad as that! I hate London. No wonder fifty thousand people, mainly Londoners, have gone to the New World."

"Yes," Lily said thoughtfully, "I've been considering Virginia as the answer to my own problem."

The devotion in Liam's eyes saved his smile from appearing condescending. "What problems have you, Lady Lily, with your wealth and position?"

"Wealth and position don't necessarily relieve one of problems." With a little encouragement she revealed her story.

Throughout her recital, Liam's mobile Irish face changed constantly in tune with her tale, which omitted all mention of Adam.

"Now you can understand that I dread returning home," she ended.

The dark Gaelic eyes showed her that Liam was planning something. "You cannot return."

"But how can I help but return? I'll be a prisoner in Jamaica until the ransom arrives, then I'll be shipped home under guard." Now was the time for him to offer aid.

"I swear before God, I want no part of the money. But of course that's not enough to free you." He ran a hand through his long black hair. Deep in concentration, he got to his feet, leaned over her and asked, "Would you let me help you if I can?"

She grabbed his arm. "Oh yes—yes—yes!"

At that moment Adam entered, and Traherne sprang back from Lily's hold. For seconds the big men's eyes measured each other. Finally Adam spoke quite casually to Lily.

"Your maid is causing trouble. Two men have just knifed each other over her favors. Kindly instruct her to stay away from the crew."

Lily rose with haughty indifference. "Lucrezia is bored with being a prisoner. She likes to wander about the ship. Nevertheless, I'll go and relay your instructions."

Through storms and mists, against adverse winds and currents, *Fearless* had crossed the Atlantic. Now in her third month out of Capri, she plowed the waters of the West Indies, but still the lookouts atop the masts spied no prize sails. Officers and crew had developed a habit of angrily scrutinizing the sea. Tempers were quickly shown and conversations dangerously argumentative. Adding to the general depression was the diet of salted oysters and dried peas. Water from the bompkin, slimy with living things, was cut to three portions a day per person.

Lily and Adam saw nothing of each other privately, and at meals their relationship was that of strangers. Her time was passed in reading. She no longer raged inwardly over his treatment of her. She had forced herself to despise him, but her mind was never free of the agony of wondering how she could escape.

All her hope, when the ship put in at the Canary Isles, and later at Cape Verde, was in ashes. Adam had locked her in the cabin with a sentry at her door.

Once at sea again she was freed, but since the day Adam had found her in intimate conversation with Liam, it had become impossible to talk to him alone. Daniel would join them, or Adam would pace within earshot. At night, to the accompaniment of fiddlers, Traherne sang Irish songs with his rich voice, Daniel sat with her so Liam could not join her. It was obviously Adam's design, damn him! Liam was the only crew member whom she considered a friend.

At the poopdeck rail, bored and unhappy, she stood

watching a school of whales break the water's surface, spouting. She glanced back at Lucrezia, who made a pretty picture as she sat with her red skirt spread on the white deck, her dark head cocked provocatively at Valentine, who was seated cross-legged beside her.

"As a boy, I didn't know there were girls as pretty as you," Valentine said.

"Were the women you knew all so ugly?"

Glad that the faithful Capriote had found some happiness aboard, Lily looked back to the sea.

"Everyone I knew was hideous," Valentine said. "Near the Scotch coal mines they're a black, savage people. If you're lucky you live in a hovel. If you're homeless the law forces you into the mines. Till I was twelve my family camped underground. But that's long ago. Now life is wonderful." He suddenly groaned. "Or it would be . . . if only we would spy a sail!"

"I'm tired of hearing you say that!" Lucrezia pouted.

"You should hear my mates. Going near insane with the empty seas, they are."

"Lady Lily," Liam's voice sounded near her ear, and she swung around to smile up into his eager face. "I've been trying to talk to you for days."

"Captain Clune has been preventing it, Liam." Her use of his Christian name was rewarded by sparkling eyes.

"I've got a plan for you." He shot an anxious glance over his shoulder at Daniel, who stood at the wheel, then spoke rapidly. "Once we reach Jamaica, you'll be entrusted to a Portuguese Jew—Sanchez. He'll guard you like a jewel, but I've a friend, a Jesuit priest, Father Dalvarez. I've done him many a good turn. With his help, I'll somehow smuggle you aboard a Virginia-bound ship and—"

"Searching the seas for a sail?" Daniel asked as he joined them. "We'd better find one soon! They're snarling below decks!"

"Yes, they swear the captain set a bad course," Liam said. "Well, I must move off." His look laid his heart at Lily's feet, and her eyes told him of her gratitude, relief, elation.

"Birds!" Daniel unexpectedly cried. "Birds!" and everyone rushed to look at the dirty white gulls dropping from the naked blue. "Man-of-war birds, which means we're near land."

"Thank God, we'll get fresh water!" Lily exclaimed. Her world was almost bright again. Liam had a plan! She would be free. Suddenly she jumped with fright as something flew over the rail and landed with a sloppy thud at her feet.

"Only a flying fish!" Daniel laughed. "We're pretty close to land. I wonder what spot it is?"

At supper, in contrast to Lily's almost happy mood, she noticed that the men's nervousness was intensified and the sailing master's rum-soaked face looked forbidding.

"I swear there's a cursed jinx on us!" Watts's heavy fist pounded on the table, and his eyes rested maliciously on Lily. "I've never known such empty seas. It's queer. Blasted queer!"

Daniel and Liam exchanged anxious glances with the doctor, then Daniel said, "The men are so jumpy, Captain, because they know your letter of marque hasn't long to go and they think—"

"To hell with what they think! The rabble!" Adam's blazing eyes swept around, resting on each officer in turn. "The first man who utters a mutinous whisper, I'll have him lashed to the mast and flogged until he's speechless! Let the men know that!"

"Aye, aye, sir," the officers muttered, busying themselves with their food, and Adam turned to Lily.

"In the crew's ignorant, superstitious minds, they have decided that you and your maid are Jonahs."

Her startled mind questioned what seriousness was attached to the accusation.

Liam broke out, "But, sir! Every time the men have dared say that to me, I've reminded them that holding Lady Lily was their idea."

"Of course, I've done the same!" Adam snapped.

THE TEMPEST LILY

"The cold fact is that the men are searching for a victim." He leveled his look on Lily. "I'm sorry, but you're their choice."

She fought to hide her apprehension. "What happens to a supposed Jonah?"

"You'll be put ashore at the first land we sight."

"But, sir!" The knuckles were white on Liam's big hands grasping the table edge. "You can't leave two women in just any desolate spot. Think what might happen to them while they wait, perhaps years, for a passing ship."

A desolate spot—waiting years! Lily's eyes darted to Adam.

"The natives around here are nearly all friendly," he said. "Damn my soul, Traherne! Do you think I *want* to maroon them? I've no choice! I've just had a deputation from the crew. They're determined to be rid of the women, even ready to renounce the ransom. Don't you realize Lady Lily and Lucrezia aren't safe aboard? Any moment some superstitious fool might do away with them."

"I still want them to remain aboard." Traherne spoke with slow determination, his face haggard with fury.

"You are outvoted!" Watts growled belligerently, and his bloodshot eyes looked murderous. "The crew has decided. For myself, I agree with them. Be rid of the women!"

For a moment Lily was sure Liam was about to spring up and grapple with Watts, but he swallowed dryly.

"But can't you as captain insist I remain until Jamaica?" she swiftly asked Adam.

"No! In God's name! I dare not cross them! Eighty men who've been without pay for almost four months! I'll tell you what that means! Along the corridors and up the rigging will go a whisper: 'Seize the ship! Mutiny!'"

"If the men rise, Lady Lily—" the usually calm doctor was agitated—"there'll be twenty to thirty dead before order is restored."

"If it *is* restored," Watts sneered.

Lily remembered tales of people being marooned, forgotten by the world, living out their lives watching, hoping, praying for a ship that never came. She must somehow save herself. She turned to Adam, and suddenly her world changed. For the shadow of a moment, the blue eyes were warm, loverlike. But she was mad! Nothing but her imagination. The eyes into which she looked were like glass, the face like granite.

"I promise you I'll leave you as well protected as I can, Lady Lily," he said. "Now I must deny you the musicians and Mr. Traherne. Songs and music might hold off the crew's ugly mood." He rose. "It would be wiser if you did not join us on deck tonight."

As the door closed behind him, panic swept through Lily. Then desperation sired an idea. With the crew so close to mutiny, they would surely follow Liam if he led them! Once in Adam's place, Liam could use force to save her. As he pulled out her chair she whispered, "Come to my cabin after the music."

He nodded, and the expression in his eyes told her he would do anything for her.

In the cabin she found a terrified Lucrezia. "Valentine says we are going to be—"

"Yes, yes, but we have a friend," Lily whispered and grasped the girl's shoulders. "Get Valentine away from the door. Mr. Traherne is coming to help us!"

"At once. I will walk so," Lucrezia wiggled her behind, "and he will follow." She darted away as Liam's voice singing an old sea chanty floated over the warm air.

He that is a sailor must have a valiant heart
And must with noble courage, all dangers undergo
In fight, in fight how e'er the wind doth blow.

Mixed with her bitter thoughts Lily visualized the scene on deck. Full white sails like gigantic wings spread across the purple heavens, stars so close they seemed to spark the mast tips. Liam bareheaded, his

THE TEMPEST LILY 75

face turned upward, Adam near the helm, inscrutable in the lantern's light. Mother of God! How could Adam sacrifice her for the crew?

Liam's song continued:

We travel to the Indies, from them we bring some spice,
And many wealthy prizes we conquer from the foe
In fight, in fight, how e'er the wind doth blow.

Now came the enormous swell of the crew's voices chanting,

How e'er the wind doth blow.

How lovely they sounded, Lily thought, these men who wanted to maroon her.

There was the shuffling of many bare feet and then Adam's voice ordering, "Rum, and a double tot for everyone on board."

Soon Liam would come, and with everything in her she would beg him to turn on Adam. She waited near the door and when he entered, she grasped his arms.

"Are you going to let Clune abandon Lucrezia and me, Liam?"

His burning eyes stared longingly down at her upturned face so close to his. "I'm going to quit the ship and stay with you. I'll protect you!"

"That's no use! For you too to spend your life waiting for rescue!" She plunged ahead with her idea. At any moment they could sight land. "You must seize the ship!"

He shook off Lily's hold, and she felt everything in Liam tear away from her as he stood staring down at her in horror. "Mutiny!" he murmured unbelievingly. "You want me to turn pirate!"

"What's the difference between pirate and privateer? Not much!" She grabbed his arms again, desperate not to lose her one hope. "You are just as capable as Captain Clune! You know that. And think, Liam, what it will mean to you. A chance to grow rich quickly. You won't have to share your prizes with a syndicate!" She saw his eyes were losing their horror, becoming ambitious. "You'll get wealth to bring your mother and sisters out of England—enough to settle on Tortuga!"

"Yes, all that is true." He shook his head. The whole thing seemed too big to grasp. "But I won't hurt the captain."

"You don't have to! Maroon him!" She spat out the words. "Then, when a ship takes him home, he can outfit another vessel for privateering."

She waited desperately as he bit his lips, not daring to decide.

He shook his head. Things were developing too fast for him. "It would mean I wouldn't have to wait for years for my family to be with me."

Lily was so relieved that he'd help that she stood on tiptoe and pulled his head down to kiss his lips. With a terrible sob Liam's arms went around her and crushed Lily to his big frame. She knew immediately that she had done the wrong thing. He had obviously mistaken her exuberance. She would have to explain right away. "Liam—"

"It's a miracle that you love me!" He pushed Lily firmly away from him. "Time is being wasted. We might sight land at any moment! I'll go into action at once. The crew blame Clune for setting a wrong course, and they'll follow me. I swear it!" His demeanor took on new strength. "Those who won't, we'll get drunk on rum, then seize the gunlocker." He slapped his chest pocket. "I've the key, so that's no trouble." With hope of power and success came boldness, and he pulled her back into his arms. "Swear that you'll marry me!"

"Liam, I can't—" Before she could finish, Adam entered and the words died on her lips.

"Not if you got the pope himself would she marry you, Traherne!" Adam's voice was a lash, and Liam swung around to face him, blanching under his suntan.

"Since when does the valiant Captain Clune listen at keyholes?"

"At the stench of treachery I listen everywhere, Traherne. In the navy you'd hang for this. On a privateer, you'll be beached!"

Lily could hardly believe what she was hearing. In her shock she was unable to react when Adam turned an avenging face of wrath on her.

"You'll be confined until we reach land."

"Blast you!" Liam burst out. "Give me a thousand lashes. Hang me! But for God's sake leave her out of this!"

"You fool, Traherne! You lovesick idiot! Save your gallantry. This woman is nothing but a scheming—"

"Curse you!" Traherne lunged at Adam, a quick blow catching him on the side of the head. Adam reeled momentarily, then, recovering, his fists pounded into Liam.

As they struck each other's heads, chests, stomachs, then dodged to avoid blows, they seemed to fill the cabin. Flattened against the wall, Lily watched horrified.

In the lantern's light the men seemed like monsters. Faces shiny with sweat, lips and eyes cut and bleeding, doublets ripped and bloodstained, they crouched around the tiny space, their eyes crafty as bears in a pit waiting for a chance to send in a decisive punch.

Then they came up face to face, exchanging thudding blows. Their grunts for breath were awful. Adam was pounding Liam's stomach while swinging his head from side to side to avoid Liam's fists. Liam landed a fearful blow on Adam's eye, but a second later Adam followed a swift left with a swift right to Liam's stomach and he folded over. Air sighing out of him, he collapsed, unconscious.

Curse Adam. He had, of course, won, Lily told herself grimly. Nothing would ever defeat the arrogant man. But blood trickled from his mouth and one eye was closing fast. He was drawing breath in rasping sounds. "Poor fool!" he muttered, shaking his head pityingly as he gazed down at Liam's inert body.

Straightening up, Adam stared at Lily, and in his

eyes she saw weariness, disillusionment, disgust. "I came here not to spy, but to say things I couldn't before Watts, because he is so against you." Still short of breath, he spoke slowly. "I wanted to assure you that wherever I was forced to land you, I intended returning for you—just as soon as I'd seized a prize. But you with your mad self-will had to inflame this poor devil to mutiny. I came the first moment I could to reassure you, but hell and damnation, I walked into your evil plan to corrupt this poor devil."

A strange laughing sound came from his throat as he knelt and carefully maneuvered the unconscious Liam across his shoulder. He glanced at Lily. "You've ruined the career of a fine officer, Goddamn you. He was my friend."

In the darkness Lily hunched on the narrow cot. What a fool she had been! How disastrous her influence on poor Liam! What scorn she had provoked in Adam! How could she have guessed he would save her in his own way? After his denial of loving her, then sacrificing her to the crew's wishes, his silence and aloofness, no wonder she had lost faith in him.

Eternity plodded by, then a seaman came to take her to the quartermaster's cabin. Lily wondered what ordeal awaited her that she should be summoned so early.

In the cabin the officers and Adam, his left eye purple and swollen, lip cut, sat behind a table. Arms chained behind his back, Liam stood facing his judges. He swung around as Lily entered. Seeing the look of adoration in his eyes, she thought it would be easier for her if he looked vindictive. She smiled tentatively, hoping it might give him some comfort, and sat in the chair Adam grimly indicated.

"Mr. Traherne," Adam began, "of course you know the articles you signed, but it's common procedure that Mr. Salter read them to you."

Daniel's face worked uncomfortably as he read from the big leather-turned book. "If one resists against another, he shall be severely punished, and I swear upon

THE TEMPEST LILY

the Holy Bible to stand one for the other as long as my life shall last."

As Daniel shut the book, Lily sprang to the table. "Gentlemen, it was at my instigation that Mr. Traherne even entertained the thought of mutiny!" Her clenched fists beat the table. "You must pardon him! I'll make restitution—"

"Lady Lily, for my sake, be seated," Liam interrupted, his face and body rigid with defiant pride. "I regret nothing, except that I didn't seize the ship!"

Lily sank back into the chair.

"You've done a thorough job of corruption," Adam sneered at Lily. "I've never had the stomach for flogging women, but you make me doubt my judgment!"

"Captain Clune!" Liam's eyes blazed. "I ask you to treat Lady Lily with respect!"

"Is it really possible, Traherne, that you don't know she was merely using you? Do you believe she cares a fig about you?" It had developed into a personal fight; they ignored the other men.

"You don't know Lady Lily," Liam retorted and turned to her. "Please answer Captain Clune."

To hell with the future, Lily decided. Liam's disillusionment could come later, when he could more easily bear it, but now she would not humiliate him. "I care greatly for you, Liam," she said quietly. "Captain Clune really does not know me."

"God and His Holy Mother bless you," Liam murmured, his heart in his smile.

She stared defiantly at Adam. He was contemplating her as he might contemplate a chess board, figuring out the next move. Then he turned to the officers.

"Is it your decision, gentlemen, that Mr. Traherne be kept in irons until we reach Virginia, where he will be beached and a record of his conduct sent to the Lord High Admiral in London so that he will never sail on a naval or privateer ship again?"

"Aye, aye, sir," they muttered, looking obviously embarrassed, and Liam left the cabin under arrest.

Next Daniel signaled Valentine to step up for sentence. A second man to be punished because of her! Oh, God forgive her.

"Your disobedience in leaving the cabin unguarded," Adam said, "shall be punished by twenty strokes of the cat-o'-nine-tails immediately after eight bells."

His jaw working nervously, Valentine stepped back to the wall, and Adam turned to Lily. "I command you to witness the punishment your actions have inflicted upon Valentine Dawson."

Adam's calm voice, his superior air of disgust, suddenly unleashed Lily's sense of injustice. He—not she —was responsible for the hellish mess, the suffering!

"I hate you, Adam Clune!" Not caring about the others, she blurted out, "I hope to see you dance the rope at Tyburn Hill, and I'll laugh with joy!"

Adam's control evaporated. "I'll see you burned first as a witch!"

Later, on the poopdeck, she stood trembling next to Adam as eight bells sounded. At a signal from Daniel, the boatswain's mate's pipes began to twitter, and Daniel roared, "All hands to witness punishment!"

From every part of the ship, men poured onto the deck and took up allotted positions. The boatswain's mates tied Valentine, stripped to the waist, to the grating. As drums rolled, they laid into him. The cat-o'-nine-tails flayed across his back. He screamed, writhing and twisting in a horrid dance.

Unbearable to watch! Lily shut her eyes. Fingers digging into the rail, she counted the strokes as they pounded through her aching head. All her fault. Oh God, give Valentine strength to bear it.

"I dislike ordering corporal punishment, Lily." Adam spoke in a low voice. "Most of all to the least guilty party in a filthy conspiracy."

"There are worse punishments than flogging the body!" she spat at him. "There's flogging the heart. I've suffered both."

"Undoubtedly you deserved to!"

She did not retort. The beating was over. A limp

Valentine hung by his bound wrists to the grating. Seamen doused his torn back with buckets of sea water before they carried him below.

"Hands to breakfast, Mr. Salter," Adam commanded. Then, turning to Lily, he muttered, "You may go down to your cabin."

"And I hope you go down to the depths of hell!"

8

WITH DEEP RELIEF Lily stepped into a bath, hoping it would also help cleanse her troubled heart. Later, enveloped in a big towel, Lucrezia helped comb her thick hair. A knock on the door made them exchange anxious glances. "See who's there," Lily instructed, securing the towel around herself. As the door opened, Adam entered, filling the cabin with his bigness and ugly mood. Surprised, Lily braced herself.

"You only escaped punishment, Lucrezia," he glowered down at her, "because Dawson swore you didn't incite him. Now go, and remember, stop wiggling your behind before the men."

Crushed by the attack, Lucrezia shot a questioning look at Lily, who nodded. The girl, looking like a hurt kitten, slipped out. Shutting the door, Adam turned on Lily.

"I've come to give you the chance to beg forgiveness for your behavior." His bruised eye and split lip made him look sinister as he smiled sarcastically.

"Beg forgiveness of you?" She flipped back her waist-length hair. "You must be quite mad even to suggest such a thing after your vile treatment of me!"

"Has your female mind no conception of the enormity of your crime?" She sensed that he spoke with an obvious effort at self-control. "You incited a man to mutiny and ruined him! Lost me a fine officer and—worst of all—you tried to ruin me. But still you don't think you're wrong! By God! After all that's passed between us! I've never known such treachery!"

"You dare to talk of treachery! Of what has passed between us!" Her months of bitterness rose to castigate him. "You, who said you loved me, then denied it. Like a Judas selling me for money! For your all-important syndicate, your rabble crew, you sacrificed me, you coward!"

The blue eyes into which she glared were murderous, and for a second she was sure he would strike her, but clenching his hands, he muttered, "Damn my soul! How right your father was to imprison you, but even that didn't make you think you might be wrong. Oh no! You risked crippling Huet, perhaps killing him to get your own way!" She had been a fool to have confided all that to him, she told herself as his denunciation continued. "You would have had murder committed aboard my ship rather than be marooned! A man was flogged because of you. Yet you still believe you have no reason to beg forgiveness." He started slowly unbuttoning the top of his doublet, then furiously ripped it open. "A woman like you serves only one purpose!"

Shocked, she watched him drag his doublet off and fling it aside. Pulling off his blouse, standing naked to the waist, he muttered, "Now, I'm going to use you for that purpose."

"Never again, you swine!"

It was impossible for her to run. He barred the way. As he came toward her, Lily grabbed her brush and hurled it at him.

She missed, and he roared with horrible laughter, "True to form, Lily! An uncontrolled wildcat!" He ripped his breeches off, kicked his shoes under the bed. In one stride he had caught her in his arms. As though she were a toy, he tossed her onto the bunk, throwing the towel on the floor. "Now you're going to pay a little for the mischief you've done!" He was climbing on top of her.

"Swine! Swine!" She fought him with clawing hands and kicking feet, but her strength was useless against him. His savage kisses were stopping her breathing. Her teeth bit into his lips; she tasted blood. Her nails dug into his back, tearing away skin and flesh, but nothing stopped him. He was like a man possessed, and seconds later, with horror, she knew her sensuousness was betraying her. It was his hands cupping her breasts that weakened her. She loved the sensation of his fingers squeezing them. She gloried in his terrible desire for her. She could not help herself as his powerful body covered hers, his long, strong legs parting her legs, the feel of his manhood's urgency huge and eager to enter her.

With a moan of capitulation she stopped fighting him, and her hands ran over the warmth of his great shoulders, smoothing down his powerful back and buttocks.

"In me . . . in me." She half-groaned as her body rose to receive him. He thrust high up into her, and she clung to him like a wild creature, throbbing with ecstasy, her legs twined around his body as he gyrated inside her.

Then glorious, wonderful, unexplainable rapture followed.

Later they lay quiet, pressed against each other's nakedness. A warm breeze floating through the window played over their satisfied bodies as the *Fearless* cut through the waters. Lily started to upbraid herself, for even while her mind and spirit despised Adam, her corrupt body had gloated in his lovemaking.

"Damnation! Lily," he murmured, "even though my mind cannot forgive you for the devilment you've caused, my body has been going insane to possess you.

It's been hell these weeks having you so close—visualizing your beautiful white body but being denied having you."

His outpouring mollified her deep hurt. But never would she admit how she had ached to lie with him. His denial of loving her was now her armor against him.

She allowed her eyes to enjoy the sight of his magnificent body. "Why didn't you come to me instead of suffering months of hell?" Lily asked dryly.

"How can you ask that? After your insults, after ordering me to leave you alone?" His hand started to caress her full breasts.

"We've both made mistakes, we've both been wrong. It's a waste of time to rehash the past."

She wanted to make love again. His caressing hand was exciting her, so she pressed her body sideways against him, ready to straddle his leg.

"Aye, talking *is* a waste of time," he chuckled, and ran a hand down her body to feel between her thighs. What a woman she was, he thought, realizing that she was ready for him again.

Lily threw shyness to the wind and grasped at his strong manhood with eager fingers.

"Oh . . . it's wonderful . . . wonderful," she murmured. "I want it inside . . . me."

"So do I, but the bunk is so narrow." He caught her around the waist. "Get on top of me—" he half-lifted her—"a leg on each side of me. Straddle me as if riding a horse astride."

"It's strange," she murmured, seated on his body, intrigued by the new position, but then he slipped his organ into her and she groaned in pleasure. "Ah . . . how wonderful . . . how lovely it is."

His hands caught savagely at her buttocks. "Ride me, Lily, ride me, ride me . . ."

She leaned down, grabbed at his shoulders and rode him as she would a stallion until ecstasy came to both of them. Then she leaned her face down on him on his great moist chest as his hands still held her buttocks.

"Whew! You may be the devil incarnate, but what a

marvelously passionate woman you are. Never have I known—" He broke off and rose on an elbow as he listened to a cry.

"Sail ho! Sail ho!" The excited voice filtered down from one hundred and forty feet of masthead through the open window.

Adam pushed Lily off him, sprang from the cot and started rapidly pulling on his clothes.

"Let's hope this is the prize we've been waiting for!" he muttered eagerly.

"Oh yes, I pray so. It would save me from being a Jonah." She jumped up to aid him, found his shoes, helped him into his doublet.

"Deck there!" came the lookout's cry again. "A sail ahead!"

Adam threw her a smile and dashed out, slamming the door, and from all parts of the ship she heard running feet clattering up the companionways. She dressed swiftly and rushed up to the deck.

The crew had darted up the rigging and hung there like monkeys, hands shielding their eyes as they searched the horizon. On the poopdeck the officers were clustered around Adam. Lily realized Liam was not there. He was imprisoned below. She made her way to the poopdeck and stood beside Adam as he scrutinized the sea with his perspective glass.

"How's she heading?" he called to the lookout at the mast.

"She seems to be coming our way, sir!" the jubilant cry floated out.

With Lucrezia now beside her, Lily surveyed the sparkling water. That far-off speck, she supposed, must be the sail. The air buzzed with speculation as to what kind of ship it might be.

"Mr. Salter, we'll heave out all sail and have a look at her." Adam's calm tone was tinged with excitement.

"Aye, aye, sir!" Salter shouted orders, and within seconds men were racing to obey.

Wonderful, Lily thought, watching figures swiftly pulling on ropes, watching the sagging canvas fill like live wings. In less than eleven minutes all sail was set with topmast housed.

"Belay!" The boatswain roared, and the crew hurried away to perform other duties. Gunners saw to their weapons, men brought boxes of grapeshot and lagrange, buckets brimming with water, small barrels of wadding and rammers and placed them in position.

As time passed, even to Lily's inexperienced eye the speck grew to be a ship. Aboard the *Fearless* all fires were extinguished, and the midday meal was served cold.

With the ship a few leagues off, Adam said, "She does not appear to suspect us, Mr. Salter. She's making no attempt to flee but coming right on."

"She's a tall ship, sir."

"Tall with riches, let's hope." Adam chuckled. "It's time to hang out the drags."

"Aye, aye, sir!" Daniel issued the command.

"Adam," Lily said, "why hang out drags when you are in full sail?"

"The ship sees us in full sail, and we want her to believe we fear her and are running from her while the drags hold us back until she comes up with us." He settled the perspective glass to his eye again. Seconds later he told Salter, "She seems to be flying the Spanish flag. Man the braces there! Clear for action!"

Salter beat "to quarters," and with mounting excitement Lily watched the men pour up on deck. Gone was their depression. Now they were excited, anticipatory, as every man expertly went about his task.

"Mr. Salter," Adam rapped, "inform Mr. Traherne I await him on deck for action."

Lily silently prayed if the "prize" were a rich one that Adam might be sufficiently mollified to pardon Liam. Unexpectedly he spun around in her direction.

"You and Lucrezia remain where you are for the moment. When the Spaniards see women aboard, they'll take us for a merchantman carrying passengers."

Then he issued a command to the excited-looking crew. "Men, take your places and lie snug. Those in the hold have pistols and swords ready and come up at my command!"

Immediately men raced down to the hold. Gunners sprang to their guns, ducking to hide behind the bulwarks.

Apprehension shadowed Lily's excitement as the approaching vessel was now so close that the name *San Anton* was easily discernible on her bow. A babble of Spanish voices floated across the stretch of intervening blue as men gathered along the sides to stare and point at the *Fearless*.

"You'd know her nationality by her smell," Adam muttered. His entire being seemed to clamp onto the *San Anton*. "Even from here there's the typical odor of all Spanish vessels—rancid oil, garlic and mold. Ah! They've spotted you and Lucrezia and that's renewed their confidence. Now walk slowly. Behave normally, but go below!"

The moment the deck was clear of women, Adam called to the *San Anton* to halt by firing his forward gun across her bow.

Realizing too late that she faced a privateer, the Spanish ship attempted to tack into the wind and aboutface. Adam shouted orders to haul in the drags and give chase. Free of the encumbrance, the *Fearless* leaped forward in close pursuit.

Below, as the *Fearless* reverberated with the shock from the first gunfire, Lucrezia fell on her knees beseeching God for protection, but Lily sprang to the window hoping to see some action. She saw nothing but part of the *San Anton*'s hull looming closer as the *Fearless* caught up with her.

Adam's guns were firing at intervals of a few minutes. The fourth shot crashed into the *San Anton*'s side, but still the Spaniards stood on defense. Through the smoke-filled air Lily saw a pink spark leave the *San Anton* as she returned fire, but the shot fell short. The *Fearless*'s guns barked again. There was a tremendous crash as the gunners scored on the *San Anton*'s poopdeck house, and triumphant roars came from the *Fearless*.

Through one of the *San Anton*'s windows men were desperately dumping satchels of letters into the sea, possibly important documents, Lily thought, that must be saved from English hands.

But she could not see enough from the window. "I'm going above," she called to Lucrezia, who remained with head bowed in prayer. Disregarding the fact that the Spaniard was now returning fire, Lily ran along the companionway. On deck, from behind coils of protective ropes, she squatted down and watched the attack.

Aiming high, the *Fearless*'s gunners made a direct hit on the *San Anton* mizzenmast. With the sound of splintering timber, the upper part of the mast keeled over; as three Spanish officers dashed wildly to escape and yards, spars, sails, ribbons, blocks, crashed to the poop delighted roars came from the *Fearless* crew.

Along the *Fearless* yards, swaying and rolling like drunken acrobats, men were lashing the *San Anton* sticks to *Fearless* sticks. On the portside Adam was directing the lowering of the longboat, crowded with armed men under Liam's command.

"Enter the *San Anton* through her lower windows," Adam shouted to Liam above the noise.

"Aye, aye, sir!" Liam yelled as the boat sank onto the water and the rowers struck out.

Adam strode back to the attack. Seeing the two ships almost board to board, he shrilled on his whistle. Immediately men darted from the hold. The sun sparked on their cocked pistols and cutlasses as, yelling curses, the boarders poured across onto the *San Anton*'s decks. The Spanish received them savagely. Pistols cracked and steel clashed on steel as men fell upon each other like furies.

Through the smoke-filled air Lily's terrified eyes clung to Adam's burnished head, which seemed ringed by cutlasses. God preserve him. Then, hearing agonized groans close by, she pulled her gaze away from the fighting and saw, far down the deck, two wounded men lying under the bulwark. She knew she must go and aid them, but she did not want to take her eyes off Adam. She had the mad idea that while she kept watch on him, he would be safe. The groans came again, and she forced herself to leave the protective coil of rope. To avoid flying bullets she crept on all fours toward the wounded.

One was a young cabin boy. He was bleeding so freely from a hole in his chest that she realized if she could not stop the flow, he would die. She bit into her skirt hem and managed to rip a strip off. Bright blood spurted over her as she tried to tie the bandage. The bleeding would not be stopped, and she despaired of saving him.

She turned to help the second victim, who was partly conscious. Half of his thigh having been shot away, his leg was a frightening sight that sickened her. Bracing herself, Lily pushed the bleeding veins, flesh and jagged bone under a form of bandage and bound it. The sun's punishing heat, beating on her uncovered neck and head, together with the stench of blood and smoke, was weakening.

"Water, water," the man croaked.

"I'll get some." She crawled past the cabin boy and realized he was already dead. She made for the companionway. Standing up, it was impossible for her not to glance across at the battle.

The *San Anton*'s deck was like a scene from Hades. Like devils, men intent on killing were lunging, dodging, weaving cutlasses, stepping back to cock pistols as they screamed curses and imprecations. Adam! Adam! Where was he? There was the red-gold hair! Adam was darting to a corner to rescue a *Fearless* man who was badly outnumbered. Now he was turning and dashing across the deck, his cutlass striking down a Spaniard whose rapierlike sword was about to run through a fallen Englishman.

All over the deck the *Fearless* men were being overrun. Where were Liam and his men? Why didn't they come? The deck seemed filled with Spaniards supposing themselves victorious. Suddenly Lily wanted furiously to avenge the dead cabin boy, wanted to help the crew. By her feet was the dying sailor's cutlass. She stooped and grabbed it. Bundling up her skirts, Lily dashed onto the *San Anton*'s deck, already dark and slippery with blood.

For a moment she stared wildly about her, then sprang to the aid of a *Fearless* man who had lost his sword in combat. Backing up to a bulwark, the man was trying to ward off his adversary's sword with outstretched hands. Hoisting her skirts with her left hand, Lily's right hand flew up. With expert skill she clashed down on the Spaniard's sword, driving it from his hand and sending it flying into the sea. The next second her sword had found the Spaniard's shoulder. She lunged and wounded him enough to put him out of battle.

"*Señorita!*" he screamed.

Other Spaniards, catching sight of her with her black streaming hair, her sword flashing, yelled, "A she-devil! A she-devil!"

Their momentary consternation gave the *Fearless* men a desperately needed respite, but then the Spaniards renewed the battle with added force.

Flashing a glance around at the satanic scene, Lily saw a Spanish sailor, dagger held between his teeth, climbing the rigging behind Adam. He intended dropping on Adam as he engaged two Spanish officers in terrible swordplay.

As the sailor jumped, Lily was ready for him. Wielding her heavy sword with both hands, she struck out wildly, hitting the man with a sidewise blow. Losing her balance with the great effort, she fell to her knees. Blood gushing from his side, dagger now in hand, her opponent crouched to spring at her. Breathless and terrified, she tried to stand. Too late. The man was upon her. It was the end!

Seeing her, Adam did not wait to free his sword from the Spaniard he had just run through. He sprang at her attacker with both hands. Adam caught him by the back of his collar and the seat of his trousers and, lifting him, hurled him into the sea.

"Shelter behind me!" Adam yelled at Lily as he grabbed her sword and went into immediate action.

Exhausted, she observed the fighting. Almost everywhere the Spaniards were triumphing. Yet Liam and his men had at last forced an entry through the lower windows and were surprising the *San Anton* crew.

Swiftly the turn of the fight changed as the *Fearless* reinforcements relieved their comrades. The Spaniards were being defeated.

Within minutes their captain struck his colors, and Adam gave quarter. The fight was over! "Thank you, God!" Lily prayed. The *San Anton*'s bloodied deck, the dead and wounded men, the sky, the sea, all melted into swirling, dark clouds as Lily swooned.

9

HELL COULD NOT be worse than the orlop deck, Lily decided as, deep in the ship's belly, she aided the doctor with the wounded. Lanterns swaying from beams bestowed little light on the fifteen mattresses on the floor. The air was stationary, and hours after battle the acrid smoke and powder odor still mixed with the stench of blood, sweat and vomit. Worst of all was the groaning of the wounded men, the rigging's vibration, rattling chains, clanking pumps, the sea's wash, the bilge emptying itself.

There was also the heat. Perspiration ran down her face, prickling her body. She was kneeling beside a man whose chest was patterned with deep splinters. Lily held instruments for the doctor as he dug and probed to remove the wood. The sailor yelled in agony, gripping the mattress sides, and when the slivers were cut out, he vomited into the bowl Lily held.

Unbearable. She must leave! Yet she continued to bathe the sailor's face and to make him comfortable. Her knowledge of caring for the sick was essential to the doctor, since his assistant had died on the *San Anton*'s deck.

For the third time she joined Dr. Moody at Liam's mattress. In the battle's finale he had received a sword thrust near the heart. Heavy and continuous loss of blood had resulted in semi-consciousness.

It shocked and dismayed Lily how, in the last hour, his condition had so rapidly deteriorated. His cheeks had sunk so the cheekbones and chin protruded; his eyelids seemed blue. Dark blood soaked his mattress, while bright blood was seeping through the bandages. About his long spare frame there was a prophetic stillness.

Removing a wad of cotton, the doctor examined the wound and gravely shook his head. "The bleeding is as bad as ever." He took fresh cotton from Lily and applied it to Liam. "He can't last much longer at this rate."

"You mean he's just going to bleed to death?" She wanted to shake Dr. Moody out of his calmness, to make him do something to save Liam. "Isn't there anything you can do?"

"I wish I could. I've sailed with Traherne for years. I'll miss him." With extreme weariness Moody rose and moved off, but Lily remained with Liam.

Gently sponging his face and neck, she was furious. Why was Moody's knowledge so slight? Why could she do nothing but watch Liam die? This man who six hours ago had been so gloriously alive? If only she could help him live, it would be compensation for the harm she had done him. She bent over him, calling, "Liam! Liam! Please answer me!" But it was impossible to call him back from his shadow world. Yet she would. She must! She grabbed a mug of rum and held it to his lips. "Drink, Liam. Drink!" She forced the liquid into his mouth, but he did not swallow and it ran down his chin.

"Liam. Tortuga. Your lovely island!" His eyelids flickered, and knew her.

"Clune," he whispered with an awful effort. "Captain."

"I'll get him!" She sprang up, making her way between the mattresses to the opening where Lucrezia squatted. "Quick, call the captain!"

Back at Liam's mattress she took his hand, leaning close, looking into his eyes. "Let's pray, Liam. Our Father, Who art—"

Adam's tall figure coming through the gloom was a help to her. Kneeling opposite her, he placed a hand on Liam's forehead and leaned close to him. "Traherne, I shall always remember you as a fine officer and a friend."

As relief showed in Liam's hazy eyes, Lily blessed Adam. Seeing the compassion riding Adam's face, she loved him once more.

"Best . . . Captain . . ." Liam forced the whisper, ". . . friend . . ."

"The *San Anton* is a rich prize, Traherne. I'll see your mother has your share."

Liam's gaze moved painfully to Lily. "Lovely . . . lady . . ." He mouthed the words and his eyes slowly closed.

The next morning in brilliant sunshine on a deck still showing signs of battle, Lily stood with Adam and the officers attending the burial of the dead. Part of the crew who had been the deceased men's friends were also there.

Against her will Lily's eyes were compelled toward the eight bodies shrouded in hammocks, a round shot sewn into the end of each. It was easy to recognize Liam, who had been taller than the others. The bodies were being loaded a pair to a grating. They were ready now, and the men glanced solemnly at Adam.

Grim-faced, he shrilled on his whistle. Activity aboard ceased, and Adam began to read from his prayer book. "I am the Resurrection and the Life, saith the Lord." The gratings were being tilted. "And whosoever believeth in Me shall never die." The bodies splashed into the sea.

With fingernails digging into her clenched palms, Lily watched as Liam's body slid beneath the surface.

"We therefore commit their bodies to the deep, to be turned into corruption until the Judgment Day when the sea shall give up her dead."

Adam closed the book. It was over. His whistle sounded; officers and crew shuffled off and activity was resumed, but Adam and Lily remained at the rail.

"You did a splendid job helping with the wounded." Adam looked weary, Lily thought sadly, older than his twenty-eight years. "You've won the respect and gratitude of every man aboard."

They meant nothing to her. That she had won Adam's gratitude and respect was all that mattered. "I'm glad I was of help."

They looked deeply into each other's eyes, probing each other's hurt souls, and their expressions told their regrets about Liam that they dared not trust to words. Then Adam glanced rebelliously at the sea and murmured, "A damnable loss!" Nodding understandingly at her, he strode away.

She stayed on, staring at the water. There was not even a sign of the infinitesimal dent made by Liam's body. Yet her suffering mind saw him plunging down, down, down, ever deeper into who knew what depths. Why had he died so young? Been denied his dream of Tortuga? He had asked for very little—a house where the sun shone, some fruit trees, the chance to fish for his meals. Was everyone's heart's desire always denied? Was this God's design? Or were some permitted to realize their dreams? Shivering in the sunlight, she left the rail.

All over the ship men were cleaning up and repairing battle scars. There was no sign of Adam, and Lily supposed he was occupied with selecting a skeleton crew to sail the *San Anton*. When she reached her cabin, an excited Lucrezia helped dispel her gloom.

"My lady, Valentine says the prize from the *San Anton* is great! Two thousand barrels of wine; fifty of gunpowder; fifty thousand pieces of eight—wages meant for the Panama garrison; many jewels meant for the Spanish king; and sugar, skins and tobacco." Lucrezia clapped delighted hands. "And, what is especially good for you and me, there's fresh meat and water!"

"What is best for us," Lily said dryly, "is that now we are no longer Jonahs."

That night the ship's court was to be held in the great cabin. Adam gave Lily permission to witness the proceedings. From her corner seat she glanced at the crew, many with bandaged arms and legs or burned faces, crowded at one end of the cabin. At the other end, behind a long table, Adam sat with the officers.

Salter was trustee for the ship's company and, with Adam, was responsible to the high admiralty court in London to produce a listing of prize goods. A line of men filed up to the table, and into two big bowls they deposited jewels, which Salter recorded. Soon the lantern light was shining on piled-up jewels that shifted gently back and forth with the ship's easy motion.

When no more men came forward, Daniel opened the book of articles and read, "Any valuable from the prize ship and the finder not delivered it to the quartermaster within twenty-four hours, he shall suffer punishment as the captain and company see fit."

Angry voices burst from the crew. "Jim Robbins has jewels!" "Yes! Search his bedding!" A thin-faced man was pushed up to Adam and the officers. "It's a lie!" he gasped.

"Robbins, jewels have just been found in your hammock," Adam snapped and glanced at the crew. "I propose he receives Moses' Law—forty strokes of the lash!"

"Aye, aye!" the crew voted vehemently, and the white-faced Robbins backed away.

Daniel again read. "He that is guilty of cowardice during an engagement shall suffer punishment—John Dawes!"

A one-legged sailor, his wooden peg tapping loudly, came up to the table. The crew muttered angrily, and Adam raised a silencing hand, saying, "John Dawes, for hiding while the others put their lives on the line, I suggest you receive the Law of Moses!"

"Aye, aye!" the crew voted, and stony-faced Dawes tapped back to his disgusted companions.

Daniel read. "Good quarter shall be given to all when asked for. George Swift! Step up!"

A huge sailor with heavy shoulders and legs bulging in his breeches swaggered up, and Adam frowned. "You killed a man aboard the *San Anton* when he begged for quarter!"

"The dirty Spaniard was trying to knife me," Swift spat out.

"That's a lie!" Adam rapped. "The man was unarmed! Mr. Salter witnessed everything. There is also another witness. Contessa Dolores da Corda, please come forward!"

From behind the crew a midshipman made way for a woman who held part of her lace mantilla across her face. Sympathy flooded through Lily for the well-born captive. Nevertheless Lily could not help being envious, the contessa was so beautifully gowned. With deliberate insolence for her captors, Dolores sat down and spread out her blue satin dress, pulled back her mantilla, showing a beautiful oval face with eyes like purple grapes that challenged Adam and his officers.

Lily suddenly disliked this woman with her full lips so artificially red. Would Adam be drawn by the mixture of purity and lewdness in the heavily lidded eyes? From his impassive face, she sensed nothing.

"Be so good, madame," he said, "as to relate what occurred."

"This man," the contessa's white hand pointed accusingly at Swift, "demanded from my husband all our jewels." Her lisping English sounded appealing. "José had given everything . . ." Dolores sobbed into a black lacy handkerchief.

"We sympathize with your bereavement," Adam said dryly, "but please continue."

The contessa straightened up. "This barbarian ripped open my gown to see if I concealed jewels. My husband tried to stop him, begging for mercy, but this devil stabbed him to death!"

"George Swift," Adam spoke evenly, "I find you guilty of murder. You will be kept in irons until we reach Virginia, where the governor will attend to your hanging." Adam eyed the crew for their decision.

"Aye, aye!" The vote came solemnly, and Adam instructed the guards to take Swift below. He glanced at the contessa. "You may return to your ship, madame."

She swept out, and soon afterward, tiring of the proceedings, Lily went to her cabin. Physically exhausted, she prepared for bed. Lucrezia extinguished the lantern, and within minutes they were both asleep.

The happenings of the last few days furnished Lily's gallery of dreams with ugly scenes. Liam and Adam fighting, Valentine's flogging. The battle. The orlop deck and the wounded. Liam's body splashing into the sea. Then a glorious picture expelled the horrors. Adam caressing her, Adam leaning down to kiss her. Then he left and she was back at the battle scene. She awoke screaming.

"Lily, Lily, ssh, it's Adam! I've sent Lucrezia out." He was naked lying beside her.

"Oh, Adam!" She clung to him as he took her in his arms. "Such awful nightmares!"

He stroked her hair soothingly. "Perhaps you're too tired. Would you rather I didn't stay?"

"No, no, stay!" She was amazed that the cabin was so light. "But it's almost dawn."

"Yes, I couldn't come sooner. The *San Anton* sprang a leak. We had to take everyone off and salvage what we could before she sank." He looked at her with affectionate amusement. "Did you actually sleep through all that commotion?"

"I suppose I must have."

"Hell to have lost a good ship!" As he slipped his muscled arm beneath her, she could barely breathe with excited joy. "It's been a cursed twenty-four hours!" He yawned deeply. "Let's forget everything for a while."

The following noon, entering the big cabin, Lily was momentarily upset to see the contessa seated on Adam's left and Dr. Moody in poor Liam's place. When Adam presented Lily to the slightly older woman, she caught the amusement in his eyes as Dolores insolently appraised her.

The women bowed stiffly to each other, and Adam said, "We've fresh meat, Lady Lily." He nodded toward a steward bringing a platter. "Until we boarded your ship," he addressed Dolores, "we were down to poor fare."

"But not in all ways." The contessa glanced disdainfully at Lily.

Damn the woman's impudence! "Madame, I also am a captive!" Lily spat at her.

Adam swiftly intervened. "You are from Peru, madame?"

"Our ship was coming from Peru, but I am from Castile," Dolores said haughtily. "My husband owned great lands in Peru." Her rounded bosom rose and fell as she sighed, "Now José is dead."

Her sorrow was insincere, Lily was sure, knowing from Lucrezia that José had been an old man.

Dolores turned appealing eyes on Adam. "Why must I be held in Virginia for a ransom? It will be so dull there."

"As you are a Spanish subject, I naturally couldn't leave you in a Spanish possession. But I assure you, for anyone as beautiful as you," Adam's admiring eyes looked boldly at her, "the gallants in Virginia will not allow life to be dull."

Why does Adam wish to please the woman? Lily

thought angrily. Anyhow, it was an indelicate compliment to someone so recently widowed, but the contessa seemed pleased by it.

"You are courteous, Captain." Dolores smiled winningly. "As a girl, I accompanied my father to London when he arranged with your king to mint Spanish silver in England. I liked the English then." Her lips turned down. "But now I know they are cruel."

"You Spanish excel in cruelty," Watts said angrily. "Your pet treatment of captives is to cut off their hands, feet and noses, smear them with honey, then tie them to trees to be tortured by flies!"

Dolores looked at Watts as if he were an unpleasant odor. "I know nothing of such things. We have always abhorred the treatment Protestant England gave English Catholics." Her heavily lidded eyes returned to Adam. "I am surprised you took a Spanish vessel. Our countries are not at war."

By Adam's slow smile, Lily sensed he saw through Dolores's pose. "The London and Madrid courts are at peace, but you must be aware that in certain seas their subjects are encouraged to make war."

"Land ho!" The jubilant cry floated through the window. "Deck there! Land two points on the starboard bow!"

Adam jumped up, scraping back his chair, and strode out, with everyone excitedly following him to the poopdeck. They stared over the blue water at a purple smear like a giant's fingerprint spread across the horizon.

"Heave out all canvas, Mr. Salter!" Adam ordered. Immediately the deck bustled with men working ropes and tackle.

"Land!" Lily said joyously. "How wonderful!" She would have felt differently a few days ago, she thought, with a resurgence of bitterness. It would be here the cursed crew would have abandoned her.

"Don't you enjoy ship life?" Adam winked intimately and, understanding his meaning, she laughed. "Oh yes, but I'm longing for fresh water! And a floor that doesn't move. You might remember I was locked up at all ports. I haven't stepped on land for almost four months."

"I'm sorry about that, but you know the circumstances."

With all sails set, the *Fearless* cut swiftly through the water. The purple smudge soon took shape into a wide expanse of beach that was fringed by masses of tall palms that shaded a village of thatched huts. In the background a wooded area ran up into high, verdant hills.

"By my reckoning, Mr. Salter," Adam said, "it looks as if we've come on Tiburon, a point of Hispaniola."

"The beach and hill formation certainly look like Tiburon, sir."

"Great luck! We'll be welcomed and get plenty of beef."

Flights of brown noddy birds twittered noisily as they circled the vessel. As the ship drew close to land, Indians rushed from huts, gesticulating excitedly as they crowded to the water's edge.

Soundings were taken, the anchor dropped and the small boats lowered. Lily went with Adam in the first one, and as it touched the beach, the Indians swarmed around. Many of them, recognizing Adam, raised their right arm in welcome. In a mixture of Spanish and Indian, he greeted them.

Carrying Lily to dry land, he told the Indians he had returned in friendship to see their chief. An old man immediately offered to escort them to the chief's hut.

Hoping to impress Adam with her adaptability to places and people, Lily smiled at the Indians, naked but for tiny palm aprons. In their ears they wore bunches of animal teeth, their sole adornment.

Hemmed in by natives as they headed for the village, Lily felt an old happiness returning. She and Adam were together again under tall trees, crunching over a beach—so like the wonderful days in Capri.

"We've got here none too soon! Thank the stars our

men can buy a woman here for an ax or hatchet." Adam chuckled. "And another good thing, they can hunt and fish here. But the Indians will victual us with turtles. We've arrived at the chief's."

Under a grove of trees was a long hut where four men, their faces gaudily painted, stood rigid, holding spears. "These are our hosts," Adam murmured. "Just copy me."

The Indians suddenly prostrated themselves on the earth at Adam's and Lily's feet. "Help lift them," Adam told her, bending over a man and touching his shoulder. The man sprang up. Swiftly Lily tapped a second shoulder, while Adam lifted the others. Then they all entered the hut.

In the shadowy interior women, their faces daubed with crimson, crowded around Lily, touching her hair, face and clothes. She managed to smile, determined to convince Adam that she would never be a burden on his travels. She was rewarded by his approving wink.

Daniel and the contessa joined them. After an eternity of powwow with the chief, Adam announced, "He's a splendid fellow. He will see that we are supplied with all we want in exchange for our hatchets and trinkets."

Back in the sunshine, heading for the beach, Adam said, "Mr. Salter, we'll fill water jars immediately and arrange the men's shore leave."

"Aye, aye, sir. How long do you intend staying?"

"Not more than a week."

Tiburon delighted Lily with the lush greenery, flowers and trees loaded with fruit. Passing a hut where bones hung at the entrance, she asked, "Has that a special meaning?"

"Very special." Adam smiled. "The home evidently belongs to a widow. Those are her dead husband's bones."

"How gruesome." Lily wrinkled her nose.

"Oh, but it's a wonderful sign of devotion," the contessa said, glancing demurely at Adam.

"I can't see any woman I know being so devoted." Lily looked pointedly at Dolores.

"Ah, perhaps because their husbands didn't warrant such devotion," Dolores said icily.

"Mr. Salter and I must return to the ship," Adam said, "but it is perfectly safe for you ladies to remain. In any case the crew will be landing immediately to start watering."

"Oh, I'll stay," Lily said. "I feel I'll never have enough of this marvelous greenery. Could you send Lucrezia ashore? She's longing to come."

"Of course, in the next boat."

"I shall return to the ship," Dolores said. "The heat here is unbearable."

Watching Daniel leave in one boat, then Adam lifting the contessa into his boat, Lily wondered why he was so solicitous to the Spanish woman.

10

THE FOLLOWING MORNING Indians drove wild cows from the hills to the water's edge with whoops and cries. Trapped there, the beasts were slaughtered. Though Lily did not see the white sand reddened, she could not escape the cries of men and animals. Throughout the day canoes came to the *Fearless* laden with joints, which were stacked in brine.

Lucrezia was ashore with Valentine, who was on leave; Adam was busy with ship's affairs; and Lily surprised herself by welcoming Dolores's company. After months with no female society but Lucrezia's, it was

THE TEMPEST LILY

good to talk to a woman of her own station. They spoke of clothes, customs in Spain, England and Peru.

"You are fortunate to be going to Jamaica. Being Spanish, it's livelier than Virginia."

Lily's stomach felt hollow. "Who told you I was going to Jamaica?"

"Captain Clune, this morning, when we were talking."

Adam had been obliged to say that to Dolores, Lily assured herself, but after their reconciliation he would never leave her at Jamaica. Perhaps Dolores was just trying to annoy her. "I thought Captain Clune was busy all morning."

Leaning over, the Spanish woman laid a soft hand on Lily's arm. "Because we are both captives, let me give you some advice. You are foolish to show how much you care for him."

Damn the woman's insolence! "He and I are old friends. He's a countryman," she spoke haughtily, "and I'm known in Wales for the number of men I've refused in marriage."

"Forgive me." At Dolores's dazzling smile, Lily sensed the woman had deliberately set out to upset her. "It was ill-bred of me to offer advice. Do tell me about Wales. I hear it is beautiful."

One of the last things Lily wished to do now was discuss Wales or remain with Dolores. As soon as she could, without exposing her chagrin, she went to her cabin.

Was she making a fool of herself before the whole ship's company, or were Dolores's remarks merely those of a spiteful woman? She must talk to Adam when he came tonight. She would not again lose herself in lovemaking until her position had been made clear.

He was late in coming that night. He and the officers were celebrating with wine from the *San Anton*. While she waited for him she stared out her window to the shore, where huge bonfires lit the night. Men on leave were roasting beef, drinking native wine, dancing with the Indians—a savage-looking scene that made her question her judgment in having allowed Lucrezia to remain ashore.

When Adam arrived, smelling strongly of wine, Lily asked, "Will Lucrezia be all right?"

"Of course. She'll love the goings-on." By the thickness of his speech, Lily knew he was almost drunk. "What a night! Water like glass, moon, flowers—wine enough to bathe in. Lucrezia will love it. But what about you?" he chuckled. "I hear you overcame your dislike of the contessa today."

"Who said I disliked her?"

"Your cat-green eyes shouted it aloud." He laughed as though it were a private joke. "Actually, she's in a bad position and making a good job of it."

"Her position is no worse than mine. She has all her lovely clothes with her. I came aboard with nothing."

"You had not been recently widowed," he teased, sinking onto the chair.

"Just why are you protecting her?" she snapped.

He stretched his long legs full-length and laughed. "Damn my soul! The beautiful Lady Lily actually has it in her to be jealous!"

"Don't be absurd!" She knelt beside him, her pale face turned up to his, arms resting on his lap. "I want to discuss a few personal things with you and—"

"Ah—ah," he shook his head, "no personal things. That would be dangerous! I might discuss a little thing called mutiny. Ever heard the word?" His face darkened. "You don't like to talk of that, do you, Lily? Then we'll make a pact—we won't talk about ourselves."

"But Adam—"

"For God's sake, don't try to see what makes our happiness together. Just enjoy it!"

Angered by his attitude, longing to argue, she told herself to wait. A tree does not fall with the first stroke. In any case he was far from sober and very belligerent. "You're right," she managed to lie lightly. "We won't examine our happiness. We'll just enjoy it."

He pulled her up to sit on his lap. "I wonder if you

mean that?" His finger traced slowly down her forehead, her nose, her mouth, then his hand closed over her throat. "You'd be a rare woman if you could stick to it. I've never known one who could."

"Stop talking generally. I hate it! I know you've had hundreds of women, but is it necessary to keep reminding me of them?"

"My lovely spitfire is still there! That delicate face merely hides her."

He was being difficult and quarrelsome. "Oh, Adam, stop talking like—"

"Blast my soul! Just let's stop talking." He rose with her in his arms and dropped her onto the cot. Then he reached up and blew the lantern out. "I'm a little drunk tonight, beloved, so don't hold that against me."

"Adam, Adam, stop talking, just come to me."

"Yes, but have you seen the stars?" He bent to look out the window. "They're gold tonight, not silver."

She held her breath, then murmured hopefully, "Gold? Like they were in Capri?" Did that mean he loved her again?

"Oh no, damnation!" he muttered. "They were *really* gold—these are tarnished." He stood staring down at her. Then he murmured as though to himself, "She tarnished the stars for you, Clune! That's what she did! But treachery tarnishes everything."

He's really drunk, Lily told herself, and I've hurt him far more than I suspected. She reached up and caught his shoulders, pulling him onto the cot. "Adam—Adam darling. Don't think. Let's just make love."

For the next few days she was unable to free herself of Dolores. "She's worse than a bad conscience," she complained to Adam, "and it's because she feels if she keeps me in sight, she'll see you."

"Nonsense; she's lonely. And why not, with only her old witch of a serving woman for company?"

"Then why doesn't she eat with the *San Anton* officers below? Anyhow, I'd like to go ashore for once without her. So far she's been everywhere we've been."

"That's embarrassing," Adam chuckled. "I thought we were alone here in your cabin."

Lily burst out laughing.

While nights with Adam were wonderful, Lily longed to be alone with him in the sunlit hours. Away from the ship with all its unhappy memories, she felt they might slip back into their Capri understanding and she could make him talk of themselves.

But she was forced to wait until the fifth day when, succumbing to the heat, the contessa remained aboard. Alone with Adam, Lily joyously landed on Tiburon. No longer of interest to the Indians, she and Adam wandered in peace. Passing a line of the crew carrying empty jars to the lake and another returning with full jars to the boats, they slowly left the village and climbed a gently rising hill.

Reaching a clearing shaded by tall fruit trees, they stepped out of the blazing sunlight, and Adam's arm suddenly cleaved through the air, catching at something.

"Open your hand, Lily. I've a white butterfly for you."

"Oh no! Let it fly!"

They watched it flutter into the matted vegetation. "Lovely things," Adam observed, "and wisely designed. Their twenty-four hours of existence from birth to death are concentrated beauty. That's how life should be lived —concentrated beauty."

In a shaded spot Lily half-lay on the earth, loving its warmth seeping through her body. She glanced up at big, oily leaves that looked almost black against the stark blue of the sky. Bees buzzed around bushes with scarlet and purple blossoms that perfumed the air. Close by, unseen water splashing over rocks sounded like music of many flageolets.

Adam had stripped off his wide-sleeved blouse and, naked to the waist, easily shinned up a tall tree. Watching his long arms and rippling back move about in the branches, she thought he looked like a boy despite his magnificent frame. If life could always be like this . . .

THE TEMPEST LILY 107

If time could only stand still; if it could always be today, now, this moment.

He slid down the tree, his white breeches stained by sap, then came to her, extending his cupped hands with golden fruit. "It's papaw, and its flavor is unique." He sat cross-legged beside her, reaching back on his hip for his knife. "I think you'll love them."

I could love anything and everything with you, she thought, her eyes on his lean brown fingers slicing the fruit.

"Open your mouth." He popped a piece of juicy yellow fruit between her lips and waited for her approval.

"Delicious." She watched him eating. "How wonderful it would be to spend one's life here."

"Even this beauty and peace would grow tiresome after a while."

"Why should it, if one had the people one loved here?"

"There's more to living than that." He spoke reflectively, carefully slicing more fruit. "You have a job, a duty to others, to your own conscience." He held out another piece of papaw.

"How serious you are," she teased, opening her mouth, then eating the fruit. "What's your duty to your conscience?"

"Ah, you're probing." He smiled. "Well, I'd like to see Catholicism back in Wales." His knife point angrily flicked seeds from the melon. "Protestantism is an alien plant for the Welsh!"

"I'm surprised. I'd no idea you felt keenly about the return of the faith."

"Because we've never discussed it before. But I believe Catholicism, the Welsh language and the people will answer for our corner of the earth on Judgment Day."

"I hope you're right. . . . I've been thinking," she smiled wryly, "since I've had so much time forced upon me at sea, that someday I'd like to work for the Catholic cause. Why don't you also work for it, Adam?"

"Why presume that I don't?" He carefully cleaned his

knife with leaves. "Perhaps the *Fearless*'s trips to Italy might be connected with smuggling Jesuit priests into England."

"Adam, how splendid!" She sat upright, eyes shining.

"Now, now, I'm admitting nothing. Smuggling priests into England is punishable by death—" he tossed the papaw skin behind some bushes—"and someday you might be angry enough with me to help put the hangman's noose around my neck."

"Oh darling, I'm sorry I said that awful thing about Tyburn, but you were just as bad, saying you'd have me burned as a witch."

"I should have added, the world's most beautiful, desirable witch." His fingers found the silver combs in her hair and pulled them out, making her hair cascade to below her waist. "That's how I love to see you." He spread her hair over her shoulders, then his hands went to unlace her bodice. "You're overdressed for such a hot day."

She warned herself not to be caught up in his lovemaking before they had spoken about themselves, but passion swept away determination. "Someone might come here, darling," she murmured.

"Don't worry. The Indians have headaches from overdrinking. Lie on my blouse, my beautiful one, the ground is too rough for you." He spread out the linen garment, then, smiling, he pushed her black hair back. "There's no one here but me, and you have no secrets from me. Let me enjoy looking at you."

She glanced at him, his physique like a gladiator of old. "It's just . . . I suppose being out here . . . away from the cabin . . ."

Laughing, he slipped his arm beneath her. "It's wonderful making love on the earth with the sun warming you. You become a part of nature."

The sun had left the clearing when they lay quiet. Lily closed her eyes dreamily as he lifted long strands of her hair and let them fall slowly.

"Listen to the cicadas," she said. "Are they also saying 'We—love—Lily, we—love—Lily,' like the ones in Capri?"

His arm around her, the whole of him stiffened, and he sat up. "Why bring Capri up?"

Staring up at his big back with muscles rippling the brown skin, she sensed with bewilderment that his spirit was withdrawing from her. "But why *not* bring Capri up?"

He reached over to his doublet and pulled his pipe from a pocket. "Because we were two other people in Capri."

"I should think we're two closer people now."

"Closer in one way. In another, much farther apart."

She sat up. For a second she watched him tamp tobacco into the pipe's bowl. Damn his moodiness. She would not tolerate it. "If you're trying to say I'm a different person because of Liam—all right. You provoked me, God knows; the blame is equally divided between us!"

"Damnation seize my soul!" he swore angrily. "I refuse to discuss it!"

"You've no right to refuse! It's unfair to keep avoiding discussing ourselves."

"We made a pact that we wouldn't talk of ourselves. For the few days that you kept it, everything was wonderful. But of course you've broken it and ruined everything."

"What do you expect? Do you think a person like me can just drift like this—not knowing how you feel about me? You loved me in Capri, even though you later denied it. For God's sake, admit it now."

"You won't be content until you've dragged a confession out of me, will you? Very well, I *did* love you. I was *in love* with you! I hoped I'd return to Capri for you. Then everything was taken out of my hands and the storm dropped you into my lap. I had the choice of holding you for ransom and satisfying the crew, or flouting them and satisfying you and myself and having us murdered."

"Darling, why didn't you talk like this to me then? Instead of denying you loved me?"

"Because you would have been impossible to control if I had. You would not have understood my position. That I had to leave you at Jamaica, that I intended to return and pay the cursed money myself to keep things in order with the syndicate and crew."

"But I would have understood! I swear it! We need not have endured all the agony and—"

"Would you have understood and done as I told you . . . keeping up the pretense? I don't think so." He laughed bitterly. "How did you behave when it looked as though I'd have to maroon you? You forgot everything but how to save your own skin!"

"I was terrified."

"I had sworn to leave you protected. Would harm have come to you in a place like this? No! But you couldn't wait. Not Lily. Oh no! You incited Traherne to mutiny! By God! Most men would have killed you for that."

"Are you going to hold that against me forever? Damnation, Adam, I've forgiven you for your treatment of me."

"I'm afraid I have not forgiven you." His voice was quiet now. "I'm sorry, Lily, and I mean I'm sorry, but I don't think I can ever feel the same about you."

"That's absurd, ridiculous. You can't get rid of love as easily as taking off your doublet."

"You seemed to do just that! You forgot your love for me when you wanted Liam to take my ship!" He shook his head conclusively. "There's an odd streak in you that always tries to dominate. You got the better of your father, Roger Huet, you twisted Traherne like a feather, but you'll not get the better of me!"

"I don't want to! Of course I'll always fight when I believe I'm the victim of injustice. Feeling as you do, how could you make love to me like this?"

"Why not? You're a maddeningly desirable woman." He stood up. "Besides, I never noticed that you objected. In fact, you welcomed my lovemaking."

She jumped up to confront him. "There's the brute in you talking again." She swung away from him and started brushing twigs and flowers from her clothes. At this moment, she assured herself, I care nothing if he loves me or not!

The sun was almost gone when, in silence, they returned to the *Fearless,* and Lily still did not know what her future was, if he intended leaving her at Jamaica or not. But no matter. If he was so unfair as to hold only her faults up for conviction and not his own, then let it be Jamaica and to the devil with him!

11

LILY WAS CONVINCED that Adam would not visit her that night, although she hoped that he would, because at last she had the strength to resist him. And he did come.

"After our conversation today I'd rather you didn't stay, Adam."

"I half-expected you to behave in this obvious fashion. Don't be a fool who starves her love to feed her pride." His hands reached to pull her to him, but she stepped back.

"A pity, Lily; I shall miss you." Damn her, he was on fire to lie with her.

"Even with your belief that life should be lived like a butterfly's? An odd philosophy for a Catholic man."

"Believing in Catholicism has nothing to do with my

personal enjoyment." He moved over and sat in the chair by the window. "The spirit is an independent entity. It has nothing to do with the flesh."

If he trapped her into arguing so that he remained, she knew she would weaken. "I'm serious. I'd like to be alone."

Adam stood up angrily. "You shall be, Lily." In one stride he was opening the door. Then he turned and grinned, but, recognizing the chagrin in his eyes, she felt triumphant. "Enjoy your newborn virtue," he commented sarcastically, and closed the door.

Lily was glorying in her own strength when she heard Lucrezia and the guard in the corridor. The door opened and Lucrezia slipped inside. Lily raised herself on an elbow.

"I thought you were staying ashore for the last night's celebrations?"

"No, my lady, I swam back to the ship."

"Swam!" In the moonlight coming through the window, Lily saw Lucrezia was sopping wet. "What happened?"

"Valentine! He tried to do things only a husband may do!" She spat the words. "So I knifed him with his own knife! I have licked the warm blood from it so I shall suffer no remorse."

"Holy Mary!" Lily sprang up, grasping the girl's arm. "You didn't kill him!"

"No, just cut his face!"

Shame flushed through Lily. Lucrezia, a peasant, had a moral strength that she had lacked. "You are a good girl, Lucrezia. Now put on a dry shift."

"My lady, I must tell you what I have seen." Lucrezia stepped from her sodden skirt. "The captain entering the contessa's cabin. Perhaps her fever is worse."

"Dr. Moody cares for the sick."

"He is ashore with an Indian woman. These shipmen are beasts!"

What could she do? Lily asked herself. Go to the contessa's cabin? Denounce Adam? She had no rights over him. She had refused him, so he had gone to another woman. Quite simple. But impossible! This afternoon she and he had lain together. Why should he be allowed to storm through women's lives, corrupting them? At least she would let him know she knew him for the low beast he was!

Cold with outraged pride, she left the cabin, sweeping aside the guard, and went to Dolores's door.

Stepping around the sleeping guard, Lily lifted the latch and entered the dimly lit cabin. On the cot was the contessa, her hair fanned out on the pillow, her low-cut shift half-exposing her breasts. Adam, without his doublet, stood leaning over her. He sprang back, staring incredulously at Lily, his face twisting with rage.

Their eyes blazed at each other. "For what hellish reason are you bursting in here? You are quite mad!"

"No! Sane at last! Now I know how truly licentious you are!"

Adam looked menacing. "This time your accursed temper has really made a fool of you!"

"Don't pretend you're here to help that woman. She's not sick!" Lily turned her fury on Dolores, who shrank back against the pillows. "Your husband's corpse barely cold and another man entering your bed! Well, let slime mix with slime." Lily swept regally out of the cabin.

Back on her bunk, she trembled over the awful scene. Her own part in the loathsome affair revolted her. "Oh, God, you have truly punished me for what I've done." She hid her face in the pillow, which was still scented with Adam's tobacco and aromatic oil. She flung the pillow on the floor. "All I want is to forget him!" Lily felt sleep would never again relieve her, but finally she drifted off.

The following day was the last day at Tiburon. Beginning at dawn Indian canoes brought piles of fruit and the *Fearless*'s boats brought fresh water. The storing away of supplies in combination with sailors returning from shore leave made the deck impossible.

Her head aching, Lily remained in her quarters, dreading meeting Adam or Dolores. By midday, however, she was ravenous, so she forced herself to enter the big cabin. Only Salter was there.

"The captain is ashore saying good-bye to the chief," Daniel said, "and Dr. Moody and Watts are enjoying their last moments on Tiburon."

"And the contessa was well enough to go?" Lily hoped her voice sounded casual.

"No, her fever is worse. She'll probably have to be bled." A joking expression lit Daniel's solid face. "Since her ransom is six thousand pounds, we're anxious that she stays alive."

Had the contessa really been ill? Had Adam been tending her in Moody's place? Impossible! Dolores had appeared more seducer than sufferer, and Adam more lover than doctor!

"I also have found the heat oppressive lately," Lily said. "Tell me, is Jamaica as warm?" She hoped that by discussing Jamaica with Daniel, he might disclose Adam's plans for her.

"Jamaica is cooler than Tiburon. I'm sure you'll enjoy staying there."

That was her answer! Like a hurricane demolishing her delicate house of hope.

As soon as she could, Lily excused herself and fled to her cabin. Pacing the tiny floor space, she told herself she would escape from Jamaica and go to Virginia. Build a new and exciting life there. But with Liam dead, would the Jesuit Father Dalvarez aid her?

Then she heard the sound of feet shuffling hurriedly on deck, the creak of ropes and tackle being worked.

"Call all hands to weigh anchor and make sail! We leave at once!" Adam's voice resounded.

Tiburon was two days behind them, but Dolores was still ill. Lily and Adam saw each other only for meals.

During the warm nights Lily stood at the window, eyes on the purple-blue sky with its filigree of stars, wondering what else life held in store for her.

The fifth night, nearing dawn, she had fallen into an uneasy sleep when Lucrezia awakened her.

"We are here, my lady! Jamaica!"

The *Fearless* had stopped sailing! She was at anchor. The moment long feared was a very present reality. Lily left the cot and joined Lucrezia to gaze out at the lofty blue mountains covered with greenery.

There was a knock at the door, followed by the entrance of the new cabin boy. "The captain's compliments. He went ashore some time ago to make arrangements for your accommodation and will you please prepare to leave the ship."

The youth left, and Lucrezia turned moist, understanding eyes on Lily. "It will be good, my lady, to leave this evil ship."

"Yes, it will! To start a new life. We'll reach Virginia somehow. I'll forget all this." Her gaze wandered over the cabin. Lucrezia was already dragging her few belongings from the chest.

It was over. She and Adam were finished. Life might contrive that they should meet again, but she and he, the togetherness, was past. Well, everything had an end. If not now, then later. You did not go under because a beloved died! You did not go under because a beloved existed only in your desire.

Lily did not know how much time had passed before there was a second knock. "The captain's compliments and the boat is ready to take you ashore," the cabin boy told Lucrezia.

Lucrezia piled their bundles onto the boy's shoulder and turned to Lily. "Come, my lady," she said softly, stepping back for Lily to precede her.

At the sight of the crew lining the rails, at the officers with Adam waiting at the head of the gangway, Lily determined to hold her head high as she walked erectly past. The men respectfully touched fingers to their foreheads. She had won their gratitude for having nursed their wounded.

Now she faced Watts, Moody, Salter, Adam.

Moody spoke first. "I hope everything will go smoothly for your ladyship." The expression in his eyes seemed to match his words, and Lily gave him her hand. He bowed over it. "I shall always be grateful to you for your assistance."

"Thank you," Lily murmured. Turning to Watts, whom she despised, she nodded curtly.

"I have the honor of accompanying you ashore," Daniel said swiftly.

She looked up at Adam, her eyes glaring into his expressionless face, half of her loathing him, half stricken knowing he was lost to her. "Good-bye? Without a private word?" she murmured through twisting lips.

He glanced nervously around at the others, then he caught her elbow and led her out of earshot of the officers. "It seemed more sensible." He let go her elbow. "Easier for both of us."

"Easier for you, you mean! Having finished with me—used me." She knew her voice was rising but she could not stop it. "It was easier for you to avoid me!"

"Quiet!" He glanced apprehensively around, and Lily knew he was dreading a scene. "It's you with your unbridled temper that's caused all the trouble."

"You won't admit that you provoked my temper?"

"What does it matter now?" He shrugged impatiently.

"Nothing! But surely I had the right to a little more courtesy."

"Why the right—after your impossible behavior the other night? Because you are Lady Lily?"

"Because I'm a woman you made love to."

"You place far too much importance on that."

"Even a brute like you might remember that, as a prize you took, I came wholly untouched. Perhaps that means nothing to Lord Clune! Perhaps as a privateersman, you specialize in seducing virtuous women!"

"You are so right, Lily," he said in a bored tone. "I specialize in seducing virtuous women."

At that moment Lily hated him. She stretched to her tiptoes and slapped him twice across the face. When she heard the gasp from the crew she had forgotten were there, she knew she had disgraced him.

At first she thought he would kill her, and an almost unearthly look came into his eyes. Then Adam laughed deep in his throat, an awful prophetic threatening sound, and Lily swung around and swept toward Daniel. Descending the rope ladder to the waiting rowboat, she was glad—glad—glad she had humiliated him.

"Passage Fort is ahead," Salter said, still looking shocked by the scene on board. He nodded toward the stone edifice on the lonely shore. "It's rather desolate here, but the town of Saint Jago is inland and it's lovely."

Desolation? Loveliness? What matter? She let Salter help her from the boat and guide her up the shore, past copper-colored Jamaicans busy with canoes, to where a carriage waited. As they neared it, an old man wearing a black robe and a skullcap on his silver head walked toward them.

"I shall hand you over, Lady Lily, to your host," Salter said. "Mr. Joseph Sanches."

The little Portuguese with brown, withered skin like a dried fruit bowed to her.

Lily warned herself, This is my jailer, I must start immediately to win him to my side. "Mr. Sanches, it is so good to be on land again, and the island is said to be beautiful." She graciously held out her hand to him. "How kind of you to have met me."

He took her fingertips and carried them to his lips. "It's an honor for me, Lady Lily, that I might entertain you in my home."

Farewells to Daniel were swiftly over and Lily, Lucrezia and Sanches installed in the carriage. The Jamaican driver flicked his whip and the horses headed inland.

The sea was left behind and the route passed through a lushly wooded area. "These are tobacco plantations we're passing," Sanches said affably. "Farther off are sugar-cane fields. Those forests in the distance are mahogany and cacao trees."

"Very lovely," Lily murmured perfunctorily.

Leaving an open plain, they approached a town with high buildings, lofty turrets and church spires glinting in the sunlight.

"This is Saint Jago," Sanches told her, but Lily had no interest in the Spanish-looking town with its colorful houses and grilled balconies decorated with boxes of brilliant flowers. Laughing people in bright array enjoyed the sunshine in open tessellated courtyards. The carriage rolled over a great square lined with handsome public buildings, passed a church with great bronze bells topped by a red and white cross.

Might this be where Liam's friend Father Dalvarez was to be found, Lily wondered, but decided it was too soon to broach the subject.

They left Saint Jago and traveled through the rolling countryside of vineyards and fruit groves. Negroes working the land waved to Sanches. "These are my estates," he told Lily.

Deeper and deeper into isolation. Escape will be difficult, Lily told herself, but I'll find a way. The carriage passed through great wrought iron gates up a drive toward a spreading white *estancia* with a portico supported on pillars. The horses stopped at the foot of wide steps, and slaves in stiff white attire sprang to open the carriage door.

Sanches ushered Lily and Lucrezia into a spacious hall where galleries and wide windows revealed a magnificent garden. "It is a pleasure to welcome you here," he said.

The lovely paintings and exquisite marble statuary pleased Lily. At least she would be a captive in beautiful surroundings.

"My house is yours," Sanches bowed. "I am your servant."

"My jailor, Mr. Sanches," she said with a rueful smile.

"To be the jailor of such beauty makes me synonymously your servant." The expression in his blackcurrant eyes seemed to plead for friendship. "Please follow me."

He led the way up a mahogany staircase, along a corridor, flung open a door and they stepped into a large chamber. Red-tiled floor, white walls, dark furniture, big windows looking toward the sea—hurtfully reminiscent of Capri.

"I hope this chamber will please you," Sanches said. "Lord Clune gave instructions that you must be most assiduously cared for."

At least Adam had worried that much for her. "Thank you. The room is charming." Now was the opportune moment to speak of the Jesuit. "After months at sea without the ministrations of my religion, I long to see a priest. There is a Father Dalvarez, I believe, who—"

"A great friend of mine, but he left yesterday for Cuba to attend a conference there."

"How long will he be away?"

"Six weeks."

What an awful loss of time. "I'm sorry about that."

"But allow me to summon his assistant."

"Thank you." She had no choice but to see the priest, to avoid arousing suspicion in Sanches.

"It is my pleasure to serve you, Lady Lily. Now I'll leave you, but someone will be always outside your door to attend to your wishes." He bowed and left, his soft padded shoes making no sound on the tiles.

He would be difficult to escape from, but nothing compared to her father, and she had escaped from Breck. She walked to the window and suddenly felt stricken. The *Fearless,* in full sail, was well out to sea.

"Lucrezia, she's going! *Fearless* is leaving!"

The girl sprang to her side. "Oh, my lady—"

The sun blazing down on the *Fearless* tinted her full sails from white to rose as she cut through the glittering water. Already she was a quarter her normal size and she was shrinking, smaller and smaller. Soon she was no larger than a bird. Then she became a speck on the mysterious line existing only in the distance where sea and sky met. Then the opal haze absorbed her, and Lily was left with only sea and time.

"I hate him!" Lily's fingers dug into the wooden sill. "I hate him!"

12

IT WAS IMPOSSIBLE to escape from an island wholly unfamiliar to her. Lily told herself that first she must learn the geography of Jamaica, so she asked Sanches's permission to wander about.

He courteously agreed, saying a couple of guides would accompany her. She refused a carriage, preferring to walk. So with Lucrezia, who was grieving at being parted from Valentine, whom she admitted she still liked, she tramped for miles looking for an escape route that she might use later. She wanted to go directly to explore the coves and beaches, but to avert suspicion she chose land routes, passing fields where hundreds of wild hogs and horses were being corraled for slaughter so their hides could be sold. Lily plodded through native villages built among fruit groves, beside sugar-cane fields and tobacco plantations. She made sure all the excursions led eventually to the sea, and became convinced that without help she would never be able to board any of the native vessels, and few European or South American ships put into the harbor. Father Dalvarez was not due back for another three weeks, so she must bridle her terrible impatience. The worst of Lily's suffering was that throughout the seemingly endless day she could not stop herself from thoughts of Adam and the contessa. Did he visit her bed each night? Where would he put her ashore to collect his ransom for her?

THE TEMPEST LILY   121

To help lighten the weight of time, she learned to play the Jamaican goombach, a hollow block of wood covered with sheepskin. She took the depressed Lucrezia to attend native weddings and other celebrations and marveled at how the languorous Jamaicans sprang into such vivacity when they danced. Lily was amused at their custom of stuffing rolled tobacco leaves in their nostrils and emitting smoke through their mouths. But her boredom and restlessness increased with each hour.

Then, one night, Sanches gave a supper party for important islanders, at which Castilian ladies were surprisingly friendly with mulatto mistresses of Spanish bachelors and inquired kindly after their illegitimate children.

As colonial gallants with glistening black eyes were presented to Lily, she saw how these men of Spanish lineage were so obviously fascinated by her beauty, and excitedly she told herself that now was her chance to enlist help to get off the island.

Lily selected one man for special attention—young Carlos Raphael. His flashing eyes held a courageous light, his athletic figure showed his strength, and he was obviously wealthy, judging from the jewels adorning his throat and fingers. Flattered by the encouragement of Lady Lily, Carlos never left her side.

As they conversed in a mixture of English and Italian, she told him how she was longing to dance after being cooped up in a ship for months. Once they were dancing, she could beg his aid.

"I'm sorry. Don Sanches had made no preparation for music tonight," Carlos said, revealing his white teeth. "But I shall give a ball in your honor at my *estancia*. It will be my greatest pleasure. I must tell you I am bewitched by you. My world is at your feet."

"A ball." She smiled delightedly. "Oh, would you? How lovely!"

"In a week, and every man in Jamaica will be jealous that I am so honored to have you as my guest."

During that week Lily did her utmost to learn some Spanish from Sanches.

On the night of the ball, she wore a gown of pale blue silk. To enhance her appearance Lily picked big pink blossoms from the garden and pinned them on both sides of her head, nestled behind her ears. She reddened her lips with cochineal.

"My lady is *so* beautiful." Lucrezia stood back to admire Lily.

"God help us, Lucrezia. I have never so desperately needed to be beautiful. My beauty must buy our freedom. But will a man I have only spent a few hours with be so quickly pliable to my wishes?"

"These Spaniards are on fire for beauty . . . like our Italian men. So have no fears, my lady, he will help you."

As Lily drove with Sanches in his carriage, he looked at her excited face. "I am so glad that you seem so happy tonight."

"The thought of music and dancing is a joy to me."

Carlos Raphael's *estancia* was a long, low building painted a dusty pink. Candles burned in all of the many windows, giving the house a fairylike aspect. Music from violins was floating out to mix with laughter and chatter as carriages pulled up and guests descended.

As she entered the house, Lily took in white walls, red-tiled floors, ornate furniture of velvet and gold-painted woods, all illuminated by crystal chandeliers.

Carlos Raphael was there to greet her, a wide smile on his attractive, dark face. He bent to kiss Lily's hand, then shook hands with Sanches and ushered his guests farther inside.

He proudly presented Lily to members of the island's eight most important families. When the violinists struck up a tune, he led her onto the dance floor and whispered, "My whole world has changed since you have come to Jamaica."

The dance was the stately pavane. The dancers took slow, graceful steps around each other, with the men holding out their cloaks like birds' wings.

"You are so exquisite, Lady Lily," Carlos whispered as they came together in the figure of the dance. "Never

THE TEMPEST LILY

have I known anyone like you. I have dreamed of you all week."

She would not waste a second. "But I am sad, Don Carlos," she said in broken Spanish, her eyes pools of appeal.

"But why? Why? I have done everything to give you enjoyment tonight."

"Ah yes, you are so kind, so gallant, so handsome." She bowed low as the dance demanded, then, rising up, looked at him with her great appealing green eyes. "I am sad because I am a prisoner."

"Aye—ec, this is an evil thing. With my heart I wish I could free you." He twirled around her.

"You can! You can help me."

His eyes widened with surprise, but before he could answer the musicians struck up a lively air. He grasped her hands and they kept on dancing.

"But if you leave Jamaica, I will lose you."

"Yet if I stay, I would always think of the island as a place I was brought to against my will, no matter how lovely it is or that you are here. I'd ask you to come with me, but I know you would not be happy anywhere else."

She was also right about his feeling for Jamaica. The woman was a stunning beauty, and frank, two qualities Carlos appreciated and found rare in combination. He would help her, though that did not mean he could not enjoy Lily Deveraux while she was still here.

"I will make plans at once."

Bubbling with hope, Lily danced as she had never danced before, with such spirit that the other guests retired to watch her and Carlos swing around the floor. There was loud applause when the music stopped.

Holding her elbow in an affectionate grasp, Carlos led her to a long refreshment table and gave her a mixed fruit punch laced with rum. "Tomorrow is a long way off—yet I shall call and we shall make plans for your journey. Now I shall take you back to Sanches. He is watching us, and we must not let him suspect."

Lily danced in turn with other admiring men. She

enjoyed the adulation of the fiery Spaniards, who moved rhythmically, and she laughed with them, almost restored to her true self.

The supper was unique, with a variety of roasted birds, rice and plantain dishes, fish roasted in fig leaves, every type of delicious fruit—mostly unknown to Lily—and fine wines.

When at last the glamorous night ended near dawn and she was back in her chamber, she whispered to a sleepy Lucrezia, "We have a friend who will help us escape!"

Don Carlos called the following afternoon, but Sanches did not leave him alone with Lily for a second.

Though Carlos came again on each of the following seven days, Sanches was always there. Burning with frustration, Lily was trying to conceive a way of speaking to Carlos alone when Lucrezia was slyly given a note by the Jamaican butler. She raced with it to Lily.

Do not despair. I shall come to your window tonight at twelve. Your Carlos.

Lily could barely sit through dinner with Sanches, she was so excited and afraid that he might notice her nervous state. They didn't retire until nearly eleven o'clock.

Not undressing, Lily and Lucrezia snuffed out their candles and sat by the open window to wait. "I wonder how he will climb to the second floor?" Lily whispered, her eyes searching the dark garden for sight of him.

"By the vines, my lady. The magnolia vine is strong. In Capri lovers use the vines like ladders."

Time dragged by as the young women sat breathing in the air heavy with flower scent. All was silent in the house. Then Lily thought she heard a movement in the garden, gravel shifting, the sound of soft footsteps. Then a figure came out of the bushes. Carlos! He dashed across the stone terrace, caught at the vine and started climbing up to the window.

As his head reached the ledge, Lily and Lucrezia

reached out with eager arms to help him up. "I have come," he murmured. He had just swung a leg over the sill when a shot rang out, splitting the silence.

He screamed, let go, and fell backward. He lay on the earth, a dark bundle.

Swiftly Lucrezia pulled Lily away from the window. "Danger. Danger. Come away, my lady."

"In God's name, is he dead? Who fired?" Noises started in the house, doors opening and shutting, feet running. "Into bed, Lucrezia! Quick. Someone may come to inquire if we are all right."

Fully dressed, Lily climbed between the sheets, listening to excited voices. Then after a while the house became still again.

What had happened? Lily longed to know. Had Sanches learned about the note and ordered a servant to shoot Carlos? Poor man, Lily prayed the wound was not fatal.

At breakfast the next morning Sanches looked very old. "You heard a commotion in the garden last night, Lady Lily?"

She shook her head. "No, I slept well."

"Extraordinary. Quite extraordinary. Don Carlos Raphael was shot in the garden."

"You mean killed?" Her voice shook.

"No, thank God, but badly wounded in the hip. It will be months before he'll walk again."

"But who . . . I mean, why here . . . ?"

Sanches lowered his eyes and busied himself in skinning a mango. "He was wounded by his mulatto mistress. These women are dangerously jealous of their lovers. She followed him to below your window. You see, he has fathered three children by her, so she is anxious not to lose him."

By the accusing expression on Sanches's face, Lily sensed that he thought Carlos had become her lover! Intolerable! He must be told the truth. "You are wondering . . . wondering if . . ." She broke off.

"Yes, Lady Lily?" His brilliant black button eyes were now fixed on her. "You were going to say?"

"Carlos was not my lover! He was coming to help plan my escape."

"Ah—h," Sanches nodded his silver head and leaned back. "If that was all, may I say I am much relieved. You see, I have already grown fond of you, and I did not want you to be deceived by Carlos. I am a true friend of yours and—"

"A true friend! If you really are, then help me!"

"Child, whatever do you need?"

"My freedom! Let me leave Jamaica before a ship comes with the ransom. Help me to reach Virginia!"

His old countenance was shocked. "Let you leave? That's utterly impossible. I cannot forfeit my honor. I hold you here on trust. Don't you realize that?"

"On trust to whom?" she demanded angrily.

"Lord Clune's syndicate. Its members have trusted me for years. I could not betray them."

"Oh, damn the syndicate! I am nothing but a prize to them, not a flesh-and-blood creature. I swear I'll ask my family to repay any financial loss you'd suffer if you let me go."

"Impossible—impossible. For twenty-five years Lord Clune's family has trusted me. I could not ruin that now."

She had failed. Now she could do nothing but wait for Father Dalvarez's return. "Very well, Mr. Sanches, and how long do you expect I shall be here?"

He shrugged and spread his slender hands wide. "That depends upon when your family receives the demand note, how quickly they send a bank draft in a ship West Indies-bound. Another six months, perhaps nine."

"I see." Never would the ransom money find her here. She would escape somehow . . . somehow.

Lily had been in Jamaica six weeks when she realized she was with child. A terrible shadow fell across her initial joy. Her child would be illegitimate.

The New World was her only answer; change her name, pass as a widow, live among strangers. The truth need never be known.

Now it was with desperation that she awaited Father Dalvarez's return—already his ship was ten days overdue.

When he did arrive, Sanches accompanied her in his carriage to Saint Jago's big square. He left Lily alone in the carriage before the once-magnificent abbey, which was now falling into decay. Sanches would come back for her later.

Shortly after he left, Lily sighted a tall, slim figure in long black tunic, wearing a four-cornered hat, walking through the courtyard. Lily could hardly believe her luck. Quickly she climbed out of the carriage and approached the elderly man.

"I am Lily Deveraux, Father Dalvarez. Your good friend Liam Traherne was anxious for me to know you."

A smile lightened his severe face. "Ah, Liam Traherne . . . a fine man." The priest's English was excellent.

"Unfortunately he died in a battle at sea some months ago."

"God have mercy on his soul." The priest's lean face looked pained. As if to ease his distress, he began walking slowly, Lily falling into step beside him.

"Liam entrusted me to your care," she said softly. "He was certain that, for his sake, you would help me reach Virginia."

"But Sanches's note to me said you were being held for England."

"Yes, I am, but . . . It's difficult to explain. I *can't* go to England! Father, please help me!"

"Suppose you tell me about yourself, Lady Lily. We have plenty of time."

Pacing up and down the shadowy gallery at the side of the courtyard, she began her story. Urged on by the priest's questions, she told everything, including that she was to have Adam's child.

"Months ago I dreaded returning to Wales, but now that my child will have no legal father, it has become impossible to return."

"I do not consider that going to Virginia would be

best for you. If Roger Huet still cares for you and, after knowing what's happened, will marry you, give your unborn child his name—"

"Never!" Lily recoiled from the mere thought of Adam's baby bearing Roger's name. "Oh no, Father, I cannot go back to Wales ever again!"

"My daughter, you are talking nonsense. Your duty is in Wales. To your family, to your child. This is hysteria, to dream of relinquishing not only your own heritage but also that of the child." His whole demeanor was growing in severity. "When your father dies, you will take up your duties as head of your family! You have no choice! God gave you this responsibility with your birth."

Looking down at Lily's stricken face, Father Dalvarez softened. "It surprises me that you've not thought of trying to send your news to Lord Clune. Even though he is deeply angry with you for your bad behavior, this news might inspire his forgiveness."

Lily stopped pacing and stared up at the priest. "I never thought there would be the slightest chance of communicating with him. I don't even know where he is."

"The last time I saw Adam here—when he was homeward bound—he mentioned that on this voyage he intended asking the governor of Virginia for a commission to privateer in those waters. A letter in care of the Virginian governor should reach him."

Her entire being surged with hope. "Oh, Father, do you believe that Adam—"

"That Adam will come to marry you?" Father Dalvarez asked gently. "Well, I've known Clune for many years. He is fiercely proud. It will be difficult for him to forget that you slapped his face before his men. Still, from all you've told me, he did undoubtedly love you. We shall do everything to send news of the child to him. The rest we must leave to God."

Later, seated alone in Father Dalvarez's study, Lily's eyes fastened on the large black crucifix hanging on the white wall.

"Oh God," she prayed with all her being, "guide me to use the words to bring Adam back, for our baby's sake if not mine."

A dozen times she wrote and rewrote the letter. She apologized for her suspicions about Dolores and for slapping him, then she gave him the wonderful news that she would bear his child.

Next, Father Dalvarez told Sanches everything. The old man was delighted, for he was truly attached to Lily. "How I wish I could always keep you here and your beloved child. God give it health when it is born. There is a Spanish vessel in the harbor loading hides and sugar. I'll bribe the captain to see that your letter reaches the Virginian governor."

Belief that Adam would come, added to the friendship of Father Dalvarez and Sanches, cheered Lily. At Sanches's insistence, she accepted money from him and visited the Saint Jago shops to buy clothes for herself, and linens and ribbons for Lucrezia to sew into baby garments. In the evenings she played cards with the Jesuit and Sanches, then entertained them by singing and accompanying herself on the harpsichord. She tried not to ask them the same questions too often.

"Do you think Adam has received the letter? Will he come in time?"

With tender understanding the elderly men tried to reassure her, but months passed without word from Adam, while the child moved slowly along the pathway to life. Marveling at the first almost imperceptible flutter, like the brush of a wing in her swollen stomach, the realization also came to her that she actually carried a live part of Adam.

It became a daily ritual for her to sit at the window, searching the glittering blue sea for hours until her eyes burned. Several times her heart leaped when she was sure she recognized the *Fearless*.

"Lucrezia! He's coming!" she cried joyously. "Quick, lay out my new clothes!"

Lovingly, Lucrezia would help dress her. Then Lily

would watch breathlessly until the sails grew into Spanish ships.

Her personal worries were banished by the arrival of terrible news: King Charles and his troops had been overcome in battle with the Scottish rebels at Berwick, and the king had been forced to sue for peace.

"I suppose now the Puritans are stronger than ever, and the Catholics' position worse than ever," Lily said to Father Dalvarez one day.

"Alas, yes, there is an enormous amount of work for Roman Catholics to do in England." Father Dalvarez looked meaningfully at Lily, and she felt his deep-set eyes commanding her soul.

"I pray Adam will come! But if . . . if he does not and I *must* return, I vow by our Lady's name, I shall do everything I can to help the faith."

For some weeks England's affairs occupied Lily's mind as much as her personal worries. After a while she became obsessed once again with her plight if Adam did not come in time.

"I believe now that he has received my letter and has decided not to come," she frantically told Sanches. "How can I return to Wales?"

"I've given this a great deal of thought," Sanches said gently. "Perhaps it would be wise to pretend that you married Liam Traherne at sea just before he died." Sanches's face brightened as he believed he saw Lily turning the idea over in her mind. "As his widow, everything will be all right for you and the child. Since only the captain and quartermaster know about ship marriages, no one else could question the story."

"Yes, yes. That *could* be a way out! Liam would have liked that . . . poor Liam."

Suddenly she stared at Sanches with blazing eyes. "So you *know* Adam isn't coming!" She rose heavily from the chair. "You know it! This is your way of breaking it to me."

"No, believe me. I swear if your letter reaches him, Lord Clune will come!" Sanches grasped her shoulder.

"It was only to soothe your fears that I conceived the plan about Traherne."

"Thank you, it's a good idea." Lily sighed, realizing she was becoming unduly distraught.

"We'll send another letter to Lord Clune," Sanches said enthusiastically.

"No, I couldn't write again. It would be too humiliating, because he may have received my letter and be ignoring it."

The long, hot days plodded by, marked by drives with Sanches, reciting the rosary with Father Dalvarez, admiring the baby clothes Lucrezia made. Eventually Lily grew too heavy to play the harpsichord or sing, and she seldom walked in the garden.

By her ninth month Lily still had received no word. She was convinced Adam had no love for her nor wish for the child. Curse his coldness; he could at least have written, she thought.

Intermittently, with the encouragement of Father Dalvarez and Sanches, hope would flare again. During the remaining days until delivery, she persuaded herself that Adam was sailing to her. "Pray, Father! Pray!" she begged the Jesuit. "Pray as you've never prayed before that he will come in time to give the child his name."

When labor began Lily cried from the bed, "He will come. He must! I'll not *let* the baby be born until he comes!" Only when the pains mounted one on top of the other, quenching her mental stress, did she surrender everything to the agony of birth.

The baby was a boy. Now that he was here and nothing could alter the fact that he would never be the legitimate heir to Lord Clune, Lily arraigned herself harshly. Wasn't it because she had loved Adam so much that she gave the incident of the child's birth too much importance? Babies were born every second. The Jamaican women casually delivered beside a river. The advent of Adam's child was important only to her.

Lily looked down at the tiny boy, with his telltale

wisp of red-gold hair. One more baby. The sentiment clutched to her for the last nine months didn't belong with a man like Adam. It would have been different with Liam, and even Roger Huet would have been transported to another plane had she borne him an heir.

Had the thought never occurred to Adam that she might conceive a child? Whether he had received her letter or not, he should have communicated with her.

A cruel, implacable man—now she would force herself to forget him.

Adam's infant son brought a measure of peace to Lily. Her delight in the child, in his need of sustenance from her, in the joy of motherhood, all helped lessen her bitterness. She swore to herself that never again would she even mention Adam's name to the patient Father Dalvarez or to Joseph Sanches, who loved the tiny boy as if he were his own grandchild. When the Jesuit baptized the infant, she chose the name of Joseph to please Sanches.

Joseph was two months old when Lily saw a large vessel drop anchor in the harbor. It was impossible for her to tell from the distance of the bedroom window what flag the ship flew.

Not long afterward a servant brought a message to Lily from Sanches, requesting that she join him in the library. Excitement flared through her. Could it be news from Adam at last? With trembling hands tidying her lustrous hair, she sped downstairs.

As she entered the library, she saw a stocky, sandy-haired man dressed in a sea captain's uniform standing beside Sanches. He strode toward her.

"Your ladyship, thank God you're all right!" At the unmistakable Welsh lilt Lily's heart missed a beat.

"Lady Lily," Sanches said, "may I present Captain Owen Llowles, master of the *Happy Lady,* the merchantman that has just arrived carrying a draft on a London bank for your ransom."

So her father cared enough about her to have paid the money. Turning her eyes from Sanches's unhappy face, Lily gave the Welshman her hand. "Captain, I'm so happy you have come," she forced through her lips.

He raised her slender hand to his lips, then straightened up. "I am relieved to see that your ladyship appears to be in good health. Your parents were worried about your state after your hardships of being a captive all these months."

"I have suffered no physical hardship, I assure you. I have been most fortunate to have been with Mr. Sanches." Lily smiled at the old man. "Shall we sit down, Captain?"

"Actually I would prefer to be on our way, begging your pardon, your ladyship," Llowles said stiffly. "These are Spanish waters we are in, after all."

"Your ship is absolutely safe while you are doing business with me," Sanches said, and Llowles's intense gray eyes raked the old man's face.

"Very well, sir." After Lily was seated, the captain lowered himself onto a chair.

"Tell me, Captain, when was it that my father approached you to bring the bank draft here?"

"I fear it was many months ago, your ladyship, when the *Happy Lady* was in Cardiff loading wool for delivery in Virginia. His lordship had just procured the bank draft from London and was having difficulty finding a ship that was West Indies–bound that would guarantee to deliver it and pick your ladyship up."

"Yes, I suppose most English ships are loath to enter Spanish seas," Lily said slowly, turning over in her mind the possibility of Llowles having encountered Adam in Virginia.

"That's one thing," Llowles agreed. "And another thing. Since the Scottish uprisings and the king's religious reforms, thousands of Puritans are so dissatisfied with Charles's rule that they are leaving England for the New World on anything that will float. Most merchantmen are making journeys as direct as possible between England and the colonies."

"I am grateful to you for having undertaken the task of my deliverance," Lily said gravely.

The captain bowed. "I am honored to be of service to you and to Lord Deveraux, who has rewarded me well." His face took on a purposeful expression. "I apologize for rushing you but I should like to leave for the *Happy Lady*. On board I shall hand the bank draft over to Mr. Sanches. I am anxious to catch the evening breeze."

An hour later Lily was ready. Her entire being was in conflict with feelings of regret at leaving Sanches and his devotion, with relief at the chance once more to join in the throb of the world, with apprehension at confronting her father, at facing her world with an illegitimate child. Father Dalvarez and Sanches accompanied Lily in one carriage. In a second, Lucrezia and Joseph followed with their belongings.

"I am happy that you are leaving, my daughter," the Jesuit said, "although we shall miss you here. Your proper place is in Wales, with your family. Remember also that there is much work for you to do there," Dalvarez reminded her when they reached the ship.

"I shall work in every way I can to help Catholicism," Lily said quietly, as she braced herself to contemplate the future with her father, and possibly Roger Huet's marriage suit.

Lily boarded the *Happy Lady* as Lily Traherne, widow of Liam Traherne, traveling with her son Joseph Traherne and her maid.

The bank draft changed hands, then Sanches and the priest bade them farewell and took their places in the small rowboat that would take them back to shore. Lily stood at the rail, her eyes filled with tears.

Happy Lady's anchor chain clanked over and over as it was raised, and Captain Llowles roared, "Set all sail! We leave at once!"

Minutes later the ship caught the breeze and sliced through the turquoise water. Lily remained at the rail waving to her friends, tiny figures on the shore, dwarfed by lofty mountains. Then they were lost to her, and soon the mountains were reduced to purple smudges against the horizon until they too disappeared.

13

FIVE MONTHS LATER the *Happy Lady* tied up at a wharf of the Thames Embankment. Lily was amazed and overjoyed to see her mother waiting there. The ship, of course, had been sighted as soon as she had entered the river, and messengers must have sped to inform Lady Deveraux of the arrival.

Lily's happiness was marred when she noticed her father. She felt relieved when he came aboard and said, "I'm thankful that you are safely back."

Before questions could be asked Lily foisted upon her parents the lie of her marriage to Liam and subsequent widowhood that Sanches had once suggested. Then she presented her parents with their grandson.

Soon afterward, at the Triumph Tavern, where she had often stayed since she was a child, Lily was climbing up the narrow stairs while Lucrezia followed with the baby. The London inn, with its low-beamed ceiling and tiny leaded windows, compared poorly with the bright, airy dwellings of Capri and Jamaica. The innkeeper bowed the Deveraux entourage into a chamber and left. Angela immediately took the baby from Lucrezia. "I simply can't believe this lovely boy is ours," she cooed. "What blue, blue eyes the darling has, and such reddish hair." She looked up sympathetically. "Liam's coloring?"

Lily nodded sadly, the deception making her feel like a criminal.

"Well, you've done one good thing, Lily." Rhys spoke with his usual brusqueness. "You've given the family male issue. Tell me about this Traherne. He must have been a damned outstanding man for you to have married him."

As she hung her cloak on a peg, Lily shot a look at Lucrezia, who was unpacking a chest. The girl's inscrutable face was reassuring; Lucrezia seemed prepared for the frequently rehearsed lies.

"Spiritually, Liam was magnificent," Lily said. "In a worldly way he was only an officer on the *Fearless*."

"Blast my soul!" Rhys exploded. "Whatever possessed you to marry such a nobody? Damned lucky thing he died."

"Rhys, don't!" Angela cried. "Consider Lily's sorrow."

"Nonsense! Traherne meant nothing to her. She married him because she was bored at sea." A sneering expression was creeping over Rhys's face. "Having been married, I imagine you won't be as fastidious as you were about men."

Ever the same, Lily thought with disgust.

"With time I suppose I'll recover from Liam's loss, but it's sad for poor little Joseph to be without a father."

"The precious darling will have all our love." Angela rocked the baby in her arms. "Why did you name him Joseph?"

"After my jailor, Joseph Sanches, who proved one of the best friends I could hope for. Also after Saint Joseph—"

"Quiet, in God's name!" Rhys snapped. "This is England, remember!"

"The Puritans have increased alarmingly," Angela whispered. "And with the Calvinists' triumph in Scotland, there's been a resurgence of hate against us. Priests have been imprisoned and let out only during the day to care for the poor and plague-stricken."

"England is in a state of chaos!" Rhys muttered

angrily. "What kind of laws have we when a British privateering syndicate like Clune's can hold a British subject for ransom? That accursed Clune had better not show his face to me! Now that you are safely back, I intend suing that blasted syndicate for the return of every penny of that money! I may have a chance of justice now that Parliament has opened again after being inactive for twelve years."

"But Father, as the king shares in the profits of Adam's syndicate, you'll have little chance of suing successfully."

Joseph started whimpering, and Lily rushed to take him from her mother. "He's hungry, the lamb." She sat on the low chair Lucrezia placed for her, and with her back to her father, loosened her bodice to give the baby her breast.

"You'll ruin your figure suckling him!" Angela was scandalized. "We must get a wet nurse at once!"

Squeezing Joseph's fat little body to her, Lily swore silently that no other woman would feed her child. "Don't worry, Mother, I've fed him these seven months and my figure hasn't suffered." Knowing how female topics would bore her father, she asked, "Will Parliament help King Charles raise funds for the next Scottish war?"

"That's his purpose in summoning Parliament, so they'll vote subsidies for him."

"Then this time His Majesty will be well prepared," Lily said hopefully.

"Well, he plans an army of thirty-five thousand foot and three thousand horse. And six weeks ago the earl of Strafford went to Ireland to raise an army of nine thousand. The king also hopes to receive arms and men from the Spanish Netherlands. Oh, by the way, that poor Roger Huet is prominent in Commons, the member for Sussex."

Surely Father won't push Roger at me on my first night, Lily bridled. "You always said Roger was England's most eligible bachelor," her voice was edged with sarcasm, "so undoubtedly he's married by now."

"Strangely enough, he isn't. Although quite a few women have tried. He's made no secret of wanting to know when you were returning. As I predicted, he's become extremely powerful, and you could thank God if you caught him! Well, I'm going downstairs, and you two had better hasten down to supper. The tavern is crowded, and there's likely to be a lack of meat."

The first thing the next morning, Lady Deveraux and Lily left the tavern to go on a much-needed shopping expedition for Lily. Stepping into the open marketplace of Charing Cross, they held rosemary to their noses in the hope of disguising the street's stenches as serving maids emptied slops into the sluices. Daintily lifting their skirts to avoid the vegetable peelings and animal droppings that litttered the cobbles, they climbed into the waiting Deveraux coach. As they set off, two outrunners in Deveraux livery trotted ahead to clear a path for the horses.

Soon they were in the traffic melee; hackney coaches creaking and rumbling along beside country carts piled with produce; hucksters screaming their wares; old hags yelling the freshness of their tripe or oysters.

On a corner a ballad singer wailing of Spanish cruelties in the West Indies swept Lily's mind back to the *San Anton,* the contessa and Adam. She began scrutinizing the traffic. Perhaps one of those tall, handsomely attired gallants on horseback might be Adam. Stop it, she castigated herself. She was in London, not Jamaica! To the devil with him. Among the city's quarter-million people, she would find men capable of making her forget Adam and the interminable questions. Had he received and chosen to ignore her letter? Had it never reached him?

Passing a painted coach filled with elegant women wearing dainty lace masks, Lily complained, "Oh, Mother, I feel so shabby in these old-fashioned clothes!"

"Never mind, darling, you'll soon be out of them. We are going to spend the entire day buying beautiful things for you." Angela patted Lily's hand. "Dear child, fancy being all those months on *Fearless* without your own clothes. I still don't see how Clune dared hold you for ransom, especially as Marion says he was falling in love with you."

"Marion is home! I thought she would be too afraid to travel alone." Silently, Lily cursed her stupidity for not having contemplated Marion's return. She would be suspicious as soon as she saw Joseph. But never having seen Liam, she must be made to believe he had the same coloring as Adam. Lily forced a laugh. "It's typical of Marion's nonsense to say Adam was falling in love with me! He was attentive to me because of Grandmother. He is a great favorite of hers."

At mention of the marchesa, Angela Deveraux's questions started anew. As she had done for hours the previous night, Lily tried to satisfy her mother's nostalgia by relating details of Capri until conversation became impossible because of a screaming row between a fishmonger and an urchin who had stolen a mackerel.

The coach was passing a narrow alley that gave a view of the Thames Embankment crowded with tall ships. Was the *Fearless* there? Angrily Lily ordered herself, Forget Adam!

Reaching the fashionable shopping district of the Exchange, Angela and Lily joined the throng of well-dressed women. As they sauntered along the upper walk, which was supported on arches, Lily stared almost unbelievingly at shops displaying satins, damasks, velvets, silks. Windows were filled with fans, gloves, feathers, ribbons, laces.

"Mother, darling," Lily giggled happily, "it's so long since I've seen lovely things I'd almost forgotten they existed." It will be the same when I meet gallants, she silently assured herself. I have forgotten how pleasant their attentions can be.

They took hours choosing glorious materials to be measured by tailors and seamstresses. Pattern makers sketched Lily's feet, glovers fitted her hands. A profusion of feathers and ribbons were chosen at the milliner's. But Lily must wait impatiently for days before the garments would be finished.

She had no choice but to wear her old clothes when, that night, her father insisted upon having a gathering of friends to welcome her home. As she entered the private room Rhys Deveraux had engaged, the first person she saw was Roger. Cynically amused, she had expected her father would arrange this.

His face flushed with pleasure, Roger came toward her. "Lily! Dear, dear Lily. Thank the good God you are safely home at last."

Such devotion after the unhappy occurrences was flattering. "I'm glad to be home, Roger." She smiled and gave him her hand. Then, as her mother beckoned to her, she left him to go and kiss Lady Clive and her daughter Mary, friends since childhood.

"How exciting that you've been in such far-off places, and with the dashing Adam Clune," Mary gurgled. She caught Lily's arm and murmured, "I want to know all the details about him."

"I'll tell you later." Lily hoped her face was not flushed. Eager to escape Mary, she turned to accept her father's introduction of a young man.

"My daughter Lily, Sir James Forsyth." Forsyth had friendly hazel eyes in a handsome face—the face of a fighter, Lily thought. "James is one of the members for York in Commons," Rhys said as he moved toward Roger.

Forsyth bowed gracefully. "I had heard of your beauty, Lady Lily, but how inadequate words are."

"Surely not when you use them." She smiled dazzlingly. "Do tell me about the Commons today. What happened?"

"The best thing that's happened today was my meeting you."

"I hope the day had more to recommend it than that." Lily laughed up at him, appreciating his impeccably tailored clothes. The red brocade doublet and wide white ruff were flattering to his black hair. "Do tell me what occurred."

THE TEMPEST LILY 141

"No sense in worrying over Westminster's muddle tonight. I'm longing to hear about you. I heard from your father that you've just returned from Jamaica. Please . . . tell me all about it." He pulled a chair close to Lily and sat down.

"All about it?" she teased. "Well, it's beautiful, mountainous." She playfully ticked the items off on her fingers. "The women are lovely, the flowers brilliant, the fruit and food delicious, the meat cooked in the Portuguese way until it's so tender it falls off the bone, and one knife serves six people, and—"

James threw his head back, laughing, revealing strong white teeth. "Wonderful, wonderful! But now what about you? Did you enjoy being there?"

"I loved the beauty, but I was lonely with just my maid."

"Adam did not stay long then?"

What malicious trick was this? Because the name Adam was in her heart, she was imagining she had heard it. "Excuse me, who did not stay?"

"Adam Clune. Your father was cursing Clune to me because of the heavy ransom he paid Clune's syndicate." James laughed. "Typical of Adam to have found such a beautiful hostage. He always was a clever fellow! We were at Oxford together. Recently I spent a delightful evening with him at the gaming tables after he had reported to the Lord High Admiral's court."

Lily's heart thumped so violently against her low-cut bodice that she was certain Forsyth must notice it. "The *Fearless* is still in London?" Her words were barely spoken when Roger joined them.

"I heard you discussing that low rogue Clune! Lily, my dear, I'd like to challenge him to a duel for his damnable treatment of you! If only I could find him!"

"I'd advise you to leave Adam alone. England has no swordsman to equal him." James eyed Roger with speculative amusement. "But if you insist . . . He's the houseguest of Sir Archibald Elliot, the enormously wealthy jeweler and Turkey merchant. There's an old romance between Adam and Elliot's daughter. If they marry, Clune gets a girl with a fortune of a dowry, and in addition the queen will assist in the ceremony of putting the bride to bed."

Lily clutched the sides of the chair. The room whirled. "It's close in here," she murmured.

"You're probably fatigued, Lady Lily. Some wine, perhaps?" James held a goblet out to her, and gratefully she drank.

Servants carried in a table set for supper, and she was seated between Roger and James. Lady Clive occupied James, so Roger was free to turn a stricken face to Lily.

"Your mother has just told me of your marriage. I cannot help but think that I might have been your husband, and your son, my son."

"Don't let's think of what might have been!" Lily blurted out bitterly, her whole being racked at the possibility that she might have been Adam's wife.

Somehow she got through the evening. Long after the guests had gone and the tavern was quiet, she still lay awake, her mind in torment. Why? Why had she been such a fool and never supposed that Adam might fall in love with another woman? While she had cherished the hope of someday meeting him and learning he had *not* received her letter, she had never contemplated that by then he would belong to someone else.

"Past three of the clock and a wet and windy morning!" came the bellman's forlorn cry. Lily turned over, trying a new position, and at last she slept.

At dawn she awoke with the realization that unless she immediately acquainted Adam with her marriage lie, Forsyth might see him and she would be exposed. Dreading possible humiliation had he received and ignored her letter, she decided to send Lucrezia anyway, though she would say nothing of Joseph. It was intolerable that knowledge of his son might bring him to her.

With the first sounds from below she went downstairs and learned that Sir Archibald Elliot's town residence was in the fashionable area of Covent Garden.

THE TEMPEST LILY 143

Once the coach carrying Lucrezia had left, Lily's heart felt as though it would burst from excitement.

Eternity seemed to plod by before Lucrezia's return. "He's gone to the country to shoot, my lady."

"When will he be back?"

"In five days."

Lily determinedly filled her time with visits to the dressmakers, tailors and milliners. Being fashionably gowned brought her a certain happiness, though she was always conscious of the five thousand pounds Rhys had paid. At dinner parties she flirted with amusing men. With several of them she attended puppet shows, theaters and supper parties. To maintain her father's approval she also saw Roger.

Lily enjoyed riding around the fashionable ring in Hyde Park in Roger's carriage, where elegant people reclined in luxurious coaches and men rode under the trees, while pedestrians wandered along the pathways.

"The trees are well in leaf for April," Lily observed. "I do love the park."

"It's one of the few good things in London," Roger agreed. "This city is a breeding ground for every vice, with its beer gardens, gaming houses, theaters and drinking inns! What's more alarming, London continues to grow rapidly."

"But with its huge port, it's become the world's mart." She remembered Adam saying that.

"The court exercises a bad influence," Roger continued. "The wives of respectable citizens ride around here encouraging compliments from idle courtiers. Then invitations to a court masque follow."

Lily burst out laughing. "What's wrong with that?"

"Ah, it's a boast of many courtiers that these women spend the evenings in Whitehall's little closets and don't return to their husbands as virtuous as they left."

Suddenly Lily sat up, her heart seemingly leaping to her throat. That man in the approaching carriage . . . it was Adam! As the coaches drew abreast, the blood pounded through her body. Against the red velvet and gold lace upholstery sat Adam! Big, handsome. The same Adam seated beside a fair girl.

In another instant the vehicle was gone. She must gather her wits, not let Roger guess she had recognized anyone. If they kept traveling around the ring, Adam must pass again within minutes.

"Tell me about John Pym, the leader of the king's opposition," Lily urged Roger in an effort to cover up her nervousness.

"I greatly admire Pym. He is a West Country squire who's served six Parliaments. His experience and fine organizer's mind make him a splendid leader. Added to everything, Pym really knows the word of God. Being a widower without ties, he lives only for his work. I am deeply honored that he's chosen me to work so closely with him."

"Yes, I'm sure." Where was Adam's coach, she wondered desperately. It should be passing by now, or had he left the park?

It was impossible for her to concentrate on Roger's conversation. They circled the ring for the second time, and with a sickening feeling she realized that Adam had gone.

"I'm tired, Roger. Could we return home?"

"But of course! You have turned pale." He instructed the driver to head for Piccadilly. "I imagine everything you suffered while you were away has undermined your health." He caught her silk-gloved hand. "I can't bear to think of what you endured aboard that privateer!" He leaned close, his thin face taut with intensity. "Forgive me for saying this, but I believe you married Traherne to escape Clune's unwelcome attentions!"

His mention of Adam was a shock. Roger's utter misconception of the past, his belief in her virtue, all made her want to burst into hysterical laughter. "You're wrong. Clune treated me well." Why did she defend him?

"I swear by God in heaven that someday I'll put Clune in the dock for his record of privateering and piracy, and he'll be convicted to hang! And it will be because of what he's done to you!"

The coach was momentarily held up by a crowd pouring out of an alley into Piccadilly, running along beside a cart carrying a condemned highwayman on his way to the Tyburn gallows. Neatly dressed, the noose lying loosely about his neck, hands chained behind him, a coffin beside him, he faced the crowds. As if grateful to him for the amusement he would soon give them, men shouted jokes to him and women pelted him with nosegays.

"That's the fate I'll see comes to Clune," Roger muttered. "It's unforgivable that he could not have saved you despite the rabble crew."

"His crew was eighty men strong. There was little he could do. But let's not talk of all that. It's finished."

Yet for the remainder of the drive Roger carefully questioned her about her life on the *Fearless*. Alarmed lest his brilliant lawyer's mind should trip her, she concentrated on answering cautiously. Their arrival at the Triumph Tavern was a deliverance, and with relief she quickly bade Roger good-bye.

⊷ 14 ⊷

LILY SENT LUCREZIA to Adam a second time, but she was unable to await the Capriote's return, for James was taking her to the Cockpit Theater in Drury Lane.

She simulated surprise that the Parisian Company boldly included females in the cast, whom the scandalized audience pelted with apples. But her mind was on Adam. She could not delay further. She must know the result of Lucrezia's call, so halfway through the play, pleading a headache, she asked James to take her home.

Rushing to her chamber, Lily awakened Lucrezia. "Did you see him?"

Lucrezia blinked sleepily in the candlelight. "Yes, my lady, also Valentine, who's his valet, and . . ."

"What did Lord Clune say?" Lily wanted to shake the girl.

"He said, 'I want no messages from your mistress!'"

Lily sank onto the bed. The same unchanged Adam. "Yes, Lucrezia," she said slowly, "and when you told him of the marriage lie—"

"I couldn't! He pushed me out of the house!" Lucrezia started sobbing at her failure.

"So nothing has been accomplished?"

"Because he was so angry, my lady. When I was waiting for Lord Clune, Valentine told me *Fearless* sails today, so the secret will be safe."

Yes, for the moment; but Adam must be warned. "Don't cry, Lucrezia. Where is the *Fearless* bound for?"

"Milford Haven. They have prize goods for Lord Clune's family."

Lily told herself she would have to send a message to him there.

As Lucrezia helped her undress, Lily tried to concentrate on the girl's happy chatter of how Valentine was so surprised at seeing her, how he loved her and wished someday to marry her.

The following night was Saint George's night, and James escorted Lily to the court ball. They reclined against velvet cushions as Forsyth's gilded barge floated up the Thames.

"A wonderful sight, isn't it?" James waved toward the city, illuminated from end to end by the high flames of giant bonfires. The sky reflected a reddish glow, against which tall buildings and church spires stood out dramatically.

THE TEMPEST LILY 147

"It's enchanting," Lily agreed.

Soon they neared Whitehall Palace and its sprawling domains. The barge took its place among the medley of craft drawing up to the royal watergates, where the pillars were hung with huge bunches of jasmine and rosemary. The stone stairway was covered by a red carpet and lined with pages and trumpeters in blue and gold livery.

As guests left the river to climb to Whitehall, the bonfires' glow highlighted jewels, satins, brocades, the men's silver shoe-roses. Along the quay the rabble pressed forward as trumpeters blared, announcing the arrival of foreign ambassadors and important personages.

"I'll be bound there's nothing as lovely as this in Jamaica or Capri," James said as he took Lily's elbow.

"Jamaica, no! But Capri's loveliness is quite special. It's beyond compare," she said softly. "In Capri the stars are gold . . . everywhere else they're only silver."

"Funny you should say that. Clune said that very thing a couple of weeks ago."

"What a coincidence."

As they crossed the red carpet to the palace entrance, she glanced up at him. His usually smiling eyes were serious, searching. Be careful, she warned herself, or James will guess the truth.

Then they became part of the throng entering the banqueting hall.

It was a glorious scene. In the light of hundreds of candles set in tinkling chandeliers, the guests' attire formed a moving tapestry that vied in color with the paintings of Rubens, Van Dyck, Titian and other masters, which adorned the banqueting hall.

"His Majesty has excellent taste," Lily said.

"You know, York is not behind London in good taste. Even though we are only the second capital, we have a center of government—an archbishop, forty churches and the most magnificent walls in England!"

"James," Lily laughed, "why defend York to me?"

He laughed at his own outburst. "I could show you

wonderful art collections, and houses and gardens in the best Italian style." He warmed to his subject. "And another thing—I assure you an ordinary meal in York is a feast in London!" He leaned down to her. "I hope you'll like York, because I want you there often. Dare I say . . . always?"

Against the hum of hundreds of voices, Lily wondered if she had misunderstood him. She gazed at him with wide green eyes.

"It's true, I've only known you two weeks!" he murmured excitedly. "But I don't need a lifetime to discover I'm in love." His voice became a hoarse whisper. "You're the most beautiful woman I've ever known. That willow satin is genius with your black hair, your white skin, your green eyes. You're like some kind of sea goddess."

How gratifying that this handsome, well-bred young man loved her. "You're very flattering, James." Despite the fact that she was still nursing Joseph, she was glad her half-exposed breasts were as lovely as those of any woman present.

"You've said nothing about the fact that I love you." James sounded reproachful.

"We're hemmed in by people."

"Forgive me. I'm behaving like a lout." He grinned like an apologetic boy. As people crowded around a new arrival, he remarked. "It's Strafford. I believe he recovered from gout sufficiently to attend Lords today."

The king's chief councillor, lord deputy of Ireland, was a tall, thin man.

"Let's go and pay our respects." Grasping her elbow, James guided Lily through the throng.

It was some years since Lily had seen the illustrious Strafford, and now she felt the same rush of excitement that his brilliant personality had always inspired in her, ever since as a child she had first seen him on visits to Breck.

The man in olive-green velvet doublet with deep lace ruff was the essence of an aristocrat. Everything about him was bred from centuries of fine stock. Thick black hair fell over a high forehead, deep-set eyes gazed with obvious impatience at the flippant courtiers fawning upon him. His expression changed to relief as his gaze fell on James and Lily maneuvering through the circle surrounding him.

"A fellow Yorkshireman—my good Forsyth!" Strafford's deep voice matched his commanding demeanor. He disengaged himself from the circle and strolled off with James and Lily.

"My lord, it is an honor to see you here tonight," James's voice was vibrant with enthusiasm. "Of course you know Lady Lily?"

With easy gallantry Strafford raised Lily's fingers to his lips. "It's not long since I left your father." Strafford's eyes narrowed. "I was trying to convince him that he should take a positive stand in the House of Lords against these accursed Puritans. These are very critical times, and every royalist must vehemently follow the king's course."

How flattering that the great man should speak like this to her. "Yes, my lord, I understand."

"I talk to you, Lady Lily, because I've always believed that women, in their soft, ingenious way can wield a large measure of influence."

She felt aglow with his confidence, as though the sun had suddenly poured down on her, caressing her with its warmth. She longed to be a man so that she could physically follow Strafford into the jaws of hell, if need be.

Strafford was talking to James now. "This has been my first opportunity to congratulate you upon winning the seat for York. We need more young men of your caliber in the Commons. I fear we are sadly outnumbered by the Puritans, and they are more militant than we are. We must be watchful, Forsyth. There are strange elements at work in our beloved England, elements that are determined to overthrow the present state of things. I do not like what I see, and—"

He broke off suddenly as the hum of hundreds of voices ceased and all eyes flew to the wide entrance. "I believe His Majesty is arriving," Strafford said. "If you'll excuse me, I'll join him." He bowed and strode away.

"He's marvelous," Lily whispered warmly to James, who nodded.

"We've nothing to fear from the smug-faced Pym while we have Strafford at the helm of state. He always looks bad-tempered," he whispered. "Although he's a fellow Yorkshireman, I must admit his dictatorial manner has made him many enemies. Still, he and Archbishop Laud are the strength of His Majesty's party."

Everyone rose from their seats while the royal party entered. In silver satin, King Charles was a small figure with a self-effacing manner, the antithesis of Queen Henrietta Maria, clad in blue brocade, leaning on her husband's arm and obviously pregnant. Behind the royal couple came the brilliantly attired entourage.

Soon afterward, on the flower-decked gallery, the music began, and the king led the countess of Carlisle onto the floor. Other couples followed, and soon everyone was dancing.

James proudly guided Lily in the pattern of the saraband. She enjoyed the slow dance and the admiring glances. It was good to receive James's adulation. She performed her figures gracefully, vowing that from now on she would dance through life, for she had suffered enough.

Then, the music over, they strolled toward two tapestry chairs. "I'll get wine," James said, going to find some. She watched his figure for a moment. Had she never known Adam, she might have fallen in love with James. She arranged her skirts becomingly about her feet, and as she looked up casually, the blood surged through her. Adam Clune! Strolling in her direction across the ballroom.

She clutched the chair arms to steady herself. There was a moment's hesitation in his stride as recognition broke over his face, and then he was standing before her, the proud head, the wide shoulders, the great height in cream silk, blotting out everything. The eyes, the

THE TEMPEST LILY 151

wonderful warm, cold, kind, cruel blue eyes were staring into hers.

"Lily . . . good evening."

She summoned all her spirit to her aid—no drama! No recriminations! Just a casual, friendly greeting. "Why Adam, this *is* a surprise!" She had managed a light tone as she gave him her hand. "I thought you had left London."

"Did you?" The old mocking tone was in his voice. His lips brushing her hand sent tendrils of warmth all over her. He straightened up. "Actually I should have sailed today."

Now was her chance to tell him about the marriage, before James returned. "I sent Lucrezia to you, Adam, because I wanted to—"

"Lily!" He stopped her with a warning tone, a warning look. "I must tell you that yesterday I became publicly betrothed."

Stricken by the news that for almost two weeks she had dreaded, she searched his eyes. Cold and detached-looking, the announcement of his engagement had brought no joy to them. It braced her to believe Adam was not in love with Jane Elliot.

"Damnation seize my soul!" James exclaimed gaily as he joined them, a fair-haired girl with him. Lily recognized her from the park. "Clune, you rascal!" James slapped an affectionate hand on Adam's shoulder. "I've just met Jane, and she's told me the wonderful news. You lucky dog!"

As the men shook hands, the women eyed each other, and a thin triumph comforted Lily. Jane was pretty in a spiritless way. Golden hair—too thin for Adam's taste, who had reveled in Lily's luxuriant dark tresses— pale gray eyes, eyes that would never spark, a constrained little mouth. A child's figure. With female instinct Lily knew Jane's only attraction for Adam was her immense dowry, which would help buy back Clune lands.

"Lady Lily Deveraux," James introduced, "Miss Jane Elliot."

"Oh, Lady Lily, I've wanted so much to meet you," Jane said with icy correctness. Lily's jealousy turned to triumph as she recognized the envy in Jane's glittering eyes as they flashed over her opulent breasts, her hair, her face. "I'm almost envious of you, having sailed for so long with my Adam." Jane tucked a possessive little hand into the crook of his arm.

At the intimate gesture Lily wanted to lash out physically at Jane, but she managed a smile that convinced Jane she was hiding some liaison with Adam. Wickedly, Lily looked at him languorously. "I don't believe Miss Elliot would have enjoyed the trip, Adam, do you?" At his annoyed expression, she bridled. "It was monotonous and tiresome."

She felt better after the oblique thrust and turned a dazzling smile on James. "The dearth of gentlemen was appalling."

"But how could that have been, with Traherne there?" James shot a quizzical look at Adam, and Lily realized her slip. "Traherne must have been quite charming for your lovely captive to have married him."

"To what!"

"James!" Lily almost screamed. "The music is starting again!"

"And I beg the honor of the dance!" Adam gripped Lily's elbow and led her off. He steered her in the graceful steps of the pavane, then demanded in an undertone, "What in God's name is going on? What the hell have you been telling Forsyth?"

"That's why I sent Lucrezia to you! When I arrived in England, I said I'd married Liam at sea."

"What devilish quirk made you do that?" Frowning, he bowed to her in the dance.

"It stopped gossip about my being so long on *Fearless* with you, and it will make life easier for me . . . when I marry." She was glad that he looked uncomfortable. The letter! She must know about that. Dancing up to him, she asked swiftly, "Did you get the commission to privateer in Virginian waters?" The dance demanded that she back away, but her eyes raked his face.

"I didn't," he said as they met again and danced around each other. "Why do you want to know?" Forgetting that the dance called for them to separate, Lily stood clutching his sleeve. "Then you never received my letter?"

"No, I never received any message from you." The dancers around them were looking in amazement at them. "We can't talk here." Adam grasped her arm and maneuvered her out through an archway into a gallery that was deserted but for a couple at its far end.

"Adam, you swear on our Lady's name that you never received my letter?"

"What nonsense is this, Lily? I've never heard from you until you sent Lucrezia yesterday, and then I was still too angry with you to accept a note." His voice roughened impatiently. "Why do you look at me like that? It's the truth." He spoke with slow deliberation. "I swear I never received a letter from you anytime, anywhere. Does that satisfy you?"

Praise God, yes, it did. She believed him now. A weakness of relief flooded through her. He hadn't known he was going to have a child. He didn't ignore me! Adam didn't deliberately reject his son!

"Why be so upset over a letter I never got?" He sounded alert, cautious. "There must have been something very important in it that you wanted me to know at the time, but which now you don't, eh, Lily?" He paused, his blue eyes searching her face. "And another thing, how did you dispatch this mysterious missive?"

Lily stood mute, staring up at him in the alternating clutches of relief and bitterness. Relief that he hadn't ignored his child, bitterness that now Jane Elliot stood between Adam, Joseph and herself.

"Lily, why don't you answer me? I asked you how you sent this letter." Adam's voice was peremptory now, the voice of a man used to being obeyed.

She said slowly, "Joseph Sanches gave it to the captain of a Spanish vessel with instructions to take it to Virginia . . . almost sixteen months ago. I suppose he never delivered it."

"If he had, by now it would have caught up with me." He studied her intently. "What was in it?"

How she longed to share his son with him. "I wrote—" But he should have come back to Jamaica for her, letter or no letter. And now he was going to marry another woman.

"Well, *what* did you write?"

"I—I—oh Adam!" The temptation to tell him, to take him to the Triumph and put Joseph in his arms, was almost overwhelming. But a man like Adam might think that she was lying, trying to trick him into marriage, when it was Jane's dowry he wanted. But if, prompted by honor and obligation, Adam offered to break his betrothal and marry her, would she want him on those terms? Never! Adam must love her again as he had.

"I wrote that I was sorry with all my heart for what I did that last day on *Fearless*." Levelly she met his eyes, probing them.

"Damned odd," he mused. "I could swear that was not what you were going to tell me at all." He gave a wry smile. "Anyhow, I'm glad to know you apologized. You'll be interested to know how wrong you were. The contessa died at sea."

"Oh, Adam." What a fool she had been, Lily lamented. Because of her display of horrible temper in striking Adam on deck, she had lost him. Music and laughter from the dancers in the banqueting hall seemed to mock her regrets.

"Well, it's good to know you were sorry. Cursed luck I never got the letter." He seemed so warm, like the Adam of Capri. Hope was restored to her despite Jane Elliot.

"Would it have made a difference? I mean, would you have acted differently if you'd received the letter?" Waiting for his answer, she could hardly breathe.

"So much has happened since then, how can I tell? Yet it would have been good to know that you are sometimes humble." He indicated with a gesture that they should stroll down the gallery.

"I'm always humble and sorry after losing my temper."

"What good is that? It doesn't restore life to a corpse, or dissipate hate. And how I hated you that last morning, and for months afterward. Every time I looked into the eyes of the crew, I could see they were remembering their captain being slapped by a wench. I could have gone on hating you if I hadn't seen you tonight. But the sight of you, Lily, always fires my blood. You're even lovelier than you were. There's a new softness about you."

Angela had said motherhood had enhanced her beauty. Lily wished she could tell that to Adam. "I'm glad my appearance still pleases you, and I'm glad we met," she murmured shakily. "It would have been awful if you had gone on hating me. . . . Listen. The music has stopped. We should go back."

"We'll wait until it starts, then slip into the dance."

If she could go now she might control this mounting longing for him. "I'm being unfair to James, and surely your betrothed will be annoyed." Mention of Jane was poison in her mouth.

"They'll be all right. Jane's reveling in all the congratulations." He spoke dryly as people started coming from the banqueting hall to stroll along the gallery. "Her father has wanted this match since she was in swaddling clothes. Our families have been in business for years. Elliot's brilliant at finding markets for prize goods."

Why was he explaining? she wondered. Was it to ask her to understand his actions?

"The queen wishes to see Jane later. Her Majesty is blessing our marriage." His smile seemed cynical. "It's beneficial for the king's cause that an ardent royalist like myself be joined to Elliot's fortune. He could practically finance the next Scottish campaign, and might do so if he were correctly persuaded."

"And you, Adam?" Lily looked up at him. "Are you in love with her?" The eyes into which she gazed answered before he spoke.

"Who is lucky enough to marry the one he loves? Jane is sweet, gentle and pliable to my wishes and—" he smiled teasingly—"she would never, never slap my face."

"Adam, don't!" Then Lily risked saying the words that might drive him away. "Do you feel about her . . . as you once did . . . about me?"

"I've never felt as close as that to her or anyone else . . . and I know I never shall again. It will please your vanity to learn that it took a damned long time and, forgive me, a great many women, to drive you out of my mind."

The background music was like a death march. It meant good-bye to Adam. She tried to laugh. "It's not lively music, not like the tarantella, is it?"

Catching her arm, he started leading her away from the light toward the shadows. The gallery was emptying again; only a few couples were left, lost in each other's murmurings.

"The tarantella was wonderful! Nothing could ever be like that night."

His bantering tone didn't deceive her. She knew he was trying to disguise his regret for a magic that had died.

Adam's fingers tightened around her bare arm. "I swore, Lily, that I would always remember you as you were that night . . . and I have. I've remembered everything . . . every wonderful detail about you."

He stopped walking and tried to draw her close. There was the well-remembered aroma of oils and tobacco from him. But she must not forget how he had left her in Jamaica! She pulled away from him.

"I always remember you, Lily, with your hair loose over your white shoulders, your cat-green eyes drowsy with desire, your open lips waiting to be kissed, the whole whiteness of your lovely body." Bending down, his mouth was almost touching her cheek.

This was the man she had begged the heavens to send back to her, the man she had loved in Capri—but she must leave him! Lily started to walk back, but he

THE TEMPEST LILY

caught her hand and, striding a couple of paces ahead, pulled her after him. Adam threw open a small door and thrust her into a dark closet. He stepped in beside her, and she heard the bolt slide home.

In the darkness he caught her savagely to him, bending her back over his powerful arm while his mouth moved hotly over her throat. Her whole being was dizzy from his kisses on her hair, her eyes, her mouth, his hands caressing her breasts. "God, how I've wanted you, beloved," he murmured hoarsely. "Wanted you so much that no other woman could make me forget you."

Wonderful words! But too late! She struggled to release herself from his ironlike arms, but he tightened his hold on her body.

"No—no! Let me go, Adam. I cannot forget how you left me in Jamaica. You are going to be married—"

His mouth silenced her with kisses, his hands squeezed her breasts. "Are you insane, beloved, to waste this chance? Our bodies belong to each other."

"No—no! I've changed. I tell you I've changed."

"You lie," Adam muttered. "I saw the look in your eyes when we danced. You are still mine, body and soul. Believe me that I had planned to return to Jamaica for you until you ruined everything between us, but I forgive you. You are a part of my blood, Lily . . . Lily, wonderful Lily."

Now his mouth was on her half-exposed breasts, kissing and licking her in the way that had always shattered her resolves. Lily grasped his head in her arms. Then he lowered her to the dusty floor. From not far off came sounds of music, voices, laughter—but nothing mattered. Adam's huge body was covering hers, his hands were on her legs, parting them, he was entering her. She moaned with joy as at last they were moving together again like one being.

15

THE NEXT MORNING Lily was in a fury with herself. Why had she allowed it? She had behaved as spinelessly as an ignorant serving wench. The moment Adam chose to crook his finger at her, she had jumped to obey like one of his hunting bitches. Disgust at herself nauseated her.

She despised him as well, for after swearing that he loved her alone, he still intended to marry Jane Elliot. Curse him and be damned to the Severn inheritance that he was sacrificing her for.

Among the attractive men she had met in London, Lily favored handsome and witty James Forsyth. He adored her, so she would accept his proposal. She would marry him before Adam married Jane. With James as her husband, Lily would wipe out even the memory of Adam.

Three nights after the ball James escorted her to the theater and afterward invited her to supper at his town house near Smithfield Market. When she hesitated to accept because of decorum, he laughed. "You'll be amply chaperoned, my darling. My great-aunt lives there. Please come. The taverns are so crowded with argumentative fellows discussing politics that I took the liberty of ordering supper at my house."

Lily made a swift decision. Marriage to James must necessarily be some months off, because she could not so soon flout her father's wishes about Roger. But she must have James's help *now!* She needed it to kill the hurt of Adam.

"Yes, of course, James, I'd like that." Being a supposed widow and not an unmarried woman granted Lily a freedom that she enjoyed. She would tell James tonight that she would marry him.

James's carriage stopped before a tall house that was well lit with lanterns burning in the downstairs windows. Linksmen sprang forward with flaming torches to guide their way to the door, where a bewigged footman in the Forsyth livery opened the door for the couple. Lily climbed a small staircase inside the hall and entered a drawing room of exquisite green and gold decor.

James took her hood and cloak while a butler served champagne on a silver salver. The room enchanted Lily; she would like to live in it.

"How beautiful, James!" she exclaimed between sips of the bubbling liquor. "I don't believe I've ever seen such a lovely room."

"I'm glad you like it. My grandmother collected most of the furniture in Rome and had it sent over. This will be your town house, beloved, when we are not living at my estate in York."

"James darling . . . but I haven't promised to . . ." She broke off as the butler returned.

"Sir James, supper is ready whenever you wish it."

"Thank you, Martindale. You may go to bed. I shall serve us. The dishes are all cold?"

"Indeed, Sir James, exactly what you ordered. Cold swan, cold turbot—"

"Yes, yes, excellent. Good night, Martindale."

As the servant bowed and left, James turned a laughing face to Lily. "He's been with my family even before my birth. He is so fond of me I believe he'd even chew my food for me!"

She laughed and surveyed him with admiring eyes. "I'm sure you inspire devotion in people, James. . . . Where is your aunt?" Lily smiled mischievously at him.

Before he could answer, the bellman's cry floated up to them from the street. "Eleven o'clock and all's well."

"There's my answer, darling one. It's no hour for an eighty-year-old lady to be up."

"You're very wicked. You knew she would be asleep when you planned the supper." Lily eyed him flirtatiously over the rim of her lace fan. She was determined to encourage him to make love to her. Tonight she was going to cure herself forever of Adam.

James came toward her and gently took the champagne from her. Grasping her elbows, he pulled her closer to him. His longing for her made him crush her in his arms. His mouth was warm on her eyes, her cheeks, her mouth.

Passionately Lily returned his kisses, and her hands clung to his shoulders. With forced abandon, she curved her body into his. Tonight! Now! She would saw away the chains shackling her to Adam. When James's hand caressed her breast, she did not stop him.

"Lily, I want you, want you." His voice was hoarse with desire as he lowered her to lie on the velvet couch, and she ran her fingers through his thick dark hair, pulling him down to lie with her. He must save her from herself, free her from her slavery to Adam.

James started to unlace the front of her bodice, sinking his mouth onto her bare breasts. This should be Adam's head she was starting to cradle. Forget Adam! Forget him! James is a wonderful man, she silently lashed at herself. Find happiness with him—save yourself.

She leaned forward to touch her lips to his hair. She ran her hands over his wide shoulders. His lovemaking was beginning to arouse her when he lifted her satin skirt to her waist. She longed for James to take her quickly so that she would not betray her resolve to give herself to him.

"Lily, beloved, I adore you," he murmured, as in near-ecstasy he felt her spread her legs to receive him. He had not dared to hope she would be so compliant. It was a dream made real.

THE TEMPEST LILY

He slipped himself into her, and Lily tried to welcome him as she used to with Adam. Her legs twined around James's hips, and she simulated passion as he moved madly on top of her, but it was Adam she was longing for.

Afterward, both fully dressed, they lay pressed against each other, James's arm around her, unable to believe this joy had come to him. Why had she made no resistance? Then a flash of stark understanding came to him as he recalled her disappearance for hours at the ball with Clune. James had suspected that it was a lie that they'd been watching the bonfires. Had she encouraged his lovemaking tonight to forget whatever it was that had passed between herself and Clune? What a fool I am! James exhorted himself. She had given him the wonderful gift of herself. Why pry into the reasons?

Lily glowed. No longer was her body Adam's alone. She was glad—glad that James had taken her. No longer was she Adam Clune's woman to take or leave as he saw fit.

"And when shall we announce our betrothal, my beloved Lily?" James's voice broke into her thoughts.

"Soon, darling James, but not yet. You'll understand when I tell you a little of my story." She told him of her father's insistence that she marry Roger, her imprisonment, the floggings, her escape to Capri—omitting her love affair with Adam. The rest he knew as the world knew of her captivity.

"Father has thrown Huet at my head from the day I returned." She gave a bitter little laugh. "And Father paid five thousand pounds in ransom for me, I mustn't forget. I must try to please him a little and pretend I'm interested in Roger—for a while. Later you and I shall marry. Do you understand, James darling?"

"I suppose so, though I'm an impatient man and I long to shout from the rooftops, 'Lily will be my wife!'"

"You will. You will soon. I promise." She pulled

his head around and kissed him, grateful that he was saving her from enslavement.

From then on she met James regularly at night or for a few hours at the charming house, and their lovemaking was now in his great four-poster bed. He was becoming a truly curative power for her and, what was most important, James would make a wonderful father to little Joseph. James would be a protection for the child, so that if Adam learned about the boy, Adam would never dare try to claim him. Concerned about her welfare, James always wore a sheath when they were in bed—a consideration Adam had never shown her. James had given her a beautiful engagement ring, a circle of diamonds and rubies. Alas, she could not wear it on her left finger yet. Instead it hung on a gold chain around her neck and lay nestled in the warm cleft of her breasts.

Although she was personally comforted by James's devotion, Lily was upset by the way England was twisting with a fury that was fast splitting the country asunder, as the king's party fought Pym's party to dominate Parliament. Now as Lily and her mother sat in their private drawing room in the tavern awaiting Lord Deveraux, Lily fervently asked Angela, *"What* can we do to help the king's cause, Mother?"

"Well, my darling, if you could make yourself marry Roger, you could secretly find ways to aid Charles."

"You, as well as Father!" Lily tried to be light. "Roger's more fanatically Puritan than ever. I couldn't be—"

She broke off as the door flew open and Rhys entered, followed by Roger and James. They were wet and disheveled. "We met at Westminster," Rhys said, shrugging his damp cloak off his shoulders. "When the cry went out, 'Who goes home?' we decided to walk together and share the same linkman."

"But why walk?" Angela put Rhys's cloak away.

"Such a delightful evening for a stroll." James grinned, shaking raindrops off his tall beaver hat.

"With such a mad mob besieging Westminster," Roger said grimly, "it was impossible for horses or coaches to approach the building."

"I've ordered supper to be served up here," Rhys said. "The tavern is crowded with argumentative fellows."

While James and Roger hung their cloaks on pegs and servants brought in wine and ale, Lily asked, "What's the news from Westminster?"

"Not good." Rhys sat down heavily by the fire. "Strafford failed to make Charles reduce his twelve subsidies to six, and Pym's party even opposed those."

"Aye, the country is going to see many changes," Roger said smugly.

"Oh, damn the changes!" James swore angrily, then turned to Angela and Lily. "Forgive me for swearing, but I want England to stay as she is. In York we're prosperous. Our clothes sell in Spain, Portugal and Italy. All the cold countries buy our wool. It even goes to Ragusa and turns up all over the Turkish domains . . . and in Russia. I'd like to go on like this."

"Forsyth represents my feelings somewhat." Rhys tossed off some wine and glanced at Roger. "Between friends, tell us if the rumor is true that Pym and you Puritan fellows are in close touch with the Scottish rebels?"

A dangerous question, Lily thought, as everyone's eyes raked Roger's noncommittal face.

"If it were true," he said slowly, "would it be wrong? Wouldn't it be fair to hear the Scots' side? Examine their religious grievances?"

"Damn it, Huet!" James exploded. "Surely like any decent Englishman you resent this Scottish uprising against authority? And despite the king's faults, he still stands for authority!"

"Ah, here's supper!" Rhys looked relieved as servants wheeled in a table spread with a white cloth and holding pewter dishes. Rhys lifted the various covers. "Herring pie, oyster stew, rabbits, swan, fruit tart. Adequate—

adequate. Come, we must eat, no matter what troubles tomorrow brings."

The next day Charles dissolved Parliament. That night James supped with the Deverauxs, and Rhys soberly told his family, "We shall leave immediately for Wales."

"I've an uncle I intend visiting in Berkshire. May I have the pleasure of riding part of the way with you?" James glanced at Lily, who smilingly nodded.

"Splendid, splendid," Rhys said. "Damn my soul, Forsyth, cursed bad luck for us, things going like this with Parliament. It means the financing of the war will come out of royalists' pockets."

At that moment the door flew open and Roger burst in, pale-faced, eyes inflamed. "Pym and his advisers have been arrested!" he cried hoarsely. "It's an outrage!"

"They deserved it," James snapped, "the way they've been trying to dictate to the king. I hope——" He broke off as angry shouting came from the street. In the chamber everyone rushed to pull open the windows to stare down into Charing Cross.

Crowds brandishing sticks were pouring from houses and out of alleys as they yelled, "Away with the papists! Let the Puritans be heard!"

Windows were being thrown open and king's sympathizers cried, "Long live the king! The king has divine right! Down with Pym!"

In the streets people shouted, "Pym speaks for the people. Let Pym out of prison!"

Pandemonium broke loose. Royalist sympathizers fought Pym's men with sticks and fists. Women pulled other women's hair, ripped their clothes.

"Damn my soul, my sword can serve Charles down there!" James cried, rushing from the room.

By torchlight it was difficult to distinguish what was happening in the marketplace, but Lily thought she recognized James in the thick of the riot.

Then, over sounds of fighting and cursing, came gal-

THE TEMPEST LILY 165

loping hooves, and seconds later uniformed civilian soldiers charged into the swaying, struggling mob. People scattered into dark doorways and alleys, carrying wounded with them. Within ten minutes order reigned.

"By God! What insolence for the rabble to criticize the king's actions!" Rhys furiously slammed the window shut.

"Don't blame the people," Roger warned. "They're tired of the unfairness of Puritan preachers being imprisoned while papist priests are favored. Their trade is suffering because of taxes and—"

James burst in, grinning like a boy. "That was good sport. They'll be sore in the morning."

"But it's impossible for people to think that Pym, an ordinary man, has the wisdom to oppose Charles—chosen by God to rule!" Lily exclaimed. Then, hearing Joseph's wails from an adjoining room, she said, "Poor mite. The bedlam has awakened him. I must go to him. Lucrezia is in the scullery."

Roger opened the door for her. "May I come? I've only seen him once."

She managed to shoot a secret look at James, asking for comprehension, and he gave a little nod.

"Joseph's always asleep when you arrive from Westminster, Roger, but come, of course." In the bedchamber he held the candle while Lily picked the screaming infant up and tried to soothe him.

"A fine child," Roger murmured. "I wish I were his father. As God has seen fit to call Joseph's father, let me try to take his place, Lily. A boy needs a man." Glancing up at Roger's face softened by love, his eyes in the candlelight beseeching her, Lily could not help pitying him. "I've waited a long time for you, my dear. Loving you despite your absence and never a word from you. Surely I've proved the strength of my love?"

His love! What a damned bore the sanctimonious man was! "Roger, I'm so recently a widow. You must understand I cannot think of marriage yet." Liam was being such a help. How it would have pleased him!

"If I have hope, Lily, I'll wait forever."

That's exactly what it will be, she thought caustically, but smiled at him while in her mind she saw Adam with his blue eyes, his strong mouth, his long fingers which brought such joy to her body. Would she ever be released from this insane passion? Would James have the power to free her? With all her heart she prayed so.

16

ON HORSEBACK ROGER accompanied the Deverauxs' coach to Hyde Park Corner and the last watchman's box, where people on foot, armed with pistols and bludgeons, were gathering for protection before leaving the city. Bending from the saddle to Lily at the window, Roger said, "It will seem like an eternity before I see you again at the Council of the Marches."

"But not really very long. The time will soon pass," she said, though grateful to be rid of him for a while.

Raising his tall black hat, Roger bade Godspeed to the others in the party, and the coach moved forward toward the Knightsbridge area.

Angela and Lily sat facing front; Lucrezia, holding Joseph, sat between them; opposite were Rhys and James.

"Huet was telling me this morning," James said, "that he feels so strongly about the Scots warranting justice in the coming struggle that he's tempted to join their military ranks." James smiled with an air of amused disparagement.

"Ah, you mustn't be misled by Huet's rather esthetic looks," Lord Deveraux said, frowning. "I don't know if you are aware that he has a fine military background."

James shook his head, surprise on his handsome face. "Indeed, I know nothing about this."

"I thought not. But soon after he came down from Oxford, he fought with the Dutch and Swedes in Germany for the Protestant cause, and acquitted himself as a fine officer." Rhys's jowly face became grim. "Roger's sympathy with the Scots represents the feelings of a multitude of Englishmen, I fear. While Strafford struggles to finance the war, the king's commander in chief is having the devil's job in raising the levies."

They traveled for hours, mostly discussing the political state, relieved by James's joke-telling, until they all slept.

Late at night Lily awoke. A pale moon was lighting an expanse of furze bushes, grassy hillocks and swampy gravel pits filled with bulrushes. Ahead, on a rise of land, a dark gibbet seemed to be painted against the wan sky. Hanging in chains, a body gently swayed with the wind. Death was the end to all sorrow and joy, Lily thought, tightening her cloak about herself.

Hours later the coach stopped abruptly, throwing everyone against each other. A rough voice demanded, "Stand and deliver!"

"Mother of God!" Angela screamed as, beside her, a mounted masked man bathed in moonlight thrust a gun through the open window.

"I'll trouble you for your purse," he addressed Rhys.

"Dog in a doublet!" Rhys's left hand swept the gun upward as his right fired a pistol at the highwayman, who slumped forward across his horse. The next second James lunged for the door, thrust it open and jumped out, Rhys behind him.

"Toss your purse to me, lovely lady," a gruff voice commanded Lily. She swung around to confront another masked man at her side of the coach. Dragging her purse from her sash, she flung it at him. He caught it easily. At that moment James, sword in hand, rushed around to seize the horse's bridle, but the robber whirled his mount and galloped into the night.

"One dog is dead!" Rhys cried as he and James got back into the coach. "Now after the other." He shouted to the driver, "After him!" The horses leaped ahead, dragging the heavy coach.

"You'll never catch him." Angela clung to the seat to save herself from being spilled.

"But we'll raise the hue and cry against him!" Rhys growled furiously.

Everything had happened with the speed of thought. Now, pulled by the madly galloping horses over the rutted roads, the coach bounced on and on until, like a sanctuary, ahead there glowed the lights of Benhurst village in Berkshire. At the constable's house the Deverauxs' outrider banged on the door, shouting, "Open for the earl of Deveraux!"

The constable rushed out and listened to Rhys's castigation of the neighborhood. "Excuse me, your lordship, but I cannot raise an alarm because between setting sun and sunrise, also Sundays, a neighborhood is not responsible for catching highwaymen or making good their thefts."

Thoroughly incensed, Rhys could do nothing but find the nearest inn for the night. The Flowerpot had two rooms. The women and Joseph shared one, the men the other. Angela, Lucrezia and Joseph were soon asleep, but Lily, although she was tired, was wide awake.

Believing mulled wine might calm her, she threw a cloak over her shift and went downstairs.

Stepping into a beamed room, she froze, horrified. Her father was holding the tavern wench on his knees. Both were oblivious to Lily in their degrading embrace. Lily raced outside, unaware of where she was heading until she reached the garden.

"Lily, why ever are you here?" James's surprised voice made her swing around.

"It was too close indoors, James. What are *you* doing here?"

"Looking for ale. I was thirsty."

She searched his face in the moonlight. Ale was kept in the room where her father was. "So you saw Father, too. It's horrible! He's just killed a man. And Mother's upstairs! Oh, James, are all men like that?"

"Don't be so upset, sweetheart. Sometimes after being part of a sudden death, people copulate as if to even up the score with nature. Once we're married, my love, you'll see all men are not like—well, not like your father."

He pulled her slender arm through his. Her long dark hair cascading to her waist and ethereal face in the moonlight made James burn with need. He walked her toward a great tree that was casting a heavy shadow.

James spread her cloak on the ground for her to lie on, and was delighted that Lily was wearing only a short nightgown. Swiftly he disrobed. Soon they were enjoying the wonderful feeling of their warm bodies pressed against each other. Lily's satiny skin always enchanted him, and she had a special fragrance about her that he loved. James covered her body with kisses as her fingers played through his hair.

"Lily, Lily, I'm besotted by you. When you're my wife, I'll keep you naked all day. You're so beautiful."

"Ah, that means you're going to keep me hidden," she chuckled teasingly.

"Absolutely! I'd kill any other man who looked at you." Then he began to fondle her breasts, and she twined her legs around one of his thighs. She liked the feel of his strength between her legs, and she pressed tightly against it until, growing very excited, he climbed on top of her and plunged into her. The first moment always made her gasp with pleasure. His hands went beneath her tight little buttocks to gather her up against his body. Then she started to move up and down against him, and he moved rhythmically with her until her nails dug into his back as she groaned aloud.

Later, in the soft air scented by summer flowers brushing over their nakedness, a terrible sadness weighted Lily. On nights such as this she had lain in perfect bliss with Adam in Capri. Now all was over; he was marrying another woman, and the body Lily had vowed was only his she now gave constantly to James. Was she a wanton?

"I'd better go in, James. Mother might wake up and miss me."

"I suppose so, my beloved." He helped her up, then picked twigs from her hair.

Anxious to be alone, she kissed him lightly, pulled her cloak on and left.

In the morning, just before they were to part, James said, "Your father has invited me to Breck to hunt buck this autumn, but the Scottish war might be in full swing by then and prevent me coming."

"Don't wait for the hunting season. Come soon." She was going to miss him.

"That's what I want to do. May I ask your father for your hand then?"

"Yes. Just give me a little time to prepare him."

"I'll live for the day that I see you again. Good-bye, my beloved. You know that you have all of my heart." He waited a moment, longing for her to say she loved him also. She did not. But she kissed him with deep fervor, and James was forced to be content with that.

Two days later, the Deveraux coach crossed the border into Wales. In Glamorganshire the heavily rutted roads slowed them down and increased Lily's impatience to see Breck Castle. At last the way twisted, and there, topping the highest hill, loomed a mass of dark masonry. Gaunt, noble, seemingly indestructible, Breck Castle stood as it had for six centuries.

Pride of heritage warmed Lily. How right Father Dalvarez had been. Joseph belonged here. Her gaze swept lovingly over meadows where fat sheep grazed. Farther off were thick forests whose mysteries had frightened her as a child, and beyond were the ugly slate quarries. Scattered along the countryside at doors of turf-roofed cottages, the tenantry waved its welcome and men sprang to their horses to ride to the village sheltered below the castle's walls to spread word that the lord and his ladies had returned.

Outriders in red and white livery trotted from the castle to escort the coach through the outer gates and the bailey to the accompaniment of blaring trumpets. Lily waved and smiled to the gatekeeper and his attendants as the coach rolled through the great gates and over the turf to the inner keep. The horses halted. Grooms sprang to hold their heads and open the coach doors. Ignoring ceremony, Lily dashed over to Geraldius, who was waiting at the stone archway, and beside him, her childhood companion, David Gwyn.

"Geraldius! Geraldius! Oh, how glad I am to see you!" She hugged the old man.

With a shaking hand he brushed tears from his eyes. "Praise God you're home, dear child. Now enough of this fuss. David is longing to greet you."

She turned to the fair young man, his sensitive face glowing. Hugging him as though he were her brother, she cried, "David, I'm so glad you've finished college. I didn't expect this added pleasure of finding you home." She realized he had grown into a strong man during the three years since she had seen him last.

"I've been back just a week, Lily, and never stopped watching the roads for your arrival." His gray-blue eyes poured appreciation over her. "Foreign travel has added to even your loveliness."

"David, from you? It seems only yesterday you were telling me what a sight I was and pulling on my hair."

They laughed at their memories, but Geraldius interrupted. "You must go, dear girl. Everyone's waiting to greet you inside."

"Yes, of course." Lily stooped to pat four dogs that were jumping and barking at her skirt. "It's wonderful they've not forgotten me."

Stepping through an archway, she reveled in the familiarity of home. How good to enter the great hall and be welcomed by the retainers. After being away so long, she realized how fond she was of them all. She climbed the wide stairs hung with her ancestors' portraits to the private withdrawing room, where her parents and Geraldius awaited her. She glanced appreciatively at walls and floors of inlaid woods, at the ceiling painted like a celestial globe; at the chimney's two columns supporting the busts of Seneca and Aristotle; at the Deveraux coat of arms of two birds holding a hand between their claws.

Rhys toasted Lily and Joseph's homecoming with mulled wine before everyone retired. Passing along the corridor, Lily glanced up at the ceiling paintings of Europa on a bull. She smiled to herself. Nothing had changed here since her earliest memories.

During the next few days she gladly accepted her father's efforts at friendliness. Riding over the land with him and David Gwyn, Lord Deveraux pointed out improvements he had instituted.

"We planted potatoes and turnips as an experiment, but they're not popular eating." Rhys waved at fields they were passing. "Also sainfoin, lucerne and clover in an attempt to grow winter fodder and so eliminate the necessity of the yearly slaughter of cattle."

"In Jamaica, cattle live throughout the year," Lily said.

"You've had good luck with your quinces, figs and apricots, my lord," David said admiringly as they rode past healthy-looking orchards.

"Yes, but now when everything's organized, I have to lose so many men to the king's forces. It's a strange kind of luck, David, that you have with your foot. It makes you incapable of military service."

Seeing the humiliation flush over David's face at the mention of his clubfoot, Lily resented her father's insensitivity. "There are other ways of helping the king's cause besides fighting."

They turned their horses toward the castle. "That's something you should remember, Lily," Rhys pointed out. "What news have you from Huet?"

"He wrote saying that Charles seized bullion in Lon-

THE TEMPEST LILY 173

don's mint, then offered the merchant who had deposited it there eight percent for the loan." She laughed superciliously. "Of course Roger is such a bigot that I hardly believe his reports."

"Huet is damned astute, and being so close to Pym, he knows more of the shape of the future than we do." Rhys's mud-brown eyes fixed meaningfully on Lily. "This business with Scotland might develop into an even more serious conflagration. If that happens we might be glad of Huet's support."

Grooms rode up to detain Lord Deveraux, and Lily gladly rode on alone with David. Passing through the inner gates, she murmured, "I'm afraid Father is still trying to make me marry Roger. You were not at Breck when that awful session was going on. It was terrible."

"Geraldius wrote me about it. It upsets me even now to think of you in the dungeons."

"Enough of me. You've had your own sorrows. It must have been terrible for you at the Jesuit college when you discovered your clubfoot prevented you from being a priest." She looked at him sympathetically.

He patted his horse's neck. "It was hard at first, but it's a good ruling that a man must be physically perfect to celebrate the mass on the altar. I've decided to devote my life to religious teaching. The Catholic Church is painfully in need of teachers in this country."

"Yes, and you can begin in Glamorganshire and continue living at Breck. I can't tell you how happy I am to have you here."

"Thank you, Lily. There've been quite a few changes in our lives since we were last together. There's Joseph. Perhaps because Geraldius is growing tired, it will be my good fortune to tutor the little fellow."

"I could want nothing finer for Joseph." With David for a teacher and James for a parent, Joseph would not miss the father he would never know existed.

Lily's days were busy helping outfit men going north to join the king's forces. There were calls to be made on neighboring gentry, her experiences to be related, Joseph to be displayed, also visits to the sick tenantry.

Then the earl was summoned by Lord Conway to Newcastle to confer upon the number of men he could put into the field.

One day, seated in her mother's Italian garden, Lily determined to tell Geraldius the truth about Joseph and her decision to marry James.

Wasting no time upon comment, Geraldius responded severely, "Lord Clune must be appraised of his son's existence as soon as possible. You have no right to keep it from him!"

"But I *cannot* tell him. He's betrothed. I don't want him to break his engagement to offer me marriage just because of Joseph."

"You must pocket your pride and let Lord Clune know about his son!"

"Oh, Geraldius, you set me a difficult task."

"To follow the righteous course is generally difficult. This thing you *must* do. Also for the boy's sake, Lord Clune must be told. The route to Milford Haven is impassable by coach. You must go by horse." He was momentarily silent. "We need a trustworthy man to accompany you."

"David can come with me." If only James were here, she would feel more secure.

"But he's handicapped by his foot. He would be little protection against highwaymen if it came to swordplay."

"He's a fine shot, though. I'll tell him I'm going to Adam's home to recover some documents I left on *Fearless* and I don't wish Father to know because of his bitterness about the whole business."

The following day, dressed in male riding attire, Lily left Breck with stocky, strong-shouldered David Gwyn. She was dreading the task ahead of her. Supposing Adam did not believe her? Thought the child was someone else's? Liam's or a man in Jamaica. And thought that she was placing fatherhood on him to force him into marriage. Well, she would have performed her duty, and in any case he could not humiliate her. She was betrothed to James. She fingered his ring hanging between her breasts.

Riding through lovely countryside, they traveled across Glamorganshire, stopping only to eat and change horses. Though she was exhausted, Lily pressed on; she wanted to have the affair over and done with. They slept at a tavern that night, and with the first light were again in the saddle and riding through Carmarthenshire.

Nearing Milford Haven, they stopped a group of peasants carrying bundles of freshly collected seaweed to fertilize the soil. "Which way to Ben Fras, please?" David asked.

"Climb that hill, sir. It's on the other side—only minutes away."

Lily burned with excitement as she touched her spur to her horse and the animal picked a footing up toward the crest of the hill. The sound of the sea, hidden from view, was tantalizing. Would she find the *Fearless* there? The horses seemed willfully slow in their climb, but at last they gained the summit and Lily looked down on empty water.

She sat trembling, staring at the vast blue-grayness. Had the *Fearless* come and gone, or not yet arrived? Far below, waves suicidally dashed against rocks. That massive stone house along the shore was Ben Fras, Lily supposed. It was sinister in its desolation, surrounded by tall scrawny trees tormented by wind. Along the deserted shore three women searched for ambergris and samphire among sea drift. They might know if the *Fearless* had recently pulled in. No. She would go straight to Ben Fras and ask if Adam was expected. Explaining to David that she wished to go alone, she set her horse to the descent.

At the great stone house she pulled the bell rope and heard the clanging sounds inside the house. A woman servant opened the door and Lily asked, "Can you tell me if the *Fearless* has called in or is expected?"

The woman eyed her suspiciously, then said, "Enter, please." She ushered Lily into a big drawing room, and

Lily wondered who would come to answer her question. Greedy for details of the house so familiar to Adam, her eyes tried to absorb everything. Which volumes had Adam handled the most among the tightly packed bookshelves covering one wall? Was that great tapestry chair his favorite? Did he often stand before the huge fireplace? Did he lean an elbow on the stone mantel? Her eyes fastened onto the Severn escutcheon and the words engraved in the stone.

> Lord Adam Clune, heir to the Earl of Severn, in 1330 was taken at midnight in the Queen's bedchamber, whence he had gone secretly by underground passage. He was condemned to death and drawn and hanged at Tyburn.

Frightening, those words. "Adam Clune, hanged at Tyburn." Shivering, Lily turned as a servant bowed in a tall woman. It was evident from her likeness to Adam that this was his mother. Her haughty beauty had an unconquerable quality. The white skin was smooth, the golden hair scarcely faded. Trembling, Lily curtsied low.

"Rise. You are of course Lady Lily." Her voice was rich with an Irish lilt.

Straightening up, Lily noticed immediately the blue eyes—like Adam's—like Joseph's! They were so distinctive that Lily bit her lip to stop a gasp.

"This is a delightful surprise, Lady Lily." The countess of Severn waved toward a chair, then seated herself next to the fireplace, and Lily sat opposite.

"I should explain, your ladyship," Lily began, "that I was aboard—"

"Fearless! But of course, I know." The chuckle was so like Adam's. "After all, I'm a senior member of Adam's syndicate!"

A servant handed Lily ale and cheesecakes. Although chafing at the interruption, she politely accepted.

"Have you heard the latest reports?" the countess inquired. "The Dutch informed His Majesty that if

English ships continue to transport Spanish troops, they'll consider England at war with Holland. If only Strafford can bring the Irish troops over, they'd restore the king to his rightful place in England." The countess was obviously no longer creating polite conversation; she was lost in her subject. "Protestant lords and gentry are out of hand. For years they've fattened on the land stolen from the crown and from the Roman Catholic Church and its followers!"

Lily was impatient to know where Adam was. "Excuse me, your ladyship, may I explain why I came?"

"But I know why—to see Adam." Her Celtic directness was unnerving. "Don't look embarrassed, child. A year ago Adam was so in love he told me all about you. For a while I was a little anxious that Adam would find you and marry you, and that would have been disastrous to our family."

Stung by the remark, Lily asked coldly, "Is Jane Elliot's dowry so all-important to the Severns?" Her green eyes glittered with contempt.

"It became so when we realized that the Severn men's swords must serve the king." The countess addressed Lily severely but kindly. "Try to understand. If the Severn men are stopped from privateering, the family will lose their lands again, because as professed Roman Catholics, we pay crushing taxes to hold our estates. Apart from what Jane's fortune brings to us, Adam has extracted a promise from her father to make King Charles a large loan. You know how vital that is."

"Yes, I do." Lily spoke dryly. "Adam made that clear to me."

"Lady Lily, forgive me—I would like you to understand my men's position." The countess spoke in a defensive tone. "So may I tell you a little of my story? As a girl in Ireland, I was about to marry the son of a neighboring family. We'd been in love since we were very young. One day my father said, 'Catherine, the Welsh earl of Severn needs to marry a Roman Catholic girl with a fighting spirit. If he does not and marries a

Protestant, the Severn family might well be lost to the faith. I have decided it is your duty to marry him!' "

Despite herself Lily was growing to like the countess.

"I rebelled inwardly and wondered why God had chosen me to be sacrificed. Later I learned that sacrifice is demanded of all of us." She shrugged and smiled wisely. "Adam, too, has sacrificed himself."

The two women stared into each other's eyes. Lily was remembering how, watching Liam's body splash into the sea, she had suddenly understood God's design, to deny everyone their dream. Rebellion flared through her. She sprang to her feet. "I'm sorry about you and also Adam. Is he here?"

"No. He's out of England for a while."

Part of Lily was crushed by disappointment, for she could not suppress her longing to see him, yet another part of her was glad not to have to tell him of Joseph. She stood up.

"I rode here to collect some personal documents I had left on board ship. I'll just have to wait for another time. I believe I should go now."

"Oh, but wait. Allow me to show you the famous Severn Chapel."

Lily could not be so boorish as to decline. "That's very kind of you."

She followed the countess out and into a stone corridor. A heavy, iron-studded door led into the small chapel. Sunk level with the floor, gravestones worn almost smooth still bore the names of Severn dead of centuries ago. Near the bell, carved in stone, were the words:

> If thou thyself shall look for grace
>   when death shall come to take thy soul,
> Then pray for others in like case
>   when they shall hear my doleful toll.

"The chapel was built in the eighth century," the countess explained. "That window's tracery bears the Severn arms. Over there are the ancient leper holes, where the poor creatures heard mass. Praise God mass is still celebrated here whenever Adam smuggles priests in from Italy." The countess's voice lifted proudly. "Since Reformation times the Severns have paid crushing fines, suffered imprisonment, death, molestation and double land taxes because of openly professing the True Faith."

Suddenly Lily felt spiritually shabby. Her ancestors had suffered nothing. Instead they had denied their religion. Even in her generation she and her mother worshiped in secret. She knelt beside the countess and said a silent prayer for Joseph, and could not help lamenting that, if life were different, she and Adam could have wed in this little chapel.

The countess saw her outside, and at the arched entranceway a groom came up with her horse. Lily dropped a curtsy to the countess. As she was rising, she flared with anger at the pity she recognized in those blue, blue eyes.

She placed her foot in the groom's folded hands and swung onto her horse. "Oh please, your ladyship, when you see Adam, tell him I am betrothed to Sir James Forsyth—a wonderful man." She dug her heels into her horse's sides and cantered off.

▻ 17 ◅

"WELL, YOU DID your best to acquaint Adam about Joseph," Geraldius said, "and it's too private a subject to write about. The letter might well fall into alien hands." Geraldius's wise old eyes looked sympathetically at Lily's face as she paced his book-lined chamber.

"Now I'm going to work for the faith." Lily swung around to the old sage. "Tell me, are there enough Catholics in Wales to be of considerable use to Charles in this Scottish war?"

"Not any longer. Although the Welsh detested the Reformation and for long afterward remained openly Catholic, most have now fallen away."

"Why didn't Wales become another Ireland?" Lily realized that meeting Adam's mother had sparked that question in her mind.

"The language was responsible. When Henry the Eighth closed our monasteries, potential priests fled abroad to study. The difficulties with language were so great they gave up, so the supply of Welsh-speaking priests ran out. In recent years Benedictines and Jesuits have filtered back into Wales, and the Jesuits courageously established the Saint Francis Xavier College, which David attended."

"I understand. I'm ashamed my ancestors accepted the Reformation so as to hold onto their lands."

"Fear also played its part with the Deverauxs." A sigh quavered from Geraldius. "A terrible power—fear. You know, dear child, once I intended being a priest."

It worried Lily to see Geraldius suddenly wrapped in sadness. "You would have made a fine priest." She went to sit near him. "What stopped you from taking Holy Orders?"

"Fear! After I saw a priest hanged at Tyburn and cut down half-dead, his stomach and chest ripped open, his heart torn out while it was still beating." Geraldius's wrinkled face twisted as though he were witnessing the macabre scene. "I knew then I lacked courage to suffer martyrdom should it come to me."

So Geraldius too had been chosen to sacrifice himself, yet he had failed. Lily knew too well that to be one's own betrayer was the bitterest gall. "Even though you didn't become a priest, you've done so much good," she tried to comfort him.

"I've tried to silence my remorse with good works.

Ah, my dear girl, time does not age a man, it's disillusionment. Worst of all, disillusionment in one's self."

"I will not permit that to happen to me!" Lily sprang to her feet. Geraldius's story had suddenly given substance to what had been, until then, a shadowy idea. "I'm going to ask David to write to Father Morgan at Saint Francis Xavier College at Welsh Newton and ask the Jesuits to try to find work for me to do to help the Catholic faith."

A few days later she rode beside David as he conducted her along the familiar route to his college. They traveled the Monmouth-Hereford road to Llanrothan. Riding through the empty countryside, they discussed Lily's intention.

"You'll find it's a great satisfaction," David said. "Even in my humble way, since I've been secretly trying to convert people, life has had a deeper meaning for me. I think with work you will overcome your grief for Liam."

Honest, guileless David. She looked over at his fine countenance that would never be marked by lies and deceit, because the corrupters would find no ingress into David's soul. She hated having to dupe him with her make-believe marriage and widowhood, but death alone would release her from that spiritual humiliation. "By now your letter telling the Jesuits I was coming should have reached them."

"I should think so. You'll find Father Morgan a brilliant man, but my favorite is Father Lloyd."

They followed a narrow, rough bridle path, riding singly until they reached a lonely hamlet. On a corner of the only street, pale-faced children stood, silently staring at them. Leaving the houses, they reached a spreading bleak edifice of gray stone and reined in.

With pride in his voice David said, "There it is! The Cym of Saint Francis Xavier. How courageous the Jesuits are to teach Catholicism in the midst of enemy land!"

Touching their heels to their horses, they rode up to

the building. There was no movement in the college's surrounding grounds.

"It would be better if you went in alone, Lily," David suggested. "I'll wander to the back and find some old friends."

Tethering her horse to a post, Lily mounted the shallow steps and knocked on a heavy oaken door strapped with iron. A grille opened, a man looked out and she gave her name. The grille closed and she heard bolts being drawn. Then the door opened and she stepped into a shadowy hall.

A small, plump priest in black robes stood aside for her, then closed and rebolted the door. "Welcome, my daughter. I am Father Lloyd." He held out his hand, and she took it. She liked him immediately. The overall impression he created was of a huge baby who had somehow become wrinkled and gray without ever growing out of infancy. The warmth of his smile lit the furnitureless hall.

"Come this way. You must be tired. You've ridden from Breck Castle?" She nodded, and he went on, "Ah, a long way, if my memory is correct." He ushered her into a cell-like room. "It's many a year since I made the journey in that direction, but that's because for many years I was abroad." He held out a chair for her to sit down and, laughing, added. "I did not choose to stay abroad, my daughter. I was exiled in a great purge of priests. But here I am again, back in Wales where I started from."

"How wonderful of you to risk returning, Father."

"Not at all, not at all." He beamed. "The air in Wales agrees with me. But I talk too much. I'll go and get Father Morgan."

Left alone, she looked around at the whitewashed walls, the black crucifix, the few chairs and the table. Severe and bare, the room was reminiscent of Father Dalvarez's chamber in Jamaica, where he had given her hope that Adam would return to marry her.

Father Lloyd opened the door and stood aside to admit a tall priest. By his quietly commanding demeanor,

Lily knew he was the head of the Jesuits, and she curtsied low.

"Rise, my daughter." From a bony face brilliant black eyes raked her soul. "I am Father Morgan. David Gwyn's letter said you wish to be of service." A thin hand waved imperiously for Lily to be seated.

She sat down, glad that the friendly Father Lloyd was there. But she must fight this feeling of inadequacy in the presence of the courageous Father Morgan. "Yes, Father, and since there are no longer nunneries in England, what can a woman do?"

"In such troublesome times, my daughter, many things, in many ways." Hands clasped behind him, Father Morgan walked slowly up and down, thinking. "Do you speak Welsh?"

"Fluently, Father." She regretted that she sounded so conceited.

"Splendid, splendid! We have too few members who speak Welsh and, alas, Catechism printed in Welsh, which means our children are left to Puritans and Episcopalians for instruction in God's word." He suddenly stopped walking and stood before Lily. "Your first work will be teaching."

"Teaching!" Like David's work. Not very exciting. She had hoped for something more adventuresome. "But, Father—"

"Not everyone can be a Joan of Arc, Lady Lily." Father Morgan's caustic tone made her flush with shame. "Teaching is vitally important. We shall have to see if you are capable of it, isn't that so, Father Lloyd?"

The little priest shook a fat finger at Lily. "Remember this—give me the child of seven and I'll have the man, but it's only by teaching that we'll get the child of seven!"

Lily could not stop herself from smiling at him. She turned appealingly to Father Morgan. "If you'll permit me to teach, I'll try to be worthy of the trust you put in me."

The black eyes softened. "Very well. You'll have to

take daily instructions from Father Lloyd for a while. We'll find you some suitable accommodation in a reliable dwelling in the village. Will that be agreeable?"

"Certainly, Father." Feeling that the interview was over, she stood up to leave, and Father Morgan took her toward the door. "There are other ways also in which you can be helpful, Lady Lily. In your position you undoubtedly hear news that might be of interest to us. Perhaps you would make a weekly report to me."

"But of course, Father. I receive constant letters from Sir Roger Huet, a prominent Puritan in London. I shall send them to you."

A few days later Lily moved into a small house in Welsh Newton, and for several weeks she received instructions from Father Lloyd on how to teach young children. In common with David, she quickly grew to love the fat priest, who seemed to possess all the Christian virtues, together with a childish sense of fun. When he pronounced her ready to start teaching, she regretted having to leave him.

Lily's work, unlike David's, was to be with children only. David had the more difficult task of trying discreetly to convert adults. On the Deveraux lands, in turf-roofed cottages, the laborers' and mine workers' children had been taught by a stay-at-home cobbler, tinker or weaver. When Lily announced that she intended to teach them now, she sensed an invisible wall of shyness and incredulity. But the children's downcast eyes looked up, sparking with gaiety at the idea of being taught by the beautiful Lady Lily, and their parents' open mouths stretched into smiles at being freed from the customary teaching fee of a halfpenny per child.

Beginning her task with an evangelist's fervor, Lily found it difficult. Whereas she liked her pupils, she disliked being closeted in the small cottage with the odors of ducks and geese in the indoor ponds, and she felt self-conscious before the grandmothers and mothers silently carding or spinning in the shadows. They seemed to be wordlessly criticizing her, but she told herself that to instruct her pupils in Roman Catholicism was her sacred charge, and within a week she was able to write and tell Father Lloyd:

> Victory smiles upon me. I'm actually enjoying the teaching and my pupils—even sharing their midday meal of pease pudding off wooden trenchers and drinking ale with them from leather bottles.

What she did not write was that the effort spent on her task was rewarded by a lessening of her personal sorrow.

The long hours she spent with the children fitted into the war pattern that now prevailed at Breck. The usual summer fetes, village sports, competitive games and musical events were canceled. Many men had gone to join the army; others were drilling and preparing should they be called. Lord Deveraux had announced to Angela and Lily that he would join the king's forces whenever he was needed.

Everywhere conversation was of the forthcoming struggle. Now in Angela's private withdrawing room, as Geraldius played the harp and Lily and her mother stitched on embroidery frames, Rhys Deveraux and David faced each other across a chessboard.

"These Scots with their Calvinistic fervor are trying to turn this struggle into a holy war," Rhys grumbled. "They've supplied their commander, Leslie, with an army triple the size of the last one, and the Edinburgh women have donated three thousand sheets for tents."

"But the king's preparations are in good hands," Lily observed. "James writes that Lord Conway has strongly fortified Berwick on the Scottish border and that great numbers of troops have gathered in York for the king." To sit quietly embroidering while there was such excitement going on in the north seemed an utter waste of time to Lily.

"I'm afraid with this campaign Charles has stirred up a hornets' nest for himself all over the country." Rhys carefully moved an exquisite ivory pawn on the chessboard. "When Barbary pirates recently landed in Cornwall and snatched men from Penzance, Charles's enemies cried, 'We are left unprotected—at the mercies of pirates while the ship-money fleet prepares to fight the Scots!' "

"I wonder if there's any truth in the rumor that the queen has appealed to the pope to help Charles with a loan?" Angela said.

"I hope she has!" Rhys blurted out. "The royalists are being fleeced to finance this war! I hate to contemplate what it's costing me to buy all this equipment and to send men north. And it won't end with that, I'll swear!"

"On my journey back to Breck today," David said, "I heard on excellent authority that the king is now raising money in London by selling monopolies."

"Damn my blood, man! Why didn't you say so earlier?" Rhys sprang to his feet, pushing the chess table from him and spilling the pieces. "Don't you see how important it is to me? There's a chance for me to buy the coal-transportation monopoly that I've been wanting!" He stared furiously at Lily. She recalled only too well that it was for primarily this reason that he wished her to marry Roger.

"It's worth a trip to London for me to look into this!" Rhys turned to David. "Give orders to prepare the coach and horses. I'll leave at dawn."

Some hours after Lord Deveraux had left, drovers brought a letter to Lily from James, saying that he would be visiting her at once in case the outbreak of hostilities later prevented him from coming. Lily surprised herself by how much she looked forward to his coming.

Several days later she was concluding a teaching session when she looked up, and through the open doorway, saw James ride up and dismount.

She rushed out to him. "James, you're here already! How wonderful!"

THE TEMPEST LILY 187

In a swift stride he had reached her and caught both her hands. She gazed up into his face—his eyes, mouth, everything about him seemed to be smiling. He kissed both her hands as his look caressed her. "I've just arrived, so forgive me for being booted and spurred. At Breck Lucrezia told me where you were." He stepped back, swinging her hands as he studied her. "You're lovelier than ever my memory told me. It's been hell how I've missed you."

She laughed happily, glad that she was wearing a becoming cream corsage with green lacings. "And I've missed you. But look, we are not alone." She pointed to the window where the children had crowded to stare out at them.

He laughed and led Lily toward her horse, which was tied to a nearby post. He helped her into the saddle, then mounted himself. She watched James, approving of his fine figure and graceful movement.

They turned their horses toward the castle. "When you wrote to me and said you were teaching, I thought you'd soon tire of it." James's eyes searched her face. "But I'm amazed. You seem to be thriving on it."

"I am, although sometimes it seems too quiet an occupation. Often I wish I were a man so I could be a part of all the war excitement."

"Thank God you're not a man!" James grinned meaningfully. "Teaching has to be agreeing with you, my darling. I swear you're lovelier than you were even in London."

"James, you'll turn my head." She swallowed the temptation to tell him that he seemed doubly attractive to her after their separation. "We'll ride home and have wine with Mother, and then if you're not too tired after your journey," Lily threw him a teasing look, "I'll take you to see some special work I'm doing."

An hour later, after James had changed out of riding gear, with half a dozen dogs accompanying them, they strolled over the velvety turf toward the stables. The summer air was scented with flowers. A dove was trilling its evensong. Glancing up at James in gray doublet and breeches tucked into soft leather boots, Lily was grateful that he was there. She had truly missed his lively personality.

"Do you think King Charles was wise in freeing priests from jail to please the queen on the birth of her eighth child?"

"No, I fear it has only added fuel to the fire."

"Wouldn't Charles naturally want to favor Catholics after the splendid way Catholic officers have rallied to his side?"

"Popish officers are hurting the king's cause. In many places the troops either refuse to obey them or murder them."

What would be Adam's fate should he lead troops for Charles? "Roger writes that in the south feeling is so strong against the whole campaign that troops are setting fire to deer forests, opening jails, and freeing criminals. What's happening in York?"

They had reached the stables, and before entering a stall he hesitated at the door. "Things are very warlike in York. The Scots are gathering in such force on the border that Lord Conway sent word to His Majesty saying the Scots would either have to disband or invade."

"It seems like madness to have stirred up all this trouble just because they won't accept the king's religious reforms." She shrugged. "Oh well, to work!"

As she passed James in order to enter the stall, he caught her to him. "Lily, let's forget the war. I didn't come to discuss that! It's you and me I want to talk of. When are you going to marry me?"

"Soon, soon, darling."

His arms crushed her to his strong body as he bent to caress her, and after being alone for so long, she fervently kissed him in return.

"I've dreamed of holding you again like this."

His lips trailed the length of her throat. James was already wild with desire for her.

She let him lower her to lie on the straw-covered earth. Lily responded to James by catching his hand-

THE TEMPEST LILY

some face between her hands and kissing his open mouth. When he started to pull up the folds of her voluminous skirts, she helped drag them to her waist.

"I want you. I want you, Lily. I can't wait," he muttered thickly as he ripped open his breeches.

"Take me, darling. Take me."

He was so excited that everything was quickly over. "Damnation, darling! I'm sorry. I'll wager that was no good for you." He rolled over into the hay.

"It was! I loved it all." She felt too embarrassed to tell him that her body had not had enough time to respond completely. "I think we should rise. Although the grooms never come to this part of the stable, someone else might."

Lily stood up, shaking out her skirts, and he helped pick straw from her hair. "You've got to arrange a date for our marriage before I leave Breck!"

"I will, darling." Why did she delay? Was she still stupidly hoping that Adam would return to her? "Now let me show you what I've been working on."

She went to lead a young stallion from its stall. "I'm training Thunder to withstand sounds of war." She patted the horse's neck, and James settled down on a pile of saddlery to watch. "He's very clever. In two days, James, he's learned not to shy at a distant drumbeat. Let's see how he behaves with noise close to him."

Covering a drum with oats, she placed it under the horse's nose. "He should eat the oats while I beat the drum." The experiment was a success.

"Bravo, bravo!" James applauded and, delighted, Lily patted Thunder. "That's all for today. Tomorrow we'll go through the same thing with a pistol. After that," she led the horse back to its stall, "I'll teach him to ride at a tree with armor tied to it until he can loosen it and throw it down—like an armed man." Distractedly Lily brushed oats from her skirts. "I've had great luck training horses to go with Father's men. At least I feel I'm helping a little." Did she dare ask him for news of Adam?

James jumped up and once more caught her in his arms. "Don't let's go yet. You're amazing. You're working as though this were your personal war. But I've just arrived. Give your time to me now." His hands started to explore her body.

"Not here again. Tonight I'll come to your room."

"Tonight is a long way off, my love." James ruefully pulled a face as she broke from his embrace.

They left the stables, with him adapting his long stride to Lily's shorter step. "James, I have more work to do. Usually in the evenings I help the fencing master teach our people how to handle a sword."

"It still amazes me to know that you fence with what Adam describes as a man's skill."

At the mention of Adam's name Lily felt her face flush. Aware that his eyes were on her, she knew he must have seen it. "I've fenced since I was thirteen. I love it."

"And has all the hard war work had the desired effect? Has it helped?"

Her heartbeat accelerated as she thought she recognized a double meaning in his question. "Helped? Oh yes, the children are learning a great deal about Catholicism as well as other subjects. And you saw how Thunder responded."

His eyes narrowed, and she sensed he was studying her. "Darling, darling, I'm not trying to lift any veils. Just remember I love you." He was silent for a moment, then said softly, "By the way, have you heard that the Clune-Elliot marriage has been announced to take place in November?"

Like a dagger the words plunged and twisted in her heart. She must make herself answer normally. "I've heard little except from Roger," she forced a laugh that almost choked her, "and naturally he wouldn't write about Adam—one of his pet hates." So Adam was really going to go through with it, and the miracle she had stormed the heavens for—that he would relinquish Jane and her dowry—had of course not happened.

"I'm glad the news does not worry you." James's voice shook with emotion.

"But why ever should it? Anyhow *my* news is that the Forsyth-Deveraux marriage will precede the Clune-Elliot marriage!" She stood on tiptoe, pulled his head down and planted a passionate kiss on his mouth.

18

FOR THE THREE nights that James was at Breck, Lily spent the dark hours lying in his arms in a big four-poster bed, and his tenderness was swiftly winning her love. It was not the same as it had been with Adam. James did not inspire the wildness in her, but he gave her a feeling of security and affection which she cherished.

During the days David had undertaken to relieve Lily of her classes so that she might spend all her time with James.

"It's the least I can do," David assured James, looking up at him as they played cribbage. "Lily is like my sister, and her happiness is important to me." He lowered his voice. "Sometimes I think she grieves over her widowhood."

"Nonsense, David," Lily chided gently. "I heard you, and you'll give James a wrong impression."

David shot her an understanding look. "Perhaps I'm mistaken." He stood up. "Well, the game is over, so I'll leave you. I've some writing to do."

Alone with Lily, James looked at her with a quizzical expression. "So you are still grieving, darling?" he asked thoughtfully, not believing that she grieved for Traherne, but did she for Adam?

"No!" she answered vehemently. "It's natural that I can't be the same lighthearted girl I used to be. After all, I have a son. I have responsibilities, and—"

She broke off as the door opened and Lucrezia came in, carrying Joseph in his night shift. "My lady, he's ready for bed."

Lily held her arms out for the fat, laughing child. His blue eyes fastened on his mother. "Ma-ma," he lisped.

She wrapped him in her arms, blowing kisses into the soft warmth of his neck. "My darling little heart," she chuckled, and covered his cheeks with kisses. "Don't wait, Lucrezia, I'll tuck him into his crib."

"Yes, my lady." Dropping a curtsy, the mischievous Capriote flashed a demurely approving glance at James and left the chamber.

James went over to look at Joseph. "What a fine little fellow he's growing into." He held out a forefinger to the baby, and Joseph's fat pink fingers wrapped around it. "May I have him?" James asked, and Lily held Joseph up to him.

Laughing, James tossed the delighted boy up and down in the air, terrifying Lily each time lest he fail to catch the precious bundle. As the happy child squealed with pleasure, Lily brushed away a vague sadness that James should be here like this, not Adam. But with a tight little smile she sat watching the play.

After a few minutes James returned Joseph to Lily and, rocking him in her arms, she softly sang a lullaby while conscious of James's intense stare.

When Joseph had fallen asleep, James asked again, "Was David right? Are you grieving?"

"David is a sweet, wonderful person," Lily said impatiently, "but his life is dedicated to God. He doesn't understand much about worldly things. He doesn't understand me, and—"

"But I do, darling! Come back to York with me. Let's be married soon, and let me be a father to Joseph." He did not touch Lily as she sat with the sleeping child, and she appreciated his sensitivity. She looked up into his pleading eyes. "Let me ask your father for your hand. Let's marry and give Joseph some brothers and sisters." James's fingers gently smoothed Joseph's hair off his forehead.

Wonderful James. Did he guess Joseph was Adam's son as he played with the telltale red-gold hair? Great God in heaven! James might meet Adam and talk of Joseph! That must not happen! Words burst from Lily. "Please, if you meet Adam, I . . . I would prefer that you do not mention Joseph to him." She raised her eyes to his. "It's hard to explain now . . . but someday I shall. My reason is—"

"Don't give me a reason. I shall certainly do as you ask." So his intuition had been correct about Adam, James told himself.

Before Lily could reply the door burst open and David rushed in.

"What's happened?" Lily demanded.

"The war! It's started! Messengers have just ridden in. The Scots have invaded England!"

Lily leaned back against the chair, gathering Joseph close. It was not only words now. The fighting, the killing would be real.

"Damn my blood!" James cried. "Every fool should have anticipated that this was inevitable." He laughed nastily. "So the rebels are bringing Calvinism to us."

"The messenger said that they're pouring over the Northumbrian hills, raising the dead with their bagpipes and psalm singing, and the English were so in sympathy with them that not a soul lifted a finger in resistance."

"It's frightful news, David!" James paced the floor. "What word of the king?"

"His Majesty has left for York."

"Good! With Charles there in person we'll stop the

blasted rebels' advance!" James swung around to Lily. "I'm deeply sorry, but I must leave for home at once!"

"Naturally, I understand!" She hated losing his strength, especially at such a time.

"I'll see to my servants and horses," he said, though his eyes told her how sorry he was to go. "If you'll excuse me."

"I'll assist you," David said, and they strode from the chamber.

Lily sat perfectly still, staring at the closed door and listening to Joseph's soft breathing. She glanced down at him. How greatly he had enjoyed James's play. Now James was going. Not an ordinary trip—but to war! Despite her father, she would marry James as soon as possible.

She rushed to the huge fireplace and pulled on the bellcord hanging beside it. She could barely wait for Lucrezia to answer the summons. When the girl came in, Lily burst out, "Pack for me—quickly! Get help from the other maids! Pack for yourself, too! We are going to York with Sir James! We'll leave within the hour. I'll take Joseph to his crib and go to explain everything to my mother."

"My lady will marry Sir James?" Lucrezia's eyes were moist, for she knew where her lady's heart really was.

"Yes, I want to meet his mother and sisters. Now hurry, Lucrezia!"

As the coach carrying Lily, James and Lucrezia clattered over the cobbles and through a gateway in the walls surrounding York, Lily smiled.

"You didn't exaggerate, James, when you spoke of York's splendid walls."

"Ah, this is only the beginning of the city's magnificence." His voice lifted proudly. "We've a wealth of castles, ancient churches and antiquities dating back to pre-Roman times."

Staring out at the street with its fine mansions and

THE TEMPEST LILY

delicate church spires like lace against the sky, Lily felt York would not be an unpleasant spot to live in. Then the coach turned a corner and everything changed. The street was cluttered with horse-drawn gun carriages passing slowly into an alley, followed by a disorderly looking band of foot soldiers.

"This militia is a pressed lot of men, as their glum faces indicate." James looked annoyed. "The whole slovenly mess will ruin your impression of York."

Lily assured him that it would not, but the journey became depressing as they were constantly held up by military troops and equipment. Disheveled-looking people gathered on corners, loudly discussing the invasion. Over the noise town criers were heard, shouting that the king and his councillor, Strafford, were expected momentarily.

Lily was relieved when the horses entered a quiet residential district of great mansions with enclosed gardens. Before an imposing stone house the coach drew up.

"My town home welcomes you," James said with a happy laugh. Enthusiastic as a boy, he jumped out, then lifted Lily down. Nodding informally to servants, who were rushing out to open the great wrought-iron gates, he guided Lily across a courtyard ringed by stables, up some steps and into a wide, marble-floored hall with statuary. Double doors opened into a large withdrawing room.

Lily had a flashing impression of luxury and excellent taste. Crystal chandeliers, imposing oil paintings, tapestry furniture, carpets and a delicate harpsichord. And then she was being presented to James's mother and sisters.

"Mother, dear." James swiftly kissed Lady Forsyth. "The outriders got here in time to tell you I was bringing Lily?"

"Yes, and I am delighted, my son." Lady Forsyth had a soft voice. She was small and plump. Her friendly hazel eyes were obviously admiring as they gazed at Lily.

Lily immediately liked her. "And I'm so happy to be here, Lady Forsyth," she murmured, feeling a bond of warmth with the charming woman and the three smiling girls behind her.

"We have been longing for the pleasure of your visit." Lady Forsyth held Lily's hand in both of hers. "It's a shame York is so crowded with military men and weapons. But there are also other people here from all over the country, so we'll make your stay enjoyable despite the horrible Scots—such uncouth people!"

"Do you know His Majesty is coming to York?" one of James's sisters broke in. James laughed and winked discreetly at his mother and Lily. "Elizabeth can't wait to meet you, Lily." As the attractive fourteen-year-old curtsied to Lily, James continued, "And these are the twins, Joan and Sybil—just turned eight."

The little girls dropped curtsies to Lily, then rushed to fling their arms around James. He stooped and caught them both in a bearlike embrace. They covered his head with kisses. James was obviously adored by the twins, to whom he had acted as a father since their infancy, when Sir Richard Forsyth had died.

Being an only child, Lily envied James his sisters' affection. "What a lovely family you have," she said to Lady Forsyth as she settled in a chair beside her.

"Indeed I am blessed." James's mother's eyes played affectionately over her offspring. "And there is also Charlotte, my married daughter, who comes just after James. You'll meet her later." Lady Forsyth caught her lower lip between her teeth. "She insisted upon accompanying her husband and his troops to Newcastle, which everyone knows the Scots will attack next."

"Charlotte has tremendous courage." James spoke with sudden seriousness while gently freeing himself from the twins' hugs. "I'm sorry, but I must see my men and give them orders. I've decided not to wait for His Majesty but to join Lord Conway as soon as possible. If the Scots are still advancing unchecked, it won't be long before they reach Newcastle, and with the pitiable

THE TEMPEST LILY

state of the fortifications there, Conway will need every man he can get."

It was several hours later when, washed and changed, Lily was playing with the twins in the nursery. James came looking for her there. "Forgive me for interrupting," he said, "but time is precious."

With alarm she realized he was leaving soon. "What wonderful tales I've been hearing of you," she said with forced cheerfulness.

"That's it, girls!" James winked at the children. "Tell Lady Lily more and more so she'll stay with us always."

"Oh, but she must!" Joan cried. Sybil's voice overlapped with, "If you ask her, James, she will! No one ever refuses you."

"What a statement." James laughed. "All right, I'll try, but run away for a few minutes so I'll have the chance to ask her."

Lily smiled at the charming children as they skipped to the door. What a happy household she would be a part of as James's wife.

Left alone, James took her in his arms. "My darling, you've captured my angel mother and my sisters just as you captured me." He covered Lily's upturned face with kisses. "Tell me before I go that you'll stay for always."

In his home rich with love and affection, she was finding a new James, not just a handsome, gay cavalier or a wonderful lover, but a sensitive, consistent son and brother. "James, darling—yes, yes! I'll stay for always."

"Thank God," he murmured prayerfully. "As soon as possible, I'll ask your father for your hand and we'll be married. Oh, Lily, I'm a happy man! Knowing you'll be here upon my return—that we'll soon marry—sends me away with added courage." He laughed like an excited boy. "Almost single-handed I could push our enemies back over the border!"

"James?" A thrilling idea suddenly occurred to her, and she leaned back to better see his eager face. "Take me with you! Many women follow their men to battle—even your own sister. I'd be useful . . . I can—"

"You might be hurt!"

"I won't be. Hundreds of women are going. I'll be out of danger just as they'll be, and I can help nurse the wounded." She reached up and pulled his head down to hers. Throwing her arms around his neck, she kissed him warmly on the mouth, willing him to do her bidding. "Say yes. Say yes! I beg you!" she pleaded in between kisses.

He crushed her to him. "It's madness, but I can refuse you nothing! Can you manage without Lucrezia? We can't take two women because—"

"Don't worry. I can care for myself. I'll leave Lucrezia here with your mother."

Joining up with other officers, their men and ladies, James and Lily left York and rode for almost two days before reaching Newburn Ford, a few miles west of Newcastle. They found Lord Conway and the best of his army—one thousand cavalry, two thousand foot and four cannon—camped near the river. Hundreds of men were constructing a breastwork at the water's edge opposite Newburn Village on the other bank, so peaceful-looking with its tidy houses and church spires rising calmly against the autumn sky.

Behind the camp, on a rise of ground with a view of the water, the women's tents had been pitched, and here James left Lily.

"I hope you'll be all right. I'll come to you as often as I can." Swinging into the saddle, he cantered down to the camp.

Grateful to be there, Lily quickly got to know wives and daughters of noblemen and gentry in adjacent tents. During the next two days, like them, she felt she was aiding the king's cause by preparing food, thus leaving the men servants free to build the essential defenses.

On the third day, in the late afternoon sunshine, the women sat outside the tents rolling cloths into bandages and looking over at the men shoveling earth onto the slowly rising breastworks.

"Will that puny mound of earth stop thousands of Scots if they decide to come this way?" a titled woman asked impatiently.

"All summer Conway has been fortifying Berwick, with never a thought for Newcastle," another noblewoman grumbled. "And the Scots bypass Berwick with devilish canniness and come this way."

"Today's messengers from York said that Charles will be here tomorrow," Lily said. "Hopefully his presence in the field will bring the rebel Scots to heel!"

"I don't hold with that." An elderly woman shook her head.

Irritated by their negative talk, Lily walked a short distance from the tent to gaze down on the camp where men and horses were milling around. A cloud of dust rose on the road from Newcastle, where half a dozen officers were arriving with their men. But more, more, more must come before the Scots marched into Newburn Village across the river.

Apprehensive of the immediate future, she watched the officers in light armor, their colored cloaks flying out as they trotted in on their richly caparisoned horses. Famous coats of arms were borne on banners by their troops clad in motley array. Where was Adam? In London with Jane Elliot or sailing somewhere on the *Fearless* on a mission for the king to bring in arms from the Lowlands or Strafford's Irish troops from Ireland?

She turned and started walking toward the tents when a sound chilled her blood and halted her movement. That shrill music coming from across the river! It was the hated bagpipes!

Men working on the breastworks stopped with shovels of earth held in midair. In the camp mounted figures seemed as still as figures in a painting. The foot soldiers stood like statuary as every soul listened. Bagpipes! Louder now. Coming closer!

"The Scots are coming! Leslie's here!" The cry went like a gust of wind across the camp. Lifting her skirts,

Lily ran to the tents for a view of the water and Newburn Village. Standing with the women, she watched in awe as a human wave started pouring into the street; colored shoulder ribbons and rosettes denoted their particular clans. With bagpipes playing and banners afloat, the enemy marched toward the water's edge.

"Thousands of them!" one of the women muttered. "Twice as many men as we have!"

"Yes, and our earthworks are not completed!" Lily said. "It's going to be a dreadful fight!"

"Pray God Charles will arrive soon with reinforcements," another woman said.

Suddenly Lord Conway's trumpets sounded and action broke the chain of fear that had been devitalizing the English camp. Orders were shouted, and pikesmen started rushing to form ranks at the river's edge. Musketeers took up positions behind them. Officers and cavalrymen were fastening on their weapons, sorting out horses, springing into saddles. Artillerymen were at the four cannon, preparing to fire. Minutes later, while the Scots were still forming rank, the English drew first blood.

Lily felt weak with excitement. Her eyes peered through the drifting smoke to the opposite bank. Small knots of men sprawled on the earth, but the cannons had caused little damage. An officer—it must be Leslie —surrounded by soldiers was issuing orders. The dead and wounded were being carried away; fresh men were replacing them, while more men swarmed to the river's edge. They were waiting to cross in heavy numbers. Other men were climbing to the top of the church tower and hauling up a dismantled cannon. Once it was in place it could aim down directly into the English camp. It would cause havoc!

Once more the English cannon barked, but with the same pitiable results. Now English and Scots were concentrated in force, facing one another across the river. The two groups paused, studying each other. Then suddenly hundreds of men from both sides

THE TEMPEST LILY

plunged waist-high into the water. There was a swirling, splashing fight as pikes were raised and flung. Men grunted and screamed as they met and fought in death grips.

At first it seemed as though the English were winning. Then the Scots fired their cannon again and sent more men into the foray. Overwhelmed and confused, the English soldiers retreated in panic.

"Cowards!" Lily cried. "If they obeyed the officers, we might hold the bank!"

"The swine must be made to fight!" another noblewoman cried.

"Let's make them!" Lily exploded. Lifting her skirt, she raced toward the trees where the women's horses were tied. Five of the younger women ran with her. Maddened by the battle's bedlam, the horses were almost uncontrollable, but with difficulty the women mounted them.

"The pikemen are running to the road!" Lily called, and, digging their heels into their horses' sides, the women headed the beasts for the spot where the camp joined the open road to Newcastle. The women galloped up and, whirling their horses side by side, turned to face the oncoming men, determined to bar their escape.

One hand holding her rearing horse as she twisted in the saddle, Lily reached down, lashing on with her whip at the fleeing men.

"Back, you cowards!" she cried. "Back and fight!"

Some bolted, but others were inspired to shed their terror and raced back to resume fighting.

Lily darted a look at the river. Scottish musketeers were in command of the high ground and were effectively wounding the English who were still in the water.

She picked out James's gold and blue cloak. He was fighting like a creature possessed, despite being surrounded by the enemy. Was she mad? But that giant with burnished hair on a black stallion . . . Adam! Half-standing in the stirrups, he was trying to rally the English soldiers.

But they were too few, these magnificent officers. Already the reddened river was choked with the dead. Adam and James would be slaughtered too! Nothing would stop the Scots. More and more kept crossing the river.

"Get back and fight!" Lily yelled again and again as she and the women lashed out at the fleeing foot soldiers. But it was useless to hope for victory. When she next looked at the officers, they were reduced to half their number. Now even some of them were retreating, galloping up the bank toward the road.

Seeing the women trying to hold the pressed men, they shouted. "It's in vain! Run!"

Whirling their horses, the women rode toward the Newcastle road. The entire camp was being evacuated.

Lily stayed on. A few dozen heroic mounted officers —Adam and James among them—continued battling. If they stayed on—a handful against thousands—it would be mad suicide!

They were turning their horses, galloping for freedom! As they reached Lily, she swung her horse around and, digging her heels into its sides, she tore along with them.

"God in heaven!" Adam cried as he saw her. "Lily!" Blood was streaming from a cut on his head.

James's blood-spattered face was amazed as he galloped beside her. "Are you all right?" His voice rose over the thundering hoofs.

She nodded. "Are you?"

"All right," he cried.

Her hair flying loosely, Lily leaned close to her horse's neck. Scottish gunfire hit the ground just short of the animal's hooves.

"Will they pursue us?" Lily shouted.

"No!" Adam called. "They'll wait until the whole force is over the river."

"The river's rising," James cried. "The rest can't cross until morning."

For the balance of the wild ride to Newcastle, no one spoke. The defeat so overwhelmed Lily that her heart could not rejoice that Adam was there. When they reached Newcastle, to their dismay they found the town being hastily evacuated. Pulling up at a corner of the marketplace to rest themselves and their horses, they watched the major part of Lord Conway's army on the march, and behind them the heavy artillery thundering over the cobbles toward Durham. Along the riverbank men worked frantically to load huge powder barrels.

"Why this hasty retreat?" Adam growled, mopping the blood dripping from his forehead wound.

Lily darted her first penetrating look at him. Apprehension filled her about his injury.

"I'll swear the Scots won't come until morning," James said. "I propose we rest here with some friends of mine for a few hours and then go on to York." He was so crushed by the royalists' ignominious rout that in his sorrow he had little room to wonder how Lily felt at being with Adam once more.

19

JAMES LED THE way to the home of a childhood friend, where they were admitted by an old groom who told them that James's friend and the servants had already fled. Glancing at the group's disheveled appearance, the groom ushered them inside without hesitation.

"Rest. I'll bring you some wine and hot water to wash in." He hurried out, and they sank gratefully into chairs. Adam and James stretched their legs out full-length. With heads against the chair backs, eyes shut, they lay exhausted. Within seconds they were asleep.

Physically spent, emotionally in a turmoil from the awful happenings, Lily reclined also. Her hands swept her flowing hair back from her face. Her silver combs were gone. From beneath lowered lids her eyes feasted on Adam.

Even in his bedraggled state he was magnificent; his bigness filled the room. His green velvet doublet and cloak were dark with dried blood. His thigh-high leather boots were slashed into ribbons by points of Scottish pikes. Her eyes flew back to his eaglelike face, marked by dust and blood, drawn in by fatigue. His hair lay damply on his forehead, part of it clotted with blood. It was almost impossible for her to sit still. She ached to rush and pull off his boots, to dress his wounds. But her pride forbade her.

She dragged her eyes from Adam to James. He looked drained. Like Adam, he was breathing in troubled grunts. Dear, wonderful James, she would do nothing to hurt him.

She looked up as the groom's wife came in carrying a bowl of hot water and linens for bandages. Now at last she could go to Adam. Leaning over him, she said, "Adam, you need immediate attention!"

He stirred. The blue eyes opened and looked at her. Warm, tender, caressing, they caused a lump in her throat. An instant later they became expressionless.

"How good of you, Lily." He sounded bored as he slowly drew his long legs in and sat upright in the chair.

The groom's wife held the bowl, and with trembling hands Lily smoothed the thick red-gold hair off the gash. "It's not very deep, thank goodness." Curse her shaky voice, it would betray her. Gently she washed the blood away, feeling James's searching look searing her soul. Her weary face must surely shout aloud her joy as her fingers touched Adam.

"Damn my soul, Adam!" James's voice was warm as always. "It was a marvelous surprise to find you in that hellish mess."

"The Scots had just entered Newburn when I rode into camp." Adam chuckled. "I hadn't expected such a reception."

"Where had you been," James asked, "that you came so late?"

"I'd just docked the *Fearless* in Hull with arms from the Lowlands. I came on to Newburn to see where Conway wanted them delivered."

"Thank God you did! It would have been an even more ignominious rout if you hadn't joined us who stayed to fight!" James shook his head disgustedly. "What a disgrace!"

He broke off as the groom came in with the mulled wine. James rose stiffly and took a goblet to Adam and held another to Lily's lips. "As both your hands are occupied, my darling, I'll hold it for you. Take a long drink. You need it."

He sounded so possessive to Lily. But why not? They were betrothed. Over the goblet's rim she stared up into his dark, questioning eyes. She stopped drinking and smiled affectionately at him. Determined not to allow doubts about her love to harass him, James winked at her and returned to his chair. She continued to attend to Adam.

The groom, who was building a fire, said, "Sir James, we've bread, cheese and onions. Poor fare for nobility, but Lord Conway's army ate everything in town."

"Cheese and onions will be most welcome," James said.

The man's wife put the bowl down, saying, "I'll go at once and prepare supper."

"Tell me, my good man, when all the others have fled, why are you still here?"

"Because I can live at peace with Scots—same as I can with English—as long as I'm left to myself."

"But the Scots *won't* leave you to yourself!" Adam said sharply. "They want to convert all England to Calvinism."

"Ah, my lord," the old man lifted a log onto the

coals, "Calvinists, Episcopalians, or papists, they're all after the same God."

"That's part of England's trouble!" James exploded. "Too many people believe they can live peaceably with the Scots."

"They'll discover too late that they can't! The Scots will dominate them," Adam said. "Besides, the Scots are rebels, overthrowing the law."

The old man pumped the bellows to encourage the flame. "Have you noble gentlemen heard that His Majesty is on the way?"

"Too late," Adam said to James, who nodded glumly.

"Well, the fire has caught hold." The groom stood up. "If you'll come with me, Sir James, I'll show you the bedchambers."

Lily sensed James's reluctance to leave her alone with Adam. Starting to wind a bandage around Adam's head, she looked up and smiled at James. She must allay his doubts.

After the door closed behind James, Adam said, "If my presence in the field surprised him, I can't tell you what your presence did to me! I thought I had been bewitched when I saw you galloping along with your wonderful hair streaming out behind you." He pulled his head away from her hands to glance up at her.

It was so hard to meet the blue eyes without dissembling and clasping his head to her breasts. "I had been visiting James's mother in York. I begged him to take me to Newburn."

Their eyes held to each other's. "Fortunate devil, James," he murmured, and bent his head so Lily could continue the bandaging.

For minutes neither of them spoke. Her trembling hands must tell him of her excitement. She fastened the linen with a final knot. "There, I think that will stop the bleeding."

"I'm sure it will. I recall how skillful you were with the wounded aboard the *Fearless*." He stood up, rising like a tower above her. His eyes fastened onto her as she pretended to busy herself folding the linens. "What a wonderful person you are, Lily. I've just realized that you must have been one of those fantastic women trying to stop the cowards from fleeing."

"What a useless effort." She kept her eyes from him. "But the heroism of you and James and the others—that at least will redeem today's disgrace."

"Alas, nothing can redeem this lost day." His fingers gently caught her chin and tilted her head back. She did not move. His touch was so bittersweet. "Lily, Lily. Look at me."

She was forced to meet the blue eyes. "Yes, Adam," she murmured.

"I want you to know that Sir Archibald Elliot financed half of this blasted campaign for the king. He wouldn't have done it unless next month—"

"I know! I went to see your mother. Perhaps she told you?"

He nodded and said, "She explained things to me. I wish to God you were not so beautiful, Lily—that all men did not fall in love with you. In particular, I wish Liam Traherne had not."

She understood what he was trying to say: If only you had not promoted the mutiny! But unfair! Unfair when he had also been at fault! "I saw you at court; I told you how sorry I was. Remember I also wrote to you in Virginia. But never have you said you regret your behavior."

"God in heaven! Regrets! What use are they? I only knew that I want you more than I've ever wanted a woman! Meeting you at court that night drove me to a frenzy!"

"Don't, please don't!" She tried to pass him to get to a chair, but he barred the way. The next second she was in his arms, molded against his thumping heart, her head on his blood-soaked chest. Then his mouth was warm on hers and peace came to her tortured heart as her lips clung to him. The joy of him—the agony that it was fleeting. There was James to think of! She must not hurt him! Dragging at the roots of her conscience, she managed to break away from the ironlike arms. Her hands flew to her hair to push it back from her face.

Adam looked perplexed. "Lily, beloved, why . . ."

At that second James entered the chamber. His eyes immediately flew to Adam and Lily, but she assured herself that he could suspect nothing. Hurriedly she picked up the bowl of water as he came to her.

"The bedrooms are now ready, my love. Before you drop with exhaustion, do go up and rest." His handsome face was more quietly serious than she had ever seen it. Then with his handkerchief he gently wiped her cheek. "You've blood on your face, darling."

The blood from Adam's forehead on her hands had been washed away before James had left. She loathed herself for hurting James. She must somehow comfort him.

"Isn't it a miracle I didn't lose my engagement ring during that ride." She pulled the chain up from between her breasts and dangled the diamond and ruby ring so both men could see it. "I'll go up now and rest." James looked so relieved, so proud that she had displayed his ring. What did Adam think? She longed to know. Did he care that James would become her husband and replace him in her heart?

In her bedchamber she ate bread and cheese. Then weariness overcame excitement, and within a few minutes she was asleep.

It was still dark when the groom's wife awakened her. Shivering, Lily left the bed and pulled on her dust-stained clothes.

James was waiting for her at the foot of the carved oaken staircase. "You look a little rested. Thank heaven the groom has managed to supply us with fresh horses. I think we should ride at once." He led her toward the door.

"Yes, of course, but what about Adam?"

"He has already left. After you retired he decided to ride directly to Hull." His voice sounded quite casual. "He was anxious about disposing of the arms aboard the *Fearless*."

"I wanted to ask him about Valentine," she lied. "Lucrezia would have liked some news."

Why had Adam gone before seeing her again? Did he fear her nearness? Or was his excuse about the arms true? Her disappointment was lightened by a perverse underlining of relief, for in her harassed state of mind it would have been difficult to have maintained normality in the presence of both men. James gave her a leg up, and she swung into the saddle, glad to be heading for York. But when would she again see Adam?

Lily had been in York for a week. Charles, having failed to relieve Newcastle, had returned to York. The earl of Strafford had also arrived to assume full military command.

Lily's time was almost entirely spent with Lady Forsyth and her daughters, as James was occupied at Strafford's war council. There had been no further news of Adam, and Lily fought to stop thinking of him. She and James had told Lady Forsyth of their betrothal, explaining the need for momentary secrecy. The lovely woman was ecstatic, for she knew how her son loved this young noblewoman.

"These war councils are depressing," James told his mother and Lily one day. "We know now that the king hasn't forces large enough to battle the Scots' huge numbers, and what is most disturbing is the fact that the enormous Puritan element in London is encouraging the rebels."

"How long will the Scots be allowed to occupy part of England?" Lily asked indignantly.

James shook his head. "Strafford is playing for time. He wants to bring the Irish troops in to subdue the Scots." James carefully crossed one impeccably stockinged leg over the other. "Some days ago Clune sailed for Ireland to help transport troops."

Lily fought to behave naturally. "Can't something be done before the Irish arrive?" she asked, wondering if Adam's trip might force a postponement of his marriage.

"Well, all the king can do is agree to pay the rebels their preposterous demand to remain where they are and not advance. Damn my blood! What a mess! Cost of occupational forces is what the Scots call it."

"And what will happen about London's demand of Charles to call a new Parliament?" Lady Forsyth asked.

"His Majesty is trying to avoid it. Instead he has summoned all the peers of the realm immediately to attend a Council of Peers in York. He hopes to be able to influence them—while he has them away from the House of Commons—to finance another campaign."

Deeply disturbed, Lily jumped up. "Since my father will have to attend the Council of Peers, I should return home at once to help govern Breck. I must tell Lucrezia to pack."

"Oh my dear, don't go!" Lady Forsyth rose and threw an arm about Lily.

"I must go. Why don't you visit us at Breck?"

"I'd love to, but with so much happening here, James will need me."

Later, alone with James, Lily had trouble convincing him of her duty. To all his pleadings to remain, she was adamant.

"As things are at the moment in London," he said, "I feel His Majesty will be forced to call a Parliament. In that case I'll be going to London. Would you like us to be married there?"

"Darling James, call at Breck before you journey to London. My father is surely not home yet, so we can be married secretly by a priest who's a friend of mine."

"Darling, thank God, at last! I shall be there soon after you."

When she and Lucrezia returned to Breck, Lily confided to Geraldius and David that she intended to marry James, then begged David to bring Father Lloyd to perform the ceremony.

When David had ridden off, Lily told Geraldius, "I think it's best not to tell Mother, because if Father finds out, he will vent his temper on her as well as on me. He still is set upon my marrying Huet, even though, if Father fights for the king, he'll be in the camp against the Puritans."

"Aye, but your father is hoping things won't get to the pass where he must openly choose sides, and in the interval he wants Huet's help with many different financial affairs." Geraldius sighed sadly. "Yes, it's wiser to keep your mother in ignorance."

Father Lloyd arrived at Breck on the same day as James. The ceremony took place in Geraldius's apartments, with Geraldius and David as witnesses. Lucrezia wore a yellow dress to be Lily's bridesmaid. Lily wore an exquisite white lace shawl draped over her head, and a pale pink gown.

Now that she was really marrying James and closing Adam forever out of her life, she trembled so much she was sure the others would notice it, but with ironlike determination she went through the ceremony.

"Do you, Lily, take James as your lawful wedded husband to love, honor and obey until death shall you part?"

"I do." The response sounded firm and strong, but the remainder of the short ceremony was lost to her. A bitter fight raged through her. It should have been Adam—Adam—Adam who stood beside her. Then she inwardly wept, God, Thy will be done.

"I now pronounce you man and wife."

James fitted a crested family ring of his mother's onto her finger. Then he kissed her. It was done! She was James's wife! Now, at last, surely God would grant her peace of soul. Now let Adam marry Jane Elliot.

Geraldius and David had champagne ready. "Sir James and Lady Forsyth." They all drank happily, then swiftly dispersed.

When they were alone, James took Lily in his arms and kissed her almost reverently. "I can't quite believe that you are really my wife at last. I have never known such happiness."

"But beloved one, you have to leave so soon."

"At dawn I'll ride for London, but no power on earth could stop me spending my wedding night with you."

"You have the same chamber as last time. After supper I shall come to you there. Now let's go and see Joseph. The little darling doesn't know it, but it's been a lucky, lucky day for him." Her eyes swam with tears. "He's been given such a splendid father in you."

"Thank you for saying that. I shall always guard Joseph as if he were my very own flesh and blood." What secret sorrow did she bear about the child? Had he really been sired by Liam Traherne, or was Adam the father who Lily's pride kept in ignorance of his son? No matter, the child was now his to care for. "I'll teach him to ride, fish, shoot, hunt—everything. Come, let's go to him."

In Joseph's nursery, Lily sat contentedly watching her happy child as he chuckled and squealed while James tossed him up, then caught him in the air. God, thank you for giving me the love of my fine husband, for my child's sake and for my own.

That night at supper James radiated good cheer upon everyone so that Lady Deveraux understood why Lily was obviously in love with the dashing, handsome man. In an aside to Lily she said, "I hope someday that you and James might marry, if ever your difficult father relinquishes his determination about Roger Huet."

Lily kissed her mother's cheek, hating the necessity of not telling her the truth.

After supper Geraldius played the harp in the drawing room. James and David sang together. There was laughter and light chatter, so that for all of them the war seemed far removed. Lily, conscious of the few hours left before James's departure, pleaded a headache and retired. Soon afterward everyone followed her example.

In the bedchamber Lucrezia was waiting to disrobe Lily. Unlacing the back of her corsage, the girl murmured, "God has taken care of you. Sir James is a husband a girl would pray to have. I am so happy for you."

THE TEMPEST LILY

"Lucrezia—" Lily turned around and caught the faithful girl in her arms—"thank you, thank you. I know that I have been blessed." The loving Capriote was well aware of Lily's suffering over Adam. "I have forgotten the past. I love Sir James. And one day you too will find a new love, or maybe you will meet Valentine again."

"That is my prayer, my lady. Valentine is the one I love."

"I'll help you all I can. Perhaps we can find work for him at Breck and make him leave the sea. Now please help me into my nightrobe. My husband is waiting for me."

That night, lying in the big four-poster bed, James kissed and embraced Lily with a new tenderness. "My wife . . . at last," he murmured, his voice thick with emotion. "Oh, darling girl, I never thought such wonderful happiness would come to me. I only pray that you *really* love me, that you share some of my joy."

"But I do! Surely you know no woman could ask for a finer husband than you." She raised herself on an elbow to look down at him, his handsome slim face and cap of dark hair bathed in a red glow from the fire's sputtering flames. But that questioning look in his splendid brown eyes—she must banish it! Leave no doubts of her feelings for him in his mind. "James, I love you. I love you. I love you, I love you, oh my darling beloved husband."

"My precious wife, that's what I've ached to hear. Oh darling, I'm going to shield you from all sorrow, all pain. I'll live to make you happy."

Their lovemaking became more intense than it had ever been. The sacrament of marriage had freed their consciences of any weight of guilt.

They hardly slept, so often did they make love, as if to compensate for the war threat that overshadowed their lives.

When the pale gray light of dawn seeped in along the edges of the tapestry curtains, he said, "I must leave you."

"Oh, James, why must we part so soon?"

He untwined Lily's arms from around his neck. He must be strong and accelerate the parting. That way it would be less painful for both of them. He left the bed and started to pull on his long hose; all his garments were on the chair beside the bed.

"The separation won't be for long, darling. I swear it. I'll send for you and Joseph and Lucrezia to join me in York, or I'll come to you."

"I don't think things in England will be too easy for any of us from now on."

"Don't allow yourself to have sad thoughts." He was pulling on his breeches. "Let's think of the life we'll have when the country is at peace. I'll take you and Joseph riding over the Yorkshire moors, and we'll gather heather, and Joseph will soon be old enough to ride a pony. We'll have picnics near my favorite lake." He was pulling on his thigh-high boots of soft leather. "We'll have snow fights in the winter. We'll build a giant snowman with Joseph." Now he was easing his shoulders into his doublet, then buckling on his sword.

"It all sounds so lovely," she said wistfully.

"It's going to be wonderful, my beloved one. Well now, I'm ready to leave."

She started to jump up. "I'll come—"

"No." He knelt on the side of the bed and gently pushed her back against the pillow. "Stay in bed. Don't come to bid me farewell. It will be easier for me to think of you lying here, warm and beautiful, while I'm riding off." He gathered her into his arms. "God keep you in His holy care, my wife."

Arms around each other, they clung together as they kissed long and fervently. Then she made herself draw back. "Go now, James darling. I know you must. God ride with you."

He did not delay but swiftly crossed the stone floor and shut the heavy oak door silently after himself.

Lily ran to the window, hoping to see him riding across the inner courtyard. She dragged the heavy tapestry curtains aside, but from this angle she could not see him. She only heard the clattering hooves of the four horses of James's small entourage.

She turned back into the chamber. It was desolate without James, just as she felt bereft without him. She sank back onto the bed, burying her face in the pillows scented by his hair pomade. Dear, kind, loving James, thank God she was his wife, secure in his affection.

Lily resumed her teaching responsibilities with a militant energy. In the hope of gleaning information useful to Father Morgan, she started to write frequently to Roger, carefully forwarding his replies to the Jesuit.

She also wrote to Father Dalvarez, saying that she was serving the Faith, and to Joseph Sanches, telling him of his namesake's progress.

One day she and David received an urgent message from Father Morgan to go to him immediately.

On the bleak October day that they reined in their horses at Saint Francis Xavier, the stone building seemed to be drifting in fog. A depressing scene, but as Lily dismounted, the idea of seeing Father Lloyd cheered her. David rapped three times on the door, the customary signal. The grille opened, but the face peering out was not the cherubic countenance of the priest they loved but a stranger's. Once they were inside, almost immediately Father Morgan strode in, his long black robes flying out about him.

He came to the point quickly. "I've sad news! Father Lloyd has been imprisoned!"

"Dear God, no!" Stricken to her innermost being, Lily sank onto a chair. "When, Father? Where?" She exchanged a distracted look with the agitated David.

"It happened some days ago, but I've only just learned of it. He had been summoned to administer the Last Sacraments to an old woman about twenty miles from here. When a night and a day passed and he didn't return, I became alarmed and sent a pupil after him to find out what had happened." The priest paused a second as though gathering himself, then continued. "The young man reported that just after Father Lloyd had given the woman Extreme Unction a crowd of neighbors burst in, yelling, 'A papist! A papist! Turn him over to the constable!' They grabbed Father Lloyd, beating him with sticks, then dragged him unconscious over the cobbled street to the constable's house."

"Horrible, horrible," Lily sobbed. "Is he badly hurt?"

"A leg broken, I believe, and his face and body terribly lacerated."

"God help him!" David muttered, his mouth twisting in anguish. "What will happen to him now, Father? With the Scots triumphant and their friendship with the Puritans, there'll be little hope of the law freeing a priest."

"But there will be!" Lily cried, springing to her feet. "My mother and I will go to London and appeal to the queen to beg His Majesty to free Father Lloyd."

The ascetic-faced Jesuit sadly shook his head. "At a moment like this Charles would not dare release a priest. Half the country is already against the king for his clemency to Catholics."

With chilling horror Lily recalled Geraldius's tale of a priest being tortured. "But we can't let him suffer martyrdom at Tyburn!"

"No! God willing, we shall save him from that," Father Morgan assured her. "I've learned that he is to be taken to Ludlow to be publicly accused and convicted at the next session of the Council of the Marches. My idea was—"

"Lord Deveraux is a judge of the council," David interrupted, then shook his head. "But I fear his lordship would not stir a finger to help a priest."

"Of course he wouldn't!" Lily flared. "And Roger Huet is the crown advocate, which means no earthly power can get Father Lloyd's release. Huet will revel in condemning him!"

"All of this I have surmised," Father Morgan said. "But with God's help there may be another way of saving Father Lloyd." The Jesuit's brilliant black eyes commended Lily. "It is possible for you to accompany your father to the Council of the Marches?"

She nodded. "I've often done so."

"Good. Then you can ascertain in advance when the trial is to take place and send me notice—at least a full day ahead." He glanced at David. "You also must go to Ludlow, but stay in an inn and, if possible, attract no attention. As soon as Lady Lily learns the day of Father Lloyd's conviction and his scheduled trip to London, she will inform you. In turn you must send me word immediately. I'll have men ready, waiting to be posted along the route Father Lloyd is to travel. They'll hold up the coach and rescue Father Lloyd. He'll be hidden until we can get him out of the country."

"But it's another six weeks, Father, before the Ludlow Sessions open," David said.

"We can do nothing but wait."

20

IN THE DEVERAUX apartments in ancient Ludlow Castle, the walls hung with gold damask, Lily stared through a long slit window at the rain-soaked vista. Although the crier had just cried four o'clock, it was almost dark. It was a forlorn scene in the valley. The river Teme divided Ludlow from Clee and Titterstone, where tops of high hills were lost in mist. Her gaze traveled over the vast courtyard that had known the footfalls of so many great people. Louis of France, before embarking on the seventh crusade; Prince Edward, who had plotted renewal of the wars against the barons; Richard, who had gathered here to begin the Wars of the Roses. Did the shrieking jackdaws, whirling against the gray skies, house their lamenting souls? A sacrilegious thought, she derided herself. What of Father Lloyd in the dungeon in the castle's depths? The nourishment and messages of comfort about his rescue that she sent by Lucrezia, who managed to slip in with the vegetable porters, must be so inadequate to him. She longed to go herself, but in such an act madness lay; should she be openly associated with a papist, it might mean punishment by death.

She turned away from the window and her gaze fell on her mother, whose dark head was bent over her embroidery. She knew of Father Morgan's rescue plan. "I saw David this afternoon at the Feathers," Lily said. "He's confident that the plan will succeed."

"I'm apprehensive about it all. We've been here for a week and Father Lloyd's case is not even scheduled. I wonder why?" Angela whispered, then her frightened eyes darted to the arras as it swung apart and in swept Roger.

Grudgingly Lily admitted to herself that he was handsome and distinguished-looking in the long black robes of the crown advocate.

Roger's eyes flew to Lily but he dutifully went to kiss Lady Deveraux's hand. "Court sessions have closed for the day."

"Good." Angela rose and laid her tapestry on her chair. "I'll go to my husband."

Roger held the arras aside for her, and as she disappeared, he turned a delighted countenance on Lily. "At last a few moments alone with you. I've seen so little of you since we've been here."

"Because you've been so occupied with the court."

"Ah, duty, dear Lily. With the country in such an agitated state, men like myself have a double duty to ensure that the word of God is enforced."

"How right you are." Sitting in her mother's chair,

THE TEMPEST LILY

Lily picked up the tapestry, carefully pushing needle and wool through the design. She must appear calm. "Surely these six-o'clock-in-the-morning sessions are exhausting you."

"No, since working with Pym I've grown accustomed to starting at four or five in the morning."

"Were this morning's sessions interesting?" She was content that her voice sounded quite casual and he would not suspect that she had a special interest.

"Ten minor cases such as carrying weapons at church or at fairs." He drew a chair up to hers and sat down. "Wearing hats on Sundays. Dueling. Tanners for not tanning according to law. People for not attending church on Sunday."

"An this afternoon's cases?"

"A man for woman-stealing, a crime difficult to suppress in Wales." He contemplated his long fingers as he tapped the tips together, a habit of his she disliked. "A woman for witchcraft and a family of these infernal gypsies from Egypt for poisoning an entire neighborhood."

Holding the tapestry at arm's length as though studying the design, she said, "In this quarter's sessions there have been no religious cases?"

"One is coming up."

"Really?"

"Yes, Father Lloyd, a Jesuit caught practicing popery." Roger's nostrils quivered angrily. "There is a resurgence of papist vermin in Wales. No one knows where or by whom they're married, how their children are christened, who their gossips are! They're taught by teachers of their rotten breed! Thumbscrews and the rack is what I'd like to give them!"

"Is there actual proof against the priest, or is it a trumped-up charge?"

"We have an abundance of written assertions against him, as well as witnesses who have seen him practicing his creed."

The day of the trial! She must know, to inform Father Morgan so he could alert his people to be in readiness.

"It might be an interesting case to attend. When does it come up?"

"Tomorrow afternoon, and immediately after the conviction I shall personally escort the Jesuit to Newgate."

Tomorrow! That would not be time enough for her to inform Father Morgan and for his men to position themselves along the London road. She must somehow delay Roger's departure. "Why must you return so soon?" She pouted charmingly in disappointment. "We've been together for so short a while."

A wave of satisfaction swept over Roger's disciplined features. Then his face fell into its habitual stern lines. "Since Parliament's opening Pym needs me immediately, and I decided to take the priest with me. The sooner he is hanged and quartered at Tyburn, the better." He smiled righteously, and Lily longed to strike him across the mouth. "Witnessing torture is such an effective deterrent to curb the evil element."

"I'm sure it is." She must go to David at once with the news. She forced a sneeze, reached for her handkerchief and sneezed again. "Oh, dear, I'm catching a chill." Lily rose and went to warm herself by the great logs in the fireplace. "Tell me more about your work, Roger. You know how it interests me."

"I wish you cared as much about me as you do about my work." He smiled ruefully as he walked toward her.

"But, Roger dear, your work is particularly demanding of my admiration and—"

"It's your love I want, Lily!" He grasped her shoulders. The whites of his eyes seemed inflamed with eagerness. "I beg you to say you'll marry me. We nearly were once so—"

"Please . . . give me a little more time. I'm seriously contemplating your most flattering offer."

"I'll not press you now—" He let go of her as the arras swung open.

Rhys, wearing scarlet judicial robes, swept in, followed by his wife. Rhys smiled approvingly at the scene he'd just interrupted. He crossed to the table, which was set with ale. "The Council of the Marches seems to be growing increasingly unpopular," he said. "Two of our bailiffs arresting a man in Wales were attacked by a mob." He drank deeply from a tankard of ale.

"Why should the Welsh be forced to travel to London or Ludlow, to be tried where the advocate and judges don't speak Welsh?" Lily asked indignantly.

Roger regarded her approvingly. "I'll discuss that with Pym. Welsh courts would also eliminate a number of people coming to London, which has grown monstrous in size and fast living."

Angela said, "Here at Ludlow the gentlemen play at tables and the inns are filled with temptation."

Realizing this discussion would continue for a while, Lily used the excuse that she needed a warm wrap and left the room. She dashed to Lucrezia, who would take her message to David.

That evening drovers brought letters from London, and at supper Roger and the Deverauxs exchanged news.

"Things look very promising for Pym's party." Roger's smugness added irritation to Lily's nervousness. "Many of the king's men were not returned to Parliament."

"You know, Huet," Rhys spoke half-jokingly, "I believe Pym not only wants to rid the country of Strafford, he wants to transfer the king's power to the High Court of Parliament."

"Today, Lord Deveraux, life depends more on Parliament than the Crown."

"Parliament has been sitting a week, but Pym still has not opened his attack on Strafford," Lily said. "Why is that?"

"Brilliant strategy," Rhys said. "Pym is first dealing with old grievances."

"Pym rightly maintains that the true religion has been persecuted, while clergy who believed in divine authority and absolute power remained protected by Charles." Roger's voice sounded strained with annoyance.

With a foreboding of what the growth of Puritan

power might mean, Lily longed to go to David to make new plans. Pleading that her chill was worse, she retired. A few minutes later, unrecognizable in concealing cloaks, she and Lucrezia left the castle. They hurried past the dungeons where Father Lloyd was. It would be cruelly cold down there on this raw November night.

The women stepped into the street and bcame part of the crowd. Ludlow was packed with judges and their families, servants, attorneys, officers, clerks and apprentices. The court served the four border counties: Shropshire, Hereford, Worcester and Gloucester. In addition to the judicial body, there were hundreds of petitioners. Despite the country's upheaval there was gaiety in the town.

Lucrezia held the lantern high to light the way to the Feathers, a black and white half-timbered building. They found David in a richly paneled room, warming himself by the fire.

Lily saw gratefully that they were alone. Without a moment's hesitation she told of the dilemma, finishing with, "I never anticipated that Roger would take Father Lloyd to London so soon." She clasped her hands in agitation, the knuckles whitening. "What can we do, David?"

His face was grim and pale. He stood up. "I've already sent someone to Father Morgan, but it's difficult to know how fast he can travel in this weather or if he'll reach Father Morgan in time to arrange for the holdup of Huet's coach."

An audacious idea flashed into Lily's frantic mind. "I know what we've got to do. We'll have to do it!"

David stared in amazement. "We? You mean you and I?"

"Yes. I remember how it's done. My family's coach was held up once on the way home from London. It only requires courage and impudence and to be a good shot."

"A desperate cause calls for desperate measures," David murmured. "You have a brave spirit, Lily."

"Tomorrow afternoon, as soon as the trial starts, I'll

send Lucrezia to you. Be ready with a spare horse and change of clothing for Father Lloyd and—"

"And a tool to cut off his awful leg chains," Lucrezia swiftly interposed. "I have seen how heavy they are."

"Yes, that's a good idea, Lucrezia." Lily laid an affectionate hand on the Capriote's shoulder and turned back to David. "As soon as Lucrezia comes, ride immediately to the giant yew, about three miles down the London road. You remember it?" David nodded. "We'll meet there."

"Then we'll ride on together and get as far as possible from Ludlow before we attempt the holdup?" David's fine face wore a scheming look.

"Yes, it's a good plan, but when we have Father Lloyd—where do we take him?"

"Back to Breck!" Lucrezia suggested excitedly.

"I'm afraid for you, Lily. This is nothing a woman should be involved in."

"Don't forget I'm both a fine shot and as skillful as a man with a sword. It'll be simple. Now I must go back or I'll be missed at supper. We'll work out the details of our attack when we're on the road."

"I still don't like you being in a thing like this. Don't forget, highwaymen are sometimes killed."

Lily's green eyes were brilliant. "We are soldiers in the cause of true justice!" She had spoken teasingly, but the knowledge that her words were true allowed no fear to disturb her.

The next afternoon Lily joined the crowd in the tightly packed Great Hall to witness the Court Sessions. Painfully nervous, her gaze played over the pinkish stone walls, which were covered with the numerous coats of arms of past monarchs and previous councillors. The president of the council was seating himself, and the lord chief justice of Chester took a cushion beside him. Then twenty scarlet-clad judges, her father among them, and four black-clad bishops took their places.

Ahead of the attorneys came Roger. His challenging

glance swept over everyone present. It was undeniable that Roger had a certain power about him, Lily thought.

The court clerk beat his staff on the stone floor and called out, "The people of South Wales against John Lloyd for the practice of popery."

The first case! Lily had not expected that. Her heart thumped violently as an excited hum arose among the spectators, who pressed forward to watch the Jesuit. Legs weighted with chains and flanked by jailors, he walked slowly into court.

At the sight of the priest she loved and revered, a gasp of dismay broke from Lily. He was hardly recognizable, he was so emaciated.

With hate and menace disfiguring his face, Roger opened his attack. "You stand accused, John Lloyd, of practicing Catholicism! There are many witnesses against you, yet the justice of the law maintains that we must listen to what lies you offer in your defense."

Half-crippled, in stained, crumpled garb, Father Lloyd miraculously remained a figure of supreme dignity. Though his face was gaunt, his cheekbones painfully prominent, his eyes were luminous with pity as he regarded Roger. "My poor man, I require no defense, as I have committed no crime when I practice my religion."

A burst of indignation erupted from the crowd, and Roger flashed a silencing glance in its direction. Obviously enjoying himself, Roger said, "John Lloyd, by saying you are innocent you convict yourself! You have committed the Elizabethan crime of felony!"

"Felony!" Father Lloyd cried out, and raised his bony hands high above his head. "Look at these two hands that have been devoted to God's work! I now hold them up against you, Sir Roger Huet, and against all the heretics of England!"

Lily almost cheered. Furious people stamped and shouted. The court clerk thumped his staff on the floor. Order was restored, and Roger, a mockery of righteousness, faced the judges. "It is unnecessary to waste the court's time, so I ask that this man be immediately convicted and sentenced to be hanged and quartered at Tyburn!"

Lily elbowed her way out of the Great Hall. Unseen, she raced up the stairs to the Deveraux quarters, where her mother and Lucrezia were waiting.

"He's just been convicted! Quick, Lucrezia, go to David with the news!"

As soon as Lucrezia had left, Lily changed into male riding attire.

"In God's name, be careful," Angela begged.

"I'll be all right, Mother. Just be sure when Roger comes to say good-bye to me or when Father asks for me, that you convince them I'm too ill to see them. Try to delay Roger so I can have a good head start."

Well cloaked, she walked swiftly across the turf to where her horse was waiting. Once out of the confines of the castle, she felt better and allowed her mount to trot normally down Broad Street, past the Angel Inn, down Butcher's Row, to the gateway in the medieval walls. Crossing the bridge, she glanced back, searching through the heavy rain to see if she were being followed. Lily saw only a couple of coaches hurrying in the opposite direction.

Soon she was in open country, traveling down the empty road flanked by dark woodlands. Lily had never traveled alone like this before, and the feel of her pistol and sword were reassuring. Reaching the giant yew, she pulled up, her eyes searching anxiously through the darkening gray vista for sign of David.

If her mission failed and her identity was discovered it would mean her death. Poor little Joseph would then be without father or mother. She must not think of that. Lily exercised her arms and legs to keep out the chill. Not long afterward she recognized a lone horseman leading a riderless mount coming down the road. Within minutes David had joined her, and they continued along the main route.

"Thank God you're here, David," she half-joked.

"I kept feeling every leaf was watching me, ready to give me away."

He laughed. "Let us ride on, Lily. It's slow going with the rain, and we must be far from here before we dare waylay Huet."

As they trotted along, they made their plans. "I propose that we head for those woods about five hours away," Lily suggested. "There, we'll wait for Huet's coach. I'll cover the driver with my pistol while you shout the command to halt, otherwise Roger will recognize my voice. You'll have to watch Huet and whoever is with him until Father Lloyd gets out. Then I'll fire next to the horses' heads."

"Yes, that should make the beasts bolt. It's a simple plan, but I don't see how we can improve on it."

"Remember, Roger is a fine shot, but so are we, and we'll have the advantage. We'll be prepared, and he won't be."

For hours they traveled south along the London road. As night came, Lily's hand flew to her pistol a dozen times. Dark shadows that were surely waiting highwaymen developed into stray cows. As they passed along the outskirts of a village, a clock struck ten.

"If Huet left an hour after we did," Lily said, "his coach should reach those woods ahead about midnight."

"Yes, I should think so. I hope Father Morgan's got the word in time so he will be waiting for us at the crossroad."

They pulled up at a thickly wooded area. Dismounting, they sheltered from the rain under the trees.

Watching the moon fighting for freedom from a mass of clouds, Lily admitted to herself that she was afraid. The waiting in the darkness was horrible. Trying to be calm herself, she recalled to David how, as children, they had pretended to be highwaymen. After a while they ate, and David unpacked the bundle of layman's clothes he had brought for Father Lloyd. Then they both tied on their masks.

Twice hooves approaching in the distance sent them springing into their saddles with pistols cocked. But

THE TEMPEST LILY

the riders were going to Ludlow, so Lily and David dismounted and again prepared to wait.

"If professional highwaymen feel as nervous as I do when they're watching for victims, they almost deserve whatever riches they steal," Lily tried to joke. "And . . ." She stopped abruptly, listening to the sound of more horses coming. "This is Roger's coach, David. I feel it in my bones."

"By the horses' rhythm, I'm sure it's a coach." They swung into the saddles, pistols cocked. "In case it's Roger's," David said, "I'll ride to the other side of the road, as we planned."

"God bless our venture, David!"

"He will, Lily, have no fear." David rode across the road.

With trembling legs gripping her mount, her pistol clutched ready, Lily's eyes searched the darkness. Far off there were two tiny red lights. Then the horses' hooves grew louder, and swiftly the lights took on the shape of lanterns. Lily's heart thumped. Now she could see the bundled figure of the driver on the high seat. Horses and coach were coming up almost level with her. She must ride—now!

"Are you ready, David?"

"Yes."

"Ride!" Lily shouted. Digging her spurs into the horse's side, she galloped into the road straight at the coach. Swerving her horse to match the four careening animals, Lily drew even with the driver's box, her pistol covering the man.

His terrified face shone in the lantern light as David yelled, "Stand and deliver!"

The driver dragged on the reins, and the horses came to a halt.

Roger shouted, "I'll kill any dog who dares to—"

"Save your threats, sir!" David commanded. "My pistol has you covered. Let Father Lloyd out at once!"

"You ruffian! You dare not interfere with the law!" the sheriff riding with Roger cried. The next second there was a deafening explosion.

Was David killed? Lily's heart jumped in terror.

"A wasted shot, Sir Roger!" David laughed. "I warn you, don't attempt another or I'll blow you to hell! Now free the priest!"

Her pistol on the driver, Lily could see none of the happenings, but clanking chains told her Father Lloyd was leaving the coach.

"Scum! You won't succeed in this monstrous plan!" Roger yelled. "I'll raise an alarm against you in every village! You won't—"

"Fire!" David cried to Lily, and she shot her pistol close to the lead horse's head. The terrified animals bolted wildly, dragging the swaying coach and yelling men after them.

As the stampeding beasts rushed into the blackness, David and Lily got Father Lloyd into the woods where the waiting horse was tethered.

"Thank you for this rescue, dear friends," the priest murmured. "Thank God! It's like a miracle!"

"Quick, Father, let me get your shackles off." David started sawing off the four-pound weights.

"We have succeeded so far." Lily's shaking hands were reloading her pistol. "But we've still a long journey ahead, Father, before you're out of danger."

Free of the irons, the priest shed his telltale Jesuit garments for the clothes David had brought.

David muttered, "We must leave this neighborhood at once. The sheriff and Huet will easily begin a search for us even though it's after midnight."

They mounted without any further discussion. They traveled for several hours through heavy rain, and Lily feared that in his weak state Father Lloyd must collapse. But miraculously he kept up. Their horses' hooves pounding the earth seemed loud enough to rouse the world, and Lily continually glanced back to see if they were being followed. From somewhere a clock chimed twelve times.

"We should be nearing the spot where we meet the relief party," David called. "If Father Morgan got our message in time. We must pass a gibbet. That must be

THE TEMPEST LILY

the one ahead. After that it's about three miles to the hill where his men should be waiting for us."

Lily's joy at being so close to another important stage of the escape turned to horror. Riders were coming up behind them! She glanced over her shoulder. Charging down upon them were half a dozen horsemen with cloaks flying out like demons.

"Huet has given us chase!" she cried, digging her heels into the horse's heaving flanks.

"Ride!" David commanded, but their animals were weary, while their pursuers' mounts were fresh and gaining fast.

"Only two more miles and we'll have help!" Lily called, to cheer herself as much as the others.

Suddenly Father Lloyd's horse stumbled in a rut. The priest yelled out as he pitched forward onto the road. Seconds later, when David and Lily pulled up and swiftly dismounted, they found the Jesuit was unconscious; a leg seemed broken. There was no time for them to get him back on one of the horses and ride off. Their enemy was almost upon them.

"I'll shoot to cripple their horses," David cried. "Save your shot until I've reloaded."

Lily took her place beside David. Pistol cocked, she faced the oncoming riders. The effort of having to stand and wait made her feel hysterical.

Then David's pistol cracked. A horse screamed, and a man shouted. Through the smoke and darkness Lily saw an animal fall and a man go over its head. Being thrown at such speed would break his neck. Now the other riders were pulling up.

"Rabble dogs!" It was Roger's voice. "Surrender the prisoner before you are shot like vermin!"

Lily heard David reloading as the sheriff shouted, "Shoot the scum, Sir Roger!"

"The priest lies between you and us," David warned, pulling Lily to squat beside him. "If you shoot at us, you'll kill him first."

"Hold your fire!" Roger commanded his men. "I want the papist to hang at Tyburn!"

David's pistol cracked again, and a second horse and rider went down.

"I'm not staying to be killed like a rat!" someone shouted before galloping away.

Three men remained on horseback and two had fallen. One seemed to be dead, but it was difficult to see the other, who could be creeping up to attack David and her from the rear. Lily did not dare shoot until David had reloaded.

"I'll let you go free and pay a rich price for the priest," Roger cried, "if you deliver him this moment!"

"How can I be sure you'll keep your word?" David taunted, playing for time to reload.

At that moment Lily heard a sound behind them, confirming her suspicion. Swinging around, she aimed and fired. There was a horrible gurgling scream and a huge body sprawled to the earth. Seconds later there was the flash of steel as another man sprang at her. With no time to reload, she pulled out her sword. The relief party must have heard the shouts. Why didn't they come?

As her assailant lunged clumsily at her, she parried his blow. A man of average size, he handled his weapon badly. Her knowledge should soon dispatch him. As she fenced, out of the corner of her eye, she was conscious of Roger swinging off his horse and making for Father Lloyd. David's pistol cracked again. There were curses and one of Roger's men fired. Fortunately the shot went wild.

Lily was aware of what was happening, although she never took her concentration off her opponent. Watching for her chance, she rushed forward and cut his right arm. His sword clattered from his hand, and she sprang to kick it away. There was little harm this man could do now.

David must be covered while he reloaded, but Roger was cocking his pistol at him. With lightning speed Lily's sword swept up and sent the pistol flying from Roger's hand. Within seconds he had drawn his sword.

"Have at you! Curse you!" he muttered, his weapon

THE TEMPEST LILY

slashing out at Lily. She parried the blow. Depleted from the previous engagement, short of breath, Roger's unexpected skill was terrifying. His additional weight favored him, but despite her weariness Lily was the more nimble of the two. As they struck at each other, she was conscious of David dragging the last horseman from the saddle and hurling himself upon the man. With his powerful shoulders David would beat the man at wrestling. They were rolling on the ground in a bear hug.

She must be careful, very careful. Her arm was dreadfully heavy. On the muddy ground it was difficult to move swiftly. Her breath was coming in gasps. Roger's thrusts were dangerously close.

Above the groans of the wounded, the grunts of fighting men, the clash of steel, she heard horses pounding the ground. Friend or foe? Slash—slash—slash came Roger's sword, and her defense had to be like lightning. If she could only maneuver toward Father Lloyd, the fear of killing the Jesuit might distract Roger. Lily dared to dart a look at the oncoming riders and, taking advantage of her momentary offguard, Roger's sword nicked her left shoulder. The sudden pain made her almost cry out and betray herself, but Lily stopped in time and somehow managed to swing her weapon to ward off his intended death stroke.

Warm blood was flowing from her wound. She was weak and felt nauseated. If help did not come soon, he would dispatch her—an awful revenge upon Roger when he discovered who it was he had killed.

Now the horsemen were almost upon them, and a deep voice boomed in Welsh, "Have you got Father Lloyd?"

Welshmen! Rescuers!

"We have him," David grunted in Welsh, and with a miraculous new strength Lily struck out at Roger as the three masked riders sprang to the ground. One hurled himself at David's opponent, and a big man swept Lily aside. "I'll finish this for you, boy," he muttered as he stepped in to engage Roger.

Swaying on her shaky legs, Lily wanted to go to Father Lloyd but the third rescuer was lifting the priest onto a horse. She looked around for her animal but it had bolted, along with David's and the priest's.

The fight between Roger and the big man was ending as the Welshman forced Roger against a tree. The man's great strength slashed down at Roger's upraised sword, breaking the blade. Then he ran Roger through the right arm. Seconds later he was trussing Roger back to back with the sheriff. Then he called in Welsh to Lily, "Mount my horse, boy! Quick, we must be off!"

Lightheaded from loss of blood, she managed to swing herself up onto the animal's back. She could only hope she would not faint. One of Father Morgan's men jumped up behind the Jesuit. Another was mounting with David, and now the big man swung up behind Lily.

"Ride! Ride!" he shouted, and whirling their horses, they galloped south, his arm like a band of iron supporting her.

Lily tried to preserve consciousness, but it was eluding her, and she slumped back in a heap against her rescuer. When coherent thought seeped grayly back, Lily was convinced that she must be dead. She *must* be dead, for Adam knelt beside her on the ground, holding wine to her lips.

"Lily! Thank goodness I came in time to save you, or Huet would have killed you. Drink some wine, my wonderful, brave Lily."

She sipped from the leather flask, her green eyes marveling at the sight of his face in the lantern light. In his mask she had not recognized him, nor his voice speaking Welsh. "Adam . . . Adam. Is it true . . . that we meet like this?"

"It's too strange to be real." He screwed the flask up and pocketed it on his hip. "When you fainted in my arms, I realized that the brave youth was a woman." He grinned in the way she so loved. "Then, damn my soul, when I removed your mask and saw your face, at first I was convinced I was a victim of black magic."

The blue eyes into which she stared glowed with a wondering admiration. "How brave of you, Lily, to have engaged in this dangerous task!"

"Thank God we managed it."

"Father Lloyd is resting in the coach." Adam nodded toward the vehicle, then caught her hand and pressed it to his lips as their eyes clung to each other. "I've bound your wound. It's not deep and I think you'll be able to ride with it." His gaze searched the darkness. "We must get away from here at once."

"Oh, not yet . . . We cannot part yet!" She raised herself on an elbow, and Adam helped her sit up.

He glanced anxiously toward a coach, beside which David and his men were waiting. "We must leave at once! We've got to put Father Lloyd aboard the *Fearless* in Milford Haven and leave England. Huet will recover and have the countryside scoured for us. Every moment here means danger to all of us."

"Of course, you're right." Adam helped her stand up, but her legs offered little support and she swayed against his supporting arm.

"Lily, come with us in the coach to Milford Haven and recover at Ben Fras. Then, later, return to Breck."

"God knows how I wish I could go with you, but I must return to Ludlow at once or my absence would make me suspect and I'd be useless to Father Morgan in the future."

"Just as long as you feel strong enough for the journey." He draped his cloak over her blood-soaked doublet. His deep concern for her encouraged Lily to madness.

"When Father Lloyd is safely at sea—oh, Adam, come to Breck for just a little while."

"That's impossible. I'm sailing with Father Lloyd to Italy. Then, when I return to London, I shall be—"

He stopped before he said the cruel word "married," but to her the word was echoing across the raw night and rebellion flared in her. Damn him and damn Jane's dowry! "Yes, James told me." She started walking toward the group where David was already mounted and ready to be off.

"We've supplied you with two of our horses," Adam said, lifting her onto the saddle. "Take care of yourself, Lily. It would be a barren world for me if you were not in it."

Words—easily uttered words of nothingness! Her green eyes blazed down at his handsome, imperturbable face, which she had never seen suffer a trace of pain. "Then your world is going to be barren, Adam, because I'm James Forsyth's wife and he's taking me to live in Virginia."

With the sudden lie, triumph flooded through her, because for a flash of a second Adam winced as though he'd been struck. Then he smiled. "Forsyth's a damned lucky man." His derisive grin was not to be tolerated.

"Lucky or not . . . he's the man I love!" Digging her heels into the horse, she galloped into the night.

21

THE COUNCIL OF the Marches was over. Rhys Deveraux had left Ludlow for London to take his seat in the House of Lords, while his family returned to Breck.

Once more Lily was occupied with her teaching. Had James been present he would have helped, but he was attending the House of Commons. The severe winter imposed almost total isolation upon Breck, so no visitors came and few drovers. The few who did come brought alarming news of Parliament's acts against Charles and their arrest of the earl of Strafford.

During the long dark months Lily, her mother, Geraldius and David had developed the habit of gathering in Angela's withdrawing room to peruse the rare letters and pamphlets that arrived.

They sat miserably listening now as Geraldius read from the most recent newspaper.

THOMAS, EARL OF STRAFFORD, LORD LIEUTENANT OF IRELAND, TRIED FOR HIGH TREASON

By the Commons. March 22nd, 1640.
At 7 A.M. the earl left the Tower by water accompanied by six barges, carrying a guard of one hundred soldiers, to go to Westminster. The House of Lords is sitting in judgment of the trial, also the House of Commons, but as a committee, not as Parliament.

With a gesture of disgust Geraldius flung down the newspaper.

"It's incredible that Pym's machinations have succeeded to this extent!" Lily exploded.

"And in only a few months," David added.

"Let's see what my husband writes." Angela's eyes skimmed over personal lines, then she read aloud:

It is 240 years since a great lord like Strafford has stood accused of treason.

Pym opened the prosecution and Strafford defended himself brilliantly against Pym's most serious charge, that Strafford wished to bring over an Irish army to subdue "this" kingdom. Strafford swears Scotland was meant by "this" kingdom—Pym accused Strafford of meaning England.

"What lies!" Lily exclaimed. "Strafford wanted Irish troops to fight the Scots!" She picked up a letter from James and read silently.

Lily, dearest love—my beautiful wife,
I long to touch your hand, to gaze into those wonderful green eyes, to hear your voice.

Realizing that the others were eagerly watching her, waiting for James's news, she revealed the rest of the contents.

I am one of the small group of officers close to the queen. We are all in Commons but, unfortunately, too few to make an impression. Puritan hatred against Roman Catholics continues, and the king has been forced to banish Catholics, except the queen's personal servants, from court, and to cashier Catholic officers from the Army.

Lily's voice trailed off as her eyes read, "Adam and Jane were married some months ago." It was done! Adam was Jane's husband! Suddenly Lily was consumed with longing to see James. "Mother, let's go to London to witness Strafford's trial!"

At the Triumph Tavern, where Lord Deveraux received his family, the change in his full-cheeked face surprised Lily. Why was life turning against the king and his followers?

"There's the stench of revolution in the air!" Rhys growled. "A fanatical determination to overthrow established rule. If Pym can behead a great lord like Strafford, who is safe?" Rhys's mud-brown eyes blazed into Lily's face. "For Christ's sake, marry Huet! This is no time for fastidious nonsense, I warn you! If you marry Huet that will at least secure our lives . . . if not our properties."

So much had twisted Lily's heart since that command had last been issued. How stupid openly to oppose him. "I sympathize with your fears, Father," she said calmly.

THE TEMPEST LILY 237

Rhys seemed content that her answer meant acquiescence, because he said no more.

At the first opportunity Lily sent word to James's house saying she had arrived.

The next day, with Joseph toddling about her knees, she sat waiting for James. When he rushed in, his mouth and eyes were all smiles.

"Lily, my love!" In one stride he was beside her, his arms enfolding her.

She returned his kisses warmly. James's delight at being with her, his good looks, his strength, sparked an answering gladness in her. James was her husband, her protector.

"What joy to see you, sweetheart." He held her at arm's length to revel in the sight of her. "More beautiful than poor memory allowed me to know."

"It's wonderful to see you, too, James." She laughed, then, seeing Joseph was about to topple over, she stooped to save him, but the little boy grabbed at James's hose.

"Well, how flattering." James chuckled. "I do believe Joseph remembers me." He tossed the happy child up and down in the air. "He's grown into a fine little man." James carefully replaced Joseph on his unsteady feet and turned to Lily. "Darling heart, when will we meet at my house?"

"This afternoon," she promised with an intimate smile.

"Darling, I long to devote my life to making you happy."

"I'm afraid the Scottish Calvinists and English Puritans have placed more important responsibilities upon you." She smiled ruefully, then lifted Joseph, who was appealing to get onto her lap. "Our lives are going to be sadly changed unless we work desperately to maintain things as they are."

James's whole demeanor had grown serious. "I know. And since the Puritans are so determined to gain the balance of power, I've become militant about preserving England as she is! Every intelligent man resents what Puritan narrowness would do to this country! It would stifle all progressive thought in medicine, science, art! In fact, everything!"

"Of course it would! Can't we do more to aid Strafford in this wicked trial? It's not only for his sake. Pym is putting our entire class on trial in the person of Strafford."

"We can't do very much." James shook his head. "It's marvelous how Strafford's conducting his own defense, but Pym has the rabble's sympathy and he's making them despise Strafford. What royalists have been doing is to mix with the irate shopkeepers and merchants at Westminster during the hearing and try to keep a balance in Strafford's favor."

"That's what I'll do! I'll go to Westminster tomorrow!"

"I wish I could be with you in the public gallery, but I must take my seat with the members of the Commons."

That afternoon, using the excuse to her mother that she must see someone for Father Morgan, she hired a carriage to take her to James's house.

He was there waiting for her, with champagne ready to be poured. "I've been living for this day." He plucked a small box from a pocket of his doublet. It was green plush. He pressed a spring and the lid lifted. Nestling in a bed of green satin was the most beautiful gold and diamond rose—almost life-size.

"Oh, James, it's exquisite!"

"My wedding present to my beloved wife. The golden rose was the greatest gift the pope could think of to bestow upon Queen Johanna of Naples when the school of cardinals acquitted her of murdering her loutish Hungarian husband. I've tried to have it copied exactly as an offering for your beauty, your wit, your indomitable courage."

Lily's eyes shone with happiness. "How generous, how flattering—alas, I have no gift for you."

"I have your love. I can ask God for no greater

gift. Come, we have so little time. I must go back to the trial soon."

They toasted each other with champagne; then he carried her to the adjoining room, where, in the great four-poster bed, they made love as if time was marking the minutes allotted to them.

Before the trial the next morning, Westminster Hall was crowded to the walls with excited spectators. Wearing her plainest clothes, Lily was pushed and shoved as she fought for a seat among the mob in the gallery. At last she managed to sink onto a wooden bench. Righting her bonnet, she looked around at specially erected scaffolding of rows of seats, topped by the empty throne. Charles was in an adjoining closet, where, unseen, he could follow the trial. Below sat the Lords of the Upper House, flamboyant in brilliant doublets and wide-brimmed feathered hats. Beside the Lords on sacks of wool were scarlet-robed judges to give advice on the law. The lower tiers held the 439 members of Commons, who were forbidden to wear hats.

At the far end of the hall, standing behind a tall desk, was a bent, thin man. That could not be Strafford! Where were the proud head, the raven locks, the air of indomitability in his carriage? Despite the spring day he wore a shawl over his shoulders, a fur cap on his now gray hair. Furious tears blinded Lily. In Strafford's deterioration she saw the end to a fashion of life she loved. Angrily Lily turned to a florid-faced woman beside her and whispered, "What wicked changes worry and imprisonment have made in Strafford."

"The poor duck does look seedy," the woman answered in illiterate tones and moved closer to Lily. The odor of the strong cheese and garlic the woman was eating was nauseating. "That's Pym and his black-clad boys next to Strafford."

Lily recognized Roger talking to Pym. "They look a grim lot," Lily said confidentially to her neighbor.

"Aye, they're not much fun."

An enormous hum of voices rose excitedly as the court clerk demanded silence, followed by a respectful hush. The right honorable steward rose to open the proceedings, bowing toward the empty throne, the Lords, then Strafford.

"My Lord of Strafford," he commented, "I am commanded by my lords to tell you that they expect your lordship to sum up your final evidence with clearness and succinctness." He glanced toward Pym and his men. "And those gentlemen of Commons will likewise sum up their final evidence."

As Strafford nodded courteously and consulted some papers, Lily whispered loudly, "Poor soul, he doesn't look like a tyrant."

The woman next to Lily agreed. "Aye, he's too weak to hurt anyone."

"That narrow-minded Pym is mad to accuse Strafford of treason," Lily said loudly.

"Shut your mouth!" the man next to her ordered threateningly. "I say lay Strafford's head on the block!"

"You big bully, me and my friend are sorry for the poor bloke!" Lily's neighbor stood up to retaliate.

"Sssh, sssh," voices cautioned.

"Have a swig, dearie." Lily's newfound friend passed a leather bottle toward her that several people had drunk from.

Girding her spirit, Lily swallowed some mix and smilingly handed it back. Then she turned her eyes away as, farther down the bench, a man openly relieved himself.

All became quiet as Strafford began, and despite his weak health, in masterly fashion he proved his innocence point by point against twenty-eight cases of alleged injustices and nine cases of general accusations.

To Lily it seemed there could be no doubt that everyone there must pronounce him guiltless. Throughout his two-hour defense, she continued whispered remarks, praying they might influence the people around her in his behalf.

Straightening his bent shoulders, Strafford prepared

THE TEMPEST LILY 241

for his final statement. Turning to the lords as if appealing to their superior wisdom and justice, his voice broke with emotion.

"My lords, with all humility and tranquillity of mind, I do submit myself to your judgments, and, whether that righteous judgment shall be life or death, *Te deum, Te Dominum Confitemur.*"

Slowly he sat down amid complete silence.

Lily turned to her neighbor. "He is innocent! All the world can see that!" She shook the woman's arm. "Tell your friends. Tell them!"

"Yes, yes!" the woman cried to the people on her other side. "Let Strafford live!"

There was an enormous rush of sound as, all over the public gallery, hundreds of voices burst into argument and people started shuffling their way toward the doors. Hemmed in by the excited throng, Lily's feet hardly touched the floor as she was half-carried into Westminster yard. Fresh air! Wonderful! But here the crowd was more furious than inside. Men were fighting. Heads were split open. Bloodied faces were everywhere as people shouted that Strafford was guilty and others shouted he was not.

"Strafford is a tyrant! He must die!" a woman was shrieking near Lily. Maddened by the injustice, Lily clutched the woman's shoulder, crying, "Fool! Strafford's done no wrong!"

The woman's dirty hands reached to grab Lily's hair, but she jerked her head away. At that moment they were both pushed sideways as the people about them heaved to make way for a giant of an officer holding at arm's length above his head a wiggling man.

"You want Strafford on the block," the huge man yelled at a bunch of black-clad men crouching menacingly before him. "But we'll have Pym first! Here, take your Puritan fellow!" And he flung down his hostage into the crowd.

As the men caught their comrade, they rushed at the officer, who quickly drew his sword. It was not until then that Lily saw his face. Adam! Almost within arm's reach. He was holding off half a dozen assailants, who were coming at him with sticks and stones.

"Get away, Clune!" two other officers cried, forcing their way through the mob to Adam. "Get away before the civilian soldiers arrive!" they shouted over the noises of the crowd.

"This is good sport," Adam roared. He pricked a Puritan on the shoulder with his sword, and the man staggered backward.

"Adam! Adam!" Lily yelled, but her voice would not carry over the bedlam. His friends were trying to stop the fight, trying to pacify his opponents, pushing Adam away, but he would not have it. Grinning like a boy, he tantalized the Puritans. "Fight! Come on, fight! I say Strafford is innocent!"

"Adam—Adam—Adam!" Lily kept up a continuous call as she struggled to reach him. "Adam! Adam!" Like a wild thing she clawed at the bodies surrounding her. At last she was almost beside him. As he lunged at an opponent, she yelled, "Adam! It's Lily!"

He swung around and shot her an unbelieving look, and at that moment, finding him off guard, one of his attackers struck Adam across the head with a heavy crop. Lily screamed and rushed to him. The officers slashed at the mob with their swords.

Adam reeled momentarily, then straightened up. "I'll get you out of here," he shouted in Lily's ear, and pulled her back against his chest. His left arm encircled her like a protective iron band. His sword in his right hand, he fought an exit to the edge of the angry crowd, where coaches and nervous horses were waiting. Then, picking Lily up in his arms, he dashed toward his coach as furious men chased him and stones whisked by his head. Adam put her inside and slammed the door. The driver lashed the horses, and the coach bounced forward. With the mob's curses following them, they galloped down an alley, slowing down as they turned into an empty street. Lily and Adam stared incredulously at each other.

"What luck to have found you in that mess, Lily."

"Yes, extraordinary!" she gasped. "Your head—is it hurt?"

"Not a bit. And you, are you all right?"

She nodded. His nearness beside her on the seat and his special scent were overwhelming, but she would not let herself weaken. Everything was over between them. She was married. "It always seems to take some sort of violence to bring us together," she observed nervously.

"I swear I'd gladly promote violence if I could be sure it would always bring us together," he said.

Lily smiled but averted her gaze from the intensity of his eyes, for she was determined to keep her resolution. She realized that she was in complete disarray and started bundling up her hair.

"Don't! It's lovely falling over your shoulders." He swept her into his arms, twisting his body to hers so they were crushed together.

Lily pressed her face to his chest, avoiding his mouth. Oh, Adam—Adam. Her buried love surged through her. Please God, help me, she prayed.

Adam stared feverishly into her eyes. "For God's sweet sake, don't pretend! Admit that you want me ... as you always have! Admit it!"

Breathless, she pulled away. "Everything has changed."

"Nothing between us will ever change!" He pressed his mouth onto her lips, and her spirit leaped toward him. His wonderful hands were moving over her body, but she tried to stop them.

"No, Adam, no!"

"Not in a coach, eh?" Breathing heavily, he grinned in the way that in remembrance had always twisted her heart with longing. "All right, I know a place." He leaned forward, calling to the driver, "The Heaven Tavern." Then Adam turned back to fold her in his arms again.

"No!" Lily shouted, freeing herself. "I'm married to James—I was married before you were."

"That's a hellcat lie to torment me! You flung it at

me the night of the priest's rescue, but I'm damned if I believe it."

"You must. It's true!" The news obviously hurt Adam. Oh, that was a satisfaction.

"I've made inquiries, and no one has heard of your so-called wedding."

"We've had to keep it secret because Father still wants me to marry Roger, and I don't want to cross Father yet."

"Down to hell with all of that! We belong together. James and Jane—neither of them can come between us. It may be years before we have such a chance as this to make love."

"I shall never betray James." She shook her head. "Never. You may betray Jane if you like—that's your affair."

"Are you in love with James?" Adam sounded so incredulous that it almost amused Lily. In his arrogance had he believed that she would never love any other man but himself?

"James is a wonderful person. He's brought me happiness—never given me a moment's sorrow. Yes, I love him."

Adam frowned slowly. "I never thought anyone would replace me in your heart."

"No? Well, there was a time when no one could have, despite our quarrels, but your betrothal to Jane for her dowry—that was too much, Adam." Lily spoke without temper or vengeance. "That crushed my love."

There was silence between them for a few seconds; then Adam seemd to gather himself and sat up stiffly. "To you, I suppose, my marriage was an indication that I did not love you—"

"That you did not love me enough to marry me. Yes, that was obvious."

"You're wrong! Damnably wrong. You are the only woman I have ever loved, but obviously your love for me is over. Just look at me and tell me so." She willed her eyes to look into his without revealing the tumult in

THE TEMPEST LILY 245

her heart, and he repeated his request. "Just look at me and tell me that your love for me is over."

"Please tell the driver to go to the Triumph Tavern, not the Heaven Tavern. I must go back to my family."

"Certainly," Adam said coldly. He leaned forward and called to the driver. Then, seated well back in a corner of the coach, he said, "God knows when we'll meet again. My next mission on the *Fearless* for Charles is a secret one with danger attached to it, so I'd like to say, should I run into trouble and not return," his voice took on a falsely bantering tone, "and we never meet again—remember always that I love you."

It was as though he had plunged his knife point deep into her heart, but Lily rallied. "You will return, Adam. You are indestructible." She dug into her velvet reticule and from a tiny jewel box she pulled out a jade figure of an Indian god, given to her in her childhood by her paternal grandmother, which she had only recently started to carry with her. "Take this. Keep it on your person. It's an ancient good luck charm. The Indian superstition is that those who carry it will never succumb to their enemies."

Adam opened his hand, and she placed the tiny token in his big palm. His fingers closed over it almost savagely. "It will never leave me, Lily."

She leaned over and kissed his cheek. "I shall never cease to pray for your welfare."

The carriage had pulled up at the Triumph. "Don't get out," she said. "Father might see you, and he still resents you for that stupid ransom money. God go with you, Adam." A groom sprang down to open the door and help her descend. She wanted to give Adam a good-bye look, and for a second the blue, blue eyes showered love upon her. Then she went into the Tavern to Adam's son, whom he would never know he had sired.

22

Rhys Deveraux, growing alarmed by the Puritans' increasing power, courted Roger assiduously. The brilliant young lawyer and politician was a constant visitor at the Triumph Tavern, where his wooing of Lily was a strain to her. She longed to make public her marriage, but she waited, hoping for a royal success to restore her father's belief in King Charles. Now, as Roger entered the Deverauxs' private drawing room at the Triumph Tavern, Lily asked him, "What is the latest word on Strafford's fate?"

"Pym has a brilliant solution, should the Lords decide not to impeach Strafford. It's a bill of attainder, which maintains by Act of Parliament that Strafford must die . . . for the people's good. It's got to be signed by the Commons, Lords and the king."

"His Majesty won't sign it!" Relief bubbled out of Lily. "He's promised Strafford that he'll not let him die at Parliament's hands."

"The king is accustomed to breaking promises." Roger's thin lips curled sneeringly. "He will sign."

Roger seemed more obnoxious than ever now that his influence had gotten stronger. Determined to give him no chance of becoming amorous, Lily poured questions at him which led to explanations of Pym's sagacity in trapping Strafford, until the evening passed.

During the next week she was thankful that Roger

THE TEMPEST LILY

spent all his time between the Commons and Pym. James also was fully occupied trying to raise sympathy for Strafford in the Commons, yet each day he managed to break away to spend a few secret hours with Lily in his London house, where he tried to calm her apprehensions about the state of the country.

Then a large majority in the Commons signed the bill to execute the king's favorite. It was immediately sent to the Lords, and Charles appealed to them to reject it, while the populace stormed Westminster demanding Strafford's death.

Pym sent an audacious demand to the king to disband the Irish troops and dismiss every papist from court. The king refused, and Pym exposed Charles's plot to free Strafford by force from the Tower.

In a quiet ceremony at court, nine-year-old Princess Mary married the twelve-year-old Prince of Orange, and the Dutch presented Charles with one hundred thousand ducats.

Then the Commons had their latest proclamation nailed on posts all over London. Lily pushed through a crowd to get a better look at it.

> The knights, citizens and burgesses of the House of Commons find this kingdom to have plots hatched against its bowels and working its destruction. Therefore, the Commons have passed resolves for security. Strict enquiry to be made as to what Jesuits be about the town. That one thousand five hundred barrels of gunpowder going to Portsmouth be stayed. That all ports be closed. . . .

Ports closed! Weak with shock, Lily moved away. When Adam returned with the *Fearless* and probably a cargo of arms, he would be apprehended.

She hid her private agitation and, like all the country, watched the king's agony as he did everything possible not to sign the order for Strafford's execution. One evening when James was visiting Lily, the door opened and Lord Deveraux walked jerkily into the room. His face was haggard.

"Father, what is it?" Lily sprang to her feet.

"The bill . . . Charles has signed it! Strafford dies tomorrow!"

"God pity the king," Lily moaned. "He'll despise himself for breaking his vow." She sank into a chair. "So Pym has won. It's terrifying!"

"Strafford's death is only the beginning," Rhys mumbled. "We might all soon follow him."

"Damn my soul!" James's clenched fists beat against his brow. "It's no longer King Charles who rules England but King Pym! I swear that blood will turn our green meadows red before Strafford is avenged and that swine Pym dethroned!"

Strafford's execution unleashed turmoil and confusion throughout the three kingdoms.

In retaliation for what had happened, Charles decided to impeach Pym. Accompanied by a party of officers, James among them, His Majesty marched into the Commons to arrest Pym and several important members of his party. However, they had been forewarned and had fled for refuge in the city.

Rhys discussed the king's humiliation with his wife and Lily. "In God's name, what next can happen? I'm trying to leave London. Since the Lords were powerless to save Strafford, to be a member of the Lords means nothing! We are dictated to by Pym and the Commons!"

"So we'll soon be going back to Breck," Lily said, dreading the very thought of leaving James.

"I'll be thankful to go." Angela nervously twisted her delicate hands. "Not only is there talk of an outbreak of plague, but there's no security here anymore. There's a fear at court that Pym might even dare to impeach the queen, accusing her of mischievous advice to Charles. Everything has changed so terribly. The Puritans seem to own London."

"That's what it's coming to," Rhys said gravely. "I've a couple of financial matters to clear up in the city, and as soon as I have, we'll go home."

THE TEMPEST LILY 249

The next day the news broke that to save her head from the block, the queen had scurried away like a criminal. It was too cruel. Lily dropped her face onto her hands, which were locked together in prayer. "Oh dear God, give the queen courage to bear her trials. Protect her!"

When news reached London that the king, after seeing the queen safely off, rather than return to a hostile London, had gone to York, Rhys swiftly closed his business affairs as best he could. James, still in the Commons, came to say good-bye to Lily at his town house.

"While I hate to part with you, I think it's best for you and Joseph to get out of London's foul air."

"But I don't want to leave you."

James took her in his arms. "You'll know that I am always with you in spirit. My love for you has made me a part of you. Don't be disheartened. The royalists' cause will triumph in the end, though it won't be long now before everything breaks into open warfare. Until then I'll hold my seat in the Commons, trying to act as pacifier in my small way. When His Majesty makes a move toward war, then, by God, I'll race back to York!"

Lily had been back at Breck for over a year, impatient at having been kept away from London. She felt obliged for Joseph's sake to remain out of the plague-ridden areas, and also James's letters begged her to stay in the comparative safety of Breck. She kept occupied by helping train men and horses for war, and whenever one of Roger's frequent letters arrived boasting of the growth of Puritan power, Lily would send it immediately to Father Morgan. But she bridled that she was able to accomplish so little when so much was needed.

When war whisperings whipped to storm strength, Rhys Deveraux decided to join the king and warned Lily that he would be leaving the governorship of Breck to her and David. James left London for York, calling first at Breck. To his insistence that Lily accompany him, she was forced to refuse. "As soon as Father leaves, all the responsibility of Breck is mine."

"But there's David. He's capable of governing in your place. It's not essential for *you* to stay."

She twisted in his encircling arms and reached up to brush the thick black hair from his forehead. "Dearest James, you must realize that I could never leave Breck if danger threatens it."

"Good God, Lily, my wealth, my men, myself, are all at the king's disposal—surely I have the right to . . . my wife!"

"Yes, but my first duty is here! I owe that to my ancestors and to Joseph. It's his heritage. Would you leave your estates if your mother were not there to run them? My poor mother has grown less capable than ever. She stays in her chambers, hiding herself from almost everything."

"How can I say your decision is wrong? I only know I want so desperately to have you with me always."

"I *am* with you always in spirit—just as you said you were always with me."

James hurried on to York, and several days later both Parliament and the king issued a call to arms throughout the country. Lord Deveraux furiously destroyed the Parliamentary document but posted the royal counterpart, which ordered men to enlist in King Charles's army.

Soon afterward the king's nephews, Princes Rupert and Maurice, arrived in England to place their battle experience at their uncle's disposal. It was then that Rhys told his family he was going to join the king at once.

Leaving twenty men for Breck's protection, and the governorship to Lily and David, Rhys, with all the troops and horses he could muster, put himself under the command of the marquis of Hertford, the king's lieutenant general for South Wales and the west of England.

To Lily and David went the responsibility of fortifying Breck to withstand attack and siege, of laying in a stock of food and ammunition, of digging an additional well, of drilling and instructing the men in the castle and village's defense. At Geraldius's suggestion they unearthed ancient armor and weapons from the castle's storerooms. Some of the pieces had been untouched for a century. The armor was oiled and polished, the weapons put in working order and distributed to villagers and servants.

Lily and David not only drilled the villagers, they also rehearsed them in the plan to be put into effect if war broke out in Glamorganshire. A constant watch must be kept a few miles beyond the village. If the enemy was sighted, the villagers were to withdraw in an orderly yet quick fashion inside the castle's protective walls.

Breck's four precious small guns were carefully tested and mounted in strategic positions upon the outer walls. Every inch of the fortifications was scrutinized, and loose stones were secured with mortar.

Occupied all day in spurring the servants and villagers in war preparation, Lily permitted herself little time to meditate on the fearsome shape of the future.

James wrote telling how splendidly his mother had assumed control of his interests, leaving him free to take his troops to Nottingham, where the king's main body was gathered. He was anxious for the fighting to start and was part of Prince Rupert's cavalry.

Roger wrote, exulting that the Puritans would soon fight "God's cause against the Antichrist's."

From Adam there was never any news.

Fourteen months after Strafford's death, Charles raised his standard at Nottingham and civil war broke out. Families were divided; fathers fought sons, brothers killed each other, and women's hearts were torn between both camps.

Those at Breck worked at their various tasks while anxiously following the war developments from newspapers, some printed by Parliament, some by royalists, which now flooded the country. No major battles were fought during the first few months of hostilities. Then, five months after the outbreak, word reached Breck of the Battle of Edgehill, reputed to be of serious size. Lily wondered if James had been engaged in it and prayed for his safety.

Lady Deveraux, so agitated by the country's travails, avoided reading the newspapers and went to her chamber when they arrived. However, Lily, Geraldius and David gathered in a small room to share the hand-sized papers whenever they came. It was on a bleak afternoon when the *True Informer* arrived and, eager to learn details of the Battle of Edgehill, they swiftly distributed the pages among them.

Standing by a long slit window to catch the wan light, Lily read aloud to Geraldius and David.

> A body of Welsh formed the only troop of infantry. Seeing the success of Prince Rupert's impetuous charge of cavalry, the Welshmen, fired with the spirit of battle, proved most valorous. Arms were the great deficiency. The men stood up in the garments in which they had left their fields and with scythes, pitchforks and sickles literally like reapers, descended to the harvest of death. Over five hundred were killed.

"It's devilish," David muttered. "Five hundred men gone. Probably some of our own villagers and miners among them."

"Yes," Lily said, "there's a list here of officer casualties—English and Welsh."

"Aye, a sinister roll call of brave men who will never respond to their names," Geraldius said sadly.

Ill with apprehension, Lily's eyes flew down the *A, B, C, D, E*s—was James among the *F*s? "Oh, God! No! No!"

"In heaven's name, what is it?" David cried.

Staring aghast into Geraldius's and David's anxious faces, she flung the paper from her, and David sprang to pick it up, his eyes immediately catching the name that had twisted her heart.

THE TEMPEST LILY

"James has been killed!"

Lily was utterly stricken. In death James became even more dear to her than he had been in life. Always honest with herself, she did not pretend that she had been in love with him as she had been with Adam, but still she loved him deeply. It was impossible to comprehend that never again would she enjoy his company. James's love had rebuilt her confidence, brought her back to happiness after the torment of Adam. It had all ended, and she was alone again. Now she was truly a widow.

Two weeks later she received a silver casket from Lady Forsyth. It contained James's heart. Lady Forsyth wrote to say that James had told her of his marriage, and it had been his wish that, should he die in battle, his heart be sent to his wife, as was customary with married people.

Lily sat in the great hall with a group of women, all of them stitching padded doublets for her father's soldiers. Her thoughts were quite removed from her surroundings. Pictures of James filled her mind—laughing, loving husband; brave cavalier; devoted son and brother. How deep must be his mother's agony. And Adam? Where was he? Leading the king's men somewhere in the war-raked land? Or bringing in arms on the *Fearless?* Was he also dead? She glanced up from her sewing to look at three-year-old Joseph playing around her knees. Poor little boy, being denied his father, he was also spared the pain of losing him—there was an odd mercy in that. Even James's love was lost to him.

Roger's letters were continual even in that distracted time. Despite the king's success in arms, Roger believed that ultimately Parliament would win what he considered a religious war. It never failed to amaze Lily that she had deceived him so successfully that he believed her sympathies were with his and that she was being kept unwillingly at Breck in territory loyal to Charles.

"Lily, darling," her mother's soft voice broke into her thoughts, "it's evening, so do put your work away."

"This doublet must be finished, Mother. It's needed in this bitter December weather."

"I know, but you've been sewing for hours. Tomorrow's another day."

Attaching her needle to the thick padding, a sigh quivered from Lily. "Another day with a repetition of the confused news we've heard for days, with both sides claiming the victory at Edgehill! Essex and his forces still have His Majesty's troops bottled up at Oxford, cut off from London!"

Lady Deveraux's dark eyes darted anxiously, and she bit her lip. The telltale signs of barely controlled distress alerted Lily. Over the past few weeks her mother had started to dissemble under the war strain. Lily forced a cheerful tone. "Oh, well, perhaps tomorrow we'll hear that the peace negotiations are being successful." She kissed her mother's cheek.

"Darling, you are such a help to me."

As Angela brightened, Lily stretched her shoulders backward to ease the ache of them and called to Joseph, "Come, my sweetheart, it's your bedtime."

"You put me to bed, Mama," he begged, throwing his strong little arms about her neck. "And tell me a story."

"All right," she laughed. Her child gave a balance to her life, which since James's death had become loveless, austere. As she carried him off, she covered his laughing face with kisses. "My dearest little heart," she whispered to the boy, who smiled up at her with eyes so like Adam's.

She supervised Joseph's supper, tucked him into bed, then sang his favorite lullabies. He was blissfully asleep when, as was her custom, she joined David on the outer walls to check the night watch. Standing beside David as her eyes searched the countryside, the rain seemed like God's tears splashing her face, the wind like devils' fingers invading her cloak.

"I hate the darkness, David. All of Essex's twenty thousand men could be out there and we wouldn't see them."

"No, but we'd hear them! On such a night I suppose I'm lucky not to be under canvas." The bitter ring in his voice worried Lily. "Still I wish I could ride in Prince Rupert's cavalry."

David's clubfoot had been a trial to him ever since Lily could recall. "Breck is small but important. If the enemy take us, they get our valuable coal mines! Don't be impatient, I'm sure you'll have the chance to fight . . . right here on these very walls."

"I've a feeling the war will end before we ever fire a shot."

"I'm sure you're wrong! We must keep our men in training. They're still hopelessly clumsy in handling the muskets."

"It's not easy to turn rough rural fellows into good shots." He led her to the tower entrance. "Let's go inside or you'll be soaked."

The following morning drovers from the south brought letters, one from Rhys in Oxford, where he was serving with Charles. He told how Essex kept the royalists bottled up and cut off from London. There was also a letter from Roger. After the usual amorous beginning Lily read:

> I am not always working from the safety of London, now completely in our hands. I am happy to say that I also take an active part in Parliamentary military affairs. It has become my special charge to discover the whereabouts of papist chapels and, whenever possible, away from Royalist forces, to organize their complete destruction.
>
> It will be my immense pleasure to go to Ben Fras in Milford Haven, the family seat of that scoundrel Clune. I shall feel I am avenging some of the wrongs done you when I leave not a stone upon a stone! I shall take a large force with me and. . . .

Shock, terror and fury engulfed Lily. Ben Fras would be destroyed! The centuries-old chapel would be razed to the ground. And what of Father Morgan's Jesuit college?

Racing from her chamber, she fled in search of David. Lifting her skirts so they would not trip her, she ran up the stone steps to the battlements. "David! David!" she called as she rushed through the tower archway.

He came swiftly to her. "Whatever is the matter?"

"This letter from Roger. He's going to burn Ben Fras . . . and all the Catholic chapels." She waved the letter at him.

He grabbed it and read the dreadful information. "We must contact Father Morgan at once. I'll get a man ready to ride."

"And I'm going to Ben Fras to warn the countess! If she's given time she might be able to raise enough support in the district to save the place."

Against David's argument that a groom should go instead of herself, Lily was adamant. She would ride faster than she would trust someone else to travel. They chose a villager to accompany her and, in man's riding attire and well armed, she left Breck for Ben Fras, desperately hoping to arrive in time.

⌘ 23 ⌘

LIKE THE BREATH of unseen demons, an early morning fog hung over Milford Haven when, after two days of hard travel, Lily and her companion set their horses to climb the hill hiding Ben Fras and the sea from view. Terrified that Roger might have preceded her and she would find Ben Fras gutted, Lily reached the summit and looked down on gray mystery. Nothing was distinguishable—not Ben Fras nor even the sea; its pounding alone told her it was there.

The horses groped their way in what Lily prayed was the right direction. Within minutes a dark hulk with diffused light took shape. Ben Fras still stood. In the damp silence, as the horses' hooves rang out, a voice challenged, "Who goes there?"

"Friends! Not foes!" Lily cried. "God bless King Charles!"

"Amen!" came the reply as they rode up to huge wrought-iron gates in the high stone walls. Peering through the grillwork, an armed man scrutinized them.

"I am Lady Lily Deveraux. Take me to the countess. I bring important news."

"My orders are to admit no strangers."

"Go at once!" Lily ordered imperiously. "Announce that Lady Lily Deveraux is here!"

From the courtyard shrouded in fog came a man's sharp command. "Open for Lady Lily!"

Adam! The blood pounded through Lily. Not for one moment had she imagined he would be here. As she rode into the courtyard, he came striding toward her, smiling.

"What brings you here?" His strong hands lifted her, trembling, from the saddle. Her feet touched flagstones, but still the wonderful hands held her, sending tendrils of warmth all through her. He wore no cravat, and his shirt top was open. The jade god she had given him, heavily mounted in gold, hung from a stout gold chain around his neck.

"Roger!" she cried. "He wrote me that he's coming with a troop to destroy Ben Fras!"

Adam let go of her. "We've only a couple of men left here! You're soaked from the fog. Come." Catching her elbow, he hurried her into the house and into the chamber where four years ago she had met his mother. She sank exhausted into a chair, her unbelieving eyes on Adam.

Taking a decanter from a cupboard, he filled a glass. When a woman servant appeared, he said, "Ask my mother to please come here at once."

As the woman left, Adam handed Lily some wine. "Every man except two old retainers is with my father and the king. The *Fearless* arrived yesterday to offload arms. That's why I'm here."

"The *Fearless!* I didn't know . . ." To see the ship again would warm her heart. "The fog hid the sea from me."

"Yes, Salter's out there." He nodded toward the hidden sea. "But with only a skeleton crew. Not enough to repulse the size troop Huet will bring."

"What about the castle on top of the hill? It's royalist. Couldn't you get help there?"

He shook his head. "You recall my father is governor of the castle, but he only left a handful of men to protect the place. We can hope for no help from there, and if the castle is taken, that means the rebels can fire on *Fearless* whenever I bring men or arms in here."

At that moment the door flew open and the countess walked in. Lily sprang from her chair as the woman came toward her with an approving smile and outstretched hands. "Lily, I've just heard that you were here. Welcome!"

Lily curtsied, then took the outstretched hands that warmly clasped hers. Sadness fought happiness at being together with Adam and his mother. She prayed she would be spared seeing Adam's wife.

"Lily's brought bad news, Mother," Adam said. "Roger Huet's bringing a troop to destroy Ben Fras."

"Merciful God, help us!" The countess's tall figure swayed, then straightened up. "The women and I have managed to repulse two small raiding parties, but they were nothing compared with organized troops."

"We'll take a couple of men off *Fearless,* and we've plenty of ammunition." Adam's long legs continued to pace the floor as he made his plans. "We'll post someone at every window, if we have enough people. Most of the women have learned how to be useful with a pistol. Thankfully the house is stone, so Huet cannot fire it. He'll not take it unless he brings cannon against it, and for such a mission as this, the Parliamentary forces couldn't afford it."

"We've still enough wine and corn left to withstand a long siege," the countess said, her anxious eyes on Adam.

"Splendid, Mother, splendid!" Adam's eloquent hands waved in approval. "Thanks to Lily's warning, Huet has lost the advantage of surprise."

"Roger wrote that he has a special assignment from Parliament to destroy all the known Catholic chapels," Lily said. "He's longing to wreck the lovely Severn chapel."

Adam's mother threw a frantic look at him. Frowning, he said, "This is all part of Huet's personal hatred of me. We'll hold him off for so long that his food and ammunition will give out." He stopped pacing and confronted Lily. "When was this letter written?"

"Two weeks ago. The drovers took a circuitous route to Breck. I left for Ben Fras the hour the letter came." The gratitude in the wonderful blue eyes was her reward for everything.

"That means that if Huet left London soon after he wrote, he could be turning up here anytime now. We must prepare at once! I'll send word to Salter immediately to start offloading the arms; then we'll summon the women, assign windows to everyone and distribute pistols and powder." He was striding toward the door when suddenly he spun around. "Lily, this sounds inhospitable," a grin lit his serious face, "but shouldn't you be leaving? You wouldn't want to run into Huet on your way out. His questions might prove difficult to answer."

Across the room their eyes met and spoke for their hearts. "Thank you, Adam, but if you've a couple of vacant windows, my escort will occupy one and I the other." Her smile was tremulous. "Don't worry about pistols; we've brought our own."

The warmth of his look wiped away the war, dissension, Jane and long separations, and Lily was sure she was the woman he loved. "Very good," he muttered, and strode out.

"Lily, how marvelous of you to have come!" There was a catch in the countess's rich voice. "Now even more so of you to stay. Come, I shall show you your window."

Together they climbed the stone stairway. Despite the urgent occasion Lily reveled in the chance to see more of Adam's home. They hurried down a narrow corridor, passing several doors.

Pointing to one, the countess said, "Jane's in there. She's not well." The beautiful, dignified face was grave. "She's confined to bed. Huet's attack will be hard on her."

What should she say, Lily asked herself. That she was sorry? Was the illness serious? She could find no words and with shaky legs hurried on until the countess opened a door, saying, "Go in, Lily. This room is a strategic spot from which to protect Ben Fras."

The large chamber had two windows. Its walls were lined with tightly packed bookshelves. The furniture consisted of leather chairs, a four-poster bed, and a *prie-dieu*. Above the fireplace marks showed where a painting had been removed. On the mantel Lily was sure she recognized Adam's pipes.

"This was Adam's bedchamber," his mother confirmed. "We've hidden the paintings and any treasure, in case we're ever seized. The room has been so long unused it's cold and damp. I'll have a fire kindled at once."

Lily walked toward a window, thinking that as a boy, Adam had occupied this chamber, as a young man from Oxford, as a mature man from Capri—after sailing with her. Had he thought often of her in here? Her eyes tried to penetrate the fog enshrouding the hillside. "Is that one of the best routes down to Ben Fras?" she asked.

The countess joined her at the window. "Unless you scale down the rocky cliffs, it's the only way but for the underground passage connecting us with the castle. The earl of Severn who built Ben Fras centuries ago was wise. The house is in a bowl surrounded by hills that protect us from wind and are far enough away so that stones rolled down from the top can't touch us. The front of the house commands a view of the sea, and the back, the hillside."

"Not in this fog! A troop of men could be descending and hiding out there and we wouldn't know it."

"Yes, such a heavy fog is an ally to Huet." The countess pointed to several small panes in the leaded-glass windows. "They open for firing through. If you see a grain of earth stir, pull that cord hanging beside the bed. The bell will alert the entire house. Now I must go. I'll send you some hot food. In God's name, watch the hill!"

Lily arranged a chair at the window so she could watch without being a target. Staring at the drifting mist, it seemed fantastic that she was in Ben Fras with Adam. But her excitement was chilled as she reminded herself that his wife was also here. A young serving girl brought hot broth, then kindled a fire. Hours passed, and no one else came. She heard sounds of hurrying feet, of voices and footsteps in the courtyard as last-minute preparations were made.

Lily stared outside, never taking her eyes from the slowly clearing mist, but fatigue, held at bay for so long, was gaining in insistence. Her body and legs ached because of hours in the saddle. Her eyes burned. Leaning back in the chair, she fell asleep.

Heavy firing woke her. What was happening? Fog still claimed the base of the hill, but on the summit it had cleared. From her position she could clearly see the castle.

The bedroom door opened and Adam strode in. "Huet's here! He's attacking the castle!" They stared up at the ancient mass of masonry.

"Are you sure it's Roger?"

The big guns barked again, and when the noise died

away, Adam muttered, "It's Roger, all right. Raiding parties don't have big guns! Damn my blood! I didn't think he'd be able to bring such weapons!"

There was an answering fire from the castle's two cannons, but it seemed pitifully weak. "If Roger takes the castle, Adam, he'll make short work of Ben Fras with those guns."

"No, thankfully we're out of range. He'd have to dismantle the guns and bring them down the hill. That's why he's attacking the castle before Ben Fras. He doesn't want them shooting down on him while he's trying to storm us. We can pick his men off. There's not much cover for them. But in his present position he can turn his guns on the *Fearless*. I must send word to Salter to stand well out to sea!"

As he left the chamber, the big guns boomed again. Would they force a breach in the castle's fortifications? An audacious thought suddenly occurred to Lily. Supposing she went to Roger and implored him not to touch Ben Fras? Would he desist for her sake? It was impossible that her plan would succeed. She was demented! Even if Roger wished to please her, he could not turn back before the troop he commanded. Peering through the drifts of fog, Lily's heart seemed to stop beating. Was it only frightened imagination or was that movement out there? Yes! Men were clambering down the hill—many of them—crouching over like beasts, hoping to escape detection.

She flew to the bell rope. Seconds later a hollow clanging echoed through the great house, followed by the sound of running feet. Lily sped back to the window. On the hillside men were creeping away, taking cover behind bracken.

The countess raced into the room, calling, "Well done, Lily. We've seen them now!" She rushed to the second window.

Lily opened a tiny pane in her window and balanced her shaky hand, holding the pistol on the leaded frame as icy air drifted inside.

The countess muttered, "The brutes must come close

to the house to fire, which will make them good targets." Her wonderfully calm voice helped steady Lily. "Watch the top of the wall. They'll try to climb over it and drop into the courtyard. They'll never force the gates. Adam is defending them!"

The big guns boomed again against the castle, and this time the answering fire was slower in coming. Had Roger forced a breach? Was the castle's defense already crumbling?

"They're moving again on the hill," the countess warned. "I've spotted them behind those bushes—just in line with these windows, and—"

She broke off as two men in Parliamentary gray-green darted from the bracken and, bending over, raced for the walls. Lily's hand shook so much she could barely aim. The men straightened up and began running at full height. They evidently believed that they were still unobserved. They were so close Lily could almost tell the nature of their faces. They were at the wall, scaling it; they were on top.

Lily pulled the trigger. A flash—a scream—a body fell to the ground. Seconds later the countess fired and the other man dropped. Now men were running from all parts of the hill, pouring toward the house as pistols cracked from many windows.

Lily had reloaded quickly. She aimed and shot again, and another man went out of action. The fight was taking on a macabre rhythm. A man ran, she aimed, he climbed, she fired, he fell. She reloaded, another man ran into her range of wall and the performance was repeated. It went on and on while on the hilltop Roger's guns were booming almost continuously, and with ever greater intervals the castle guns answered.

But, her spirit rising with elation, Lily felt that if things continued like this they could pick off all of Roger's men with no harm done to the great house. Again and again Ben Fras defenders brought down the enemy.

"We'll beat the devils!" the countess muttered as she brought down a man.

"What's happening at the castle?" Lily cried in terror. "There's been no firing for so long."

"Perhaps a sallying-out party has destroyed those awful cannons! Or—God forbid—the enemy has the castle!"

The short winter day was fading. Darkness would be another enemy to Ben Fras. Under its protection the Parliamentarians would have a good chance to gain the walls. Roger's musketeers were advancing, leaving themselves vulnerable, but they were determined to get within firing position of the house. Aiming at a musketeer training on her window, Lily missed, and his fire shattered the window. Flying glass cut her hands as the shot hit the floor beside her.

Peering from the side of the window, Lily fired again, and seconds later the man was sprawling on the earth. On and on the hellish pattern went, while more and more Parliamentarians kept coming.

Then a wild-eyed serving girl burst into the chamber screaming, "The castle has surrendered! We've been betrayed! The enemy is pouring into the connecting passage!"

"Come with me, Lily," the countess cried, running into the corridor. Racing down the stone stairs, they heard the clatter of many boots on stone, then a wild hammering on wood.

"They are trying to force the connecting door," the countess panted. "It leads into the chapel."

Bursting into the chapel, Lily's terrified eyes fastened on two elderly retainers and Adam with the strength of a creature possessed dragging a huge closet up to the oak doors. Sweat poured down Adam's face and soaked his blouse as, with a final heave, he got the closet into position to barricade the doors, which were shaking now from the violent hammering of the enemy's musket butts.

"Open up, in Parliament's name!" The angry voice was Roger's.

"The pews! Drag them up to support the closet!" Adam commanded one of the retainers, his mother

THE TEMPEST LILY

and Lily, as with a giant's power he lifted a pew and carried it toward the barricade.

With all her strength Lily helped pull at a heavy wooden bench while the pounding grew heavier. "Adam, shall I bring the women defending the windows to help here?" the countess cried excitedly.

"No, they must continue to protect the walls!"

For desperate, agonizing minutes they struggled savagely to strengthen their defenses while the pounding of musket butts intensified and the heavy wooden door began to crack.

"The doors won't hold!" the countess groaned.

Roger shouted, "Open, in Parliament's name!"

The heaped-up furniture was slowly shifting as the double doors began to separate. "The swine are coming in!" Adam muttered. "God knows how they'll treat women." He grabbed his mother and Lily. "Hide down in the leper hole! Quick!"

"Let me stay, Adam," Lily begged. "I'll implore Roger to—"

"No!" Savagely Adam pushed her down after his mother, then dropped the heavy grillwork into place, securely hiding them. Then he sprang to the doors.

Crouching in the hole where centuries ago lepers had been permitted to attend mass, Lily and the countess peered through raised grillwork. They could see the altar, the barricade of furniture and Adam, sword in hand, waiting. The elderly retainers, also armed, stood beside him.

What could they do against the overwhelming numbers forcing an entry? Lily agonized. The furniture was shifting more easily now, giving way with the hammering. The doors were parted, soldiers were coming through the narrow aperture, climbing over the barricade. Three of them were in the chapel.

Adam stood to the side, both hands grasping his raised sword. As the men scrambled in, he brought the sword down on their necks like a hatchet. Horrible! He almost decapitated the men. Drenched in their spurting blood, he straightened up, his sword ready for the next figures jumping over the barricade. He was like a frightful spirit from another world as he stood with his great height balanced on legs spread apart, as again and again he struck out. But he was alone! God help him! Lily implored as the two retainers fell victims to musket butts.

"Why don't you remove the barricade, you fools?" Roger's furious voice ordered. "What are you doing in there?"

Roger's advance guard did not answer. They lay at Adam's feet. Seconds later, with a final push, the last of the barricade was shoved aside and Roger, like the God of Wrath, led his men into the chapel.

At first he did not see Adam, who was fighting off three musketeers trying to split his head open with their gun butts. Springing up on the wrecked furniture, Adam wielded his sword and with lightning skill caught one man on the shoulder and put him out of action.

Lily's terrified eyes darted to Roger as he shouted in an ecstatic voice. "Destroy this idolatrous temple! Hack that crucifix to splinters!"

Men jumped to obey, but they were not fast enough to satisfy his hate. With a face distorted with venom, he rushed with raised sword and slashed at the wooden altar. Madly he cleaved at centuries-old carvings of Christ and His Mother.

Lily had to clasp her hand over the countess's mouth as she cried out in furious grief.

"Away with popery and its trappings!" Roger screamed as, in a frenzy of righteousness, he hit out at the tabernacle. "I'm doing God's work! You men smash those windows!"

The soldiers gleefully shattered the ancient stained-glass windows. Then Roger spun around to continue his havoc and his gaze fell on Adam, covered in blood, dead men at his feet as he battled two new assailants.

"Clune!" Roger cried triumphantly. "So you didn't sail with the *Fearless!* I never hoped to take you when I demolished your idolatrous home!"

"You've not . . . done . . . either . . . yet, Huet,"

Adam panted, never taking his eyes from the men he was fencing.

"I'm going to arrest you, Clune, for treason against Parliament!" Roger shouted to soldiers near him. "Arrest that man!"

With drawn swords they rushed at Adam, but he sprang higher upon the furniture wreckage that was piled against a wall. As the four men tried to reach him, with almost magical skill he leaned down and pierced one and then another in the shoulder. But the others were climbing up. Roger was motioning men to help him pull the furniture from beneath Adam's feet. When he lost the advantage of fighting from the small height, he would be overpowered. He scrambled up to the top of the heavy closet.

"How many men must you have to take me, Huet?" Adam scoffed. "Are you still afraid to engage me?"

"I'll subdue you in single combat, Clune, if you'll stop being a coward and come down!"

The furniture was falling level with the ground, and men were pushing the huge closet over despite Adam's sword slashes. It was toppling when Adam sprang to the stone floor before Roger, and seconds later their swords crossed. The soldiers backed away, leaving the antagonists space in which to fight. Stepping over dead men and debris, Adam and Roger circled around each other, swords clashing as they lunged and parried—big men, superb swordsmen, well matched. Lily had seen them fight over Father Lloyd, but then Adam had been fresh and Roger fatigued. Now it was the reverse.

Unexpectedly someone sprang onto Adam's back, legs gripping Adam's hips, hands encircling his throat. Adam staggered momentarily from the man's weight. Then with a swift movement he reached behind him, grabbed his attacker and flung him over his head. He turned back to confront the point of Roger's sword quivering against his chest.

"Move, Clune, and you're a dead man!" Roger muttered. Never taking his eyes from Adam, he shouted at the man who had attacked without orders. "Fool!

Idiot! You robbed me of the chance that for years I've been waiting for! I didn't need help."

"Don't berate the fellow," Adam half-chuckled. "You owe him your life."

Roger's thin lips curled. "I'll trouble you for your sword, Clune."

Lily's arms held the countess or she would have collapsed as, still grinning, Adam handed Roger his sword.

"I arrest you, Lord Clune," Roger snapped, "in Parliament's name!"

"I don't recognize them as an authority, but what are the charges?"

"Of aiding the queen in her escape, when she also took her jewels with her—all against the interests of Parliament and the people."

"A most complimentary charge, but I'll wager you'll never prove it!"

"Keep your bragging to impress the crowds who'll watch you dance the rope at Tyburn." Roger glanced at his soldiers. "Secure the prisoner."

Diffidently they approached Adam, who was still held at sword point, and grasped his arms. Lily called on all her wisdom to stop herself from rushing out and beseeching Roger for mercy. But she knew too well the folly of that. Later, when Roger's fury had cooled, she would go to London and plead with him.

Men were rushing in from the house side of the chapel, calling triumphantly, "The building is entirely ours!" An officer approached Roger. "Only women defending, and they've fled to the hills, sir."

"Good. Remember I want no looting!"

"There's nothing left worth carrying off. The royalist scum have already removed it all."

"Make haste and set fire to everything that will burn, then meet us on the hilltop. We ride at once for London."

The officer and his men hurried back to the house, and Roger signaled for Adam to be marched out.

As Adam turned to leave, his gaze flew for a second to the leper hole and his hand felt for the Indian god around his neck. Then his eyes with a flash of agony surveyed the havoc of the ruined chapel. "You've done a thorough job of vandalism, Huet. Seven centuries of piety, love and exquisite taste destroyed in one barbaric hour. God have mercy on England if men like you ever come to power." He turned and strode from the chapel.

The Parliamentarians marched after him. Roger was the last to leave. As his pale eyes glanced over the wreckage, he slowly smiled. Lily shuddered. His venomous triumph was the worst part of that tragic day.

Lily and the countess listened to the footsteps fading away as the smell of smoke drifted to them. "They've gone," Lily murmured. "If the horses are still here, we can leave at once for Breck."

"First we must see if Jane has fled with the women."

They needed all their strength to lift the grillwork off the leper hole. Then they stood listening. Nothing but a crackling sounded as furniture and woodwork went up in flames. The house, being stone, would not suffer too much damage.

Rushing past burning doors, they reached Jane's room. The bed was in flames. "Mother of God!" the countess screamed.

"They didn't want to kill women!" Lily reminded her. "Jane must have fled with the servants." They were racing from the room when moans stopped them. "She must be hiding here," Lily said.

"Jane! Jane!" the countess cried, and an answering moan came from Adam's wife, who was lying beneath the burning bed. They dragged her clear of danger, and to Lily's dismay she saw that Jane was with child.

"I was hiding," Jane murmured, "under the bed when they set fire to it, then I fainted."

Grabbing a blanket that had not yet caught fire, Lily threw it over Jane's shift. Then she and the countess half-carried Jane to the stables. Fortunately the horses were still there.

"She has already lost one child," the countess told Lily. "God knows what will happen after this shock."

Through days of fog, rain and bitter cold, they rode only as long as Jane could endure. At night, in taverns, while Jane slept, Lily did all she could to comfort Adam's mother, assuring her that there must be a way of freeing him. An idea, horrible but perhaps practical, took shape in Lily's mind. Added to her agonizing over Adam, it was a cruel torture for her to be obliged to care for Jane, who carried Adam's legitimate child. She was glad when at last they reached Breck village.

"It is I—Lady Lily," she called to the scouts she knew would be hidden close by. They rode up to the castle, and as the gates swung open, David and Lucrezia, followed by other servants, ran to help the travelers dismount.

"What's happened?" David questioned, his worried eyes on the rain-soaked women.

"Roger sacked Ben Fras!" Lily murmured. "Carry Lady Clune to my chamber. She's ill."

As David and a servant lifted Jane from her horse and carried her upstairs, Lily took the countess to an apartment adjoining her own, then sent a serving woman for dry garments and wine. Then, certain that the countess was being cared for, she hurried to Jane.

Lying inert on the bed as Lucrezia undressed her, Jane seemed incapable of movement, as though her last strength had gone in the effort of reaching Breck. Her face was an unearthly color, her eyelids bluish. Was she going to die? God! Stop me thinking about it! Lily silently prayed, but she could not control her thoughts. If Jane died, Adam would be free! Free to . . . No! Such ideas were almost murderous. As Lily stepped out of her sodden clothes and pulled on dry garments, she glanced at Lucrezia, who was stripping Jane's swollen body, and jealousy consumed Lily. This pale, bloodless-looking woman was no mate for a man like Adam. Her tiny breasts would not fill his wonderful hands—not like her own breasts. Jane's weak thighs could not support— Enough!

"Give her mulled wine," she whispered to Lucrezia as she helped pull the bedclothes over Jane. Lucrezia nodded, and the glitter of her eyes told Lily that the Capriote's mind had been in tune with her own.

Going into the adjoining chamber, Lily found that the countess had changed her clothes and was pacing the floor. She had evidently permitted her agitation some rein while she was alone, but at the sight of Lily, with habitual strength, she assumed a measure of calm.

"Your ladyship, ever since the tragedy of Ben Fras, I've been planning a way to save Adam."

"How? A twenty-thousand-pound bribe would not open the Tower gates for Strafford!" The countess's spirits seemed suddenly to drain away. "In any case, we couldn't raise a huge amount to offer for Adam."

"No, but we can offer me," Lily said softly, staring into the countess's amazed face. "I'll explain. Roger Huet has been in love with me for years—obsessed with the desire to marry me. I don't know whether his hatred for Adam can be overcome with the bribe of having me for a wife, but I think perhaps it might. Anyhow, I'm going to London to barter for Adam's life."

"Pray God you are successful! Do you really love Adam so much that you would marry that zealot, become part of the Puritan camp for his sake, perhaps even risk your life by begging for Adam's?"

"Despite all the awful things that have passed between us, I still feel Adam is part of me," Lily said softly, "like the dawn, the sunset, wind on a mountain, the sun sparking the water. I can't explain." The tears coursed slowly down her face, and with a shaking hand she brushed them away. "I love those things and all beauty with my senses as I love Adam, but I love him also with my soul. If Adam died, of course my body would go on, but my soul would die with him. I'd marry Huet or even Pym! I'd make almost any sacrifice just to know the world holds Adam, even if my eyes were never to see him again."

"Mama, you're home!" Joseph called as he toddled across the chamber, and Lily rushed to clasp him in her arms.

"Oh, my darling, darling. Yes, I'm home." Momentarily she had forgotten the countess and, looking up, after half-smothering Joseph in kisses, she saw the astonishment in the woman's face.

"I didn't know you had a child," she murmured, almost in awe, as her eyes became riveted on the boy.

Paralyzing emotion silenced Lily as Joseph's grandmother gazed at eyes blue as her son's and red-gold hair so like his. Then Lily recovered enough to murmur, "Yes, this is my son Joseph."

She dared to look into the countess's face. No need to wonder if Adam's mother had guessed the truth. The expression of fierce love lighting her face convinced Lily that she had.

"May I hold Joseph?" She held out her arms.

With a feeling of relief, as of reaching shore after a battering voyage, Lily placed her son in his grandmother's arms.

"Nice lady." Joseph smiled and touched the countess's cheek with his fingers. Her eyes were bright with pride as she possessively hugged his fat little body.

"Care for him," Lily said chokingly. "My mother is already badly affected by the war, and worse times may be ahead. If I succeed with Huet I may not return for a while and—"

"My dearest girl, I shall always care for Joseph as if he were Adam's child," the countess said softly. Looking into each other's moist eyes, the women silently told each other much that they needed to know.

24

To avoid Parliamentary forces Lily's coach followed a little-used route over rutted country roads, which inevitably lost time. Her apprehension was fraying her nerves, and again and again she told Lucrezia in agony, "I hope I'm not too late to save him!"

When they reached London, a sentry at Hyde Park Gate inquired why they had come. Lily's answer—that she was visiting Roger Huet—secured immediate entry. Not waiting to go to an inn to change from her travel-stained garments, she freshened up in the coach and went directly to Roger's chambers at Westminster.

Progress was slow. Because of a rumor that the royal forces were advancing from Colnbrook, chains had been spread across narrow streets to stop a possible rush from Prince Rupert's cavalry.

Out of a multitude of plans she had torturously reviewed and discarded of how mentally to seduce Roger, Lily had eventually settled on one. Now as the coach stopped at his door, she prayed it would be successful. A much-impressed clerk ushered her into Roger's book-lined study. Roger's body seemed incapable of movement as he stood staring at her in surprise. Then he rushed to her with outstretched arms. "Lily! You! What unbelievable happiness!"

Forcing herself not to think about the brute he had been at Ben Fras, she allowed him to embrace her and controlled a shiver as he kissed her. Lily willed herself to return his kisses. Let them stupefy his reason. At the excited thump of his heart, at his trembling hands, she became nervous. That too she pushed out of her mind, realizing his excitement was the first step toward gaining what she wanted.

Drawing her head back, Lily smiled up at his face that a few minutes ago had been so disciplined but which now radiated desire.

"How wonderful that you're here, Lily. What brings you in these distracted times? At the moment we're a bit upset, downcast because things are not going too well for us. But Charles will soon grow short of ammunition, and we'll achieve our goal. But about you—why are you here?"

She gently disengaged herself from Roger's arms and went to sit on a straight-backed chair. "I was tired of being at Breck, but actually I came for two other reasons." She assumed a demure diffidence she knew he would appreciate. "The most important one was to see you. I'm so proud of your political success, and from your letters I've realized how you've also developed in spiritual strength."

"My dear Lily, I'm unworthy of this." His words and the deprecatory gesture of his hands did not disguise his pleasure.

Encouraged that her plan to flatter him had been wise, Lily continued. "It's true, and I longed to see you—to tell you so. I suppose you're also filled with a great pity for mankind."

"Ah, anyone who struggles to follow in the Master's footsteps must acquire a measure of pity."

"Exactly. That brings me to the second reason for my visit." She dug her fingers into the chair and plunged ahead. "I've heard of Adam Clune's arrest. I want your help in freeing him."

The words seemed to hang in the air interminably as Roger stared unbelievingly at her. Lily held her breath. Suddenly he started laughing, loudly and heartily for him, but a terrible sound that seemed to clutch and

THE TEMPEST LILY

twist her vitals. "Yes, I suppose it does seem a strange request," she managed to say quite normally, "and a surprise to you that I'd help a man I despise."

"That's one thing," his laughter began to die down, "that seems so extraordinary. And then, after all my work to bring Clune to justice, well . . ." Roger shrugged, "the idea of freeing him is really too absurd!" Puzzled admiration was growing in his pale eyes. "How merciful of you to want to help this beast who dared place a price on your head. Only in heaven's name *why* do you wish to?"

"Silly, it's not I who wish it." She busied herself taking off her silk gloves. She dare not let him see her face. "I don't care if Clune rots in Newgate!" Her voice was convincingly disdainful. "It's simply that years ago Clune's mother rendered my mother a vital service, and now she has appealed to Mother to beg you for mercy. You see how widespread your fame is?" She stared at him with admiring eyes. "Geraldius says you possess one of England's most brilliant legal minds."

"That's praise indeed from Geraldius." He leaned over her chair. "But all the success and fame mean little if I don't have you to share them with me. Oh, Lily, tell me you've come to London to be my wife!"

She smiled mysteriously. "You know what my feelings are for you—how nearly we were married once. Yet before we can talk of ourselves, I must keep my promise to Mother about trying to help Clune. Tell me, what is he charged with?"

Roger's face tightened with annoyance. "He is charged with being a professed papist, with transporting arms from Holland to England to use against Parliament, also of aiding the queen to escape with her jewels. For these acts of treason against the people, he will hang!"

Lowering her eyes in case Roger read the agony in them, Lily said, "The countess of Severn swears those are trumped-up charges."

"The mother of even such an Antichrist as Clune would lie for her son. I'm amazed *your* mother would try to aid a man who victimized you. I delight in bringing Clune to Tyburn, if for no other reason than his ill treatment of you on board his ship."

"As a true Christian, I bear him no malice . . . nor does Mother." Lily rose on trembling legs, elaborately shaking out her wide skirts. "And that's how *you* should feel, Roger. You've done your duty in destroying the chapel at Ben Fras. But what will be accomplished in taking Clune's life?" She forced a stiff little laugh. "Surely I wasn't wrong when I promised Mother that you would free Clune?"

"How could you promise such a thing, Lily?" His voice was coldly furious.

"But, Roger," she stared up at him in feminine surprise, "naturally I surmised that because of your love for me you would do a little thing to please me!" She started pulling on her gloves.

"A little thing! To free a man I've hated for years! A man accused of treason?"

"Wrongfully accused, or so his mother swears." She was losing. She must make one last attempt. "Forgive me." She started moving toward the door. "Perhaps in seeking your aid to free Clune, I've embarrassed you by asking you to do something beyond your power. Undoubtedly I must go to see a man who can—"

In a stride he was beside her. "It is within my power!" he said pridefully. "I will not let you go to anyone else!" Roger grasped her shoulders, his fingers digging into the flesh. "I have as much power in London as anyone but Pym!" His eyes narrowed suspiciously. "Is it possible that you were going to Pym?" He spoke slowly. "Do you know him that well?"

With a shaking hand Lily played with the edge of his white ruff, looking up from under her long lashes. "Roger, don't be jealous. If you refuse to help me, why do you care if I go to—others who will?"

"I do care! And if I wished, I could free Clune tonight!"

"Then why don't you?" She moved so that her body touched his, but not blatantly so as to scandalize his sense of propriety, just enough to inflame desire. "Forget your old hatred of Clune. Arrange his release so our thoughts can be free for ourselves."

His arms crushed her to him. "Oh Lily, when your green eyes look at me like that, God pity me, but I'd do anything for you, even against my better judgment."

Merciful God, thank you, she prayed. "Clune's mother promises he will leave the country forever—go to the New World."

"I shall not let the swine go unpunished!" In his anger Roger let go of Lily. "I shall have him tied by his wrists to the back of a cart and dragged through the streets!" His eyes became brilliant as he delighted in his plan. "That's it! And he shall receive a lash for every bead of his accursed rosary."

Fifty-nine lashes, dragged behind a cart. Enough to kill a lesser man than Adam, but he would not hang! "That sounds like a punishment Clune will never forget," she murmured.

"Indeed he will not! And afterward you and I will visit him together so he'll know that it is at his victim's hands that he has received mercy! What a lesson!"

Joy and relief flooded Lily. Adam was to live! She would see him again! "Roger, you are so clever."

"I can think of nothing except that at last you will be my wife!" Catching her in his arms, he stared possessively at her. "Lily Huet." He murmured the name like a prayer. "You don't know how I've longed for that name to become real."

"It soon will be," she said softly, squirming in his encircling arms. She must get away or she would collapse. The fight for Adam's life, the relief of victory, had drained her strength. The horror of the future as Roger's wife she dared not envision.

Though aching for a glimpse of Adam, Lily knew she could not witness his suffering; she might be mad enough to implore his torturers to spare him. So she sent Lucrezia, who, pale-cheeked, returned to report that a crowd intoning biblical admonitions had followed

Adam from Newgate Prison to Tyburn and back again. His magnificent physique had stood up well to the dragging over the cobbled streets and to the lashings.

Hoping to escape the criticism of his fellow Puritans in freeing Adam, Roger had decided to go to Newgate by night. Now, as Lily sat in his coach traveling through the empty streets, mysterious in the January fog, she shivered with excitement.

Beside her, Roger was happily anticipating their future. "While the war lasts we'll have to live in London, much as I hate the evil place. But when Parliament has won its holy fight, we'll join my mother at my place in Sussex. You hardly know Mother, but with time you will grow to admire and respect her."

"I'm sure of it, Roger," Lily murmured, recalling how the thin Lady Huet had seemed to bring a movement of cold air with her whenever she entered a room.

"Mother has had numerous conversions resulting from her prayer meetings." There was pride in Roger's clipped tones. "She will instruct you, and you'll learn to aid her in the holy work."

"I shall be glad to," Lily answered mechanically. Her eyes strained through the fog. That great bulk of masonry looming ahead must be Newgate Prison. The horses trotted beside the massive walls inset with barred windows.

The coach stopped at the great gates, and Lily, longing to dash out, was obliged to let Roger courteously help her down and guide her over the cobbles as the outrunner held a flaming brand to light their way. At the grille in the gates, Roger called, "Open for Sir Roger Huet!"

A guard shone a lantern in their faces, examined Roger's papers; then a door in the great gates opened and they stepped into the prison yard.

"Take me to the governor," Roger commanded. Bowing, the guard led the way to Newgate's main building.

Her legs seemingly turned to water, Lily walked down a dimly lit stone corridor reeking with the stench of unwashed humanity. They passed an open cell where a practically naked man lay spread-eagled on the floor, his hands and feet tied down. A board on his chest held great iron weights.

"That's a highwayman," the guard explained. "There's a weight of three hundred and fifty pounds on his chest. Instead of hanging, he chose to be pressed. If he survives, he goes free." The guard laughed. "What man survives pressing?"

Lily avoided looking into the other open cells they passed. It was hellish enough to hear the agony of men being crushed to death.

Reaching the governor's chambers, the guard announced, "Sir Roger Huet." The governor left a table covered by papers, lit by a tall candelabra and came to Roger with hand outstretched.

Roger addressed him in tones inaudible to Lily, but the governor nodded energetically, returned to the table, wrote a hasty note and handed it to the guard, who left at once.

It all seemed so easy. Or was Roger tricking her? Instead of Adam's release, had Roger ordered his execution? Agonizing suspicions flashed through her mind. Roger indicated that she should sit on a wooden bench. While Roger and the governor conversed in low tones, she fastened her gaze on a trickle of moisture seeping down the wall. When the drip reached the adjoining stone, perhaps Adam would come. But the trickle had passed over half the wall before she heard footsteps in the stone corridor: the confident steps of the guard, then a half-dragging step. That surely could never be Adam's virile stride. But an Adam who had been lashed and dragged over cobbles might shuffle now. There was the guard, and now an enormous man behind him!

Unseen by Adam, Lily sat with fingers digging into the wooden bench from her place in the shadows. She must not cry out because Adam's cheek had been severely lashed, nor because his crumpled clothes were dark with dried blood. Adam was alive despite everything, and the blue eyes glittered with scorn as they stared at Roger standing stiffly before him.

"To meet you again, Huet, is a pleasure I had not allowed myself to hope for." The rich voice was dangerously sarcastic for being directed at a captor. "Do you intend personally to put the noose around my neck, or have you devised some other pleasant little form of suffering for me? Yesterday's affair was quite novel. I trust you enjoyed it?"

"The sight of you at no time brings me enjoyment, Clune!" Roger answered furiously. "It offends me in every way. But to fulfill a promise I have given my betrothed, I am here to free you."

"Free! What new deviltry is this, Huet?"

"You are free of the hangman's noose, but you will be banished from England!"

Adam's whole demeanor seemed alert with suspicion. "Why should your fiancée bestow such a service upon me?"

"Because of her pure Christian spirit," Roger snapped. "The lady who is extending such mercy on you was once victimized by you." Roger held his hand out to Lily. Placing her icy fingers in his, she left the dark corner and came into the pool of light.

"You!" Adam cried, and swayed toward her. Then he checked himself. "Lady Lily, I am indeed indebted to you." The wonderful blue eyes were amazed, grateful, adoring, and she tried to answer with her eyes.

Her dry throat and her heavy tongue obeyed her. "Because of your mother's old friendship to my mother, I begged Sir Roger to save you. He has generously complied."

Somehow she moved to the door. With Adam and Roger following along the dark corridors, her heart cried out so that Adam *must* feel its message. Not long now, beloved, before you will be free.

Outside the prison gates three of Roger's servants waited with his torchbearer. Roger turned to Adam. "My men will escort you to Blackfriars Wharf, where the frigate *East Wind* is waiting for you. Immediately

THE TEMPEST LILY

upon your boarding she will sail for the colonies. I warn you never again to set foot in England!"

"Your generosity is extraordinary, Huet." Adam smiled slowly. "You've burned and gutted my ancestral seat, made my women homeless, had me publicly flogged like a common thief, and now you banish me from my birthplace." He swept his arm out as though doffing a hat and executed an expansive, mocking bow. "Your hatred of me must finally be satisfied."

Why did he risk his luck like this? Lily could not wait for him to be off. Roger might have a change of heart.

"Play no tricks, Clune!" Roger said with dangerous calm. "My men are well armed, and it would be a pity if they had occasion to run you through after the trouble I've taken to save your worthless life."

"But I'm unarmed, Huet. Have you forgotten how you robbed me of my sword at Ben Fras?" Adam turned and bowed swiftly to Lily. "My deep gratitude to a generous lady. It's foul weather tonight, but three months from now, in heaven, the stars will be gold again." He signaled Roger's men. "Come, my brave bodyguard . . . away!" He moved out of the torchlight into the fog.

He had gone! He was almost free! Lily was flooded with relief as Roger helped her into the coach. In the only way Adam could, he had told her he loved her.

"Clune is truly a scoundrel!" Roger settled beside Lily. "I hope I have not committed an awful error in not hanging him." The coach began to move. "What the deuce did he mean by that last remark? There's absolutely no sense in it. Even at Oxford he affected absurd speech."

Lily suddenly saw the sense in it, and she almost cried out. Adam had been giving her a message. By "heaven," he had surely meant the Heaven Tavern—that in three months he would meet her at the Heaven Tavern. He intended to return to England to carry on his part of the king's fight—to meet her again!

25

LILY HAD BEEN Roger's wife for almost three months. He allowed her as a special concession to keep Lucrezia with her as her serving woman. Joseph, of course, was still at Breck. Not only did Lily suffer at not seeing her child, but being Roger's wife was more horrible than she could ever have imagined. He considered her a chattel and was excessively dictatorial. Due to his religious beliefs he had known no woman before. Now the acquisition of a wife gave his long-frustrated desires unbridled run.

He developed into a strange beast with terrible lusts, which he condoned by twisting biblical phrases to prove a man might do as he wished with his wife. Roger forced her to satisfy his craven needs until she sickened. Each night he made her strip and parade nude in front of him with her waist-long hair falling like a cloak around her, which he reveled in arranging so that her breasts poked through the locks. As she wearily walked up and down the bedchamber, his eyes, glittering like an animal's, moved greedily over her white-skinned body.

My suffering, my degradation bought Adam's freedom, she would silently remind herself. Sometimes, however, she rebelled against the payment she must make. "Roger, I refuse. This is disgusting!" She cried out and reached for her shift.

He dragged it from her hands, shrilling in a half-insane voice, "Oh, no! You will obey me! For years I dreamed of seeing your nakedness. I ached to see your white body. Now I'll stare at you. I'll examine you for as long as I like."

He so nauseated her that sometimes Lily feared she would lose control and kill him. Somehow she must escape from him and return to Breck, but the dreadful days and nights plodded by, and she remained in her misery.

Acute longing for Joseph added to her suffering. She hurt for news of her child. Since her marriage she had received only two letters from Breck, almost incoherent missives written by her mother, which convinced her that Roger in his jealous possessiveness had intercepted her correspondence. Lily often wondered whether her father was satisfied at last that she was tied to the monstrous Huet, but she heard nothing from him. In the afternoon, when she took walks with Lucrezia, she found London sadly changed from what it had been when the king and queen had held court. The brilliantly gowned women and handsome smiling officers were now nothing but shadows cast on the wall of longing memory. And of those who had danced, sung and laughed, some were beheaded, some forgotten in the Tower, the queen homeless, the king fighting, the lively men, like James, moldering to dust, the women shut up as she had been in Breck, waiting to defend their property and lives. Theaters, pleasures and beer gardens were closed. London seemed like a virile man's body being eaten away by a malignant internal growth.

At times, when Lily accompanied Roger to Pym's home, where she was part of the inner circle of powerful Puritans, she occupied herself with the question: If she killed them, would the war terminate? Probably not. Oliver Cromwell, the bright star of the Parliamentary forces, would carry on despite the loss of his London allies.

Lucrezia's sympathetic devotion, the thought of Joseph and the hope that Adam would return to meet her were the only things that made life bearable. As the time grew close for her rendezvous with Adam, Lily told herself that now that she had lost James, she would take what happiness came to her—Adam, be he married or not. At any moment he could die as James had.

On the day she was to meet him, Roger remained at home with a chill. Furious and disappointed, Lily was forced to remain with him and to send Lucrezia in her place.

The Capriote returned with eyes glittering, her mouth curling into smiles. "Lord Clune was there!" she whispered. "He says he will come soon again, and we must watch daily for him."

"He will come again. Thank God!" Lily squeezed Lucrezia's shoulder.

"Yes, my lady. Oh, it was wonderful. Valentine was attending him." Love lit Lucrezia's pretty face, which under Puritan discipline had been forced into an expression of gloom. "He works with his lordship in secret somewhere in London. Oh, my lady," her ecstatic sigh was like music, "is it not good to know that Valentine and Lord—"

She bit off her words as the door flew open and Roger stood in the entrance. It was a habit of his to come in like this, as though he always anticipated surprising people committing some sin.

"Ah! And just what are you two whispering about?"

Lily managed a laugh. "There's nothing to whisper about, Roger." She threw Lucrezia a look to go. Convinced that he could not have overheard the conversation, she turned to a mirror to tidy her hair.

"Your hair is quite perfect, my dear. Now please dress for outdoors. We must visit Pym. He's ill again." Roger went to the closet and pulled out a black corsage and skirt and laid them on a chair.

Lily dutifully began to take off the rose-colored gown she was wearing. Hating his eyes on her as she undressed, she moved swiftly.

THE TEMPEST LILY

"The prolongation of the war is draining Pym's health. Who would have believed Charles could have held out like this?" Roger started walking toward her. "We must pray for the return of Master Pym's good health, Lily. We must pray!"

There were the dreaded signs of lust in his face: the loosening of the tight mouth, the glitter in his eyes as they fastened on the white swelling of her half-exposed breasts.

Not today! She could not tolerate his touch, his body next to her, when the whole of her rebelled at having been denied Adam. "Yes, we must do that." She stepped back from his outstretched hands reaching to grasp her shoulders.

Passion was reddening the whites of his eyes as always. "Why do you try to avoid me?" His voice was shrill. "I am your lawful wedded husband—remember? I shall have you whenever I wish." He grabbed her breasts, making her wince with pain. "You belong to me—you understand? You are my property!" He was ripping her shift off. "I waited all these years for you, and now you are mine!"

He dragged her to the bed and flung Lily on her back. Laughing aloud, he spread-eagled her arms and legs. "Ah, what beauty—what wonderful nakedness, and it is all mine."

She tried to close her legs, to move her arms against her body, but his hands roughly stopped her. "Stay like that. Stay like that. Oh . . . how it excites me."

The next second he tore open his breeches, and, gloating at the size of his manhood, he half-screamed, "Look! Look what I bestow upon you!"

She shut her eyes to blot out his maniacal face, his disgusting body as he flung himself onto her. Lily felt hysteria taking hold of her as he thrust his organ into her and started to gyrate on her body, which was made numb with revulsion. There was a sickening odor from him that increased her disgust when he kissed her mouth, forcing his tongue into it. She endured his puny passion while thinking that he was surely driving her to murder him someday.

For the next few weeks Lily sent Lucrezia daily to the Heaven Tavern for news of Adam. There was none. In her miserable state she grew to believe that her deliverance from Roger would come when the royalist cause was successful.

Her hopes flared when the king's forces defeated the Parliamentarians at Chalgrove Field, slaying the Parliamentarian hero, Hampden, in the battle. Success seemed imminent to her when the besieged city of Bristol surrendered to Prince Rupert. But these royalist victories were swiftly balanced by Oliver Cromwell defeating and killing Cavendish at Gainsborough.

The Puritan party rejoiced with this success, and with renewed belligerence their Roundhead soldiers swept through London, seizing suspected royalists and accusing them of plotting to overthrow Parliament. Many more king's men lost their heads on the block.

This last bloody event shook Lily out of her lethargy. She must do something, if only to quietly foster discontent among the people.

Each day when Roger was at his chambers or in the Commons, she walked around the crowded streets well hooded and cloaked, dropping words of dissatisfaction about the Parliamentarians. Wherever she went, she encountered Puritan fanatics. Claiming divine inspiration, they audaciously preached what they called the word of God; tinkers, tailors, buttonmakers, laundresses and dairymaids publicly rebuked each other for negligence in observing God's laws. After the self-styled prophets had passed on, many angry citizens whispered about their disappointment that Pym had rejected the king's repeated peace overtures. Others grumbled at heavy taxation imposed by the war and the disturbance to overseas trade.

While Lily worked at her self-imposed task, she continued to send Lucrezia to the Heaven Tavern for news of Adam. Always they met at a certain alley, and always Lucrezia's answer was disappointing. But a day came late in July when one look at the girl's radiant face told Lily that Adam was waiting.

Rushing into the black-and-white half-timbered tavern, her voluminous skirts sweeping over the sawdust floors, Lily's greedy eyes saw a man standing in a discreet corner, wide-brimmed hat pulled far over his face. Adam! No other man had the width of shoulders, such great height. Unexpectedly weak, she stood still as he walked toward her with outstretched arms. Lily put her icy hands in his strong clasp. The wonderful blue eyes were staring down into her shiny eyes.

"Adam . . . oh, Adam!"

"Beloved. At last!"

His gaze swept the entrance hall. They were alone now, but at any second people might enter. "Shall we go up?" he asked, and she nodded. Hurrying toward the narrow stairs, she had the awful feeling that Roger's pale eyes were following her. She glanced back, but at the doorway there was only Lucrezia smiling into Valentine's delighted face.

The room was all scarlet and gold with velvet hangings. They bolted the door. They were alone again. It seemed impossible. Flinging his hat on a chair, he wordlessly crushed her in his arms. His heart thumped against her body, his mouth was warm on hers. She clung to his great shoulders. They were together at last! Was it real that she was in his arms again? Or was it imagination gone wild with longing?

"Lily . . . my love . . . my heart. What can I say to thank you for what you've done for me?"

"Hush." She placed her fingertips on his lips. "You're alive. Nothing else matters."

"But you married that slimy creature to save me. For years you fought against marrying him. You don't have to tell me; I can see by your eyes what hell you're suffering."

"Let's not waste our wonderful moments talking of that. Tell me what you are doing in London. Is it safe? Don't let anything happen to you, for God's sake!"

Adam started taking off her shawl. "Don't worry, I won't fall into Huet's hands again!" He spoke softly but excitedly. "I'm organizing a plot to seize the Tower of London! We've got to bottle up the river traffic and regain control of the city!"

"But if you're discovered! It would mean death without a trial!"

He was plucking the combs from her hair. "Don't worry, sweetheart, the scum won't catch me again." He spread her black hair out over her shoulders. "There . . . how lovely. Now let's forget the war for a while, I'm hungry—thirsty—starving for you!"

With swift fingers he unlaced her bodice. His lips found her breasts, and she clasped his head with its burnished hair against her as her spirit soared with delight. Then he lifted her onto the great four-poster bed. "The skirt, beloved—take it off," he murmured, easing his wide shoulders out of his velvet doublet.

Within minutes they lay on the feather bed, their nude bodies clasped in each other's arms. "Oh, Adam, Adam, is it true?"

"Aye, beloved, we're together again."

His greedy hands played over her body, bringing it back to life again, wiping away the degradation she had endured with Roger. She had almost forgotten the wonderful strength of Adam's magnificent body, the hardness of it.

"Everything is changed now I'm with you," she murmured, her lips against his.

He kissed her wildly, on her eyes, her mouth, her throat, her breasts—all over her burning body, and when he took her, the urgent flame of his lovemaking swept her up into the joy of complete togetherness so that their souls and bodies merged as one being.

So often before, after lovemaking, they had lain together in luxurious lassitude, but today the world intruded. From the streets below came sounds of marching men leaving to join Essex's Parliamentary forces. The sounds cruelly dragged Lily back from her personal heaven, and two questions sprang to her mind. What

THE TEMPEST LILY

had Adam's mother written to him regarding Joseph? Had Jane's baby been born? "Darling, what news have you from Breck? I've had none for months."

"Nor I. I've been in Holland with the queen, helping her raise money in order to buy ammunition and guns."

"However did you get away from the ship Roger put you on?"

"Easily." There was the grin that always made her heart sing. "The *East Wind* was still in the Thames when I managed to jump overboard and swim to a royalist's house by the wharves. London has many king's men; they only lack an organizer."

"Oh, Adam, how much longer will the war drag on?"

"God knows! One of the troubles is that Charles has so few sea routes open to him. And now if Pym succeeds in his Scottish alliance and gets reinforcements of eleven thousand men, it might prove fatal to us. Lovely, lovely Lily. There is a sadness about you that hurts me, even though it enhances your wonderful eyes, your wonderful mouth. You must know that all my happiness comes through you. For me, you are the blue of sea and sky. When you came to help me at Ben Fras—when you made Huet free me—I knew I loved you more than my life."

"But, beloved, we must part again. Oh, Adam, our world has so altered. The things we thought secure have all been swept away. I sometimes wonder if Capri and those golden days ever really happened. Or are they only my make-believe?"

"I know what you mean. But you must not feel like that. While there are stars in the sky, while the sun rises, there is hope. How can I get you out of Huet's clutches? Somehow I've got to."

"Don't even think of it. He has grown so powerful; he's so close to Pym. I must go. If Roger comes home and I'm not there, his suspicions will be aroused."

Adam held her in a grip that hurt. "Tomorrow—will you come tomorrow?"

"Yes. The same time."

For the next two weeks they met daily, and for the stolen hours they had together, they managed to create a cocoon of pleasure that temporarily shut out the world.

Then one day he said, "My love, I'm afraid this will be our last time for a while. I'm going on a mission soon."

"You will be careful?"

"For your sake, I shall. If we do not meet again, is our love not strong enough to continue through time and distance? If I fall in battle, remember my spirit will always be with you, and—"

"Stop! Stop! I can't bear it! Those were James's words. Is it not enough that I have James's heart in a casket! All that is left of the man is like a dried piece of—" Her voice choked.

"Sshh, beloved," Adam soothed her, stroking her hair. "I shall always come back. It's only the good fellows like old Forsyth who go. Devils like me can't be killed."

"Just be sure and send me word somehow that you are alive. That's all I ask."

"I promise I will."

She glanced at the sky. By the light she knew it was late. "I must go soon. If I'm not there when he returns, he will be furious."

"Blast his soul! I can't tolerate the thought that he can take you whenever he wishes!"

"Don't speak of it." She buried her face on his shoulder.

He lifted her head and kissed her savagely. Adam's hands on her body were demanding. His lovemaking became a desperate thing, as though he was trying to absorb, to use all of her so that nothing of her would remain for Huet. Reveling in his embraces. Lily pitied jealousy. She was familiar with its torturings.

Then the depth of their love and their joy in being together brought a blessed forgetfulness that blotted out Roger, Jane, jealousy, war and death.

"My lady! My lady!" Lucrezia was whispering frantically at the door. Lily and Adam sprang up, pulling on their clothes. Then Adam silently unbolted the door, and a terrified Lucrezia slipped in. "Sir Roger is downstairs!" she gasped as Adam rebolted the door.

"Is he looking for me?" Terror clutched Lily.

"No, no, he is with some civilian soldiers. A royalist plot to take the Tower has been discovered."

"It's me they're after!" Adam strode toward the small casement window in the sloping ceiling, and Lily rushed after him. "How can you get away?"

"Over the rooftops. Don't worry. Will you be all right?" She nodded. "Hold them off until I'm gone." Springing onto a chair, Adam started easing his shoulders through the small aperture at the same time that feet could be heard ascending the staircase. "Where is Valentine?" Adam asked Lucrezia.

"He told me to say he has gone to the place you know of," Lucrezia whispered as loud knocking shook the door.

Adam's shoulders were already through the casement. Seconds later he was swinging his legs onto the roof. Then he leaned down to take his sword from Lily, and in an instant he was gone. Lucrezia quickly shut the window and removed the telltale chair while Lily's trembling hands bundled up her hair.

"Open in the name of the Commonwealth!" a voice commanded.

"How shall I explain my presence here?" Lily whispered frantically as she arranged her shawl over her hair.

"Say I met a man here and you came for me."

"No. Sir Roger will punish you. I can't let you—"

The pounding was going to break the door down. "You must. You must say it!" Lucrezia dashed to unlock the door. It burst open, spilling soldiers into the room.

"You!" Roger exploded as he saw Lily. "Why?" His eyes swept the room. The rumpled bed told its story. The soldiers were searching beneath it, in the closet. Lily must delay them and give Adam time to get away.

"I suspected this bad girl of meeting men here,

Roger." She spoke with deliberate slowness. "So I followed her. Really, my dear," she smiled, "I'm perfectly capable of dealing with an immoral wench without the aid of soldiers."

"There's no one here, sir," the captain told Roger, then turned to Lily. "Your ladyship, why did you take so long to open the door?"

Lily's green eyes surveyed him as though he were a stupid lout. "Naturally I had to allow the girl time to dress before admitting men. To spare yourself further trouble, Captain, the man who was with her left some time ago. A mariner; French, I should think. He won't return after the reprimand I gave him."

The captain, so obviously impressed by her beauty, bowed obsequiously. "Forgive me for worrying you, your ladyship." He signaled the soldiers to leave, then addressed Roger. "That was a false clue, Sir Roger, about a royalist plotter being here."

Roger had recovered from his shock. "Evidently," he snapped. "Come, my dear," he said to Lily, standing aside for her to precede him from the room.

Shaking to such an extent that she was sure he must notice it, Lily descended the narrow stairway. Had Adam gotten safely away? Had her deception worked, or, once they were alone, would Roger scream, Adulteress!" at her?

They had been back at Roger's dark house for an hour, and in the cellar Roger was still laying the lash across Lucrezia. Pacing her chamber, Lily felt she could no longer bear the girl's screams. She must tell Roger the truth. But that would expose Adam to danger. If only Charles would be victorious and return to London. Then she could reward the devoted Capriote who was being punished for her sins.

Her sins! Her sins! "Oh, God, merciful, forgiving, all-understanding. Was it really sinful to have made bright a few moments out of my days of darkness?"

Several weeks had passed and there was no word from Adam. Lily worked with savage energy to increase

THE TEMPEST LILY 293

the dissension spreading among the populace. When crowds of women of every class, weary of taxes and war privations, stormed Westminster for peace, Lily went with them. White ribbons bedecking their hats and shawls and fastened into their curls, they chanted, "Peace! We want peace!"

A clerk appeared in a doorway and ordered them away.

Lily, her face concealed by a lace shawl, cried, "We won't leave until Pym promises us peace!" The women took up her cry, and the man closed the door.

Minutes later Pym's famous guard poured into Palace Yard, firing powder at the throng.

"Bullies! Cowards!" the females screamed. "Stone the bullies!"

Pelting the guard with stones, they drove them back to their barracks. Then, flushed with victory, they surged up to Westminster, pounding on the doors, yelling, "Away with Pym! We want peace!" Before long the civilian soldiers appeared on horseback. The women's fury wiped away discretion and they flew at the soldiers, beating them with sticks, trying to drag them from their saddles.

Lily grabbed at a Roundhead's doublet. Suddenly the August sunshine sparked on swords that slashed down on the women. Screams rose above the shouting, and blood seemed everywhere.

The flat of a sword struck Lily across the back and sent her sprawling face down in the dust. Catching her breath, she tried to rise, but a body falling across her legs pinned her down. A gray-haired woman, blood spurting from a heart wound, succumbed almost immediately.

The women fled to alleys, their peace demonstration over except for the dead and wounded lying in Palace Yard. The soldiers were departing, and aid was being sent for the injured from Westminster. Lily struggled to her feet. She must run or her identity would be discovered. Retrieving her shawl from the dust, she threw it over her head. When will order be brought to this demented land? she wondered.

But months passed with little alteration in the stalemate, first one side seeming to hold the advantage, then the other. Essex offered to negotiate a truce, which was rejected by the Puritans. The single possibility for a decisive change would be if Pym stepped down due to an internal abscess that was extremely painful and might prove to be malignant.

Winter came, and Pym, though suffering acutely, was still alive. Lily had received no word from Adam, but letters did come from Breck. Hungry for news of Joseph, she tore open her mother's letter. "The boy is well," Lady Deveraux had written. "He is chattering like a sparrow and is a joy to everyone."

The awful longing for her child brought tears to Lily's eyes and blurred her vision as she looked at the countess of Severn's writing. Wiping her eyes, she read, "Some months ago Jane succumbed in childbirth. Her baby daughter also died. May they rest in peace."

God have mercy on her soul.

Lily angrily tried to shake off a feeling of guilt. She should not be so callous; she should feel some sympathy, for Jane had meant nothing to Lily until she had married Adam.

From then on a new torment was added to her life. Adam might meet someone and fall in love while she remained chained to Roger.

Unexpectedly Pym's health declined rapidly, and Roger moved into Derby House to keep vigil at his master's bedside until Pym succumbed. For five days Pym lay in state while thousands viewed his corpse, following which, with every Puritan member of the Commons in attendance, he was buried in Westminster Abbey among the remains of England's royalty.

For weeks afterward Roger grieved so extravagantly that Lily believed his mind was unhinged. Again and again he would cry out his sorrow. Then, burying his face in his hands, he would weep uncontrollably.

Six weeks after Pym's death, because of exorbitant payments he had made, the Scottish army crossed into England. Not long afterward Irish troops landed for Charles at northern ports.

Had Adam transported some of them, Lily wondered, lying in bed in the dark and trying not to hear Roger below as he mourned over Pym in an orgy of self-pity. Would she ever be released from her hell with this half-crazed man?

Silence from below told her Roger had temporarily purged his spirit and would be coming to bed. Hearing the door open, she closed her eyes. Pray God that tonight he would not want her. But the yellow flare of a candle held close to her made her open her eyes. She looked up at Roger's pale face leaning over her. He was staring at her with a strange intensity.

"Roger, whatever are you doing?"

"Looking at how beautiful you are with your hair spread out about you like an evil cloak." He carefully placed the candle on a nearby table and sat on the edge of the bed. "Ever since the loss of that blessed Pym, I've known I had a duty to perform. Alas, being weak, I've neglected it. But I must deny my physical desires."

What heaven-sent words—if they meant he would never touch her again. She started to sit up, but he roughly pushed her to lie down again.

The unearthly look in his eyes was terrifying as anger crept across his face. "I'm going to stop you from exercising your evil power over me, Lily! It's your hair that does it! That long, silken black hair cloaking your white body. I'm always thinking of you like that—always—when I should be concentrating on the fight for King Jesus."

He had gone insane! She must get away. With a sudden movement Lily tried to spring out of bed, but he was too swift. His knee caught her in the stomach and pinned her down while he pulled a pair of scissors from his pocket.

"Don't struggle, my love." Quickly one of his hands

dragged her by the hair until her head was hanging over the edge of the bed. She fought like a wild animal, but he had an insane man's strength and she could not free herself from his grasp. He started cutting off thick strands of hair.

"Roger, Roger, stop! Stop!" Screaming for help, she clawed and beat at his knee crushing her. Would Lucrezia hear her screams?

He was cutting savagely, wildly. "You are a bad, voluptuous woman! You hide sin with your hair." The scissors were snipping close to the scalp, grazing her ear. She must stop struggling or he might kill her. Her hair was strewn over the bed and the floor. Without warning he ceased and stared at her in agonized horror. He flung the scissors on the bed. "It's all off—your lovely, lovely hair is gone!" He began whimpering like a child. Then, picking up a handful of hair, he sank his face into it.

Be calm, Lily commanded herself. She must be very calm. He was gentle now, but like a mad dog, he could turn savage any moment. She must trick him into letting her get up. Then she would dash to the door.

"Don't weep about my hair, Roger dear. You were right to cut it off, it was sinful and stimulated your desire, but that's all over now."

"Is it?" He looked up, dropping the hair from his hands. "Are you quite sure that I'm free of you?" With a swift movement he caught and ripped off her shift. "Daughter of the devil! Temptress! Your evil has not gone with your hair! It is still there—in the wicked whiteness of your naked body. I must destroy you—free myself of you!"

As he ranted, her eyes found the scissors and, struggling desperately, she tried to grab them, but he caught them first. She summoned breath to scream. "Lucrezia! Lucrezia!"

He clamped a hand over her mouth and raised the scissors daggerlike to plunge into her breast. She bit into his hand, and as he snatched it away, she gasped, "You will kill your child if you kill me!"

THE TEMPEST LILY 297

The lie worked. He dropped the scissors and stared down at her in wonder. "My child!" he muttered in a thick voice. "A son to bear the name of Huet!" The change in him was miraculous. Roger smiled tenderly and released her. "Now I must go downstairs to offer special prayers of thankfulness!"

As though no near-murder scene had just occurred, he straightened up and went quietly from the room.

Lily lay catching her breath for a second, then she grabbed the scissors. He might return to kill her, deciding a child of her womb would be evil. As the door catch lifted, her fingers tightened on the weapon. It was a terrified Lucrezia who slipped in.

"Are you all right?" As Lily nodded, her hand running over the wild tufts of her hair, Lucrezia rushed to the closet and dragged out a heavy cloak. "We must leave at once. I hid as he passed me in the passage." She was pushing Lily to the door. "Go in bare feet. I have your pattens."

They tiptoed along the dark corridor and down the stairs. In the hall Lucrezia silently drew the big bolt on the door and pulled it open. They stepped out into a snow-covered world. Lily was near collapse, but with Lucrezia's arms supporting her she managed to run to an alley.

"We must leave London or he'll have soldiers after me."

"Let us go to the Heaven Tavern, my lady. We'll get help there."

The innkeeper gave them mulled wine and warm clothing, but he was anxious to be rid of them. "I'll supply you with horses, money and food, and at dawn my son will take you to the City Gate that troops are leaving from. He'll get you out as camp followers."

26

GAZING AT HER reflection in the mirror in her chamber at Breck, Lily impatiently dragged the painted wooden comb through her hair, which curled cuplike around her head. So much had happened since its growth. Roger's first letters had upbraided her for her desertion, for lying about her pregnancy. Later they had ordered her immediate return, otherwise he would find a way of punishing her. Finally he had written saying he had actively joined Oliver Cromwell and was serving God's cause in the field.

Adam, having called at the Heaven Tavern and learning that she was at Breck, had also written. The letter soothed her aching being, quieted her secret dread that, being free, he might meet and love another woman. He and his father were serving with Prince Rupert. Adam was optimistic about the future, believing that most of the country was behind Charles, that His Majesty's Parliament, sitting at royal headquarters in Oxford, was an asset and that a victory seemed assured.

After that one uplifting letter months of silence stalked by, not even his mother hearing from him. Added to anxiety over Adam's welfare, the tenor of the war had been reversed by the Scots. Hired by Parliament, eighteen thousand foot and three thousand horses swept down from Scotland to dominate northern England.

THE TEMPEST LILY 299

Charles's commander in the north, the marquis of Newcastle, badly outnumbered, was threatened on one hand by the Scots, on the other by Parliamentary forces under Cromwell and Fairfax. Since early spring the city of Newcastle had been besieged. If it fell the effect would be disastrous; King Charles would lose the north.

Lily sprang up from a stool. It was cowardice for her to remain in the comparative safety of Breck while the royalist cause cried for aid. She ran her fingers through her thick curls. She must do something to help. Following a lifetime habit, she sped to Geraldius's chamber to seek his guidance.

Suffering the weight of age, the sage now spent most of his time in his book-lined sanctuary. At Lily's hurried knock, he called, "Enter." Glancing up from his book, his wise gaze assessed her. How well he knew the brilliant green eyes, the pink spots high on the pale cheeks. They meant her spirit was in revolt.

"And what is worrying you, dear child?" he asked gently.

"The war, mainly! It seems wicked for me to sit here, hardly doing a worthwhile task, when every pair of hands is needed to help relieve York! James's city is being bombarded and ruined! Heaven knows what has happened to his mother and sisters." She laced slim fingers together, tightening them so the knuckles whitened.

"But my dear child, what can you do? Lead men into the field like the queen did?" He shook his silver head. "Soldiers follow her because she is the queen. Besides, there is a Deveraux already serving the king. Leave active fighting to your father."

"Do you call sitting in Parliament at Oxford active?" she asked in disgust. "Why doesn't Father fight like the earl of Severn? Even at his age he's with Adam in the field!"

"Dear child, who knows what your father thinks?" Geraldius nodded thoughtfully. "The main reason you want to go to York is the hope of finding Adam, isn't it?"

Lily did not answer immediately, but walking to a long slit window, she stared out at the benign summer day. She spoke thoughtfully. "I don't know the truthful answer to that. I want to help, of course. If I can't fight I can nurse the wounded, but naturally I want to see Adam!" She spun around to face Geraldius. "For months I've been contemplating doing something. Now that Adam is free—and I am not—isn't it an opportune time to tell him about Joseph? He can hardly doubt me or think I'm lying to trick him into marriage, because I'm tied to that fiend Roger. It's all too difficult to write him about. In any case, half my letters are never delivered."

Geraldius carefully laid his book on a table as he reflected. "Yes, I agree. Though if you go, what about Breck's defense?"

She waved an impatient hand. "You know I'm not essential here. While I was in London Breck was attacked twice, and David and the countess successfully repulsed the rebels." She hesitated. "Of course there's Mother, but we both know that her mind seems to be deteriorating. She just can't sustain all the sorrow and trouble. She's retreating daily into her own world, protected by her wall of prayers and memories. Thank God old Marion is so devoted to her."

"Aye," Geraldius sighed. "It's fortunate for Joseph that he has the countess, his 'Aunt Catherine,' as the boy calls her."

"Don't you wonder, Geraldius, if Adam's mother suspects about Joseph, why she's never written to Adam about him?"

"She may feel that Adam has enough to contend with at the moment without burdening him with news that, while it might elate him, must also give him a sense of guilt. You know, there's another facet to your going to relieve York." Geraldius spoke teasingly, but his eyes were serious. "Your path may cross Huet's. He can then claim you, make you return and fulfill your conjugal duties."

She shuddered. "That's a risk I must take. At least

THE TEMPEST LILY

Father won't be there." Retrieving the shawl that had slipped from his shoulders, she draped it around him, and he reached up and caught her hand between his mottled hands.

"I shall be anxious about you. Who will accompany you? There is not a man to be spared."

"No, but there is Lucrezia. With her spirit she's worth any man."

Geraldius smiled. "The girl will enjoy the excitement, I'm sure. And from all she's told me of her life in Capri, she's skillful with a dagger. Still, I wish there were a man—"

"Don't worry, hundreds of women have followed the troops to battle. Lucrezia and I are no less brave, no less resourceful than they are." She bent and kissed his withered cheek.

He blessed Lily, and she sped away.

For several days Lily and Lucrezia traveled through countryside controlled by royalists. Although there was a food shortage, they ate and slept adequately at inns along the way. As they neared the north the scene changed. Fields and roads were empty, as though a giant hand had plucked all living things. Death was master. Houses were gutted, farmyards burned, carcasses of cattle and sheep lay covered by flies. Fields of burned crops like brown stains were an affront to the land. Great trees, nurtured for long centuries, had been caught by, but defied, the flames. Robbed of leaves and branches, their scorched trunks stood like huge spears pointing skyward. Here and there a stray fowl ran shrieking from the women's horses.

Lily was stricken to her innermost being. "This is the work of local raiding parties—neighbors who for years enjoyed the same sunrises, the summer twilights, suffered the same frosts and rains!" She shivered. "But because they worship God in different ways and have different ideas of government, they wreak this havoc."

"The hate of brothers for each other is more deadly than the scorpion's bite." Lucrezia's despairing eyes wandered over the desolation. "My lady, do you really hope that we shall find Lord Clune and Valentine? The country is so big."

"God willing, we shall find them. If we can reach the King's Arms tonight, where we once stayed with Sir James, we'll be close to York and Prince Rupert's army."

Though nine o'clock, in the summer twilight it was light when they rode up to the inn Lily had mentioned. No fowls pecked in the courtyard, no dogs barked at their approach, no stable boys came running to hold their horses' heads. The iron sign reading King's Arms, beaten and twisted, lay at the entrance. Over everything was a silence Lily and Lucrezia had grown to recognize.

"I'll look inside and see if any food is left." Lily swung to the ground. "You stay with the horses." Pistol in hand, she approached the stone house.

The wooden door, strapped with iron, swung on its hinges. She pushed it open, then waited to see if any movement followed the noise. Nothing. She stepped across the threshold but backed up as her foot touched a dead body. It was the erstwhile proprietor, only in life she remembered his face had been jovial. Now his wide-open eyes stared up in horror. Around his twisted mouth wasps were buzzing. A sword thrust had found his heart; he appeared to have been dead for some days.

She shooed the wasps away, then, dropping her handkerchief over his face, stepped across his body to search for food in what once had been a gay chamber. The looting had been complete. Even window frames had been ripped away and benches wrenched from wall fastenings. Closets stood open, their wooden shelves gone. Among empty leather bottles littering the stone floor were several white rosettes. So this was the work of rebel soldiers—perhaps the troop was still in the vicinity.

Longing to run from the macabre building, Lily forced herself to climb the spiral steps. Food might still be hidden upstairs that the rebels had not discovered. In the chamber where she and Joseph had slept, she found the innkeeper's wife. The woman's skull had been battered in by musket butts. On the floor beside her were the crushed remains of a rosary. This woman had cuddled Joseph; she had been a laughing, friendly soul, but a Catholic.

So the Puritan soldiers really killed women! It was not just royalist propaganda. Fired with hate, Lily ached to avenge the dead woman. Racing down the stairs, she rushed from the sepulcher of a house to the horses.

"Only corpses are in there," she told Lucrezia, and swinging into the saddle, whirled her horse. "We've got to get to the royalist forces soon!"

They spent that night in a ditch and quieted their hunger with wild blackberries. With the sun's coming they were again in the saddle and had been traveling for an hour when they confronted a party of anxious-faced women and children. Unkempt, dust-covered, loaded with bundles, they still looked of high birth, and Lily sensed that they were not rebel families.

"God bless King Charles," she called, reining in.

"Amen," they muttered, looking furtively behind them, but crowding around Lily as she swung to the ground.

"What's happening?" she asked. "Where have you come from?"

A gray-haired woman with sad eyes said, "Rupert and his army have fought their way into Lancashire and on all sides they're punishing the rebels."

"Grandmother, tell about Latham House," a small boy said excitedly.

"Yes, the countess of Derby was defending it against two thousand rebels. Rupert lifted the siege!"

A heavily pregnant woman said, "Rupert's cavalry is invincible! He's plundered Stockport and Bolton, and last week Lord Goring joined him with five thousand horses, and together they took Liverpool."

"But with such victories, why in heaven's name are you going south?"

"We've had too much war." A woman holding a baby on her hip spoke bitterly. "Before Rupert's arrival, the Scots wrecked our entire village. Burned our houses, killed our men. We hid in the woods or they would have slaughtered us too. They don't spare women or children. If we go south, close to the king, we shall be safe."

"Surely with Rupert and Goring going to relieve York, everything will be all right again?" Lily said.

"But will they arrive in time to save York?" The gray-haired woman shook her head. "I fear not. The walls are mined, and the marquis of Newcastle is treating with the rebels for terms when he surrenders the city. Why are you going to York? There'll be awful bloodshed when Rupert meets the Puritans outside the walls."

"England's drenched in blood," Lily said angrily. "You won't get away from it by running." Bidding each other Godspeed, they parted.

Lily and Lucrezia were two hours closer to York when a thudding of horses' hooves and blur of men's voices made them pull up.

"An army!" Lily muttered. "God knows if they're ours or the enemy! Quick, dismount and hide in the ditch!"

Pulling their horses into the woods, they held onto the reins while crouching down. Protected by bushes, they watched the road. Over a rise of land came a stream of cavalry in gray-green Parliamentary uniforms. As they drew closer, their conversation was audible.

"Why did Cromwell lift the siege on York just because Rupert is coming?"

"He didn't want to be caught in a vise—Newcastle in York before us and Rupert coming up behind!"

"I don't understand Cromwell. He's traveling with his coffin and winding sheet because he's sworn to take the north or die, but he runs from Rupert!"

"York has been relieved," Lily murmured to Lucrezia.

The front men passed on, and great numbers poured after them. The cavalry seemed thousands strong, and

THE TEMPEST LILY 305

Lily searched their faces, to see if Roger might be among them. Following the horsemen came endless numbers of foot soldiers, grim-faced, sweating men with the Puritan short, round haircuts.

When the clouds of dust had begun to settle and the road was clear of the last man, Lily sank back on her haunches. Her soul was warm with gratitude.

"Soon we shall see Lord Clune and Valentine." Lucrezia was rapturous.

Pray God Lucrezia was right. Remounting, they traveled through the woods; the road was too dangerous; they might meet another Parliamentary force. For several hours they moved cautiously, and at last the woods ended on a ridge of land from where they gazed down on York, with its lovely towers and church spires. Its magnificent walls were scarred from the bombardment, but they still stood. The king's standard floated from the highest turret, and camped below the walls was the royalist army!

Spreading over the green, tents like huge mushrooms were topped by the brilliantly colored banners and standards of the noblemen serving with Prince Rupert. Milling around were their personal troops, clad in their lords' family colors. In the galaxy of greens, reds, silvers, blues, yellows, purples and golds, it was impossible for Lily to pick out the Severn banner of green, black and gold.

"Quickly, Lucrezia, help me unstrap my bundle. I must wear my cloak to cover this mannish attire." Lily freshened her face with rosewater from a small bottle, ran the painted wooden comb through her hair and descended to the camp.

Three months of the besiegers' living had marked the land. Piles of refuse, rags, rotted vegetables, dead animals and bird carcasses, animal droppings, empty water barrels, sacks and paper littered the ground. Fresh mounds showed where soldiers had been buried, possibly victims of the pox, and small wonder, Lily thought as she and Lucrezia passed ditches reeking with pestilential stenches. On the camp's outskirts two sentries stopped them.

"We are king's people," Lily spoke haughtily. "I am Lady Lily Deveraux, with my maid. Kindly direct me to Lord Clune, in Prince Rupert's cavalry."

The sentries evidently decided that her superior voice and manner supported her words. "The cavalry is not known to us, your ladyship. If you'll ride through the camp, you'll reach the noblemen's tents."

"Thank you, my good man." Digging into her doublet pocket, Lily tossed him a coin and rode on, leaving Lucrezia to follow close behind as befitted her station when they traveled in public.

As they trotted through the camp, soldiers ran toward them, whistling and calling out lewd remarks. Loud, ribald laughter followed, and a number of women climbed down from carts and dashed to see what was happening.

"Don't mind these louts," a full-bosomed woman called to Lily. "There are only a few women in camp, so new females excite the fools."

Nodding perfunctorily, Lily hastened toward the opposite side of the great camp, where horses were milling around. Trying to hide her excitement, she reined in before a clerk sitting at a table strewn with papers and set in a tent's opening. She said imperiously, "I am Lady Lily Deveraux. Kindly direct me to Lord Clune's tent."

The man stood up. "We've only just encamped, so I must refer to my lists." He seemed deliberately slow to Lily, but at last he looked up. "There's no Lord Clune listed."

"There must be! His lordship is serving with his father, the earl of Severn, and I know—"

"Ah yes! The earl fell in Liverpool, so that's why Lord Clune's not listed. He's now the earl."

Adam was here, thank God! But heaven pity him for having lost his father.

"If you'll dismount, my lady, I'll conduct you to the tent."

THE TEMPEST LILY

He led them down a row of tents to one topped by the Severn standard. Lily had to restrain herself from rushing in, but the tent was empty, and the clerk went in search of Adam.

"Go and find Valentine," Lily said, laughing at Lucrezia. "Don't stand there waiting, you silly girl."

Lucrezia was gone in a second, and Lily stood at the side of the tent flap watching the clerk continue down the lane of tents to a group of men and horses and . . . there was Adam! Head and shoulders above the others. The clerk addressed him, and he looked amazed. Then he came rapidly striding toward her, though she was concealed by the tent flap. Bursting in, he grabbed her shoulders. "In God's name! What disaster brings you? My mother, is she—"

"She's well. I don't bring bad news." His face lost its anxiety, and she said gently, "I heard about your father. Oh, darling, I'm sorry."

"Yes." He nodded grimly. "A cannonball." His distress was obvious from the way his fingers dug into her arms. "But you, why are you at York?"

"I couldn't stay bottled up at Breck when everyone is needed to help." Why did he go on questioning? Why didn't he just take her in his arms? "We've been separated for so long . . . and now you don't seem glad to see me."

"Glad!" His eyes moved eagerly over her face. "Glad is a poor word to describe what sunlight means after months of darkness. But my love, my heart, it's dangerous here! Although we've made the rebels fly from York, it doesn't mean we won't fight. Prince Rupert this minute is waiting for the marquis of Newcastle to join us. He has a letter from King Charles telling him to find the enemy and engage him!"

"I've come such a long way to find you that—" Disappointed and furious, she stopped before she betrayed too far her longing for him. Drawing herself up, she said coldly, "May I at least sit down?"

He grinned suddenly. "No. Not until I've embraced you." He reached back and dropped the flap over the tent's opening. Then he crushed her to him, his heart pounding against her cheek. With her lips clinging to his, the world suddenly became a lovely place. But what about those women she had seen when riding in? Of course they were the footmen's women; the cavalry would have their own. Ladies of the highest rank followed Prince Rupert's forces. She must discover if there was a new woman in Adam's life. She pulled her head back to look up at him, and her cowl fell off.

"Damn my blood!" Adam stared in distress. "Your hair! What in hell happened to it? Have you suffered the pox?"

Her hands flew to her tight curls. "No. Let's sit down and I'll tell you about it."

He guided her to his straw mattress, which was stretched on the furze, and made a backrest for her from piled-up saddlery. "This is Roger's work," she said. And as she told him of the awful scene, his face took on such an expression of hate that for a second she almost feared him. He had looked like that when he and Liam had fought on the *Fearless*.

"What a score I've got to settle with that animal!" On his clenched fists the knuckles whitened, and she pulled Adam's face down and kissed him. "Don't worry, my darling, my hair is already growing back."

He looked at her strangely. "There was no truth in what you told Huet?" His voice sounded strangled. "That you were going to have his child?"

"None whatever."

"I'm glad. I couldn't bear the thought of you carrying a child of his."

Now she would delight him and tell him of Joseph. "Adam, darling, I've come a long way to tell you that—" she felt choked and tremulous—"to tell you—" Why did she still hesitate?

"To tell me what?" His eyes narrowed. She hated his sudden suspicious tenseness. "To tell me what?" he repeated impatiently, staring at her with such angry amazement that the words died in her heart where they were born. He went on, "I hope to God you're not going to say that you and I—in London—at the Heaven—" He stopped as though not knowing quite how to continue, then went on. "Because this is the most damnable time for—"

"Stop!" she almost screamed, and jumped up. "I'm not trying to tell you anything! But if I had been, would it have upset you so much? Would such news be so distasteful to you?" She bit the inside of her lip.

"Don't talk nonsense or weave dramas. Leave that to the playwrights. It's just that at such times as these a man dreads further responsibility. Can't you see that? Besides, you're still Huet's wife. What could be more bitter gall for me than to learn you had given birth to a child of mine while you bore Huet's name? A son, perhaps."

She knew now she could not tell him about Joseph. Sick with disappointment, she reflected caustically that the secret of Joseph had been hers so long that she could continue to maintain it. Adam's face was drawn and marked with fatigue, and her heart longed to comfort him. She forced a smile.

"It's you, really, who is the weaver of dramas, not I. I came to see you, my darling, because neither your mother nor I has heard from you for months."

"I'm sorry, but when a man's fighting and moving about, I suppose the letters get lost or mislaid." He held his arms out to her. "Come to me and I'll tell you how courageous I think you are for coming to York. I'll tell you how I've longed for you and—" He broke off as a trumpet sounded. "That is the signal that the marquis of Newcastle is riding into camp." Adam got to his feet. "I'll be needed to receive him." He grinned in the way that always made her spirit soar. Then as the tent flap lifted and Valentine looked diffidently in, Adam said, "Come in, Valentine."

With his strong face puckered into smiles, Valentine bowed respectfully to Lily. Then he hurried to a leather chest holding Adam's weapons and lifted out a sword in an exquisitely carved scabbard.

Adam started buckling the weapon on as Valentine knelt before him, brushing his long leather boots. "Will you wait here, Lily? I'm afraid it's the best hospitality I can offer. The reception for the marquis won't last long. I regret that he and Rupert are not overfond of each other."

Valentine jumped up and preceded Adam from the tent, holding the flap up for him. Then it dropped back.

Ostensibly Adam occupied a pallet with another officer and gave his tent to Lily. Chaperoned as she was by Lucrezia, her presence created no amazement in the camp where titled ladies visited noblemen whenever it was practicable. Many wives moved with the army, their coaches traveling behind the troops.

Lily and Adam reveled during three wondrous days and nights, for when darkness came, Lucrezia slipped away to join Valentine in the field behind the camp, enabling Lily to lie throughout the night in Adam's arms, a circle of love shutting out the world, to hear him murmur how much he wanted her. This was her spirit's essential substance.

It was that magical time that has no name, when night's ancient darkness succumbs to dawn's virginal light, when for a space there is no sound, and, hushed with reverence, the earth awaits sunrise.

Stirring in Adam's arms, Lily's eyes opened and she looked up into his granitelike face just above hers. A little smile gave a lift to his strong mouth.

"I was looking to be sure that you're real," he whispered. "Do you know that until you arrived here, it was almost five years since we'd spent an entire night together? Otherwise we've only been allowed to snatch at hours."

"I know." She nodded. "And it's such exquisite happiness to reach out and feel you there in the darkness. I treasure the night hours so much. It's a waste to sleep through them."

Chuckling deep in his throat, he kissed her chin.

THE TEMPEST LILY 311

"Who are you pretending to? You must admit we've done very little sleeping."

"That's because I'm not an experienced soldier." She wrinkled her nose at him and laughed softly. "And the straw pallet is so flat, I feel the prickly furze pushing through. Also I've a terror of spiders crawling over me."

"All right, my love." He smiled teasingly. "I'll gallantly accept your explanation." He touched her hair, letting it curl around his fingers.

"You know, you look like a beautiful boy with your hair curling around your pale face. Luckily for me, from the neck down you are still my most feminine, glorious Lily."

Bending down, his mouth covered hers and he gathered her to him. She ran her hands over the smooth skin of his shoulders and down his back to squeeze his buttocks as she curved her body into his.

"Hm-mm, beloved Adam, have I ever confessed to you that I could spend my whole life in love play with you? I suppose it's because we've had to be parted so often that I have such an enormous appetite for your caresses."

"You're an absolute hussy at heart," he chuckled, "and am I glad!" Then he climbed on top of her, and as he thrust himself into her, she moaned with delight and her spirit soared to meet his.

Cocks had finished crowing, sentries had changed watch, grooms were watering and currying horses, boys kindled fires and the camp was actively awake when Lily and Adam lay side by side chained in an immense lassitude. After a while she murmured, "Oh, darling—darling—darling. Why was I such a fool as to stay shut up at Breck longing for you? Why didn't I come to you months ago?"

"Much as I would have wanted you, it's as well you didn't. I've been fighting with Rupert up and down and across the country. You couldn't have dragged after me." He sighed. "We'll be fighting very soon again, so I'm sending you off to Breck today."

She suddenly sat upright, pulling the blanket up to her chin to cover herself. She felt as though she had received a physical blow. "You are not serious, Adam! You can't be!" Her great green eyes clouded in dismay, but he nodded soberly.

"Yes, I am. We move on today, and from what our scouts report we'll be meeting the enemy's main force not too far from here. They are evidently waiting for us."

"I beg you, don't send me away because of that."

"Please, Lily." He sounded as though he were controlling his patience with an effort. "I can't keep you with me! You are married—the wife of a prominent member of the enemy. A fair amount of moral laxity is indulged in during the stress of war, but we can't spit in the face of propriety."

"But if I'm prepared to sacrifice my name to stay with you, I can't see why you should care about—"

"That's just it, my darling. I know the extent of your generous love. You married Huet to save me. I haven't forgotten. Yet I can't have you exposed to such scandal. Lily, you are my only love! There has never been another to equal you in my heart. Let's be grateful for the hours we have known. Some people live all their lives without even experiencing a single hour such as we have had by the hundred. Go back to Breck. I beg you—for my sake! I'll fight a better war if I know you and my mother are comparatively safe."

She could not stay unless he permitted her to. She had no choice but to comply.

"Come soon to Breck! If the war drags on throughout the year, then come at the winter cessation of activities at Christmas."

"I shall. I promise you, beloved." He left the pallet. "Now I've much to do. We march at noon. I'll tell Valentine to send Lucrezia to you so that you can both soon be on the road to Breck."

"Adam, let me come a little of the way with you?" she begged.

He was dressing swiftly, the man of action now, as though by leaving the pallet he had discarded his lover's role. "Very well, but you promise that when I give the word, you'll leave?"

"I promise."

27

MISERABLE AT HAVING to part from Adam so soon, Lily and Lucrezia walked their horses up to the group of mounted women who were excitedly watching as the army got on the move. Soldiers swarmed over the meadow like ants, the sun sparking their long pikes and muskets as column after column climbed the slight rise.

From the direction where the cavalry was preparing to advance, Adam came riding toward Lily. He was magnificent in light armored breastplate, green breeches and long, soft leather boots reaching to the steel tassets protecting his thighs. A lobsterlike helmet, the visor open, covered his head. His horse's caparisons were in the Severn colors of gold, black and green. Reining in beside Lily, he pointed to the marching men.

"Those are Newcastle's men wearing the white shirts that they've sworn to dye red in rebels' blood."

On and on came the various regiments of pikemen and musketeers proudly holding high the standards of ancient lineage. In steel caps the thousands of heads moving in close formation seemed like a river flowing over the land.

Then came the artillerymen with great guns, eighteen-pounders, the Culverins, drawn by teams of twenty-six farm horses. Closing the ranks came the baggage train; carts piled high with sacks of food, barrels of wine and water and the noblemen's special equipment.

Lily flashed brilliantly excited eyes at Adam. "It's a wonderful show of power."

"Aye; pray it will suffice to vanquish the Parliamentary power. They have almost twice as many men as us."

"That's terrible." She was apprehensive. "Is the enemy close at hand?"

"About seven miles ahead, encamped on a ridge of Marston Moor." He shot a reassuring smile at her anxious face. "Don't worry. But now I must rejoin my men. Travel with the women, and when we halt to make camp, I'll send Valentine for you and Lucrezia."

She tried to return his smile as his forefinger touched his forehead in salute and the sun sparked his ring with the Severn crest in diamonds. Then he whirled and cantered over to join Rupert's dashing cavalry.

Wearing a scarlet cloak embroidered in gold, Prince Rupert led his seven thousand horsemen, magnificently attired, as they trotted after the footmen. Lily's eyes found and for a few minutes followed Adam at the head of his regiment, then in the mass of mounted men she lost him, but the Severn banners told her where he rode until the cavalry disappeared over the rise. When the dust they had raised began to settle, they were followed by the forlorn women.

Two hours later the royalist armies reached Marston Moor, and like a sudden wind excited comment gushed from thousands of mouths as everyone stared across the intervening land to another ridge. There among the waving rye the rebel armies sprawled in terrifying masses. A heavy downpour of rain, like a sheet of gray silk, diffused the royalist view of the enemy, and with frantic haste Rupert's armies pitched camp.

There could be no major conflict while the rain lasted. Lily watched the hasty activities around her as the regiments took positions. Waiting impatiently for Adam to

THE TEMPEST LILY 315

send for her, Lily joined with Lucrezia and the women in frightened speculation as to when the fighting would start.

The rain cleared as suddenly as it had begun, and Valentine came to escort the two women to the officers' site, down narrow lanes of tents, until they reached Adam's, but he was not there. Lily gladly shed her wet cloak. Standing to the side of the tent's opening, sure she could not be seen, she watched for Adam.

Noblemen were gathered in groups as one among them with a perspective glass scrutinized the enemy and gave reports to his companions. Lily looked at a large tent, where, through the opening, she saw a figure with a scarlet cloak pacing back and forth. Rupert's tent! The leaders were in conference! An hour passed with intermittent rain and sunshine, and then Adam emerged from the tent and came striding toward his own.

As he entered, Lily threw her arms about him. "Oh, darling, what's going to happen?"

"Don't worry. From what we've seen they're in no hurry to attack. Unbuckle my armor, will you?" She started to undo the leather straps, and he continued, "Our scouts brought in a couple of prisoners, and they say that Cromwell and his cavalry have left, but when we arrived, Cromwell was asked to return. It's his regiments that are causing all the movement in the rye." She helped him out of his breastplate and laid it on an upturned wine barrel. "Ah, that's better," he said, stretching his shoulders. As she smoothed the wrinkles out of his wide lace ruff, he caught her in his arms. "How I wish I could keep you with me always." He held her against his heart and she clung to him, too deeply stirred to talk, feeling as helpless as a butterfly in a storm. His mouth was warm on hers. When again would she feel his lips, his arms, his heart's beating? After a few seconds he released her.

"Rupert wanted to attack at once, but Newcastle would have none of it." Adam shook his head. "When the prince told the marquis, 'My lord, I hope we shall have a glorious day,' Newcastle retorted that he had mutiny in his ranks because he had no funds to pay the men, and he considered it wiser not to fight at all!" Adam angrily tamped tobacco into the bowl of his silver pipe. "I reminded him that Prince Rupert's cavalry has never met horsemen they can't scatter!" He squatted on his heels. "Come here, and I'll try to explain the battle formation."

She knelt beside him while with a stick he traced a semicircle in the trodden-down grass. "Here is the moor, with the hill at the back, the woods on the far end, we at this end. The Scottish infantry hold the center of the enemy line. On the right is the Parliamentarian horse. Over here is an enormous troop of horse and infantry commanded by Oliver Cromwell."

"Cromwell! Roger was with him! Is it possible he still could be?"

"Definitely, unless some bullet has rid the world of the vermin. Now, facing the enemy's center we have Newcastle and Eythin, the German expert who commands our pikemen and musketeers. On the left is Lord Goring's cavalry. Rupert and his men face Cromwell on the right."

"That's where you will be." Lily prayed aloud, "Oh, God give us victory . . . we are so outnumbered."

"We've often been outnumbered, beloved, and have won the day!" He stood upright with the quiet strength of a big man, confident in his power. "As soon as we have eaten meat this evening, I want you and Lucrezia to be off."

"Let me stay, I implore you! There'll be wounded. Lucrezia and I can be of help."

"No, Lily!" His demeanor was implacable. "Don't even ask me that."

She did not burden him by begging, and almost in silence he finished his pipe and then returned to Prince Rupert's tent. Left alone, Lily told herself she would remain without his permission, but to cross him at such a time might invoke his anger so that he would never forgive her.

The afternoon passed with cruel swiftness. A little

THE TEMPEST LILY 317

before six o'clock the cooks started lighting fires. Lily hated the drifts of smoke rising in the summer air. It was the signal that she must soon leave.

Adam strode back from the war conference. "Well, everything's arranged," he told her. "His Highness has decided that it's too late for anything to happen today. We shall charge the enemy the first thing in the morning. He's ordered supper, and Newcastle has gone to his coach to solace himself with a pipe, and that's what I'm going to do."

As he pulled out his pipe, her sad expression settled on her small saddlebag. Within the hour she must be gone, and then God alone knew when they would meet again.

Suddenly there was a thunderous sound—the charge of thousands of horses' hooves! The earth under her feet trembled. Screams and shouts rose in the air, trumpets blared, drums rolled and Adam sprang to his armor, shouting, "The enemy is attacking!"

Lily rushed to help him fasten his armor. He fitted his head into the steel cap, grabbed his pistol, felt his sword hanging by his side and within seconds was dashing outside. At the opening he turned for an instant. "Leave at once! Ride, Lily!" Then he was gone.

She ran to the edge of the camp, where the white-faced women were flocking to watch. Cromwell's cavalry was charging down the slope to the ditch, where Rupert's red-clad musketeers held the all-important ground separating the rebels from the royalists.

A volley of shot blazed from the musketeers and the front row of enemy horsemen toppled to the ground. The terrible charge was halted, but only momentarily. The enemy regrouped and, whirling their horses to face the royalists, yelled, "Religion! God with us!"

His scarlet cloak flying out behind him, Rupert with Adam on his left was leading his cavalry. With swords waving they galloped at the foe, shouting. "For God and King Charles!"

They made their way around their own musketeers to attack Cromwell's rear guard. The clash of swords, the oaths and the screams sent the birds in the nearby woods screeching from the trees. Lily's frantic eyes tried to hold onto Adam as he fought, but it was impossible in that mad melee of men and horses.

For a while it seemed as though Rupert's men had the advantage. Lily found it difficult to discern the details of what was occurring because the air was filled with black gunpowder. When the haze lifted, the tide had altered. It was horrible! The king's men were being massacred.

Was that fair-haired rebel who had lost his steel cap actually Roger? The face was drowned in a thousand maniacal countenances before she could be sure. Hordes of enemy infantry were pouring into the all-important ditch. Rupert's men, outnumbered three to one, struggled for their lives.

"The devils are gaining!" a woman screamed, and another cried, "If they do, they'll advance to this very spot!"

White-faced with terror, Lucrezia implored Lily, "Let's leave this hell before we're killed!"

The great guns roared, and their foul breath darkened the moor again. For terrible moments the women were left with only the soul-chilling noises of violent slaying. When the smoke cleared the second time, they saw that the battle had swayed a distance from them. The green grass was dark with blood and prostrate bodies.

"My son! My son!" a woman called in agony and rushed from the camp toward the battlefield. Other women, catching courage from her, ran forward to succor the wounded.

Brave creatures defying the horsemen nearby, the women bent over the dying. Pairs of them started dragging men back to camp. Adam might be lying out there! Lifting her skirts, Lily darted from the camp, dodging around the horsemen. With his great size she would find Adam. She searched and searched. He was not there.

She stopped beside a dead pikeman whose legs lolled over a young soldier's head whose eyes were still mov-

THE TEMPEST LILY 319

ing. Working frantically, she managed to free the boy. He was almost drowning in his own blood from a stab in the throat. She propped him up against a dead horse and turned to aid a man whose calf had been halved by a hatchet. It was a hideous sight. She clumsily bundled his leg up in her cloak. A terror-stricken Lucrezia joined her, and together they moved among the dying, roughly binding the wounds and trying to lighten the men's last moments in the inferno raging over the moor.

Close by, the horsemen's savage battle was ending. The outnumbered royalists were in retreat, circling about the women and wounded. The enemy galloped their horses straight across the field. Women screamed and fled, others ducked. Lily tried to run from the foaming horses but slipped in the mud.

"Holy God!" A voice of wrath sounded above the bedlam. Scrambling to her feet, Lily looked up at Roger's demonic face. "Harlot of the king's army!" Roger roared. "Is that what you've become?"

Picking up her skirts, she ran wildly, straight toward the main scene of battle. She would be trampled beneath horses' hooves, killed by slashing swords. Anything was better than being caught by Roger. As she ran, jumping over mounds of dead, rushing into riderless horses that frantically searched for escape, Roger caught up with her.

"Jezebel!" he screeched, and leaned down and struck her with his revolver butt across the shoulders. She staggered from the awful blow, and in an instant he sprang to the ground and grabbed her. Her struggles were nothing against his strength. He threw her facedown across his saddle, swung up and started galloping toward the rebel camp.

Her shoulder bones felt broken, but she squirmed and twisted to get to an upright position. She must get away! His pistol butt cracked down on the nape of her neck and it was all she could do not to faint as the ground flashed by beneath her hanging, bouncing head.

They had left the battleground. They were at the rebel camp. What would Roger do with her? He pulled up, and cooks and women ran to him as he jumped down, yelling, "Hold my horse! The Lord hath delivered mine enemy into my hand!" He dragged Lily off the animal and carried her toward a cart. "Leather thongs! Quickly, so I can secure the Jezebel to a cart!"

People rushed to obey him. In his crushing hold Lily struggled to straighten up, but as she lifted her head his open hand struck her savagely across the face. The women around her cried out, but he swiftly struck her again with the back of his hand on the other side of the face. "Adulteress!" he screamed, and holding her up with one arm, he kept striking her until her neck seemed broken. Her head roared and she collapsed, unconscious.

It wasn't until Lily's mind began to work coherently that the awful truth beat through her aching head. She was Roger's prisoner. He had found her among thousands of people. She was bound to a wheel of the cart, standing with her back to the camp. Her mouth was filled with blood and her ears throbbed from Roger's dreadful blows. The hell of battle was still going on. It would never end. She would die tied to this cart. How long had she been there?

"God has rewarded his own! Rupert has fled!" some women cried, excitement in their voices.

Others laughed. "Newcastle's famous white coats have been wiped out! They dyed their coats red in their own blood!"

"Thousands of royalists are dead! Victory will soon be ours!"

Was this news true? Lily twisted her head around to see what was happening. Bearers were bringing in the wounded, laying them down in rows. Scottish and Puritan women were tending them. The stench of blood was stronger than the smell of smoke. The long twilight was falling, so the debacle would soon end. Charles had lost! Had Adam been hurt? Roger would return to torture and kill her.

Suddenly a royalist horseman charged like a madman into the camp, disrupting the care of the injured.

THE TEMPEST LILY

The great horse's caparisons were filthy; the rider's breastplate was splashed with red where pikes had found flesh; blood seeped from under armplates and the tassets on his thighs. And though his face was hidden by his visor, as soon as he set his horse to jump a low cart to gain the camp, Lily immediately knew it was Adam.

When he landed in their midst, men rushed at him with drawn swords. Adam slashed at them while he whirled his magnificent horse to elude grasping hands. "Lily! Lily!" he shouted.

"Behind you! Tied to a cart!"

Using his sword like a rapier, he cleared the air around him, cutting down anything in his way. Then he charged at the cart. Rearing his horse, his sword tip cut the thongs binding Lily. "Quick! Mount!"

His left hand pulled her up and she managed to seat herself on the saddle before him. At the same instant the Parliamentarians, recovered from their surprise, rushed forward. Adam dug his heels into the horse, and the beast broke into a blinding gallop. The rescue had been so audacious, so swift, Adam had not given the enemy time to think.

Adam was alive! Lily rejoiced in his pulsating heart against her back. But what carnage littered the moor! The big guns were quiet now. Fighting had ceased, but royalists were in retreat.

"Our armies have been routed!" Adam called in her ear. "I'm making for the woods! We'll get through to York. I've sent Lucrezia there."

So he and Lucrezia had met. That's how he knew Roger had taken her. Lily could not shout at him. Bullets were whizzing all around them. They were being pursued. They flattened against the animal, but with their extra weight it was losing the lead.

At the edge of the woods, Adam whirled to confront the Roundheads.

"Into the woods! It's Huet and two others!"

Lily dropped to the ground and raced for the trees as she heard Roger roar, "Clune! The devil incarnate! I knew you were back!"

Lily kept running as steel clashed on steel, and Roger shouted to his men, "This man is mine! Get the woman! Don't let her escape!"

Turning to look back, Lily saw the men ride after her. No use her running—they would catch her. She must hide. Her frantic eyes fixed on a deep hollow in a great oak. Rapidly she lowered herself into it, pulling at furze and ferns as a covering. She heard the searchers' horses coming closer, closer. They were almost at the giant tree.

"Why hunt for a woman when there's all the royalist troops to follow and plunder?" a voice grumbled. "They've not gone far away."

"You're right. There'll be fine loot in the noblemen's baggage carts."

With her heart thumping so violently she could hardly breathe, Lily listened to their horses' hooves fading away. Convinced that they had gone, she sped from her hiding place and, protected by bushes, her frantic eyes watched the fight between Roger and Adam.

Adam's visor was closed again, giving him the advantage over Roger, who had lost his helmet. With amazing skill the tip of Adam's blade played about Roger's uncovered head. Roger was panting, terribly on the defensive, and Adam with his superior weight and strength was suddenly increasing the pace. As Roger's weapon went up to protect his head, Adam struck down with such force that he split the steel and it flew off. Stunned, Roger stared at the hilt of his sword. Like the lash of a snake, Adam's long blade plunged into Roger's shoulder, and within seconds he collapsed.

Lily dashed from the woods. At sight of her Adam cried, "Mount! Mount!" He lifted her over his saddle and swung up behind her, setting his horse to a path in the woods as merciful night began to drop a shroud over the carnage. All around them there were voices shouting as rebel soldiers pursued royalist troops.

"Will they chase us to York?"

"No, they need time to recuperate. They also have wounds to lick."

THE TEMPEST LILY

"Adam, it was the devil himself who led Roger to find me, but you've killed him. I'm free of him."

"Yes, one of the chief rats is gone, but that's nothing! Today's disaster is the worst King Charles has suffered. God help us, we've lost the north! We shall never forget this damnable day—July second, 1644—it will be written in blood in England's history."

The stallion picked its way through the darkness. They rode in silence until Lily touched Adam's hand on the reins. The warm, sticky feel of blood struck new terror in her. "You're hurt! Is it serious, darling?"

"No, just many small flesh wounds. I've been tremendously lucky."

"God's been good to us," she murmured, and after that they spoke no more. They were too physically spent and spiritually crushed by the defeat to do more than just manage to ride to York.

Thousands of royalist troops had already found sanctuary behind the city's walls. The city so recently relieved from months of siege was in a turmoil. There was neither food nor accommodation for the refugees. Noblemen and retainers were lying side by side in fields. Adam found places for Lily and himself, and with hundreds of others they slept on the wet grass.

With the first light Adam awakened Lily. He wore a fresh doublet and breeches. He helped her up, and she got stiffly to her feet, tidying her hair, shaking out her rumpled skirts. All around them the other people in the fields were awakening.

"I've located Valentine. He managed to save my equipment, and he's also found Lucrezia," Adam said. "I've secured two horses, and I want you to leave at once."

"Now? Oh, darling, let me stay with you a few days! I also want to see James's mother, and—"

"Lily, this is not a social call in York!" he snapped irritably. "There's no food here for visitors. In any case, the enemy will soon take the city." He spoke with dry bitterness. "Rupert does not intend remaining here to be bottled up. We shall re-form our armies as fast as possible and then march to the king for new orders."

"Can't I stay until you march?"

"No! No!" He looked exasperated enough to shake her. "I've only time to help reorganize our armies. This morning our scouts told us that we lost four thousand men at Marston Moor yesterday!"

"What a frightful loss!" Her great eyes sought comforting words from his, but his weary face was drawn.

"You see why I've no time for anything but our cause!"

She nodded. "Of course, darling; I'll go immediately."

Their farewells were brief. Adam and Valentine accompanied the women as far as the city gate. "Come to Breck in the winter?" Lily asked. "Promise!"

"I will if I can. I promise." A shadow of a smile lit the wonderful blue eyes, but Adam was all warrior now, anxious for the chance to fight and avenge the royalist dead. "Godspeed, my love," he murmured, and with that she had to be content, and she resolutely moved forward. As she turned a bend in the road, she looked back to wave, but he had gone.

⇔ 28 ⇔

HIDING BY DAY, traveling only by night lest they meet the enemy, Lily and Lucrezia at last reached Breck. The hideous news of the defeat at Marston Moor had preceded them, but Lily was not spared the sad duty of telling the countess of the earl's death. With immense courage Adam's mother did not burden others with public grief. Yet over the course of days, Lily saw the mark of sorrow upon the brave woman.

While everyone in Breck tried to cheer themselves that Charles still held much of the west and south, Lily enjoyed a secret comfort: Roger would no longer worry her, and when hostilities ceased for the winter, Adam would come to Breck.

Six months dragged by, with the king losing open ground but holding isolated fortresses and castles throughout the land. The winter of 1644 was so severe that fighting almost stopped, but Rhys Deveraux decided to remain at Oxford with the king's dwindling forces. From Breck's ramparts Lily kept daily watch over the bleak countryside for the first sign of Adam. The only callers were occasional drovers or royalist soldiers who had been separated from their regiments, or peasants seeking shelter after rebels had driven off their cattle and burned their huts.

In the lonely land of snow and sleet, Breck seemed a forgotten place where Lily was tortured by apprehension and disappointment. Why had Adam not come to Breck? Was it true or an excuse when he had written that he was sailing the *Fearless* to Ireland to bring in more Irish troops? Why had his few letters been so unfeeling? Did this all point to a new woman in his life? If so, then this was the end between them. She could never tolerate another female between them.

With the coming of spring the war was resumed, and still Lily watched from the walls for Adam.

On a warm day Joseph came looking for her, calling, "Mama! Mama! Come quickly. Geraldius won't talk. He just lies in his bed with his eyes closed."

Behind Joseph was Adam's mother. She and the child were seldom separated, and Lily's worried eyes questioned her. "He's very weak." The countess mouthed the words.

Fear gripped Lily. A month ago Geraldius had suffered a stroke, but she had deceived herself into believing he would recover. She looked down at Joseph. The sight of the boy, tall for his six years, with the same straight shoulders as Adam's, challenged the gloom of her soul. "I'll go to Geraldius, darling." She kissed Joseph's upturned face. "Don't worry about him."

She hurried away. Entering the familiar chamber, Lily was braced by the presence of Marion sitting silently praying. The old big-bosomed nurse, Geraldius and she were here again—together as they had so often been when Lily was a child. The same threesome, but one look at Geraldius's face and she knew death made a foursome.

Kneeling by the bedside, she despaired that there was no priest nearby whom she could summon to administer the Last Sacrament. Geraldius must enter the shades without the comfort of Extreme Unction, but surely God's own hand would be extended to the good man. Lily did not call her mother. This added grief might make her collapse entirely.

"Is there anything you wish for, Geraldius?" He had no relatives; her family was like his own.

Slowly the heavily veined eyelids opened. "Go . . . with Joseph," came in painful gasps. "Colonies . . ."

"You mean leave Breck? Now?"

"At once." His struggle for breath was torturous for her to watch helplessly. "King . . . never reign . . . again. . . ."

His frightful prophecy, his fading life were not to be borne. "Oh Geraldius, get well!" Lily pleaded. "Please get well!"

"Don't grieve . . . all cannot . . . go together . . . we'll meet . . ."

She bent closer to catch the whispers, but Geraldius was dead.

On a warm June day with a mockingly benign blue sky, in the cemetery within the castle walls, a little apart from the crowded-together tombstones of centuries of Deveraux dead, Lily stood by Geraldius's newly dug grave. With the exception of men posted on

THE TEMPEST LILY

watch and Angela Deveraux, everyone in Breck was there as David read the funeral service.

The coffin, suspended on leather thongs, was slowly lowered into the ground. The gravediggers' big shovels started tossing earth onto the coffin. It fell with heartless thuds, covering the beloved old man and with him Lily's infant laughter, her first steps, her discovery of fairies. Thud-thud-thud—the grave was filled level with the grassy ground. Now all those who loved Geraldius were sticking the wildflowers they had brought into the soft grave. The bed of color hid the scar where the coffin had descended.

The countess put an arm around Lily's shoulders and guided her away. Their heavy steps halted at the graves of Jane and her baby daughter. A part of Adam would forever lie at Breck. Who could have visualized such happenings when, wandering over Capri's verdant hillsides for a space when mercifully there seemed no time, he and Lily had been sprinkled with magic?

Several weeks later, after placing fresh flowers on Geraldius's grave, Lily and the countess were returning to the castle when a stable boy rushed forward, bowing to the countess. "Your ladyship, the earl of Severn and his attendants have just ridden in."

"The earl!" All color drained from the countess's face, and for a moment Lily feared the woman would crumple. "It's not possible!" she murmured. "The earl was killed at—" She stopped and the color flooded back to her cheeks. "But of course—it's Adam!"

"Adam! Here!" Lily stood absolutely still. Her legs felt as if they would never move again. The countess started hurrying away, then turned around. "Lily, are you ill?"

Shaking her head, Lily muttered, "No, I'll join you later." She must be allowed time to absorb the fact that Adam had finally arrived. Nodding understandingly, the countess walked hurriedly into the castle.

Suddenly Lily could not wait to see him, and she sped to her chamber. As Lucrezia helped her change, she was ashamed at her happiness so soon after Geraldius's death, but at last . . . Adam would see his son! Would he believe the child was his? Would Adam want him? Would Adam want her because of the boy? She could not bear that. If he loved a new woman, he might deny that Joseph was his son. "I must act wisely," she told herself as she flashed a final glance at her pale face in the mirror.

"That lemon-colored gown looks lovely on you," Lucrezia said.

"I hope the countess won't think it too frivolous of me to wear it so soon after Geraldius's death. Oh, my hair . . . it's still short, and Adam was so upset about it the last time he saw me."

"Oh, my lady, his lordship will not care. He loves you too much. Be happy together, and when you can," Lucrezia smiled impishly, "discover where Valentine is."

"Go, you foolish girl, and see who the earl's attendants are. Valentine is probably among them." Lily laughed as Lucrezia cried, "Oh, thank you," and flew from the chamber.

Gathering her skirts, her heart thumping from excitement, Lily raced down the stone corridor to meet Adam. When she was at the door, she warned herself to be calm. He had not come during Christmas, and his letters had implied something that altered his feelings for her. She forced herself to walk slowly into the room.

Adam was bent forward in his chair, talking earnestly in low tones to his mother. They were sitting under a long slit window, and the light was falling on his hair. He turned and their eyes locked, but there was no warmth in his eyes. Instead, they shone with a terrible blue-glass look. This was no man coming to claim his lover. He rose slowly, and his great height and ugly mood filled the small chamber. Though travel-stained, he was still magnificent in cream doublet and red breeches tucked into thigh-high leather boots. His sword clanked as he moved indolently toward Lily with an outstretched hand. She put her icy fingers in his

THE TEMPEST LILY 329

strong clasp, and he perfunctorily raised her hand to his lips.

"I'm happy to see you, Lily. It seems that despite the severity of the times, you maintain your standard of fashionable beauty. Obviously the privations of war don't bother you."

Damn his impertinence! "Does one have to be bedraggled to show one suffers from the war?" she asked haughtily. "Breck has withstood attack and privations. Thanks to thoughtful planning we're not down to eating our cats and dogs or horses like many garrisons are, although I assure you it's months since anyone felt comfortably fed!" She shrugged elaborately. "Of course, to a man like you who has seen so much action, life at Breck may appear luxurious and courtesy may have become superfluous."

"Lily," the countess swiftly interposed, "Adam has been telling me the latest news."

Surprised by his mother's sad expression, Lily's anger lessened and she sank into a chair.

Adam lowered himself onto a loveseat. "None of the news is good. Although Charles still has some strong garrisons left, he'll have to raise a new army to put into the field if we're going to win."

"Then His Majesty should go to Ireland and bring back a great Irish force!" the countess exclaimed.

"You forget, Mother, all the big ports are closed to us. *Fearless* had to hide in a cove near Milford Haven. We've just brought over as many Irish as we could carry and smuggled them across the beaches." He shrugged. "But these small numbers are nothing against what Cromwell now has. In the last year he has organized a well-disciplined and splendidly equipped model army, while ours has dwindled to almost nothing. Of course, as long as the castles and fortified garrisons hold out, the revolutionaries will never get control of England. Yet by the same token we shall never overcome the rebels with our scattered forces."

"What will be the outcome?" Lily asked, almost afraid to hear the answer.

"Peace, I hope, on honorable terms."

"Is the rumor true," the countess asked, "that the Scots are quarreling with the revolutionaries because they are trying to impose Calvinism upon them?"

"Yes, but it's not serious enough to split the union." He looked meaningly at his mother. "I believe this is as good a moment as any to attend to our personal affairs, because I've not much time to linger at Breck." Adam unfolded his great height and stood up.

The countess of Severn shot an anxious look at him, as though she wished to counsel him. Then, as if deciding not to, she rose, and Adam strode to the door to open it for her. As he shut it, hope flared in Lily. Now that they were alone, he might change. But his demeanor remained the same when he sat down again.

"Oh, Adam," she burst out, "why are you behaving so strangely?" If he loved another woman, let him tell her and be done with it. "You've changed so terribly. Whatever has happened?"

He leaned toward her, elbows on his knees. His face was taut, his eyes narrowed. "Yes, I've changed, and it's because I've been the victim of the worst bitchery a man has ever been subjected to! It's your vile deceit—your having lived a lie for years that is responsible for the change!" Angry words rushed out of Adam. "How dared you pretend you loved me? It is yourself you love! No one else!"

Half-stunned by the sudden vicious attack, Lily sprang up. "Just what am I accused of? What have I ever done in connection with you," her throat tightened painfully, "except marry that monstrous maniac Huet to save your rotten life!"

"Aye, you saved me from the hangman's noose, and I'm grateful, but by God, the wrong you've done me outweighs the good. And—"

He broke off as the door opened and his mother and Joseph came in. Lily's glance flew to Adam. His eyes were riveted upon his son. She looked back at the six-year-old boy, at his strong, lithe body, at his straight shoulders in the blue silk doublet, his fine legs in knee-length breeches and long white hose. With the burnished hair, the flame-blue eyes, it seemed to Lily that she had never seen the resemblance to Adam so sharply. The boy was a small edition of the man. She felt ill and sank into a chair.

"Mama," Joseph rushed excitedly to Lily, "Lucrezia says there's a great hero in the castle, the earl of Severn. She said, I think," he turned shyly toward Adam with eager blue eyes. "Is it *you*, sir? How many rebels have you slain? I'm ready with my slingshot to get them when they attack Breck!" He reached inside his doublet pocket. "Would you like to see my slingshot, sir?" He started to drag the sling from his pocket.

"Yes, indeed I would." Adam's voice was thick with suppressed emotion. His gaze was pridefully, possessively bathing the boy with warmth. Suddenly Lily realized that Adam already knew Joseph was his son! Of course his mother had at last written to him telling him her suspicion that he had sired Joseph. Well, the countess could not be blamed. Now seeing the boy's likeness to himself, Adam was convinced of the truth. What right had Adam to be furious with her?

"Won't you please tell me your name?" Adam was saying to his son, leaning down with an outstretched hand.

Joseph laughed gladly. "Oh, I'm Lady Lily's son, Joseph Traherne." He placed a small hand in his father's huge one, and the strong fingers tightened over the young fingers.

"Traherne!" Adam spat the word at Lily, his eyes blazing derision at her.

"Oh please, my lord, do tell me, *are* you the great hero Mama's told me so much about?" Joseph's excited voice bubbled on. "She says you can bring a ship safely through the worst storms there ever were! That you've taken hundreds and hundreds of Spanish vessels and you've killed thousands and thousands of rebels with your sword. Mama says that you—"

"Wait! Wait!" Adam burst into laughter.

"Joseph, darling," Lily said softly, "aren't you talking a little too much?"

"Let the boy talk!" Adam snapped at her.

Lily's temper flared. On the strength of supposition that Joseph was his son . . . how dare he tell her how to treat her child? Wanting to send Joseph away, she did not because of the boy's enjoyment of being with Adam.

For a few minutes she suffered an exquisite hell, vacillating between joy and despair as she watched Adam kneel on the floor beside Joseph as he showed the boy how best to handle the slingshot. This was the moment she had prayed for—in which she would show Adam his son. But everything was all wrong. Instead of it being a moment of fulfillment, it had inspired hate in Adam for her, which in turn was resurrecting her bitterness and antagonism for his arrogance. Lily could bear no more. She must have the wretched affair out with him.

"Joseph, now you really must go. His lordship has ridden a long way and . . ." Her voice trailed off at the disappointment in Joseph's blue eyes, at the sight of the puckered mouth. She gave him a consoling look, then coldly addressed Adam. "Will Joseph have the opportunity of being with you tomorrow? Do you intend staying the night?"

"Oh do—do—do, please, do your lordship," Joseph begged, and Adam grinned happily at him.

"I shall, Joseph. Then you can show me over Breck's fortifications and I'll tell you about some of my battles."

"Oh thank you. I'd *like* that."

Lily threw an appealing look at the countess. "Would you accompany him, please?"

"Of course, my dear." She smiled gently. "Come, Joseph." Hand in hand, she and the boy left the room.

As they went, Adam followed them with his eyes, and as the door closed on them, he whipped around to Lily. "Why didn't you tell me I had a son?" he asked crisply. "How dared you keep it from me?"

THE TEMPEST LILY 333

Her blood soaring to her face with rage, she cried, "How *dared* I? What impudence for you to use such a word to me! You left me in Jamaica without a thought that I might have a child of yours. Did you ever return to see what had become of me . . . and a child, if there had been one?"

"I was wrong about that." He waved his hands to dismiss the subject. "That's over and done with. Whatever possessed you not to have sent for me? You should have scoured the seas to find me before the birth. Don't you realize I would have married you, given Joseph his rightful name?"

"You . . . would . . . have . . . married . . . me. How generous of you, Adam! You might even have foregone Jane's fortune." She gave a choked laugh. "Has it occurred to you that after your treatment of me I might not have wished to marry you? But you . . . Oh, this is too much. If you'd known about a child, I would then have been acceptable to you, despite the mutiny—"

He bent his face close to hers. "For God's sake, don't speak in the embroidered language of courts. Try to understand. A woman is one thing, and a son's another —changing everything. Had I known about Joseph, I would have dealt with you differently, have no fear of that."

His eyes were like ice. Now, she thought, at last I no longer love him. "Your memory is very poor. Try to throw your mind back. There was my letter to Virginia, which never reached you, but in it I told you I was expecting your baby." Her green eyes blazed up at him as bitter remembrance welled in her. "Then, in London, Lucrezia came to you with a message from me, but you were too implacable to hear it."

"All right, I'm sorry about that, too." As Adam paced the floor, he burst out, "What stopped you from telling me later—when we met at court?" He halted and towered threateningly over her. "I'll tell you! You knew I was going to marry Jane, and you knew I should claim my son from you. In your selfish possessiveness of my child, you kept his very existence from me!"

"So that's it! You think you could have taken Joseph from me. *If* he were your son, I'd have died before I'd allowed you and another woman to have him. It's typical of you to think you'd have the right to take him from me after you left me alone to arrange about his birth—about a name for him!" His eyes looking into hers were filled with hate, but she didn't care now. "This you can believe or not, as you wish! It was to spare you from pain that I always kept silent about Joseph."

His clenched fist beat against his forehead. "When my mother wrote telling me her suspicions, I was insane with rage at your trickery, but today, after seeing the boy, I realize how much I have wanted a son." He turned to Lily with truce in his eyes. "Don't you think he already has some of my strength, my ways?" Adam seemed diffident, asking her for approval, through the boy, through the son who was theirs. He became eager. "Oh, Lily, I'll teach him everything—to handle a sword, a ship . . ." He paced rapidly back and forth. "He'll carry on in the Severn tradition at sea! I'll adopt him, give him his true name. Don't you realize that this boy," he pointed vehemently toward the closed door, "is Lord Clune now that I am the earl?"

Lily vacillated, touched by Adam's joy in fatherhood and annoyed at his conceit. "You might recall at Marston Moor I tried to tell you something then, and with horror you backed away from the thought that I might have had a child of yours." She spoke with bitter sarcasm. "It would have added a responsibility to you."

Suddenly Adam halted in front of her. "Don't use that as an excuse! You should have forced me to listen to you," he grated. "I shall never forgive you for keeping me without him for all these years. The boy belonged with his father . . . not his mother. I could have watched my heir grow from babyhood to boyhood. Despite the war I would have found a way to guide him that you never could and—"

"Curse you, Adam! All you are thinking of is your own sacred feelings and your heir! What am I—a peasant girl who has borne a child to the great earl? The Deveraux name will suit my son every bit as much as the Severn name!" Now she would teach him what suffering was, teach him the torture of uncertainty. "In any case, aren't you taking a lot for granted, Adam? Because that child has red-gold hair and blue eyes, you and your mother have decided that he is yours. But Liam Traherne was Irish, remember? The same coloring is common in Irish stock." Instantly Lily discerned the danger signals in Adam's face.

"What bitchery is this? You swore to me years ago that you never had anything to do with Traherne." There was some compensation in seeing him riddled with doubts. "Did you lie to me then, or did you give yourself to Traherne so that he would mutiny?"

"Why ask me? You seem to know the answers to everything."

"This pretense about Traherne is a new devilishness, Lily," he muttered thickly. "I tell you that boy is mine! He's the image of me. He has my ways, my look. He is my son, I tell you!"

She stared blandly up at his suffering face. So Adam was telling her that her son was his! She said nothing. She just stared at him with enigmatic eyes. She would enjoy her power, tormenting him with uncertainty.

"He is my son, Lily." Adam bent over her. He was pleading with her. "Tell me he is my son!" His voice was taut.

Lily knew he was shaken to his depths. She eyed him coldly. "Sit down, Adam. Don't hang over me in that threatening way. It's taken you over six years to even ask if I had a child by you. You'll be gallant enough to allow me six minutes to give you my answer?"

He sat down tensely. "Do you require six minutes to say yes or no? Is Joseph my son or not?"

"It's painful not to know, isn't it?" All the suffering in Jamaica, then over his marriage, the last year of coldness, demanded that she should milk to the last drop what she could by twisting his heart as he had twisted hers. "If wondering about Joseph hurts you, Adam, then you are going to be hurt."

"You haven't changed!" he spat at her.

"Really? Take a look at yourself for once. Was it your wounded pride, your precious work only, that kept you from calling at Jamaica or sending some word to discover if there had been a baby? Most men feel some responsibility to find out what happens, but not the great Adam! I upset your ship's morale, gave you a humiliation which you provoked, so to hell with me and a child if one resulted!"

"For God's sake, Lily, what's all this to do with us now?" He looked as though he would spring at her. "Things have changed for us. We must take things as they are. The past is dead. That boy is mine, and I plan to have him. Do you understand?"

"You forget that this is Breck, not the *Fearless*. I am not a captive taking orders, rather the mistress . . . giving orders!" He might be planning to take Joseph in the night. She must assure herself he would not. "Besides, Adam," she smiled, "what a fool you'd be riding off with another man's child, just because suddenly you are aglow with the fires of fatherhood." She laughed. "It's really all too funny."

His face was drawn with hate. "Enjoy your moment, Lily," he said angrily.

"I am, and who can blame me? Not once have you said, 'You've done well with the boy.' Tell me, Adam, *if* this were your son, can you have some small idea of what I went through returning to my home, my parents, with a fatherless child? I was not a wharf rat whom you left but a woman of ancient noble stock, with the world's eyes turned on her. Can you visualize the extent of my desperation? My planning, my lies? My carefully built-up deception to protect my son's name? You've obviously not thought of any of this. So, you see, I feel you deserve a little suffering." Lily stood up, shaking out her skirts tantalizingly. "Perhaps Joseph is your son, perhaps he is Liam's son."

"Many men would kill you for this! Whatever you feel about the past, you have no human right to deny a boy his father! This is another of your tricks! I haven't forgotten the machinations of your intriguing mind. Whatever you say, whether you like it or not, I mean to have my son! He's mine and I know it!"

"Really? What makes you so sure?" Let Adam torment himself. "Liam Traherne was close to your build, almost matched your strength." She smiled and said softly, "And he often spoke of his blue-eyed mother with blond hair."

Adam sprang at her, seizing her and shaking her furiously. Her teeth chattered and she thought her neck would break. "You bitch!" he shouted. "Is he my son? Is he? Is he?"

"Perhaps."

His hands flew to her throat, tightening around it, squeezing the breath out of her, hurting, hurting. His eyes were demented. "Answer me! Answer me!" The chamber around her darkened. He was killing her. . . .

Then the alarm drum rolled. The frantic sound warned of the enemy's approach. Suddenly Adam let go of her. Gasping, Lily fell backward onto a chair, and he strode out of the chamber. Would he stay and aid in Breck's defense, or take his mother and go at once? She must be sure that he made no attempt at snatching Joseph. Massaging her aching throat, she rushed to Lucrezia to instruct her to keep the child in a locked room. Then she sped to the battlements.

29

RACING UP THE stone stairway, Lily's heart agonized at the sounds of frantic villagers fleeing from their homes, crying to each other to hasten. They poured into the castle's yard, driving cows and hens before them.

She saw Adam on the battlements with the countess and David. Fortunately they stared anxiously down at the forest, which was spewing forth masses of enemy cavalry and footmen. Teams of farm horses were dragging lead-colored gun carriages toward a field where the men were assembling, out of range of the castle's guns.

"Revolutionaries, all right!" David exploded. "Religion is embroidered on their banners, and they've white ribbons in their hats."

"They're certainly not king's soldiers with those hair trims." The cynical amusement in Adam's voice lessened everyone's apprehensions.

"There are hundreds of them!" the countess murmured as the late-afternoon sunshine glinted off a mass of steel.

"They've brought an army against us this time," David said. "And look at those weapons!"

"They're the new type Cromwell has equipped his model army with," Adam observed. "What is the strength of your force, Gwyn?"

"Thirty musketeers, well trained, and about twenty

women able to hurl stones and hot embers over the walls."

"Not nearly enough!" Adam snapped. "They'll build earthworks and mount those huge guns on top of them and pound the walls until a breach is forced." Hard-faced, he turned to Lily. "I suggest you immediately send scouts to scour the countryside for royalist bands who might be able to help. You can use three of my men."

It was an order, not a suggestion, but at least he intended to aid in Breck's defense. "David and I would be grateful if you'd take command here." Lily's eyes begged for a truce, and the lines of his face softened.

"Very well." He swung around to David. "Come with me, Gwyn." They strode toward the tower door. A few minutes later, on the opposite side of the castle, the watch guards saw Adam's men ride out of the castle's precincts.

Adam and David went to examine the fortifications, and an hour later two unarmed rebel messengers rode up to the outer gate and presented the revolutionary summons. Lily was in her room with Adam, his mother, and David when she received it. At the sight of the handwriting, her heart almost stopped. A shiver ran down her spine.

"Adam!" she gasped. "It's Roger's writing! It's not possible—he's dead!"

He stared at her unbelievingly as her shaking hand gave him the letter. "Damn my blood! The swine did not die! My sword thrust must have missed the lethal mark." Frowning, he read aloud:

Madam,
It has pleased God to put me in charge of the Parliamentary forces now before you, and I am well able to defend myself and offend my enemies. I am sent here by Parliament to demand the deliverance of Breck. As your allegiance binds you to your country, I advise you not to inveigle those

innocent souls in your care but to deliver the castle. I desire your resolution, yes or no?

Roger Huet

"He's here to punish Lily," David exclaimed, "as well as to take Breck!"

"Huet is a doubly bitter foe," Adam said reflectively.

Lily tried to rally herself out of her shock. She would not permit herself to be overly afraid because Roger was alive and in command outside. She dipped her quill in the ink and looked up at Adam. "What shall I answer?"

He hesitated for a second, his eyes narrowed. "Nothing! I'll answer him!" Lily gave him the quill and her place at the table. He wrote rapidly.

Sir,
  I am now at Breck. We intend holding the castle in the king's name.

Severn

After the letter was dispatched Adam went to assure himself that the castle's four cannon were in the most strategic position and to give everyone last-minute instructions.

Roger sent a second note within the hour.

To the Earl of Severn,
Sir,
  Once I committed the error of saving your life; in return you almost took mine. I presume that you do not know that my disposition is neither to give nor take quarter. I advise you to deliver the castle. In so doing you shall be received into mercy, but if you resist, our intention is not to starve Breck but to storm it and then hang you. Think well, because relief is denied you. If you are not aware of it, Lord Deveraux is prisoner in the Tower of London awaiting trial.

"That's why we've heard nothing from Father for months!" Lily exclaimed, pity stirring in her being for the man who had never felt comfortable in displaying his parental love.

"He's possibly as safe in the Tower at the moment as he would be anywhere else," David said gloomily.

Adam had continued reading and now looked up, ashen-faced. "Huet has enclosed a warrant from the king. If the wording wasn't so like Charles, I'd swear Huet had forged it." Adam paused a moment as though to collect his emotions before continuing. "King Charles surrendered to Parliament at Newcastle on June tenth."

Too shocked for speech, everyone just stared into each other's stricken faces. The countess sank into a chair, a hand covering her eyes. Lily was numb. Nothing that was happening seemed real. Adam was the first to recover enough to speak.

"If this document is true, it's two weeks old, so I should have learned about it before I came here. I have to believe it's an invention of Huet's!"

"The man must be insane to think we can be so easily duped into delivering Breck!" David pounded the stone wall with his fist. "How shall we answer him, my lord?"

"In only one way." Adam smiled slowly and strode to a long slit window.

The others followed him to look down at the village. In the evening light red-coated soldiers were carrying baggage into the turf-roofed cottages so recently vacated by the villagers.

"They'll soon start gathering for evening prayer." Adam sounded amused. "While they're thoroughly occupied assuring God how pure and sinless they are, we'll sally out and surprise them. After that we'll sent them our official answer!"

A few minutes later, standing at a small gate, Lily watched in trepidation as Adam and fourteen men prepared to ride out to attack hundreds of Parliamentarians. It was brave, wonderful madness! She wished she could stop Adam, but she dared not interfere. The setting sun glinted on the men's armor as they sat tautly on their nervous horses. Their hands held pistols already cocked. All eyes were on Adam, waiting for his signal to go.

Suddenly the sound of hundreds of male voices singing a hymn rose on the evening air. Adam waited a moment, then raised his right hand. Despite their hideous quarrel, surely he would not ride to such danger without a glance at her. He started forward, then glanced down at her—warm, caressing—and he was gone. Oh, God, let him return, she beseeched before speeding back to the ramparts.

Most of Breck's inhabitants were on the walls excitedly watching as the fifteen horsemen, screened from the enemy by thick shrubs flanking the road, descended like lightning to the village. At the bottom of the road, they swiftly formed a line and charged into the mass of Parliamentarians. There was a volley, and men screamed. Smoke diffused the details of the action from those at Breck, but even in the confusion they saw bodies fall. Now the riders whirled their mounts. They were galloping up the road out of range too fast to be pursued. Success! Breck had taken the offensive. On the wall people hugged each other, even though they knew the success was infinitesimal.

Within minutes Adam and his men were striding breathlessly onto the ramparts. "Every shot went home," Adam announced to the grateful audience. His eyes found Lily's flushed face. He mopped his sweating forehead. "The attack was a complete surprise, but one they won't permit us to repeat. Now we'll give them our official answer!" He turned to the man nearest him. "Hoist the flag of defiance atop the tower."

There was silence as all eyes watched the flag being raised over Breck.

"Nothing will happen tonight," Adam said. "It's too late. They'll begin tomorrow."

Everyone but the men on guard left the walls, some to pray, others to try by talk and drinking a little wine to dispel their apprehensions. The countess suggested to Lily that Adam should occupy the small room leading from her own. Thus Lily was relieved from having to talk personally to him about his quarters.

She went first to comfort her mother and to try to reassure her that all would be well. Lily found Angela's mind had made a complete retreat from the cruel present into the happiness of her Capri childhood. While the mental deterioration added to Lily's burden, she realized it came as a merciful release to her poor mother.

Lily walked to the great hall to supervise the sleeping arrangement of the village women and children sheltering there. Afterward she returned to her suite, and in a locked room found Lucrezia trying to make Joseph go to sleep. He was so excited about the impending battle that it took all of Lily's persuasion to calm him down.

When he eventually slept, Lily whispered to Lucrezia, "Have you seen Valentine?" In the candlelight Lily saw the girl's pretty face break into a wide smile.

"Oh yes, my lady. It was wonderful. He's waiting for me in my chamber. I hope you're not angry."

"No, of course not. I'm glad that you're happy." She affectionately squeezed Lucrezia's shoulder.

"So *very* happy, my lady. He swears he still loves me, and someday he will leave the sea forever and we shall marry."

"Go to him, my dear Lucrezia. I shall remain in my room next door to watch over Joseph."

"Oh thank you, thank you." Lucrezia grasped Lily's hand and kissed it fervently before she sped away.

Lily picked up the two-branched silver candlestick and went softly to her own chamber, leaving the connecting door slightly ajar.

She went to stare out a narrow window at the Puritan camp below, where fires glowed like menacing eyes.

It was terrifying that Roger was alive, almost as though some evil power had brought him out of the grave to confront her. Without Adam at Breck, she did not dare think of what the outcome of the siege would be. Even with his experience in war, his tremendous courage, could Breck withstand that force out there? She was not going to think of that! And Adam the man, if he had time to reflect—would he regret his argument with her? Would he learn to understand what she had endured?

There was a rap on her door and she held her breath. She gathered herself and said, "Enter."

It was Adam, his face serious. In the candlelight they stared at each other across the room. She did not speak, and he quietly closed the door after himself.

"May I talk with you, Lily?"

"Of course."

He stood with his hands locked behind him. His demeanor was too calm, and it did not hide his inner turmoil from her. Had he come to ask for Joseph when the siege ended?

"Lily, despite the urgency of the hour, I'd like to talk of ourselves." He waved to a chair. "Come and sit down and forget those people out there."

He was ordering her again, but she did not demur. She settled in a favorite chair where for years she had often sat, praying that someday he would know his son.

"About this afternoon," he began slowly, "before the rebels came, I apologize for having hurt you." His granitelike face looked ashamed, but it was not for physical hurt she wanted apology.

"I realize how furious you were, Adam," she said, pitying him, for apologies came hard to such a proud man. She tried to help him. "It does not matter."

"I know now what a brute I've been, not only this afternoon but for years—from the very first time we met." His mind flashed back to the night he had violated her virginity. "Forgive me, Lily, for everything— I beg you—whether Joseph is my son or not, I'll be a good father to him. But it's *you* I want. I love you. I want you for my wife." He dropped on a knee beside

THE TEMPEST LILY

her chair. "Somehow you will be freed from Huet ... and we'll marry."

The blue eyes into which she looked were filled with a new kind of love. At last! It had happened; Adam wanted her for his wife. Lily was so deeply stirred, speech seemed impossible. She could only stare at him.

Her silence terrified him. Had he lost her? "Lily, tell me I haven't killed your love. Say you will marry me as soon as it's possible. Lily! Lily!" His arms went around her waist, and he buried his face in her lap.

Suddenly her suppressed love rose in great waves of forgiveness. She clasped his head in her arms, cradling it against her breasts. She sank her lips in the thick burnished hair. "My love, my dearest love. In my heart I have always been your wife."

Adam lifted his head and kissed her fervently but tenderly. "Thank God. I'm a lucky man." Then he grinned in the way that always wrenched her heart. "You've given me a rough passage, my darling girl. It's been a bloody, stormy voyage—no easy task to bring this ship to port."

Now Lily felt shame at having made him suffer over Joseph, and the old aching longing to share their son with him burst into words. "My darling, we've reached port at last." Her voice choked on sobs. "We are safe in the harbor—we three."

He said nothing for a moment while his brilliant blue eyes raked her tear-filled eyes. "We—*three?*" he whispered.

Lily nodded slowly. "You, I ... and Joseph. He *is* your son."

In Lily's big four-poster bed, the curtains half-down against drafts, she and Adam lay in each other's arms. Both had reached the height of emotion, and now nothing was hidden between them. Their love for each other was fully revealed, and the shared joy of their son bound them together as never before.

In between their fervent lovemaking she tried to help

Adam recapture in words the events in Joseph's life. His questions were endless, her answers gladly given. Then at last they lay side by side, as through an uncurtained window they watched the sky for the first light.

Lily's thoughts turned fearfully to Roger, separated from her by only a short distance. She was absurd to fear him so much, she told herself, yet she was obliged to control a shudder. How strange was God's design. Roger outside, she lying in Adam's arms, her heart's longing satisfied that Adam knew of his child, but also only just before they must face an attack that could be lethal.

"I must rise now, sweetheart," Adam said gently, disengaging himself from her arms and swinging his feet to the floor. Silently she watched him dress. When he was ready, he leaned down to kiss her and their souls met in complete union. Then he left for the ramparts, and she rose to face the terrors of the day.

By noon Roger had split his forces into two orderly camps. At one of the castle's precipitous sides, gangs of men were working in nonstop shifts, erecting earthworks. The second camp was in the village, where his cavalry was stationed. His intention was obvious—to storm up the road and force an entrance at the castle's most vulnerable spot.

Weighted down with pistol and sword, armored breastplate worn over her cotton robe, Lily stood on the walls with Adam and David, watching their musketeers trying to pick off the rebels building the gun enbankments.

"How many of the dogs have you hit?" Adam questioned a musketeer.

"About five, my lord, but they're very cautious and work just out of our firing range."

"Sniping isn't going to stop those earthworks from rising," Adam told David and Lily as they stared at the swiftly growing mounds.

"If only we could flatten what they've already built,"

THE TEMPEST LILY

she said, "before they can mount their blasted guns on them."

"We *shall* flatten them," Adam said quietly. "Tonight a couple of men and I are going over the wall. Once down there we'll blow those fortifications into clods of dirt."

Fear clutched Lily's entire being. The drop to the valley was sheer, but she dared not remonstrate. "What about your return? How will you scale up the walls without being brought down by enemy fire?"

Adam grinned. "We shall not come back at once. We'll hide in the forest until the excitement has died down, then in answer to my signal David will lower ladders for us."

"An ingenious plan, my lord." Admiration lit David's harassed face.

"We've got to do everything possible, Gwyn, to delay Huet's attack. It's obvious from the activity down there that he plans a full-scale assault for tomorrow. Once his big guns are in position, he hopes to effect a breach in the walls. His cavalry will make a simultaneous charge from the village, and they'll be followed by pikemen and musketeers."

To Lily, longing for night's friendly protection so that Adam and his men might destroy the earthworks, the summer twilight seemed unending. But at last a dark secretiveness covered everything. In the Puritan camps all movement ceased; only their fires glowed like vindictive eyes. Standing on the ramparts beside David and a group of men, Lily watched Adam, Valentine and other men go over the wall, their hands gripping the leather thongs by which they would lower themselves. The group on the walls braced themselves to take the loads as the men descended hand over hand. The three figures were like flies clinging to the ancient edifice until they disappeared.

"His lordship's down! He's let go the ladder!" a man grunted and started hauling the ladder up.

"The others are down!" another voice whispered.

A seeming eternity of silence followed. At last a flame

split the darkness, followed by an explosion shattering the quiet. Men shouted; then came a second explosion. The Puritan camps were in turmoil. There were sounds of a chase as pistols cracked.

"They've done it," David muttered.

"Pray that they've reached the forest," Lily murmured.

After several hours the Puritan camp settled down again, but it was only just before dawn that Lily's anxiety was relieved. An owl hooted three times. Adam's signal! The leather straps were lowered, and within minutes Adam and his men were safely back inside Breck.

30

DURING THE NEXT two days, while Roger's earthworks rose anew, Adam occupied the defenders with further preparations for defense. David was in command of the musket fire atop the walls. Lily and the countess were in charge of the women, whose business it was to hurl stones onto the enemy when they came within striking range. Adam took the vulnerable village section of selves against the shock. Simultaneously with the firing, he organized his mounted party for an eventual countersally.

On the third day Roger's replacements had risen to the desired height and the big guns were mounted upon them. When the Puritans' morning prayers and

THE TEMPEST LILY 349

psalm singing ended, the soldiers noisily took up allotted positions.

The attack began with the big guns opening fire. The ancient foundations trembled from the enormous impact, and atop the walls the defenders braced themselves against the shock. Simultaneously with the firing the cavalry charged up the long road, pikemen and musketeers marching behind them.

Lily watched with sickening fear as Adam and his men waited to charge outside. Next to her she could almost feel the hammering of David's heart as he strained to judge the exact moment to order the musketeers to fire. Closer and closer the terrifying cavalry came. Now they were within musket range, and David shouted the command. Seconds later a volley rained down on the enemy, while at the same time the castle's three-pound guns roared. Rebel cavalrymen dropped from their saddles, horses pitched forward and the charge was momentarily broken. But whirling their crazed horses around, they hastily formed ranks and galloped forward.

It seemed an eternity to Lily before the second round of bullets was released, and still the enemy pressed forward. They were coming dangerously near. Now the gate opened, and Adam and his men raced forward to grapple with the enemy. But what chance had they? Twenty men against a hundred?

Lily's terrified eyes fastened on Adam's figure. He was ringed by pikes and slashing swords, and he seemed to be fighting everywhere. There was an inferno of men trying to kill each other as they struck with lances, swords and hatchets. Bodies of men and horses were covering the road, and the big guns incessantly pounded the walls.

"Scaling ladders for the walls! Bring the ladders!" came the dreaded cry.

Lily knew she must rush to aid the defenders in throwing the ladders back, but she believed if her eyes left Adam he would be struck. It was a foolish idea that almost chained her to the spot. Lily made herself dash to the castle's other side. David and the musketeers were already taking up new firing positions, and the countess, commanding the women, was hurling stones at the climbing soldiers.

"Don't let them up!" the countess yelled. "Stop them!"

Grasping stones from a pile, Lily flung them down. Her aim was good; she hit several men, who fell off the ladders, but others immediately sprang to replace them. Along with the women, she kept hurling stones until her hands were cut and bleeding. Yet as swiftly as the women acted or the musketeers loaded and fired, the enemy persisted, scaling the walls under the protection of their guns. Some of the women were knocked unconscious by flying masonry from the bombarded foundations.

Lily could not go to their aid because Roundheads were almost level with the ramparts. "Don't let them get a footing!" she shouted, but her cry was lost as the guns boomed again, shaking the castle so violently that it seemed to totter.

Directly before Lily was a ladder covered with men swarming up it. Their hands were reaching for her skirts to drag her off the walls. Somehow she eluded them and pushed at the top of the ladder. Using all her strength, she shoved the ladder back . . . back . . . back! It stood straight for a second, then toppled over.

All around Lily Breck's defenders were battling for life. There was Adam among them. He must have beaten the enemy from the village. Now he was encouraging everyone as, sweating and panting, he poured hot oil over the ramparts.

The fighting raged for seemingly endless hours. Suddenly a loud cheer broke through the chaos. The enemy's drum was beating retreat! Lily slumped to the stone floor, exhausted.

"Everyone! Here! Quickly!" Adam shouted. "The walls are breached!"

Scrambling to her feet, Lily staggered along with

THE TEMPEST LILY

the others to help push beds and mattresses, furniture, sacking, boulders—anything—into the hole.

"We've beaten them off for the moment," Adam panted. Blood was seeping through his breeches from a thigh wound. "But we've lost five men, and many are injured!"

Roger took half a day's respite to bury his dead and to hold prayer meetings. In Breck Castle they prepared in every way possible to withstand another savage assault, while their desperate eyes searched the countryside for signs of help.

Ten days of hell followed, during which Breck's stones and powder became depleted and the weary defenders were obliged to do battle with only swords and pikes. Half their number was lost, and the remainder miraculously withstood continued attacks.

Throughout the ordeal Adam and Lily snatched at a few private words together. "Shouldn't I prepare Lucrezia to escape with Joseph?" she asked. "In case we don't live through this?"

"Yes! She must somehow get to the *Fearless* in Milford Haven! She must tell Salter that it is my wish that he take Joseph to your grandmother in Capri!"

On the eleventh night, when darkness again mercifully brought on a few hours of cessation of hostilities, Lily sought Lucrezia and Joseph in the great hall, where the children slept together so they could be easily cared for.

Struggling not to appear too upset, Lily told her serious-faced little son, "Soon, my love, you and Lucrezia must leave here." She turned to the Capriote. "You know the plan, and you have the gold I gave you." Lucrezia nodded gravely. "If you fall into rebel hands, you must swear Joseph is your son. Then no harm will come to him!"

"But Mama, I don't want to leave here! Something awful might happen to you. Let me stay with you." Joseph's arms tightened around her neck. "I could fight too. I have my slingshot ready!"

Lily crushed her child in her arms. "I'd love to keep

you here, but it will be much better if you visit your great-grandmother. She's very kind and will take good care of you."

After Lucrezia had solemnly sworn that she would try to reach Capri with Joseph, Lily lay down to try to rest.

Just before dawn she took her place on the walls. In the hollow eyes of the unkempt people, Lily read what they all knew. They could withstand one more assault, no more. Those too weak to stand sat in chairs with both hands grasping swords and pikes. The undefended spots were hidden from the enemy by standards.

At sunrise the Parliamentarians' singing filled the air. As soon as the hymns ended, their war drums rolled and the great guns boomed. The soldiers swept up both sides of the castle. There was little that could be done to prevent them. They were gaining the wall. Suddenly a face corrupted by hate appeared over the edge—Roger! He was battling hand to hand with a wounded man.

"Keep them off!" Lily yelled to those fighting near her as with leaden arms she struck—on and on—but next to her, people had fallen. Lily tried to cover every point by rushing wherever she could.

Revolutionaries locked the royalists in a death grip.

"Help has come!" a woman cried unexpectedly above the sounds of battle, and both sides paused to look.

Spilling out of the surrounding forest, a group of armored horsemen galloped up, crying, "For King Charles!" They fell on the rebels' rear, forcing them to turn from the castle to defend themselves.

"Fight on!" Adam shouted on the ramparts to the tired defenders. "Don't stop until the relief force is inside!"

Lily was agonizing to know if Joseph had been harmed by the flying stones that shattered windows. She picked a footing over the dead and fled to the tower.

"Watch out, Lily!" David warned. "Some of the enemy are in the castle!"

But she ignored him and rushed down the stone stair-

THE TEMPEST LILY 353

way to her chamber, where she found Joseph and Lucrezia. "Thank God you're both all right." She bent and threw her arms around Joseph.

"Mama! You're all over blood!" Joseph's face puckered in anguish. "Are you hurt?"

"No—no, my love. Nothing but cuts. God has heard our prayers. Help has come, and—"

Joseph wasn't listening to her. He was staring angrily at something behind her. Then, with amazing speed, he lifted his slingshot and shot a stone.

There was a grunt of fury, and Lily spun around to confront Roger, a mesmerizing figure of avenging wrath, his sword raised. Joseph's stone, striking Roger's wrist, had averted the blow meant to kill her.

In Roger's eyes there was insatiable hate. Escape through the doorway was impossible. She must get to the arras connecting with the adjoining room.

"Ah, Lily, it's taken a long time, but I have come as God's messenger to punish you for the witch that you are!"

"Don't call my mama those awful names!" Joseph exclaimed indignantly. Lily tried to push him behind her skirts as Roger's look swung to the child.

"Your mother? Ah—yes, you have grown a lot." Comprehension seemed to be dawning in Roger's eyes as recognition, then murder, crossed his face. "So that's it!" he exclaimed in fury. "I'm amazed I never realized it before!" He started laughing like a man possessed. "That boy—he's Clune's bastard! Now I know the real story. I see it all—he's the image of his evil father! And you, Lily ... adulteress ... Jezebel ... deceiver ... you are going to die with your bastard!"

As he lunged at her with poised sword, she thrust Joseph aside. "Roger, wait!" she screamed, and ducked down to dodge the blade, but he was too quick. The tip caught her high on the arm. Roger raised the lethal blade to inflict the death stroke.

"Huet!" Sword drawn, Adam burst through the arras and sprang between Lily and Roger.

"Murderer! Fornicator!" Roger gasped as Adam's sword crashed across his blade.

Both men flung themselves into savage combat in the beautiful tapestried room. Barely breathing, Lily crouched, watching, with Joseph now clasped in her arms and a sobbing Lucrezia clinging to her.

The men lunged and parried, with eyes crafty as bears in a pit watching for the chance to kill. The clash of their rapiers was the accompaniment to their death dance, as years of hate drove them on in frenzied fury.

They were well matched, but Adam was taller and heavier; he would dispatch Roger before long. Then to Lily's horror two rebels with drawn swords ran through the arras to strike Adam from the rear.

"Adam!" she screamed. "Behind you!"

Adam spun around to defend himself, and his assailant lunged at him, but Adam jumped aside so fast that the blade meant for him plunged into Roger's stomach, running him through.

"Fool . . . fool!" Roger gasped as his sword clattered to the floor. Clutching his stomach, he staggered a moment before pitching face down on the floor, while Adam continued to engage with the other rebels.

For a flash of a second, Lily wanted to go to Roger. No matter how he had treated her, she could not let him die like an animal. Yet he might be faking that he was badly wounded, and if she got within his reach, he would kill her. Her eyes swung from his body to Adam.

He was backing his opponents to the arras. Lily sensed his intention. He was going to trip the men in the long curtains. Suddenly, with enormous strength and amazing speed, his sword crashed down in flying blows on both their bodies. With the awful impact they lost their footing. The younger antagonist collapsed on his weapon with a groan. Swiftly Adam pulled the arras down on the other man, who was just scrambling to his feet. The heavy tapestry covered him completely.

At that moment a young officer rushed into the room. His face lit with pleasure as he saw Adam. "Damn my soul, Adam! Thank goodness they haven't gotten you! We came as soon as your scouts reached us!"

"Willoughby!" Adam almost chuckled as, bending over the bundled rebel, he caught his breath in gasps. "I've never been so glad to see anyone. Help me truss up this rogue, will you?"

"It will be a pleasure." Willoughby laughed and pulled the arras cord from the wall to tie up the rebel. "All of our men, excepting for a few casualties, managed to gain the castle. You're doing what we are—fighting on despite the king's warrant to stop action."

"Damn me, Willoughby!" Adam paled under his flushed face. "You don't mean that blasted warrant is genuine?"

"Yes. Charles is a hostage of Leslie's." He secured the cord around the rebel's feet and stood up. "Temporarily, our cause is lost." He strode toward Roger and rolled him over. "Bravo! That rat Huet is dead! That cheers me. Adam, in God's name, get away! There's a heavy price on your head. You're one of the most sought-after royalists! Unless you want to land on the scaffold, go . . . before we must make peace with that scum outside!"

"No! I'll fight to the end, thank you!"

Lily was going to rush to Adam to plead with him to leave when his mother burst in. Blood bespattered her loose hair. She dashed to Adam. "You've heard? The cause is lost! Escape at once and live to fight for another day!"

"But I can't leave you here!"

"They won't hurt an old woman, and I'll care for Lily's mother. For my sake, go! Save yourself, Lily and Joseph!"

Adam pulled the child to him, and as Lily swayed giddily, his arm went about her. "Are you strong enough to travel?" She nodded. "Then quick, get Lucrezia to pack a few things and prepare to accompany Valentine. We'll leave at dark."

The defenders were still in possession of Breck when Lily and Adam, Joseph asleep on a saddle, Lucrezia and Valentine cautiously made their way from Breck. Terrified of detection, they walked their horses slowly. Not until they had reached the security of the forest did they believe they had escaped.

"We'll travel only by night," Adam murmured to Lily, "and hide by day until we reach *Fearless*. Once aboard, we'll sail to Virginia."

By dawn they were a safe distance from Breck. Dismounting beside a stream, Adam gently laid Joseph under concealing bushes. Lucrezia accompanied Valentine as he took the horses to water them at the stream.

Lily watched Adam for a moment as he made Joseph comfortable. Then with her heart bursting with gratitude that the child at last had his father, she came and knelt beside Adam.

"My son." Adam slowly shook his head in wonder. "My son . . . and you his mother!" His arm went about her shoulders and he drew her closer. "Never did I ever hope for such blessings." He sighed heavily. "We've lost everything—the war—Ben Fras—Breck—"

"And my father a prisoner in the Tower."

"Don't fear for his life. When the king capitulates entirely, your father will be spared."

"I pray so." She hesitated, not knowing how to voice the depth of her feelings. "Long ago I believed that God's design—His pattern—was to deny humans the realization of their dreams." Then her mind swung to poor Liam, dear James, unfortunate, half-mad Roger. "But I was wrong! God has realized my soul's deepest wish. We three are together. In the colonies, where there is no religious hate, where there is freedom of thought, we shall find happiness."

"You're right, beloved, and someday we shall return to aid England to restore the king to his rightful place."

ABOUT THE AUTHOR

HELGA MORAY, who was born in Capetown, South Africa, is the author of over twenty-five novels. She began her career as a screen actress and was also Hollywood's first camerawoman. After Hollywood she turned to writing and has had stories published on a variety of themes.

American readers will be most familiar with her best-selling *Roxana*. Ms. Moray writes prolifically from her home in Cannes, France.

GLORIOUS BATTLES OF LOVE & WAR

Romances of Strange Lands and Distant Times

Read about the dazzling women and bold men whose passion for love and excitement leads them to the heights and depths of the human experience—set against flamboyant period backgrounds.

Look for Richard Gallen Romances from Pocket Books—

___ 83504	SILVER LADY Nancy Morse	$2.50
___ 83524	SWEET NEMESIS Lynn Erickson	$2.50
___ 83560	THIS REBEL HUNGER Lynn LeMon	$2.50
___ 83561	SAVAGE FANCY Kathryn Gorsha Thiels	$2.50
___ 83562	THIS TENDER PRIZE Nancy Morse	$2.50
___ 83366	THE FROST AND THE FLAME Drucilla Campbell	$2.50
___ 83636	TOMORROW AND FOREVER Maud B. Johnson	$2.50
___ 83564	TANYA Muriel Bradley	$2.50

POCKET BOOKS/RICHARD GALLEN PUBLICATIONS
1230 Avenue of the Americas, New York, N.Y. 10020

Please send me the books I have checked above. I am enclosing $_____ (please add 50¢ to cover postage and handling for each order, N.Y.S. and N.Y.C. residents please add appropriate sales tax). Send check or money order—no cash or C.O.D.s please. Allow up to six weeks for delivery.

NAME_____

ADDRESS_____

CITY_____ STATE/ZIP_____

Romance & Adventure

New and exciting romantic fiction—passionate and strong-willed characters with deep feelings making crucial decisions in every situation imaginable—each more thrilling than the last.

Read these dramatic and colorful novels—from Pocket Books/Richard Gallen Publications

___83164	ROSEWOOD, Petra Leigh	$2.50
___83165	THE ENCHANTRESS, Katherine Yorke	$2.50
___83233	REAP THE WILD HARVEST, Elizabeth Bright	$2.75
___83216	BURNING SECRETS, Susanna Good	$2.75
___83331	THE MOONKISSED, Barbara Faith	$2.50
___83332	A FEAST OF PASSIONS, Carol Norris	$2.50
___83445	THIS RAGING FLOWER, Lynn Erickson	$2.50
___83446	FAN THE WANTON FLAME, Clarissa Ross	$2.50

POCKET BOOKS/RICHARD GALLEN PUBLICATIONS
Department RG
1230 Avenue of the Americas
New York, N.Y. 10020

Please send me the books I have checked above. I am enclosing $_____ (please add 50¢ to cover postage and handling for each order, N.Y.S. and N.Y.C. residents please add appropriate sales tax). Send check or money order—no cash or C.O.D.s please. Allow up to six weeks for delivery.

NAME_____

ADDRESS_____

CITY_____ STATE/ZIP_____

RG 11-79